Another Place to Die

It was the secret China didn't want the world to know, 200,000 people died suddenly in Jiangsu province. A new lethal flu virus is literally flying around the whole world. Everything your Government said would protect you is a lie.

There will be no effective vaccine for six months.

Make a choice. Escape to remote islands – or try to tough it out. There's growing panic in the city, people are literally falling down dead in the streets. There are rumours of mass graves being dug. Europe has already succumbed as emergency systems are overwhelmed. Despite mass vaccination, will the same happen in Canada and the USA? People are scared – martial law is certain.

Fen, aged 15, is dragged by her family to a tiny Gulf Island off Canada's west coast to 'ride it out.' Deka, an immigrant cabbie in Vancouver, is convinced he can survive the flu, thanks to his vaccination by Dr Borov, another immigrant. The Russian, Borov is a former virologist who will treat anyone desperate enough to fill their veins with his home-made antiviral soup. Arno Lakis, an analyst with 'Futuretank Inc' in Toronto, has seen all the emergency scenarios – hell, he wrote some of them. He knows just how bad it's going to get. He heads west to Rachel. If everything is unravelling, he wants to be with her to the end.

Do you stay? Stockpile enough food and water for sixty days and pray the looters don't get you, or escape and hope the virus doesn't get there before you? As the world economy collapses and every certainty is swept away *Another Place to Die* exposes the real horror of surviving the Great Flu Pandemic of 2009.

Where would you go? Are you prepared?

ISBN 978-1-84753-899-4
Lulu Publishing ID 472938

First published in the UK & USA 2006.

1 3 5 7 9 10 8 6 4 2

Another Place
to die

Sam North

Lulu Press
lulu.com

Another Place To Die

A vivid account of individuals caught up in a world flu pandemic – a terrifying scenario of people facing the horror of a killer virus that will kill millions.

This is Sam North's seventh novel; the first set in his home city of Vancouver BC. Sam is the Course Leader for the Masters in Creative Writing Programme at the University of Portsmouth. He divides his time between the UK and Canada. Sam is the founding editor of www.hackwriters.com – an award winning international writers' magazine and he is a member of the Writer's Guild of Great Britain.

Also by Sam North

(Fiction)
209 Thriller Road
Ramapo
Going Indigo
Diamonds – The Rush of '72
Eeny Meeny Miny Mole* as Marcel d'Agneau
The Curse of the Nibelung – A Sherlock Holmes Mystery
(a new 2005 edition of the title originally written under Marcel d'Agneau nom de plume)

(Radio Dramas)
The Devil's Dog
Final Accounts
Adventures with Randolph Stafford
Copycats
The War in Drab Nebula

(Screenplays)
The Pushover
Got it Bad

Acknowlegements

To George R. Stewart for paving the way so long ago. Appreciation must also go to Allen Gibson in Vancouver for his many helpful suggestions and insider knowledge. I am especially grateful to Sara Towe for providing a base for me to work from in Vancouver. Thanks must also go to Tabytha Towe and Koko the wonder dog, both of whom who enabled me to understand Fen and Red so much better. A special thanks to Carine 'Kit' Thomas who designed this book and whose patience and encouragement was invaluable throughout.

1

The 'National Strategy for Pandemic Influenza: Implementation Plan updated in May 2006 led to the US Congress appropriating 3.8 Billion dollars for 300 critical integrated federal actions; covering transportation and borders, law enforcement and public safety – including a global epidemiological standard for triggering an international containment response to a potential pandemic. Stockpiles of counter-measures were pre-positioned for rapid deployment to some 75 million persons. This, along with Project Bioshield that guarded again bio-terrorism, meant that many felt reassured that the US Government was thinking hard about what might happen and how to contain it during the next great disease outbreak. Although some were concerned that the government was, as usual, 'fighting the last war,' and the next great biological threat could be from a totally unexpected vector.
Extract from 'Strategies for coping with the onset of a pandemic' by Arno Lakis
Futures: Journal for Structural Futurologists – Winter Edition 2007

Coquitlam, BC. Canada – September

'Are you even started?' Frances demanded to know. 'Do you have any idea how serious the situation is, Fen? Do you?'

Fen adjusted the volume on her iPod and let *The Killers* drown her. She slammed the door. She hated being shouted at and all that seemed to go on in this house lately was that everyone shouted at her. She so appreciated being endlessly told that she was ugly, lazy, stupid and apparently most likely to suck at everything in life. Well fuck her. Didn't everyone get zits? Didn't every girl have an ugly stage? Shit, not Diane, Frances' daughter, she had never had an ugly phase. She was born beautiful and probably never had one zit in all her life. Even got the man of her dreams. Of course she was dead now. Even died beautifully, most likely; except that most likely wasn't true, not with the virus making you cough up your lungs like that. Such a gross way to die. Fen hadn't appreciated Frances hooking up with her father and she guessed the feeling was entirely reciprocated. Didn't appreciate that they met at Diane's funeral either. There was something sick about that.

The door opened again slamming against the cupboard, (one of Frances' first moves was to remove the lock) and there she was staring at her with malign hatred, the veins on her neck pulsating with tension. Fen removed an earpiece, adopted an aggressive posture. 'You agreed you would knock, Frances.'

Frances was so mad she wanted to spit. She loathed this rat of a fifteen-year-old girl. Since she'd got engaged to Mercer, every disagreement she'd had with him was about Fen. 'You agreed to answer when I called.'

Fen offered a withering smile. 'No. I think that was an agreement you made with Red. I am not the dog. This may have escaped your attention, Frances.'

Frances did not respond to the sarcasm. 'I don't care for your tone, girl. I don't care much for you period. You might think you are your father's favourite, but you are not, Fen. Believe me you are not. If you want to stay with this crappy family, pack! We are leaving in fifteen minutes. With, or without you. One case but pack for three months. That means you might want more than one set of underwear and jeans. OK?'

'Three months? You said one, last night.'

'Things change. Pack sensibly. It's going to be winter soon. You have,' (she checked her watch) 'twelve minutes.' Frances turned away and went back to her own room.

Fen slammed the door shut. She went over to her cupboard and stared at her clothes. Three whole fucking months on the island with her. Jesus. Forget the clothes, just pack an axe.

Her cell rang and she grabbed it. It was Leone. Status: best friend.

'Waz up?'

'We're leaving too. Dad reckons it'll be safer in Baja. Took us out of school and everything. Home study now, as if.'

'Mexico? You ever seen a Mexican hospital, Leone?'

'We're not going to wait to get it, Fen. We're going before it gets here. My Uncle's got a place, it's really remote, it's gonna be safe. You still going to the Island?'

'Yeah. They're saying three months now.'

'Fuck, three months? You'll go crazy girl. Wish you could come with us.'

'Yeah, believe me *they* wish I'd go with you.'

Leone laughed. 'Got to go, Fen. See you at Christmas OK? Dad says it could burn itself out by Christmas.'

Fen registered that useful fact. 'Well he should know. Fuck, Leone, I'll miss you.'

Leone was distracted the other end. 'Got to go. Bye Fen. Bye... good luck, bitch, you'll need it.'

Fen turned off her phone and threw some sweaters into her case. Leone was a crazy girl but her closest friend since third grade. If Dr J thought it would be over by Christmas that was closer to four months. Fuck. Mexico. Drastic move. Made sort of sense, though. People were less likely to catch a cold down there.

It seemed lots of people were planning for the worst now. Her own Dad had got all excited by it when the first people began to die in China. Hell he'd been plotting its progress since two years before when the first outbreak began and everyone was saying millions would die. Of course no one did and everyone got kinda bored by it. Not him though. Mercer always predicted it would be back and there'd be mutations. He said everyone would think they were safe and then, just when they weren't looking, it would strike hard. He had Catherine make them all masks and insisted they wore gloves in public so they didn't touch anyone.

Mercer made Fen go over to the island to help him fix up the cabin there. Over a period of eight months on weekends, they put in a new well, and a shower, complete with solar panels, so there would hot water for Catherine and his girls. Mercer had even dug a pit for storing emergency food. It was like all his life he'd been waiting for an opportunity to 'survive' a major disaster. Must have watched every season of 'Lost' on DVD a hundred times.

Fen had been interested at first. It had seemed the right thing to do. Stocking the cabin, fitting it out for the four of them and Red. The island was small, but it would be safe. Each month the news got worse and Mercer felt more vindicated. He wasn't going to wait for the virus to hit town, the statistics indicated that there was no way the Government could contain it and only fools would stay behind to await its arrival.

He hadn't figured on Catherine dying though. She only went back East for a day for her Grandma's funeral. They wouldn't let her fly back. The heat scanners at the airport picked up her infection and she was dead in two days. Mercer had been devastated. Fen too, in her own way. Everyone wanted her to cry and be upset, but Fen just couldn't. Didn't know how to grieve. Never really seemed real to her that her mother had died back East. She never saw her die and it just didn't take as an idea. Her sister May was the same. She went away and somehow they spent the next two months waiting for her to come back. Then Mercer met Frances at her daughter Diane's funeral and life turned to shit. It had been a whole year of tension in this family since the first wave of the virus took Catherine away.

Later, when a thousand people died in a week in Montreal, Mercer quit his job at *Chapters* and started taking all their stuff to the cabin. He was determined to save them all. Had her and May quit school so they wouldn't mingle with 'the infected'. He didn't want to take any risks and he got them psychologically ready to leave at a moment's notice. He kept repeating that 'saving the family unit was job number one.' Both Fen and May noticed how quickly Frances had become 'family' and both resented it and didn't accept the explanation from Mercer that 'God' wanted him to make sure the girls were taken care of. It was sex, pure and simple. He just couldn't do without it and Frances quickly made it plain she couldn't stand either of them.

There was a tap on the door and it opened slightly. Mercer stood there, looking anxious, his lank hair sweaty from loading up the truck. Fen took the earpieces out and sighed.

'I'm packing, Dad.'

'We gotta go, Fen honey. We'll miss the ferry. We're not the only ones leaving y'know.'

'I'm almost done. Did you get the dog food?' Fen didn't care much about her family but she did care about Red, the setter, the world's worst gun dog who worshipped her and had never cared much for anyone else in the family.

'Yeah. He's in the truck. Did you hear the news? They found a whole city apartment full of dead people in Hull.'

'Hull is 2500 miles away, Dad. I know my geography.'

'It's getting more potent, Fen. We're getting out just in time.'

Fen threw some books into her rucksack on top of her underwear and then, spotting her other sneakers stuffed them in there too. She turned to Mercer and shrugged. 'I'm done.' Zipping it up and squishing it a tad to make it fit.

Mercer looked relieved and took the case from her. He paused, remembering something. 'Hat, coat, gloves. Island gets cold, Fen. I know you don't think it's cool but...'

Fen grabbed her army surplus coat and slung it over her shoulder. 'I'm on it, Dad. Let's go. We've got a ferry to catch.'

Mercer backed away from her. He didn't like to get close to anyone now, not even family. Fen marched down the stairs ahead of him. She needed to get some chips. Something for the journey. Shit something to last three whole fucking months.

Outside Fen saw them all sitting in the truck. Red enthusiastically wagging his tail when he saw her and her sister already tuned out listening to her shit. Frances was staring straight ahead. Fen turned around and wondered when she'd ever see the house again. Wondered if they'd even come back. She suddenly remembered something from childhood. A moment on another day when she'd been told to pack by Mercer. Catherine and her father were having a rough time in their relationship and she threatened to leave. She wanted to go south – Fen remembered her own excitement because she had been promised gigantic waves. She guessed Mercer had given in, because soon after she packed her little case they were in the old camper van headed south to California.

Fen had been five. What was for a couple of weeks turned into a year. A whole year just surfing, picking fruit when the money got low or (she didn't know it then) dealing shit to UCLA students on campus and at the beach. They lived in the camper van at first, then an abandoned beach shack near Manhattan Beach with the sound of airplanes from LAX constantly ringing in their ears. Fen had learned to surf, grown stronger, bigger and more confident, but May, her sister, had never really taken to the life and when she got sick from something in the water (according to Catherine) they realised the dream was coming to a rapid end. Paying for a Doctor was impossible. Mercer took her to see a health worker he'd met on the surf and they even stole some antibiotics from a pharmacy with his help, but May didn't recover. She was constantly short of breath, coughed all the time and broke out in a rash. No one ever got to sleep anymore and Mercer and Catherine fell to arguing again. One night, when she couldn't stand it anymore Catherine grabbed May and took off. Mercer panicked and went looking for her. That was when Fen, six now, decided she wanted a different family. She was quite clear about it. She wanted to live in a proper house and go to school and be normal. Fen walked away from the beach house and headed north.

A day later, exhausted and hungry she was in Santa Monica and when a man asked her if she was lost, she told him she had run away from the orphanage. Stephen believed her, fed her. He took her home and she wasn't afraid because she didn't know anything bad could happen to her. Stephen introduced her to Joley and they asked her some questions (which meant she had to tell quite a few lies and describe life in the orphanage, which she liberally borrowed from seeing *Oliver Twist* on TV). Then, as if it was pre-ordained, they showed her to 'her' room filled with dolls and there was a proper bathroom with a shower and everything. She moved right in. Became their kid and they treated her like bone-china. She'd never felt as loved and appreciated as that time with those men who quickly became her Uncles. They took her with them to San Francisco when Joley changed jobs and she even started school there. She loved the place, the little apartment in an old block perched on the side of a hill, and the little *Red* school she went to. She made friends, and her two Uncles bought her anything she ever wanted and never ever touched her except to hug and make her watch old musicals with them. (She saw a lot of musicals and was probably the only kid in the world who knew who Ginger Rogers and Cyd Charisse were). They even taught her how to tap dance. When out in the market one day she saw a poster with her face on it and a number to call. It was a shock, she had never thought they might actually look for her.

That night she made them cut her hair like a boy and they liked her even more. Joley worked in city planning, Stephen in a department store and they never once missed collecting her from school or taking her there. She didn't mind at all that they never let her out of their sight or speak to strangers. She wanted to stay forever and when she had a seventh birthday they let her have a party. She chose five friends, had them over for tea and then they went to see the *Ice Capades* at the Forum. Only Stephen came along to supervise, and when all the parents had come and taken their precious monsters back, she and Stephen caught the bus home where Joley had promised to make a big cake whilst they were out.

Fen had known there was something wrong the moment they got to the bottom of the hill. The crowds, the noise, the fire trucks.

The fire destroyed the entire block and all Fen remembered from that night was the shouting, the water cascading down the hill and Stephen running away up the hill towards the fire shouting Joley's name. She stood alone, soaked, scared, crying because she knew Joley was dead. Didn't know how she knew but she knew and Stephen didn't come back. She waited there for four long hours.

The cop asked her where she lived and she told him. Before she knew it she was under the care of some woman who stank of sweat and she couldn't call Stephen because there was no home to call and he didn't show up for work the next day, or even the next week. They didn't believe her anyway and explained that if he existed he would be going to jail anyway, which made no sense to Fen as Stephen had taken real good care of her.

A month later they had traced her to Vancouver and it was Catherine who came to get her. A blonde Catherine. They had both changed so much they hardly recognised each other and it was like two strangers hugging when they finally released her. Catherine took her back by *Greyhound* and once in Vancouver they lived in a squat and Mercer was getting by dealing dope he grew on the island. May had recovered but she still didn't speak much to Fen or anyone. Fen had realised then, even at seven, that she wasn't hippie material. No one ever discussed her 'leaving the family' and she never talked about it, although she did write some letters in secret to Stephen to let him know where she'd gone, but he never replied. She experienced her first sense of loss and that stayed with her a long time.

Seven years on – she'd been packing again and she knew, with instinctive certainty that her life was about to change all over again. Mercer was locking up the house as Fen stuffed her rucksack into the back of the truck between Red, his bags of dog chow and the tins of soup and stuff Frances had thrown in there. Mercer ran over to join them.

'Get in, Fen – we're running late.'

'OK already.' Fen climbed in, had to perch beside Red on top of the dog chow and Red whined, putting out a paw to her. 'Hey, boy. Ready to live on the island?'

Red put his head down beside her and Fen shot a look at May who'd managed to squeeze herself into the truck cabin. May had her face stuck into the pages of 'Catcher in the Rye' and was just nodding her head to the music, oblivious to anything. As ever. They only time she ever came alive was in the Mall and she wasn't going to see one of those again for a while.

'We've got forty minutes, Merc.' Frances declared.

'We can do it.'

The truck lurched forward, laden, it rolled a little, but it was strong and Mercer was a good driver. If he had one quality, it was his driving.

Fen looked back at the house, the vine that hid most of one side of it and she had a strong feeling she'd never see it again. Nothing decisive but it was a strong feeling nevertheless. She'd already decided that if she got the virus she'd make sure she'd kill herself. She'd read about the symptoms and how almost no one survived and those that did couldn't even breathe on their own anymore. You'd be a cripple with a huge ventilation machine attached and all your joints would swell and people screamed when they tried to walk, the pain was so bad. No fucking way. If she caught it she'd make sure she died and take the evil Frances with her.

'Don't look back, kids,' Mercer was chirping. 'This is a big adventure and we're going to survive this thing.'

May looked back at Fen then and pulled a face. Fen shrugged. Both of them knew it was bullshit. Even if they survived, what would they come back to? Empty malls? Empty schools, empty cities, it'd be like that movie 28 Days Later. A city full of fucking zombies. What was the point of surviving exactly?

2

Office Pandemic Defense Kit:

The Office Pandemic Defense Kit can be easily stored in a locker, a vehicle, classroom, workstation and may even be carried in a backpack to assure you have immediate access.

1. (1) Box of (20) N95 Disposable Respirator Masks, Non-Valved (exhale) to protect others and for entry into facilities not allowing valved Masks.
2. (1) Box of 25 Pair of Nyplex (non-Latex) Disposable Medical Quality Gloves.
3. (1) Box of 100 5" x 8" Sani-Dex Sanitizing Hand Cleansing Towellettes. Kills 99% of Germs
4. (1) Box of 50 5" x 8" Sani-Cloth HB Bactericidal, Fungicidal Virucidal Disinfects Surface Wipes
5. (1) Pair Indirectly Vented of Anti-Fog Full Protection Goggles
6. (5) Medium Size Red Infectious Waste Bags with Bio-Hazard Symbol
7. (6) Packages of 20 each Pocket Two-Ply Tissues in Resealable Pouch.
8. (1) 7" x 15" Nylon Carry & Storage Bag with Cord Lock, assorted colors only

http://www.safetycentral.com/ofpadekiavbi.htm

Vancouver – Early October

'That's the third one I've seen today.'

'Huh?'

'Look over there, by the coffee bar. See the woman crying?'

Arno followed the direction of the stubby finger and indeed saw a woman holding a small dead dog in her hands and weeping hysterically. Two other women fashionably underdressed looked uncomfortable as they frantically searched their own handbags for their own dogs, no doubt fearing the worst.

The taxi sped on towards the bridge. Arno looked back at the women with concern.

'Getting so I see at least one a day.'

Arno was tired and the flight had been fraught. He hated flying, even though with all these health scares most flights were running half empty now, filled with passengers looking suspiciously at one another, all sitting the regulation three feet apart, the middle seats always unoccupied. Going through the process of fumigation before you got on the aircraft was distinctly unpleasant and probably redundant. It was just PR protocol to make people feel as though something was being done. It was worse arriving with everyone being herded into screening areas and no one allowed to leave until temperatures had been taken along with saliva samples. Two-three hours waiting to get on a flight that would last five hours and another two hours just to get out of an airport, no wonder no one wanted to fly.

He adjusted his N95 face mask. He hated wearing it. Hot, made his face itchy and it was redundant. He removed it, let it sit on his neck. Made him look stupid, but he was in a taxi for god's sake and who gave a shit how he looked.

'They suck. You get it, you get it. I only wear mine when I have to talk to someone. I heard that you can catch it if they touch you. You hear that?'

Arno looked at the taxi driver who was staring at him from his mirror. He noted the cabbie was wearing his mask loose as well.

'It's just a palliative that's all. Won't stop it. I heard that about touching too, but it's skin on skin. Virus lives on the skin. No one shakes hands anymore. What's with the dogs anyway.'

'Handbag dogs. It's an epidemic. Why women got to keep stupid dogs in their bags beats me. Must stink.'

Arno was confused. When did this thing cross over to dogs? Could be just a coincidence of course. Could be natural, dogs weren't supposed to live in a woman's purse. They could catch anything in there. His ex, Monica, used to keep her dog in her bag. Yapped all the time. Used to want to zip it up in there. She cried for a week when someone snatched her bag back in Montreal. The bagsnatcher must have gotten a surprise. Hope the dog bit him at least. Had nasty sharp teeth. At least it should have bit him.

'You're right,' he told the cabbie at last, 'not a healthy environment for a dog.'

'Damn right.' They were finally crossing the bridge in slow traffic, going around a truck that had stalled. Arno was yawning when he saw the ambulance, the guys in full HAZMAT decontamination suits hauling the driver out. Looked like all the blood had drained out of him. Wouldn't last ten more minutes.

'His number's up.' The driver muttered as they moved on, picking up speed.

Arno looked at his own hands. What the hell was going on in this city. He'd been told the virus hadn't reached here; yet in the space of five miles he'd seen dead dogs, a dying trucker.

9

'You wanted The *Sheraton* on Burrard, right?'

Arno nodded. 'Yeah.' He was staring right at the *Wall Centre*. Looked to be one the tallest buildings in the city. He'd hoped for a nice discreet old fashioned place with balconies. Not something with thirty-five floors. Never ask a secretary to book a hotel for you without making it clear what you wanted.

'They just reopened it. Had two hundred quarantined for sixty days. Shit, wish I could get quarantined in a luxury hotel.'

'I guess if you have to be...'

'Two people blew their brains out, I heard.'

'Sixty days of *Days of our Lives* and I guess we'd all go a tad crazy.'

The driver smiled. Yeah, that would do it for sure.

Arno put his mask back on, took out a hundred and put it in the slot. He wouldn't get change. No one liked to actually touch money anymore. You had to have it cleaned at the bureau. Always some bastard who figures out how to make money out of misery.

The driver pulled up outside the hotel portico and looked around. He saw the money in the slot and nodded. Arno grabbed his overnight case and then paused with a hand on the door. 'You might want to consider a different job whilst this scare is on. Not a good idea to be so open to the virus.'

The driver laughed revealing gleaming white teeth. 'I'm inoculated. No bug is going to get me.'

Arno was about to say something more but thought better of it. He knew there was no effective inoculation yet. TCH-5 had manifestly failed to halt it. The virus was still mutating. There was no inoculation, no cure. A new derivative of Tamiflu was out there and being distributed, but that had never been designed to combat H5N1 – or this, whatever it was going around now.

'If you need a driver whilst you're here. Name's Deka. Take a card from the box.'

Arno took one, gave him a brief nod and exited the cab.

He was immediately approached by the masked doorman who made no attempt to take his bag. 'Good evening, sir. You have a reservation?'

'Yes I...'

The doorman cut him off. 'If you would go into the ante-lobby.'

The cab sped away and Arno strode uncertainly in the direction indicated, knowing with a sinking heart that he was going to be fumigated again.

He wondered if anyone had tested this stuff for allergies... dammit he didn't want this shit, not twice in one day.

He got to the ante-lobby and was surprised to find no one there. The door closed behind him and he turned to protest when he suddenly understood. A private ambulance had driven up – a guest was leaving on a stretcher.

He looked a moment too long, saw her distorted face, looking drawn and misshapen, a mess. He experienced a flash of sudden recognition as their eyes met for a second. Desperation and fear. Surely not? The mask covered her mouth but he knew it was her, he'd seen at least three of her movies. He knew in a second he wouldn't be seeing anymore.

'She jumped.' An emotionless woman's voice declared from behind him.

Arno turned around and saw a uniformed girl from the hotel. 'Jumped?'

She shrugged. 'Her husband died last night. Got the virus on location, I guess. She went crazy, all night long, I hear. She jumped a couple of hours ago, landed on a delivery truck. It's a shame.'

'So not the virus.'

'No.' She sighed and picked up a clipboard. 'You arriving?'

'Yes'.

'Better get you checked in then.' She smiled and Arno still slightly bewildered at the latest tragedy meekly followed her into the main lobby. He couldn't believe it. It would be all over the news soon. He reflected that he'd come here to escape the oppression of back East. Here, he'd thought, would be optimism – this was still the city of the future at the edge of the new world. City on edge more likely. Back East people were jumping when they got the virus, better to get it over with fast. But it takes courage, even knowing you might be dead in 24 hours, it takes courage to jump.

The receptionist turned and attempted a smile, inviting him to speak.

'Arno Lakis.' He told her and she flipped open the desktop screen to search for his name.

'Welcome, Mr Lakis, I hope you will enjoy your stay in our city. And good news, you have been upgraded. We have a suite with an adjoining sitting room for the same price. It's a really nice room.'

'I'm sure it is. As long as the shower works. It's been a long day.'

She smiled as he offered his credit card. Arno just wished the check-in would go faster. He really wanted to wash the flight out of his system.

'Top floor', she added. 'Great view.' She handed him a keycard. 'Enjoy your stay.' She was about to give it to him when the computer dinged. 'There's a message for you.' She opened the message.

'Oh'. She didn't have time to hide her surprise. 'It's from the Premier's office. There's a number to call.' She printed it off.

Arno took it. He doubted he'd call. He'd hoped to arrive anonymously. Someone in his office must have arranged it. Damn. This was a personal trip, damn it. 'I hope you have a pleasant evening,' he told the girl.

'Diane,' she informed him. 'If you need anything, it's Diane.'

Arno already knew that from the name badge on her lapel. He just wanted his room. 'Thanks, Diane.' He walked to the elevator. The sign on the door said *'Please for the security of all of us wear your mask at all times when in public. We can beat this'*.

Not this time. He didn't think they'd beat it at all.

Rachel waited a while – watching the sky from her 30th floor window. She'd never wanted to live so high but Candi had arranged it whilst she was in Europe. Now Candi was gone and the damn apartment nothing but a stupid liability. Since the virus appeared all construction had stalled. Now the Olympics looked like being cancelled, real estate values were in free-fall. What use is a half-share in an apartment that no one wanted? The realtor told her it was worth thirty percent less than when they bought it and this was supposed to be the big investment. Property was never going to go out of fashion right? No one was building land anymore. Well who knew the virus would kill the market so quickly?

Rachel hadn't even lived in the place for most of the time they owned it. She'd gone to visit her Mother in Cloverdale when Candi arrived sick from her vacation in Cambodia. That was back in the first wave. They never even saw Candi. They stopped her at the airport – took her to quarantine and she was dead in a week, her lungs turned to water they told her. Then they quarantined the entire building because some guy from Korea collapsed in the lobby. Four months on, she was finally back in the apartment and facing bills she couldn't pay. In four months half the city was on welfare, the other half in nice safe government jobs. The banks were calling in loans, the whole economy was spiralling down and no one had come up with even a suggestion of a cure. Got to burn out the experts were saying. 'Natural phenomena,' they said. Hell why they didn't stop international travel earlier? Surely they had plans to deal with this shit?

All Rachel *was* sure about was she'd sunk thirty grand of her own savings into this one-roomed apartment and she was going to lose it all, if she couldn't pay the mortgage on the 1st. Didn't help that it was now known as the plague tower. But then, almost all the towers had plague now. Martin, the prick she used to work with, was really excited by these 'buying opportunities' and couldn't wait for the prices to bottom out. He'd sold just before the virus struck and was planning on buying a penthouse for next to nothing. She told him. 'What's the use of a penthouse, Martin, if there's no one left to impress?' But he didn't get it. No one did. No one was thinking straight. Arno would understand, he'd predicted this, told everyone who'd listen that this economy couldn't survive a pandemic, but no one really listened. It takes imagination to understand that if enough people die or get scared the opposite of capitalism occurs. Hardly anyone was left alive who could remember a real recession, a time when prices went down.

Her cell vibrated.

'I'm here.'

Rachel smiled, an audible sigh of relief on her lips. 'Take a shower, go to bed. I'll be there in an hour.'

'I showered already. Come now. Ask for the Penthouse Suite.'

She laughed. 'Take a cold shower then. I don't want you over excited.'

Arno smiled and hung up. He'd come a long way to see Rachel. Taken this early vacation. Even though they didn't want him to go. Considered him vital. But he knew, as they didn't, that vital meant nothing now. Either they went with the plan, or they didn't. Nobody was vital anymore. The virus saw to that. Everyone was singularly redundant now. He'd sat in a meeting on Friday listening to all the plans to keep the economy going in the face of the virus and he'd come to a decision. Just one thing mattered to him. Rachel. A young woman he'd been with once, for a day and night in Kelowna. Neither one of them had wanted to be there. Just another stupid conference. She was assisting Draycott with his presentation and Arno was giving a paper on risk in the real estate market going forward to 2012. All history now. Draycott was dead and the financial world was like a snake consuming it's tail. His pandemic model was ignored until it was too late to implement it with any real meaning or impact. No one really wanted to face that. You drive around cities in the world and you can see the high tides of economic prosperity, different peaks and troughs, each one marked by the architecture dominant in the last phase of prosperity. You could see it in London, New York, LA, old European cities like Valencia or Newcastle, every city had a tidemark of peak prosperity and now, just like other times in history, this would be another. Who knew how long before confidence would be restored?

Already the news was full of riots in cities right across the world, all the certainties had gone and people were scared. The virus had barely got started they should save their breath for later.

Rachel was his big plan. If you can't rescue the world, save yourself. Save the one you love. Selfish, but at least it was a plan he could make happen.

Deka was on a break. Two good fares in an hour with tips. Coffee was long overdue. He liked the Korean run Metrocafé on Main Street because he could sit in the window and watch his cab. He wasn't obsessed, but lately people were taking more risks and he'd been held up at gunpoint once already. Right now he was saving up for a bullet proof window between him and his fares. Bullet proof.

Germ proof. Whatever.

'Chicken soup?' Margi asked smiling, her Korean accent still quite pronounced, despite having been in Canada for twenty-five years. 'Chicken guaranteed disease free. From organic farm in Cloverdale.'

'You know I'm vegetarian,' Deka replied

'People change. Soup's good insurance against cold.'

'You may not have noticed Margi but I'm the only freak in this city who doesn't have a cold.'

'Or mask.' She remonstrated from behind her grease-stained and completely useless mask.

'Can't eat with a mask.'

'They say I may have to close next week.' Margi told him, wiping down the server counter with extra strength disinfectant.

Deka frowned, he hated the smell of disinfectant around his food. 'Why? Where will we all eat if you close?'

'Virus – they close all the café's. Even the ones on Robson.'

'They can't close on you. Hell you're an institution. All the cabbies eat here, and the cops.'

'Closed movies already, soon restaurants. I heard it on the radio. Bad business.'

'You'll survive. You must have made millions here. Margi, I know you live in a fancy house in Richmond. Been there remember.'

Margi shrugged. 'Big house cost more. If we close, we not open again. For sure.'

Deka frowned. If the restaurants closed, then so would the hotels and then there'd be no tourists. No one came from the States, as it was, since the border closed. If Margi closed, then how long before they halted the cabs? Just how bad was this thing? Come to think of it he hadn't heard the latest numbers over the radio and TV. Used to give out numbers every day at noon, but lately nothing. Then again maybe he hadn't been listening.

Another driver entered. Reece, big man, big fading ginger hair, lots of big opinions. Deka didn't like him. He was removing his gloves and shoving his mask to the top of his sweaty head. 'Schools closed in Richmond. Looks like they'll close all over. Bus drivers gonna strike for spacesuits for sure.'

Margi poured him a coffee.

'Soup smells good, Margi. Shit,' he turned to Deka and acknowledge him. 'If someone even sniffs near my cab they ain't getting in.'

Deka muttered something that sounded like agreement.

'Did you hear about Mishy?'

'The black guy, Ethiopian I think.' Deka ventured.

'Whatever. Got a fare to Langley right. Woman was sneezing. He had a headache when he got there, by the time he got back to the city his nose was bleeding and he called in, said he couldn't drive and when they got there he was dead. They wouldn't even open the cab to get him out. Ginny was all for burning it. Fucking virus is lethal man. One hour and he's dead. Like the plague. Worse there's more people now.'

Deka had heard some of this story over the radio earlier. Didn't know it was Mishy. 'I keep telling you, get yourself inoculated. Go see the Doc in Gastown.'

Reece shook his head and rolled his eyes to Margi. 'Margi is keeping me safe with her soup. Aren't you, Margi.'

Margi smiled. 'It's the ginger – lots of ginger. My Grandpa – he say long life much ginger.'

'Ginger might be good,' Deka acknowledged, 'but I tell you if you want to survive this thing you got to get inoculated. Doc says...'

Reece groaned. He'd heard it all before. 'If it's so good why doesn't everyone get it? Why just you?'

'I told you, he's willing to do all of us, he's looking for volunteers.'

Reece smirked. 'Fill our asses with junk, all have a good laugh at that.'

'He's a Russian Doctor and everything, had ten thousand patients over there.'

'Disbarred probably. What did he do? How many patients did he kill Deka? Huh? You seen the state of Russian hospitals? That's where all this shit that's killing us probably grows. You seen the HIV figures for Russia for christsakes? It's scary. It's way out of control and they don't give a shit. All that oil money in Moscow and what did they do with it? Buy Europe that's what. Don't get me started.'

'He just don't have the papers to practice here, that's all.'

Reece laughed again, sitting down to spoon up Margi's chicken soup. 'That just makes us all Doctors. I can cure AIDS. Just put some of this soup on your dick and hey – magic.'

Margi cackled.

Deka finished his coffee and stood up. He knew he couldn't convince anyone anymore. Not here. Not anywhere, but he knew. He'd been inoculated. The virus wasn't going to get him. He'd be the last cabbie on the road and they'd all be dead, chicken soup or not.

'Gotta go.'

'Yeah'

'See you tomorrow,' Deka told Margi as he picked up his hat. She shrugged like she wasn't so sure about that. Deka paused a moment like he was going to say something important, but then just smiled and left.

Margi watched him go and checked the time.

'I never liked him, but he my best customer. Why he think this thing not going to get him huh? He think he special.'

Reece chuckled, breaking his toast into the last of his soup. 'I hate everyone who gets in my fucking cab, but they're all my best customers, Margi. Make that a coffee to go. Got to stay out there longer now, pretty soon everyone's gonna be so broke they'll start walking everywhere.'

Margi frowned. That was what she was thinking too.

Rachel glistened with sweat. Arno peeled himself off her and looked down at her perfect body. She was a little pale, but he enjoyed seeing the balls of sweat gathered on her chest spread over her stomach. Loved the scar that crossed her belly from when she had been climbing as a child. Loved her tiny brown nipples erect as she savoured the moment, her eyes closed as she found her breath. One of her hands pulled him down on top of her again and she squeezed him tight, the other hand squeezing his right hand, lacing slippery fingers between his like she wanted to merge.

She opened her eyes and laughed, burying her face in his hair. Then pulled away as she suddenly realised something was different. She looked again and Arno made a face.

'My God, your hair.'

'Not a word.'

'I like it. I really do.'

'I don't. Woke up last month and suddenly I was silver, or at least...One day black, another day silver. I was in a state of depression for a week.'

'I'm gonna call you skunkhead. Wow, just one side?'

'You think I'm a freak?'

Rachel smiled, sliding her hands down to his ass and squeezing him affectionately. 'God I've needed this for months. I'm too scared to date, to even stand next to anyone now. Shit, I didn't realise how much I needed you.'

Arno smiled, tracing a finger around her face. 'No one kisses anymore, no one does anything intimate. It's like everyone is suddenly married.'

Rachel laughed and pushed him off her, pulling at his head to get a closer look. She kissed the back of his neck – pressed his head to her breasts and held him tight.

'I'm kissing hungry now.' Then, asking the question she didn't really want to. 'How long have we got Arno?'

Arno didn't reply immediately. He wasn't sure what she meant. He unwound himself from her grip and kissed her full on the lips, lying back on the bed and drawing her close to him. He was overwhelmed at just how much he loved this woman, her smell, her everything. 'How long?'

Rachel ignored it. She frowned trying to be logical instead. 'This is crazy. We could be dead in the morning. You've been flying, who knows what you breathed in. You know they aren't releasing the figures here, right? When it hit a thousand a day they kind of stopped letting us know.'

Arno stroked her hair and sighed, reluctant to let this moment slip away to reality. 'I wore a mask. Sat alone, was fumigated, took two showers and I'm taking TCH-6, twice a day.'

'TCH-6? They're still giving out TCH-5 here.'

'It's useless. TCH-6 is ...well probably no better. I brought a supply for us.'

'But flying...it's...'

'There were only ten people on the flight Rachel. The airline won't survive the winter. Only government people are flying and we all take precautions.'

'Did you really come just to see me?' There she had said it. Insecurity out there. What would he do with that she wondered?

Arno smiled and then reached for the bedside table and a little red box. Rachel had noticed it. Kinda box that contained serious sentimental shit. She'd seen boxes like that before. Never got one, but seen them.

'If I open it?' She asked, knowing there would be a price to pay.

'You say yes.'

'If I don't open it?'

Arno pursed his lips, then bit her gently on the nose. 'I came for you, Rachel. I don't want to spend another day without you.'

Rachel rested her head on his chest and stared at the box lying not more than two inches from her face now. She thought of her mother who longed for her to be married and be normal and yet...

'You don't love me?'

'I...' Rachel closed her eyes. 'Describe it to me.'

Arno stroked her hair and placed one leg over her to keep her tight to him. He understood her reluctance. After all, this was the only second time they were meeting, and he was older, probably much older than she figured she'd end up with. 'It's a blue sapphire, set in white gold. It has five faces and it used to belong to Princess Grace of Monaco. It was given to her by Alfred Hitchcock when he wanted her to come back to him and make another film. Her husband, the Prince, naturally didn't want her to wear it. In fact he was probably insulted. So secretly, it was sold to a Dr Raphael Lakis of Nice and he gave it to my mother when he met her one January when she was taking the air.'

'Your stepfather?'

'My father. He died a year after I was born. Enter the rather aloof Mr Holness and hence yours truly raised in New York, Geneva and then Africa. A UN child through and through, fluent in everything except living in my own skin.'

'Your mother?'

'Smoked, drank, played bridge, lived liked a princess. She told me once that if she lived past sixty, I was to take her out and shoot her. I am happy to say she died in her sleep at the *Ritz* in London and was mourned by many.'

Rachel felt immediately intimidated. God it was so European. Her mother used to play bingo at the Legion until last year. Never left Cloverdale except to go to White Rock once a year to paddle.

'Of course I could have bought the ring at Jerry's Pawn and he'll take it back for half the price as long as you don't get it tarnished. Not quite as interesting, but...'

Rachel smiled. 'I'll open it later. I think I'll mull on the princess and the pea story for a while.'

Arno just closed his eyes and let things be. Rachel lay there listening to their hearts beating. 'I never want to leave your side. You didn't need a ring, Arno. If I had known how to find you I would have come looking. I felt so stupid. I didn't even know your name. Nothing. I could remember everything but your name and when I called the conference people, everyone had left and of course the stupid conference speeches were confidential, so no one was going to tell me anything. I thought I could find a list of speakers or something, but even that was secret. Then I got this call telling me to back off and.... That's when they stopped delivering mail of course and so I just prayed you'd contact me by email.' She drew breath, he held her tight. 'I didn't even know if you knew my name. I thought about you every day. Draycott promised he'd tell me who you were; but when he collapsed four days later...it...'

Arno kissed her forehead. 'I flew to London. I knew on the flight there I had already fallen in love with you. I thought you were married. You were wearing a ring.'

'I always wear that at conferences. It keeps the men off – mostly.'

'I don't think I looked at your hands, not until later.'

'I looked at yours. No ring. No watch, no nothing.'

'Never liked them. Time's on my phone. I had my secretary try to trace you. But although she came up with a name – I knew you weren't an Audrey.'

'I replaced Audrey. I had to use her security clearance because mine wasn't ready. Mr Draycott didn't think anyone would notice.'

Arno felt a momentary annoyance. Aside from the security breach his secretary should have picked up on that. There was a digital picture of everyone there, how had...?

Rachel opened her eyes. 'I signed her name for everything. Even wore her glasses in conference. I don't even wear glasses. Remember? You were puzzled when I read you some of his pompous speech. I tried rewriting some of it, but where to start?'

Arno had a vivid impression of their night together in the hotel, the creaking bed, the shower head that fell off, the lizard that crawled across the ceiling.

It had been on the flight back to Toronto from London when he had suddenly remembered seeing her name. It was right there on her car reservation Rachel Geary. RACHEL. He had let out a cry of joy when he remembered and disturbed everyone, but it was a moment of intense pleasure. He'd called the moment they landed and he got her number and even though he only got her answerphone just hearing her voice gave him hope.

'It's funny I never really knew I needed anyone till I met you and now I can hardly breathe without you.'

Rachel allowed a smile to spread and dug her fingers into his arm. It had been the same for her, exactly. Just one night and she'd let him go. She'd known the moment she got in the car and drove away that she'd made a huge mistake in not asking his name. By the time she'd reached Hope she was sick with regret and tried calling the hotel back in Kelowna, but of course, even as she dialled she realised she didn't even know his room number. Draycott was useless, didn't even pretend to be interested in her problems.

'And then came this plague.'

'And then came this plague.' She acknowledged. She suddenly reached out and grabbed the box. 'I'm going to open it.'

Arno watched her as she broke the seal and gingerly opened it up. She snapped it shut immediately. She looked at him with surprise and wonder. 'It's beautiful.'

Arno smiled. 'Like you.'

'Arno – it's worth a fortune.'

'It was designed to lure a princess back to Hollywood, Rachel. It better impress.'

Rachel stared at it again, allowing more light on it this time. 'I don't know why I'm so scared of it.'

'Because it means our lives, your life, is going to change.'

Rachel shut the box again, thrusting it under the pillow and turning inwards, curling up like a child. 'Arno, I'm broke. I don't have a job. I'm going to lose my apartment and the money I invested in it. I got unpaid bills stacked twenty feet high. I'm just worthless...'

Arno put a finger to her lips and shook his head. 'No, I'm worthless. I should have asked you to marry me the night I met you. I'm the one who made the mistake and besides, you think money is important right now? Didn't you listen to my paper? The only thing of value we have is our health, Rachel, and our love. Nothing else matters. Absolutely nothing.'

Rachel snuggled up to him. She didn't really have anything to say. She felt as though she had been wrapped up in a warm rug and she was five years old again, trusting, feeling loved and secure. If Cindi had been still alive she knew what she would be saying. 'He's too old for you. Just because you like him doesn't mean you can stay with him forever. Think about it Rachel, he'll be like seventy when your fifty. He'll be old. Sure he makes you feel safe, but can you really imagine a future with this guy?'

Arno was stroking her head. 'You worried this is going too fast?'

Rachel pressed her back into him securing his arm around her tighter. 'I was thinking about Cindi. My roomie — we bought the apartment together before she died. She was always preparing herself for disappointment, y'know? She'd find potential flaws in every relationship and work at them until they happened and then she'd be happy. She almost took satisfaction in seeing it all crash around her. She used to laugh at me because I'd just sort of adjust. Meet a guy, he'd want to spend half the winter watching ice hockey or most of the summer sailing or something and I'd know I was just the bit of his life he'd fit in between all that. I mean Cindi would fight it, demand attention, but you'd know the guy was thinking about the game he was missing, or the guys down at the bar. Then they'd start resenting her and in the end, she'd be that meat in the sandwich, they'd be there for the sex and nothing else. I just didn't want that.' She paused a moment realising something. 'I guess I wanted this.'

'Back in Toronto, my job is to second guess events about the future, as you know. I was sat in yet another a stupid meeting listening to everyone speculating about how bad this pandemic is going to be. We were discussing whether there was enough of the latest vaccine to go around and who was going to get it first and what would be the best way to protect our investment portfolio. Suddenly I realised that if I had any future at all, it had to be with you. I just got up, left the meeting and booked my flight. I don't know anything about you, why you matter so much to me, but you do.' He smiled to himself and hugged her tighter. 'That scare you?'

'No. A bit maybe.'

'I sold my house the same day. There's a guy back in Montreal buying up all the quality houses he can find. Got backers in Saudi I think. He makes an offer, maybe thirty percent less than what it's worth, or what they were worth last year. I took the cash. My realtor figures I lost half a million but I believe I made on the deal. Bought gold. I'm either stupid or...'

'You think you did right? I mean, now you don't have a place. Hard to give up a home.'

'Who knows?' He shrugged. 'But the way I see it, they threw their money away. Besides I'm here now.'

Rachel half turned. 'You're not going back?'

'No. You'll see. Rachel, I've seen the mortality figures province by province, the ones they aren't telling you about. They are truly scary. It's far worse in the States of course. I left just in time. I believe that in a day they'll close all the airports and stop interstate travel completely. Once the trucks stop, the economy will nose dive right across here and North America. Everyone is really nervous to make that decision, but if they don't close the highways soon, it's game over. Everyone believes they are immune to the virus because we had this mass inoculation programme. But TCH-5 only held the virus back – in fact it is probably responsible for why the virus is so virulent now. It had to overcome H-5 first and now it's lethal. We got TCH-6, but can we roll it out with a mass inoculation programme without actually spreading the virus further and faster? I don't think it's come in time. Meanwhile everyone continues to go to school, go to work, shop, In fact they have to, they have to pay the rent, pay salaries, maintain the status quo or give in. But every extra day people get on the Skytrain to go to work, or just stop to get a sandwich and coffee, the virus makes a friend.'

'But that's the problem.' Rachel agreed. 'Everyone has to go to work to get money to pay the rent and buy the food. The antivirals make everyone feel safe at least! Who can stay at home? I mean once you've exhausted your savings, who'll pay the damn rent or mortgage? What's to stop the landlord from throwing you out or the bank repossessing your apartment? How long do you have to hoard food for and then how do you stop going crazy? Even now, if I ever see another repeat of *Friends* I want to scream already.'

'I heard they already shut down most TV series production in LA after an outbreak in Burbank. This is the tipping point, Rachel. The exact moment when we should shut everything down and hope for the best and it is most likely a month too late. That's why I knew I had to make my choice yesterday.' He took her hands. 'It's you, Rach.'

Rachel buried her head into his chest. He really had come for her. Burned his boats and everything. She should feel pressured, but it still felt like relief. Like she'd been on this desert island and he'd finally seen her desperate waving. She pulled away a moment, taking a good look at him. She smiled. 'You think you could make love to me again?'

Arno shook his head and laughed. 'No, but I can try.'

Rachel put a hand onto his lips. 'No history of heart attacks? I just got you, I'd hate to have to send you back broken.'

Arno kissed her and she responded with some force. He was thinking that this was how love should be. It was hard to find a soulmate in the best of times, now it was perfect. Now, no matter how bad it was going to get – he'd be with her.

'They closed the airport,' Reece told him over the radio. 'I just got the last passenger. Port and Train stations closed too. I heard they are closing the highways into BC as well. All of them. No one out, no one in. Schools next. The universities are talking of suspending this whole semester, but the students are already here. They're going to go crazy.'

Deka muttered something. He had known this was coming. Everyone was scared.

'Had a guy in my cab from the hospital. They admitted twelve-hundred today. Twelve-hundred, Deka. It was about a hundred a day last week. He says they've opened a mass burial pit right by Deer Lake and another near Port Moody.'

Deka hadn't heard that one. 'I had a doctor in the back who says they don't burn the bodies. Got no time, just dump them in a pit add some chemicals and go back for more. She was heading up to Quesnel. Says the virus hasn't reached there yet.'

Reece snorted on the radio. 'If it ain't there now, a doctor's gonna to take it up there. Fuck being a vegetarian. Start with the chicken soup, Deka, really. I mean it.'

Reece signed off and Deka was sat in his cab waiting for the next customer. Chicken soup. He was tired of telling people he was a veggie and besides chicken soup was the last thing anyone needed. Wasn't it chickens where all this had gotten started? Fucking Bird Flu! How many times did they say it wasn't going to spread to humans? Only just about everytime some kid died from it. Then something knocked it off the news and people forgot all about it.

He was bored. Been on duty now since 5 am. He liked to quit around seven. Only did the nights on weekends. No fares for an hour now and he'd read the paper, digested all the bad news he could manage, done the crossword. He was about to quit when he saw a guy running. The man looked a little bit crazy, even if he was wearing a suit. There were some people chasing him. Deka locked his doors. He didn't like the look of this situation. The man wasn't wearing a mask, the men chasing him were. They looked like security guards.

The man reached his cab. Tried the door and when it wouldn't open banged on the window shouting for him to open up. One look and Deka could tell the man was sick. Anyone could see that. He was sweating and his eyes looked hollowed out. He held up a hundred dollar bill, screaming now for Deka to get him out of there. But Deka shook his head. The security guards were joined by a doctor and a male nurse in HAZMAT space suits. They had the man surrounded, guns levelled at him.

The man turned again to Deka and held up several notes. 'A thousand. Take me to the airport.'

Deka looked past him to the doctor who was preparing a syringe. 'Airport's closed.' He yelled at the man. 'No one can leave now.'

The man's face fell. He knew it was over. He tensed as the needle went in, right through his suit and everything. The second guy in a space suit grabbed him, turned him around, and cuffed him. The shouting had stopped and they began to lead him away. The Doctor gave Deka a thumbs up, a thanks for co-operating he guessed. But Deka felt dirty somehow. Instinctively you wanted to help people, but not with this thing. Even the money was contaminated. A thousand bucks. That man must have been really desperate. Deka didn't want to think about it.

He unlocked, got out of the cab, grabbed the disinfectant and went around to the other side of the vehicle and began to clean every spot the man might have touched. Sprayed the window where he breathed on it and in particular the door handles. That's when he saw the notes. Ten of them, lying in the gutter. A thousand bucks.

He frowned. A thousand bucks off his payments would come in handy. He looked around. No one was looking. He sprayed them where they were and withdrew some tweezers from his pocket. He took them around to his side, placed the notes in a plastic bag; careful not to breathe the whole time he was exposed to them. He felt sorry for the guy; but then again, in twenty-four hours he'd never need money again.

He drove to the bank. The tellers all wore masks and gloves. The notes, like the coins, all had to go into a microwave to get zapped before they'd even look at them. Even then they picked them up with tongs and put them into a counting machine.

He'd put all the day's takings in with it. Almost eighteen-hundred with the thousand. He left himself two hundred to live on, put the rest in against his loan and felt a momentary lightening of the pressure. It still left five grand owing on the cab, but the bank would be happy for a while. He knew they were calling in loans all over the place, it was killing business as they instigated repossessions all over the city. Stupid. They should be lending more as business dropped. By the end of this plague the banks would end up owning everything and everyone would be beggars on the streets outside.

'Thank you, Mr Deka,' the bank teller said. 'You stay well now.'

From the corner of Deka's eye he saw a bank employee sneeze and several of the girls behind the counter wince behind their masks. They all looked trapped and scared.

'You too.' Deka countered and quickly left. He hated being out in public now. It was too dangerous. Time to go home.

Arno awoke at 4am. The time difference always got you. Even if it was only three hours. He often woke too early and it irritated him. Mostly he never got back to sleep and he watched CNBC or BBC NEWS 24. But not today. He had company.

She lay there, beautiful, even in her sleep. He loved this woman. Each inch of her. He knew he'd been right about her the moment she arrived at the hotel. She just clicked. Whatever that meant. No shyness, no uncertainty, she just knew, as he did.

At 4.30 he got up to pee. He didn't switch the light on and gazed into the bathroom mirror, which reflected light back from the city. Something about the quality of the light, it wasn't quite right somehow. He put the lid down (didn't want to flush either in case it woke her) and walked over to the window.

There was a building on fire. Looking east onto the slopes overlooking the city some miles away. Arno opened the window as far as it would go and immediately the sounds of sirens flooded the room. Rachel stirred and then opened her eyes. She saw him standing naked at the window; his face illuminated red from the streets lights. She slowly remembered where she was and who she was looking at it and smiled as a feeling of intense comfort flowed over her.

He must have heard her move. 'There's a fire. Many fires,' he whispered.

Rachel joined him at the window and realised with growing apprehension that she was looking at The Drive in the distance. The bohemian side of the city – her favourite side. 'Commercial Drive. Lot's of old timber homes. That's big.'

'Ten homes, maybe more from the look of it.' Arno remarked.

Rachel shook off the memory of sleep. 'Shit. I've got friends there.'

'Wake them,' Arno told her, the urgency in his voice emphatic. 'If they don't know, wake them. It could spread.'

Rachel ran for her cell. She had Tasha on quick dial and it dialled the number. It rang five times before a sleepy voice answered. 'Fuck, who is this?'

'Tash, look out the window. Now. It's me, Rachel. The Drive's on fire!'

Even Arno heard the screech from the phone as Tasha went to her window.

'Fuck, Rachel, the whole Drive is in flames.'

'Grab your things, get the cat and leave. Wake your neighbours.'

'It's huge, Rach, it's fucking huge.'

'Don't talk, leave. Get out now. Call me later. OK?' Rachel disconnected, shaken. Arno comforted her. 'You want to go there?'

Rachel shook her head. 'Only get in the way. Oh shit. Everything's turning to crap, Arno. The Drive will never be the same. Can't believe it.'

Another fire truck set off, sirens blaring. Arno went to close the window. 'You don't live near there? I don't really know where you live I guess.'

'Used to. I'm in Coal Harbour now. Till they repossess.'

'It's a bad time.'

'Is Toronto like this?'

Arno nodded and sighed. 'Nowhere to hide.'

Rachel nodded. 'I was going to go up to Nelson. Hide out there. I figured I could at least be a waitress or something and wait for the whole thing to go away. You kind of think it's far away, the cold winter will kill whatever it is that's spreading. Then I heard it got there on a school bus. Kids coming back from a hockey game in the States. Practically the whole town died.' She looked away a moment, sensing vertigo as she recalled her emotions. She didn't even know anyone in Nelson but somehow it had choked her up when she heard.

'That's why I'm here. I've rented a yacht.'

Rachel looked at him with surprise. 'A yacht?'

'Motor yacht to be precise. It's safe. I'm a good sailor. Actually I had a hard time getting it. Apparently they're all rented. I don't know what state it is in but she's seaworthy – apparently.'

'For us? I mean...a yacht?' This had truly surprised her. 'If I hadn't come?'

'I was banking on it. Come on. Let's shower and have breakfast. We have a lot to do. You ever been to the islands? I'm counting on you knowing which is which.'

Rachel stared at him a moment. She'd just been hoping to see him again, she'd made no plans whatsoever. He'd made so many plans. What else? But then again she recalled how just the night before she'd actually prayed, got down on her knees and prayed for the first time since confirmation, years ago, for God to send Arno to her and let her live out her life with him. She'd felt embarrassed doing it. Her mother would have slapped her. 'Never pray for anything for yourself,' she'd say. 'Prayer never works if it's selfish.' But not one of her prayers had ever come true as far as Rachel could ever tell. But then again knowing her Ma she might have prayed for everyone else to be as miserable as her. Rachel smiled a moment. She suddenly realised how lucky she was that Arno was there and it was him planning everything for her. She smiled.

'You really have been thinking about this haven't you.' Rachel told him, as she ran to the bathroom. 'Got to pee. Shit. I can't believe the Drive is burning. It's the last bit of the city with character. I hope people have gotten out in time.'

Arno turned to watch the flames in the distance. He wondered if it had been set deliberately. Lot of people who couldn't sell now were going for the insurance money. Things were worse than he thought out here. Time to put his plans into action. Put some distance between them and people.

Arno was about to join her in the bathroom when an explosion rocked the night air and sent flames shooting up towards the sky over the Drive. Windows everywhere in the cityscape lit up and some rattled with the force of it, even at this distance. He instantly knew what *that* was. 'There a gas station up by the Drive?'

'Is that what that was? Shit. There's a *Shell* station on Hastings, beyond Victoria Drive. Oh shit, that's going to be bad isn't it. You don't want it spreading that way, there's all kinds of storage tanks by the docks and...'

Arno was watching the flames. Saw the pinpricks of secondary explosions all around it as parked cars ignited. The firemen would have their hands full down there. The gas station would blow itself out in time with an explosion that big, but all the timber buildings nearby would have been blasted. He hoped people had gotten out, but had a bad feeling about it. 'Definitely time to go,' he muttered.

'Shower first,' Rachel called out. Arno nodded. Yes, shower first. Weird. On this side of the city people slept on, oblivious to the panic over there on the Drive and here they were about to take a shower. They should be there, helping, getting people to safety but then, that's how the virus operated. Gets people when they are vulnerable, forced out in the open. Arno entered the bathroom, to be enveloped by steam. 'Let's go somewhere where no one gets ill or dies.' Rachel was saying as he joined her under the hot spray.

Arno looked at her, saw her glowing skin with tiny freckles on her shoulders and just held her a moment, letting the water cascade over them both. He felt a real thrill in just holding this women. Felt her body again his and then noted how perfectly they seem to fit. He lifted her chin. 'This paradise where no one ever gets ill. Does it have a name?'

Rachel shook her head and buried her head into his neck. 'No.'

'I'm sure there is a place out there, but right now there's a few hundred thousand people headed towards it. Just take one to be ill and...'

Rachel frowned. It was probably true. Only now was she realising that there was no escape. Not from people.

'I brought you a book to read.' Arno was told her when they were drying. 'It's about medieval Europe. *A Distant Mirror* by Barbara Tuchman. First edition. It's about the 14th Century. If you think things are bad now. It's just amazing how organised everything was five hundred years ago. Then the plague came and it just swept everything they knew for certain away. Created opportunities too. People used to pray for the plague to hit the next village, not theirs, so they could annex farmland.

'I think everything they teach us in school about the past is wrong. Absolutely wrong. Of course everything people knew about disease back then was utterly wrong too. We at least don't have to march across Europe flaying our skin raw with sticks to drive out the virus. Apparently sailors walked off ships, breathed on people and they dropped dead. It was incredibly virulent. Stupid thing is, with all our science, we have no idea how to stop the virus and neither did they with none. Of course they thought Europe was crowded back then with just a few million people. Who could have imagined the world would have six billion souls five hundred years later.'

'Nice light reading then.'

'Plagues come, plagues go. Whole cities die but someone always survives.'

'Let it be us.' She held him tightly.

'Amen to that. We're aiming to survive. That's my plan.'

Rachel laughed. 'It's a good plan, Arno. The best plan.'

Arno smiled. 'Yeah.' He kissed her neck. 'A good plan.'

Deka woke with a sore throat. He was not really concerned. He knew he snored and this often made his throat sore. It came with the territory of a sinus problem and his mornings were always difficult until he showered and generally neutered his 'condition.' The shower pressure was down he'd noticed. There was a distinct smell of burning in the air. He no longer listened to the news on the TV and the radio just depressed him. He opened his window and now he could see smoke in the distance. He went to the living room window and pulled the curtains. Even he, who could not be easily surprised, was taken aback. Jesus. The whole skyline towards Commercial Drive was black with smoke. There must have been a huge fire. He couldn't believe he'd slept through it. His cell rang. It was Mandy from the garage. They'd dated once or twice and he'd been serious for a while about her but nothing came of it. Entirely his own fault.

'Did you hear?'

'I can see smoke. A lot of smoke.'

'From Charles Street on down to the old Indian cinema, and then it jumped up Pender right over to Victoria Drive and took out the *Shell* station up on Hastings. It took out thirty homes before they got it under control. Silinky says three-hundred are homeless and the Drive is devastated. Firemen and volunteers were literally falling down with exhaustion. I saw it on the news.'

'What caused it?' Deka asked, trying to stand on a chair to get a better view from his balcony.

'Arson. Probably an insurance job. Some pizza joint was about to be repossessed, I guess they got pissed.'

'Silinky told you that?'

'Reece says it's arson. He heard it from a cop.'

Reece, always Reece. Deka resented the man's name, everything about him. 'What about the airport. It official?'

'No airport, no trains, no tours, no *Greyhound*. The *Four Seasons* is going to close. Gave notice to all the staff this morning. I guess a few other hotels will close.'

Deka swore. How was he supposed to make a living? They couldn't close down everything could they? Business still has to go on. 'What about you, Mand?

'Might as well call it quits. I'm going to my brothers in Langley. He can still fish. I can cook. Well he can cook better than me, but ... it's all turned to shit, Deka. Can't believe it. You won't forget me will you?'

Deka sighed. 'No. You know I won't. What about Banff? Didn't you have a sister in Banff? Might be safer up there in the cold.'

There was an awkward silence. Deka knew what that meant. 'I...'

'You didn't know, Deka. It took about a thousand out there last week. Some conference. She was catering and...' There wasn't much more to be said about that. 'Besides they got the army on the road. No one can get out or into BC now. Alberta's got a shoot to kill policy and they mean it.'

Deka coughed. 'Smokes coming this way, Mand. I got to go back inside. Go to Langley OK. You'll be safer there.'

'I'm going today. Deka?' She sounded emotional now.

'What?'

'I wish I'd had that inoculation you was going on about. I was stupid. You have to risk things. You live a good life, Deka Fortun. OK? You're a good man. I know you are. You don't heed what Reece says about you. He's a mean man, always will be.'

Mandy rang off, leaving Deka looking at his cell with confusion. Mandy getting sentimental? Damn virus mocks us all. What had Reece said about him? Bastard. Always mouthing off, always in his face. He had few regrets but Mandy was one. She'd been good to him, let him know she was ready for something permanent, but he'd been worrying about debt and ... well the moment passed. He didn't know why but he figured that was a goodbye call, in more ways than one.

Deka needed some breakfast. Needed his Rooibos tea, needed to pray. Everyday he prayed – he just hoped someone was listening. He wanted to pray for the people of the Drive. A lot of homes lost. Beautiful homes. One of the last heritage places of old Vancouver razed to the ground. He thought of his homeland then, of the problems that had driven him to Canada in the first place and then shook his head. Never cross a rising politician. He'd refused to teach the new history syllabus that was clearly a distortion of the truth. He made a stand that suddenly became headline news in the Argus and on TV. Suddenly he'd become an enemy of the ANC and unemployable. All the bitterness forgotten now. No point in being in the new world and remembering the old. No point at all.

The tea helped, but not as much as he had hoped. His throat was still raw. That wasn't right at all. He felt OK otherwise but there was a nagging doubt there. He thought about Doc. Could this inoculation wear off? Of course it didn't have to be the virus, hell anyone could wake up with a sore throat right?

He ate some toast and found it was pretty painful getting it down, even when he dipped it in his tea.

The trouble was, if you went even near a doctor with a sore throat they'd automatically put you in quarantine. They had powers. He's seen it with his own eyes the day before. He thought again of the sheer incomprehension on the man's face as he had beat on the side of his cab window. He had no idea that the virus lost you the right to be human the moment it started. Now almost no one reported a cold and that only made things worse. Even going to the pharmacy to buy a cold remedy put you under suspicion. They'd grab you on the way out. Or so he'd heard.

Deka made up his mind. No work today. He'd go and look for the Doc. Find out if he needed a booster or something. Yeah, that was it, he needed a booster. Reassured, he put on his shoes.

Sam North

3

Government studies completed in 2006 predicted that fully 40% of the population in the USA would be unable to work, or get to work during an influenza pandemic. A worst case scenario was predicted of 2 million mortalities in the lower 48 states alone. Civil infrastructure would be severely affected, delivery of all services impeded, some quite drastically and a prediction was made that some $600 billion would be wiped off the GDP in a pandemic year.

National Bank – pandemic impact analysis survey 2006

A Premier Calls

'The Premier isn't here?'

'No, er... he's here, I mean, on conference call – on screen.'

'Ah.' Arno smiled. He couldn't blame the guy. It was likely to be a lot safer in Victoria than Vancouver right now. There would be no courageous walkabouts in front of the TV cameras to reassure the public all was 'safe' then.

'Sit here, Mr Lakis. The Premier will be with you shortly.'

'I can't spare much time,' Arno reminded him.

The personal assistant smiled revealing straight white capped teeth that looked just a tad too bleached. 'He particularly wanted your input on this crisis.'

'Faith Popcorn not available then?' Arno joked mildly.

The assistant ignored him.

Arno had heard these words many times before. The government always wanted to 'sound out' people, particularly people they would normally have to pay a $5000 consultation fee to see. Arno wasn't impressed. The office was fitted out lavishly. The mahogany and maple Glendale architectural desk would have cost a bomb, as did the slew of Aeron chairs (though he was envious of those at least). The huge wall screen plasma screen was impressive too. No taxpayers money had been spared on making sure this space was impressive. He was studying the carpet. Wilton Claremont sapphire blue. Had to cost plenty. Very presidential.

'Wilton?' Arno enquired innocently.

'100 percent wool. Premier has allergies.' Came the explanation.

'I guess the office is meant to impress.'

White teeth looked a little put out. Probably chose the decorations himself. 'The Deputy Premier uses it and the Lt Governor when she's in town.'

'Well it's handy, that I grant you. He on-line yet?'

Arno studied the blond assistant in his Paul Smith suit and Church shoes and decided that the public purse was doing well out here in the West. Getting real value.

White teeth was fiddling with the PC, trying to get Arno lined up and the Premier on the screen so they could see each other.

'With you in a second.'

'No problem, I'm sure he's busy too.'

Arno scanned the Vancouver papers, noting that the morning edition was half the size he remembered with hardly any advertising. Most of the stories were supplied from Reuters and he wondered where the regular columnists were. It cost $3.50 as well. It was going to be impossible for printed papers to continue. They were particularly vulnerable in this crisis. He'd already made the prediction that most papers would fold. It was the law of unintended consequences. A combination of newsprint costs rising as pulping was affected by the virus and local distribution problems, staff shortages, as well as the huge drop off in advertising as retail went down the tubes. He was surprised they tried to stay in business at all. The progressive migration of news to the web and the cell phone would finish them off. People wanted their news fresh.

The screen suddenly came to life.

'Mr Lakis. Really appreciate you making the time for us.'

'My pleasure, Premier.'

'We got ourselves quite a pickle.'

'As you say.'

'I read your report you gave to Premier Bernay in Nova Scotia. Pessimistic.'

'I'd like to say realistic.'

'It's all in a word I guess. You think the new vaccine TCH-6 will fix it.'

'No.'

'Why not? We're going to be spending millions rolling it out right across BC.'

'Too late Premier. H-5 raised the stakes. The virus got tougher and smarter and TCH-6 will could raise it to something else entirely. At best you can save key workers, but the very act of another mass inoculation will just mean you spread the virus further faster.'

'Point taken.'

'I might add I was surprised that you hadn't closed the schools and universities.'

'The Prime Minister specifically asked us not to send panic signals and that would be a big one, Mr Lakis. Getting all the kids vaccinated was trouble enough with all kinds of religious groups wanting to opt out. We couldn't allow any opt outs. It was tough politically, but it kept the schools open. As it is, getting the East Indians to wear face masks over their beards is practically impossible.'

'The N95 respirator masks don't work over facial hair anyway, save yourself the trouble. Pretty useless on kids too.'

'People are frightened, Mr Lakis. They need answers.'

'Well, things have changed. You have to close this city down. Lock everything down. Airports, ports, everything.'

Arno studied the man who had been elected twice to the principal office in British Columbia and wondered if he was getting the message. He looked tired and harassed.

'The economy is already at breaking point, Mr Lakis. Retail is suffering real pain. We have record numbers on sick leave. We can't afford to capitulate.'

'You can and you have to. I know you have prepared mass burial sites. People aren't stupid. Believe me, they feel better about a government that is seen doing something than one that pretends nothing is happening. There's no easy way out of this.

'I saw dead dogs on my way in yesterday and a trucker dying on the road. Last night you had Commercial Drive burn. It might be connected, it might not. But every crisis enables the virus to get a bigger hold. We let H-5 lull us into thinking we weren't going to get it bad and now we have. Close everything down now, Premier. Impose curfews. Make sure people know you intend to enforce them. If you're not getting the true picture, get someone who can read the mortality figures. It caught everyone by surprise back East, no need for it to happen here.'

Arno could see the man was irritated by his remarks.

'We don't have the manpower for city wide curfew, let alone province wide, Mr Lakis.'

'People will stay indoors out of fear, Premier. They do in Toronto anyway. But you have to get contingency plans in place fast. They will need food and they will need electric power. If you can't get food distributed right, they'll go looking for it and then you'll see the virus grip hard. Remember modern cities are just three days away from catastrophe. Get the people to stay home and keep the power on at all costs.'

The Premier look upset now. Uncomfortable with this frank exhange.

'I read a memo that said we can expect the pandemic to last around 60 days. Do you agree with that analysis?'

'I wish it was so neat. Premier, this event could last five or six months here with peaks and troughs. No one really knows. In England they had a whole scenario worked out. 58 days from the first breakout to exhaustion, with a possible million deaths a week at the worst case. They could handle 45,000 deaths a week max.

I saw official documents from Fleet House. Their billion pound National Health Applications and Infrastructure system was overwhelmed. In a week they were on emergency power of only fours a day and software failures that meant they lost fifty percent of patient medical data nationwide. They stopped counting bodies after the first ten days and they say it might take four months or more to get around to burying their dead. It's a nightmare there and it isn't over yet. Everything they planned for failed in the first few days. I might add that the World Health Authority is overwhelmed already, they are short of manpower.'

'We have very robust emergency action plans in place, as you know.'

'Then action them. People are dying now. Close the city down. Prepare for something that might not peak until February.'

'You're talking about putting sixty percent of the population on welfare.'

'Better welfare than funerals, Premier.'

The picture suddenly went dark. No signal flashed up on screen. The assistant looked puzzled. 'We lost the link.'

Arno shrugged. 'You think he was listening?'

'He heard you, he's been taking views all day.' The assistant remarked.

'Well it's not a view. It's the only way to go.' Arno stood up. 'Got to go.'

He nodded, looking at Arno with a frown. 'You really believe this is it?'

'Absolutely. And you better hope he does or it's going to get nasty out there. Maybe too late already.'

Arno put on his mask and headed to the bathroom. He needed a leak. Moments later, when washing his hands, he had a bad feeling that the Premier wasn't going to action anything. Who wanted to be the one guy who would cause a financial meltdown? But he had to do it. That's why he was there, that's why politicians were elected, someone had to take the tough decisions.

He was annoyed. Futuretank strategists had predicted that the virus would peak back East first, but overwhelm all of Canada in time. Ignoring the obvious about closing BC to the Far East the moment the virus mutated had been a big mistake. The fact was, the virus had a direct line into the Western Provinces via the South Asian immigrants, and then with links to Eastern Europe too, where one of the first outbreaks had occurred in Turkey at the beginning of the Bird Flu, before it mutated. All places where people lived closely with birds, their immediate source of food.

Everyone had had enough warning but party politics and sensitivity to the large immigrant population – who were not keen to be identified as the source of the virus – meant they fudged it, and now the shutters were coming down on the whole economy.

The Premier was lucky. With restrictions on movement they couldn't hold an election and get rid of him. Equally, saying goodbye to the Winter Olympics meant hello to billions of dollars of defaults as private enterprise went belly up. *Now* they wanted advice – but other than swallow the barrel of a gun before you couldn't lift one...

He knew that the vaccination programme had failed. When the virus mutated, not once, but twice over a period of six months, they were overwhelmed. *Sanofi Pasteur* in France believed they had a fix, but that was there and who knew what new strain was developing in Europe. Damn thing seemed to adapt so quickly. Rumours down in Washington State were blaming complications with West Nile virus and this new influenza virus combining to make a perfect killer, but Arno didn't think that was possible. Didn't matter shit anyway, as his expertise was future planning and for that to be possible there actually had to be a future.

He wanted to get back to Rachel. It was definitely time to leave this city. His phone rang. He looked at the number. He sighed. He really didn't want to take this call. He had no good news for this client either.

Rachel was in the *Marketplace* store on Burrard. Mask on, like everyone else, nervously keeping away from others as she filled her trolley. She considered herself lucky to be among first ten allowed in – access was limited now since the first food panic a month ago. A rush of people invaded a Safeway on the North Shore and several people were killed in the crush. All because a talkshow host went on air speculation about food rationing. Now you took a number outside the store and waited, keeping your distance. There were at least four hundred in the line outside this store with armed guards in HAZMAT suits watching.

She had a list from Arno, mostly dried and tinned food, pasta, sauces, and sugar, stuff that would last on the yacht. She had to work out what they'd need for a month on the water. A worst case scenario Arno had told her. They would want to stop by the liquor store for wine if there was time. A month at sea without booze sounded damn bleak. She stopped by the long life milk – careful to check the dates of all the products. Now you had to calculate backwards to buy stuff that was made before the virus took hold. It was complicated and involved a lot of guesswork, and most of the foods were sterilised to hell and gone anyway, but one couldn't take chances. She wished Arno was with her but the Premier's office had called just as they were leaving and they insisted on meeting with him. He had no choice. Now they were together at last she was nervous to be apart from him. She wanted to be gone, on the yacht, away from the tension and daily exposure to people.

She had already been home, grabbed some clothes, switched off the electricity. There were bills outstanding but they would be taking the apartment back from her anyway...they could keep the bills too. Luckily they were in Candi's name and she wasn't paying anyone.

She saw a man coming towards her with his trolley and she quickly reversed out of the aisle – awkward now that her trolley was full. She saw him take out a small disinfectant and spray the area she had been in. She stared longer than was polite but this was what it had come to now. Each one of them terrified of the other.

Flour, she needed some flour, some pancake mix. Lemon juice. She had a sudden vision of herself aged ten packing for her first trip to camp, trying to figure out what would last a whole summer up by Osoyoos in the Okanagan valley. She smiled at the memory of swimming every day, her first yucky kiss from a boy called David Warblington (who grew up to be a gay priest). It was her first taste of freedom from her mother and father and despite all the rules of camp, it was as if she had become a butterfly. Going home to the oppressive manic depressions of her mother was as painful as having her wings clipped. Funny to think that Camp had been the only happy moment of her childhood.

Her cell buzzed. She looked down. A text from Arno.

'Got wine. Get some dried beans. On way back now. See you back at hotel.'

She sighed. Well at least they'd be together soon. Dried beans. She remembered something else too. Water. They'd need bottled water. Mustn't forget to check the date on that too and make sure the water was from the west. It didn't guarantee anything but ...how much? She looked again at the sticker. 'Guaranteed Purity. Government tested.' This was going to cost a fortune. That was another thing that had happened recently. Prices had practically trebled, more in some cases. Just how could people afford to eat, let alone stock up?

She made her way to the till. This would cost a grand. At least. A year ago three hundred dollars, if that. She wondered if anything would ever return to normal again.

'Not keen on fresh food huh?' The woman at the cash register remarked, looking at her trolley. She had a double mask on, hair net and wore cocktail gloves. Risky business being on the till these days. She was checking a new list a latest prices. 'The coffee is sixty-six a can, not thirty-four. You still want?'

'Yes.' Rachel barely hesitated. $66 bucks for ground coffee? Prices were going crazy now. This was the cheap stuff. She'd thought thirty-four was robbery.

'We're camping – big family. Can't get by without our coffee.' Rachel informed her, feeling guilty under her stare.

'Well, I hear bugs carry the virus, so I hope you know what you're getting into sweetie. Wouldn't get me out there.'

4

As Indonesia and Cambodia struggle to contain outbreaks, officials there are warning that failure could put the entire world at risk. Indonesia's flu Czar warned in the *Financial Times*, "Avian influenza is not only a problem for Indonesia. If we succeed, it will be a significant contribution to success for the world. If we fail, all the world will probably face the problem." Last autumn, a World Health Organization regional spokesperson speaking to Australia's *Sydney Morning Herald* warned that "There is no incentive for somebody who raises chickens to report infected chickens if he is not going to be compensated on the day government authorities come in and kill all his chickens."
Caging Bird Flu – Embassymag.ca

The Old Ways

Deka found parking and stopped by the corner store to buy some lozenges. He was remembering the day he got the inoculation and what the Doc had told him last time he saw him in Gastown. 'You know what is crazy, Deka Fortun? The only people who are going to survive this virus are the whores, the crack addicts, me, you and the winos. The only people who'll let me save them. Think on that, Deka, the meek shall finally inherit the earth.' Then he laughed, loudly, shaking the floor, revealing his two gold teeth. Deka liked to watch the Russian laugh. For him it was all about irony. Deka felt he understood the Russian. Over here bureaucratic bullshit wouldn't recognise Doc's qualifications. In Russia he'd been a respected (if

Sam North

slightly eccentric) virologist, a specialist in respiratory disease. In Canada he was a
lowly part time cab driver and caretaker for an artists studio in Gastown. In South
Africa, Deka had trained as a history teacher but he'd never found a teaching job
in Vancouver. They wanted him to do his qualifications all over again and even
then there would be no guarantee of a job at the end of it. Driving a cab was
regular and paid more. He, like the Russian, didn't understand why a country
would let them emigrate then not let them practice their trade.

The Russian wasn't at their usual coffee shop. Deka didn't like to wait around.
He didn't like to leave his cab on the street too long. Nothing was safe now. If
they couldn't steal they were just as likely to burn it. His throat felt easier now he
was sucking on the lozenges. He knew it was just temporary though and he really
wanted to see the Russian. Get some reassurance. That's what he needed. Just
some words that would let him continue believing. In the end words would either
save you or kill you.

Gastown was deserted. The stench of the smoke from the Drive was still heavy
in the air, but he'd heard over the radio that it was under control. Only five dead,
but many homeless. He felt sorry for those people, but maybe they'd be rehoused.
After all there were a lot of empty apartments available. People were reluctant to
go into a place after someone had died there, but you couldn't just sleep rough,
not in a city famous for its rain.

He decided to drive up the street to the Ironworks on Alexander street. The
gallery and studios were closed now. The area wasn't always safe at the best of
times, being so close to Hastings and all the junkies and their craziness. Doc Borov
ran his clinic there. It was a secret affair. Even the owner didn't know. One of the
rumours was that he'd taken off to the safety of the Okanagan when the first wave
of virus appeared a year before and showed no signs of coming back. Another was
that he'd taken off in his yacht for a remote Pacific Island. Whatever the truth, as
long as the place was safe and business ticked over he didn't bother Doc. Deka had
many fond memories of lively evenings of jazz concerts in this old building during
the Jazz Festival and he'd even tried Flamenco dancing once the previous year. Best
acoustics in the city and built like a battleship about a hundred years earlier. A real
survivor this building.

He noticed three cruise ships in the harbour and another two anchored in the
Burrard Inlet beyond. They weren't going anywhere anymore. Not since one had
arrived in Alaska with two hundred dead passengers and the rest dying. It had
been one of the first horror stories of the virus. Alaska wouldn't let them dock, they
had to anchor and wait until the virus burned out. Three hundred more died and the
survivors were damaged for life, their lungs scarred from the coughing. It was
dubbed the 'Ship of horrors' on the news and the world watched with shame as

they watched choppers drop food and medicines from the air onto the ship. Doctors were airlifted on board but they too succumbed and then no one else would go.

Now here the ship was, anchored in the inlet, maybe never to be used again.

He parked directly outside the building, locked and checked doorways for sleeping bums, saw none. Deka knocked on the gallery door. Got no response. He could see there was no one around. There was a bum walking crooked along the road, a brown bagged bottle of rotgut in his hands.

'You seen the Russian?'

The man looked at Deka and spat, revealing blackened teeth. 'Clinic back.'

Deka didn't quite understand for a moment, then realised what he meant. This was one of the Russian's many clients, the meek. The man didn't look as though he'd eaten food in months. He abruptly turned and started walking back the way he'd come, staggering across the road to stand with his back against the far wall, pinning himself up against it as if he was holding it up by his will alone. Deka turned away. Yes, saving the meek had its disadvantages.

He went down to the rear of the old building, under the road bridge that loomed right over it. He found a burned out truck down in the parking lot. Someone was going to be pissed about that. Scorch marks scarred the concrete above it. The property ended at the fenced off railway line. There was a sturdy wooden fence to the side. He thought he heard voices on the other side, but wasn't sure. A freight train slowly trundled by hauling a heavy load. It was kind of reassuring that something was still functioning. Deka pushed opened the gate, surprised to find it unlocked. Normally Doc kept it secure. He mounted the stairs. The back door was open, a boxer dog sat across the entrance, eyeing him suspiciously. 'Hello, Wylie.'

The boxer stood firm, he had orders. No one in or out unless told to. Deka let him sniff him. Wylie stood like a rock. Deka wasn't getting in unless invited. He was a big strong dog and he could knock a man down and hold him there if he had to. Deka wasn't afraid. He'd grown up with dogs – had one of his own back in the Cape. A Ridgeback called Solly. She'd lived eleven years and they'd been great pals. The trick with dogs was to treat them with respect. Solly knew every hiding place in the neighbourhood and had a burning hatred for cops. Just couldn't abide the blue police vehicles that were never far away. He and Solly ran wild in the mountain forest for years, never tiring of roaming. Deka had considered becoming a forester for a while. His rarely seen sober father despaired of him every getting his matric but study came easy to him and he passed with high scores. He never mentioned to his dad that sometimes he took his textbooks up there to the mountain reservoir with Solly and studied. It wasn't cool to be seen studying.

'Doc? You in here?'

A face appeared from within the darkness. A kid, pale face, shaved head. About twelve. Looked scared. He held the curtain in front of him so Deka couldn't see his body. 'Who wants to know?'

'Deka. Tell him it's Deka Fortun.'

The kid disappeared. Wylie nudged him back from the doorway, wanted him to know he was ready for anything. Deka just looked at him and smiled. 'It's OK, Wylie. I know you're doing your job.' The dog relaxed a little. Deka's voice was non-threatening, held no fear. Deka could hear some whispering inside. A curtain twitched. Doc's distinctive voice was heard. 'Let him pass, Wylie.'

The dog instantly lay down and Deka stepped over him.

He immediately noticed a burning smell. It troubled Deka as his eyes adjusted to the darkness. He moved into the inner room and the candlelight. The kid was sat on a chair in his skimpy underwear. A woman was prostrate on the floor naked; her skin seemed to be on fire, small blue flames burned all over her body. The Russian was protecting her hair as he dribbled more fuel onto the flames.

Deka said nothing. He was used to crazy things happening around the Doc. He just stood and stared as the Russian rolled the woman over and poured what looked and stank like paraffin over her and the flames spread over her belly. She didn't seem to be in any pain, didn't react at all. She seemed to be asleep in fact.

Deka continued to stare as the flames spread down her legs, between her legs, burning the stubble of her shaved pudenda. She wasn't young, a mother around forty. She was totally rigid, as if a force held her in place the floor. The Russian looked up a moment, their eyes met. He acknowledged his presence with a nod. 'She's going to be fine. I hope. Paralysed. Been like this for four years the kid says.'

'The fire?' Deka enquired, as he watched in fascination as her feet suddenly flared for a second. He figured that if had been *him* on fire he would have been screaming by now. The woman showed no reaction at all.

'Old Russian cure.' The Doc said, as if this explained everything.

'Like burning witches?'

The Russian snorted, appreciating the little dig. 'No, not like burning witches, Deka. That's what they do where you come from?'

'Sometimes they kill witch doctors. Mostly it's the other way around.'

'Paraffin.' The Russian indicated the bottle, now almost empty. 'It has many healing properties. She burns yes, but I didn't strike a match. Ask the kid.'

Deka didn't have to. The look on the kid's face was enough to know that he knew what was going on. As if to demonstrate the Doc poured the rest of the bottle over the kids back and instantly it flared blue as it burned across his flesh. Deka watched as the kid arched his back and stood without pain, almost as if the heat was welcome and eased his suffering. He hastily removed his underpants, which were in danger of burning. The Doc grinned but said nothing as the flames died on the boy's legs.

'Kid is OK.' He declared, tossing him his sweater. He put a hand out to the kid.

'Get dressed. Get some water. Your mother will be thirsty.'

The kid ran to the back of the room and into the darkness, happy to be released. Deka watched as the Doc poured some vodka over his hands and then ignited them over the candle. They flamed for a brief moment as he flicked them around to make sure he was sterilised completely. He grinned at Deka a moment. 'We resort to the old ways, Deka. Things we know that work.'

Deka watched as the last of the flames burned across the woman. 'I've got a sore throat,' he told him at last.

The Russian didn't react immediately. 'Red raw?' He asked after a while. 'Hard to swallow? Any temperature?'

'No fever, just hard to swallow.'

'Me too.'

Deka frowned. That wasn't what he'd come to hear. 'You too?'

The Russian stood up and eased his shoulders. At six foot three he was imposing. Always seemed to act as though a camera was recording his every move. Even now. He beckoned Deka to the corner where he dug out his half burned cigar and he lit it, taking pleasure in the moment as he got it going and blew smoke over the comatose woman. 'You know, Deka, I smoke the cigar because tomorrow I might die. Besides, this crazy virus only likes healthy lungs. Funny isn't it, my friend, something they don't tell the people. It's the smokers who are the least likely to get sick – that's kinda interesting don't you think. For years we have tried to make the world healthy enough for the virus to kill us all.' He smiled. 'Do not look so alarmed, Teacher. If your throat is sore, it means my little soup is fighting. The virus is strong, Deka. Very, very strong. It kills with ease. You are stronger. We all are. We have the scabs to prove it yes?'

Deka instinctively rubbed his arm. 'Ya.'

The Doc shrugged. 'You want a cigar?'

Deka shook his head. Hadn't smoked since he was eighteen. Wasn't about to start again now. He doubted starting now would save him.

'Well, I'll smoke a cigar, my teacher friend, whilst we await a decision. Victory or defeat? You'll know one or nothing of the other.'

'I heard it was over twelve-hundred yesterday.' Deka told him.

'Nothing. It is nothing. When you tell me it was two million and we are still standing I will shout for joy. When we stand alone in this whole ghost city we shall both get drunk and fight over who gets what, hey?'

'Two million?'

The Russian pulled a face. 'I said half the population could get it, Teacher. Back in 1919 perhaps 50 million died of influenza, maybe more. This time they say a hundred million. Perhaps more. Think of that, my friend. How could you design something that would kill so many young and healthy people so quickly, so precisely? So much skill in Mother Nature don't you think.'

'If it was Mother Nature.'

'Ah conspiracy theories.' He turned to look at Deka for a moment, eyebrows raised. 'You think something like this could be man made? Such a good design could be God or nature. Never man. Never man, my friend.'

Deka saw him wince as he swallowed. So he really was suffering.

'Read your history, Deka. Thucydides recorded a terrible plague that struck Athens in 431 BC. A year long, it killed all. Rich, poor, children, old women. It devastated the whole economy in Athens. He talked of violent hot headaches, eyes swelling, throats and tongues on fire, bloody spit and a powerful stink of the breath. It could be caught instantly and so many were dying they couldn't find anyone to bury the dead. Sound familiar? Everyone always assumes every plague is bubonic, but it could have been this virus. Then, as now, coming from Asia on infested ships. People went mad, Deka. Some spent all their money on parties and week long orgies. No one obeyed laws because no one expected to outlive it or to be brought to justice if they did. All this we can expect. And more. No one reads history but you and me, but it's there, handed down to us if we care to pick it up.'

The Russian moved to a cupboard on the wall and took out a key from his pocket. 'I've got something for you my, South African friend. It won't cure you, but it will make it easier, help you fight it. Something we borrowed from Thailand. I developed it a little. Got extract of Nime oil in it. Very powerful natural drug. The best cures grow on trees, you might say. People in India swear by Nime to cure almost anything.'

He unlocked and opened the cupboard, took out a small dark blue glass bottle.

'Tiny sips, no more than two – three sips a day and absolutely no driving for thirty minutes after. OK? You understand. You cannot drink this and drive.'

Deka stepped forward and took the bottle from him. No label. He unscrewed the cap and sniffed it. Just like cough syrup but something bitter in the background. 'You use this?' He asked him.

The Russian gave a short snort of derision and then coughed. It sounded wet and phlegmy. 'I'd never give you something I don't use teacher. Try it. Guarantee you will hate it. Soldiers used it in Chechnya to stay alive.'

Deka took a swig and nearly spat it out. It was like liquid tar. The Russian laughed at his expression and slapped him on the back. 'Tastes bad yes? Like proper Russian medicine.'

Deka felt like puking it up, but slowly warmth spread out across his whole chest and neck and like magic he felt almost well again. The Russian could see its effect. 'Only sips. OK?' He reminded him. 'No more until you are at home'.

'I don't suppose you want to tell me what else is in it?'

The Russian just smiled then turned his attention back to the woman on the floor. The very last flame flickered out. Deka could see that she seemed to have suffered no ill effects, save now he looked more carefully, her skin seemed waxy and covered in goosebumps. Deka noticed the kid was back in the room, dressed again and nervous, remaining just out of reach.

'Medicine is mostly about illusion, Teacher. A mere trick to fool the mind or the body that the pill or liquid we swallow will make us feel better. The mind can sometimes be fooled and then – poof – you feel better.'

'And this woman?' Deka enquired.

The Russian squatted down beside her. 'Ah there we have it. There's no fooling her. She requires the best medicine money can buy. She has it – right here.' The Russian rolled back and grabbed the boy, pulling him towards him. The kid looked terrified. 'This boy loves her, Deka. It is important to love your mother. Even if she hasn't spoken to you in four years. That's the best cure there is. Kid's got ingenuity. Brought her to me himself in a shopping trolley.'

Deka suddenly sat down. The liquid he had swallowed made him feel slightly dizzy. The Doc wasn't kidding that it was powerful stuff and he'd only had a tiny sip. He watched in silence as the Russian took down a large magnet from a shelf and swept it across the woman's body in a circular motion. He did this several times, addressing the kid who was watching his every move with the intensity of a small bird. 'Ben – hand me that needle I told you to keep.'

The kid didn't respond immediately. The Russian turned to look at him.

'Now, Ben.'

'She hasn't moved,' he protested.

'No,' the Russian agreed. 'She hasn't moved. You remember when you came in that I told you she wouldn't feel anything?'

The boy nodded.

'So no matter what we did she would feel nor remember nothing?'

'Yes.'

'Well now we need to wake her up, Ben, and I believe she'll walk. I need you to believe that too, Ben. She might not talk, but she *will* walk.'

Ben reluctantly took a long needle out of his pocket. Deka watched carefully. It was huge. Weirdly there was a sudden memory of his own there. A hut, up above Tamberskloof in Cape Town. A medicine man. A huge long shiny needle. His stepbrother who wouldn't talk. Never talked and was nine already and his mother, in desperation, had gone to see the shaman who lived in a small hut high up in the mountain slopes. A Malay man with a long blue robe and many shiny needles. He remembered closing his eyes as the man stuck the needles into his stepbrother, one by one and then he hit each one with a tuning fork. His stepbrother shrieked and then just as suddenly, clearly and as if he'd spoken all his life asked the man to stop. It cost all of a thousand back then, when the Rand was still worth something, but his stepbrother never stopped talking from that day on.

The Russian was sterilising the needle in the candle flames. He smiled at Deka, then abruptly plunged the needle smack into the woman's chest.

Her eyes popped open. Certainly she was feeling something now!

'Mrs Tooley. Your heart is in my hands. You want to live, Mrs Tooley? Your son Ben wants you to live. Can you hear me, Mrs Tooley? Blink if you can hear me.'

She blinked. Ben gasped.

The Russian turned the needle, then brought the candle very close, warming it, abruptly giving the candle to Ben to hold. 'Mrs Tooley, when I take the needle out of your heart I'm drawing out all the pain in your body. Every last pain. All your troubles and fears will go and you'll be able to walk home with Ben. Is this what you want, Mrs Tooley?'

She blinked again.

'On a count of three. Ben...count it down for me.'

Ben was shaking with fear and dread. 'One.' He could barely speak. 'Two... three.'

The Russian pulled out the needle and just as quickly slapped a plaster over the little hole to stop the blood, which spurted from the puncture wound.

An instant later a scream pierced the gallery and seemed to fill the entire space with an awful pitiful screech that was gushing from the mother's mouth.

The Russian raised the candle to her mouth and the scream became a flame that flashed across the room and then died in mid-air. There was only silence.

Ben was shaking so much Deka thought the boy would collapse, but in that moment of stillness Mrs Tooley groaned, then unexpectantly sat up, looking around her, surprised to discover she was in a room full of strangers. She looked at the boy who was staring at her.

'Is that you, Ben?' Her voice was hoarse.

Ben dissolved into tears and fell into the woman's arms. She folded her arms around him, dazed and unsure of herself. 'How did you get so big? What's going on? Who...' She saw the Russian and Deka watching for the first time. She realised she was naked. 'Good God, I'm...' She used Ben to cover herself but he was too big and she was too weak. She croaked. 'Will someone for the love of God tell me what's going on?'

The Russian walked to the next room as Ben broke free and grabbed his mother's clothes. Deka thought he should say something. 'You were ill. The Doctor helped you. Your son is a good boy. A very good boy.'

Mrs Tooley looked at Deka as Ben gave her a top to put on. She didn't seem to comprehend anything. Deka looked away as Ben tried to get her up on her feet to dress her completely. He was quite expert in dressing her, been doing it for four years now.

'Just get dressed, Ma. We're going home.'

Deka left to join the Russian who had a kettle on the boil already and was making coffee. Doc looked drained. This had been a miracle and Deka felt honoured to have witnessed it. 'I have a cab nearby. I'll take them home.'

Doc put an arm out to him and nodded. Deka was curiously glad to be able to help, do his bit. The Russian sighed. 'I need money Deka. Running out. No one pays. Everything costs more. You bring me patients yes?'

Deka drew out his wallet. He opened it up. There was the two hundred there. 'Take it, Doc.'

'I can't take your money.'

'I'd be dead without you. Take it. There's more if you need it.'

'You still might die.'

'Then tomorrow we shall eat and await death, Doc. I'll be here at seven. I'll cook you the best curry you ever had. Don't worry I'll bring all the food. I'm an excellent cook.'

The Russian offered him a tired smile. 'Da. Bring dog food. At seven then. Key's in the usual place. I need sleep and I have to lock up.'

Deka nodded acknowledging the trust. Doc kept a key hidden under the bridge for emergencies. Some Russian habits never die. 'Remember what you said, Doc. Each of us must save our corner of the world. Well this is our corner.'

Ben appeared with his mother leaning on him for support.

'I have a cab,' Deka told him. 'You have your mother again.'

'We live near Burnaby. I can't pay.'

'No matter. Doctor just paid.'

Ben looked at the exhausted Doctor for confirmation and the Russian just nodded. 'Go with him. He's a friend.'

Mrs Tooley allowed herself to be led away, still confused by the size of her young son and why she was in this strange art gallery. She stopped to look at the Doc. He turned away. Ben urged his mother on. 'We have to go.'

'Let them pass, Wylie.' The dog moved out of the way under his master's command. Deka followed, looking back, disturbed to see the Doc sway by the kitchen sink.

'Close the door, Teacher. Don't drink that medicine until you are home, remember.' He looked in the mirror and regarded his red raw throat and didn't like what he saw. 'There may be no tomorrow, Teacher, bring lots of dog food...'

But Deka was gone and the door was closed.

The Russian poured his coffee and tossed a biscuit to the dog. 'Who will fix the Doctor, hey, Wylie? Who's gonna fix me?' He looked sadly at the dog a moment. 'Who will save you?'

5

Computer models run by *Nature Journal* and the Department of Infectious Disease Epidemiology at Imperial College in London in April 2006 were very discouraging. They showed that the number of people getting sick in the U.S. could be as many as 102 million – dropping to 84 million if even one quarter of the population was vaccinated. The plan was to have a minimum of 81 million people vaccinated by 2008 with key workers getting priority. Even though antivirals such as Tamiflu (also known as oseltamivir) were being distributed to private companies in blister packs of ten pills per person at a wholesale price of $61 a pack, U.S. Health and Human Services stated: 'We don't recommend that individuals stockpile antivirals.'

The Dead and the Dying

Arno arrived back with wine and some foodstuffs from the deli. He was glad to see Rachel was safe and preoccupied. She had a cab and was busy loading the food she'd bought. The cabbie watched from a distance, unwilling to get near them. Arno noted the cab had a makeshift barrier between the driver and passenger, just like the old cabs. 'You checked the dates?'

Rachel looked back at him, annoyed. 'Sure. There's a premium on out of date stock. Can you believe that?'

'I can.' Arno put his suitcase in the trunk alongside the food. It was a pretty tight squeeze. 'You got everything you need?'

'I hope so. You get a first aid kit and Tylenol?'

'Pills, potions, blades, bandages, the lot.'

Reece, the cabbie, had been watching carefully. 'You planning on going a while?' He was thinking that he had better stock up on stuff himself if everyone else was doing this. Do it soon too, he had this damn violent headache all of a sudden. Been on the road too long today. Needed some food and some sleep.

'Going out to our cabin.' Arno told him. 'Stock up every year.'

Reece nodded. It was a great idea, only they didn't look the cabin sort. Unless the cabin was in Whistler or someplace. Road was closed up there now since...

Arno saw it happen first. The cabbie turned when he heard a car horn sound and as he did so he stumbled. He didn't utter a sound, but, as if he was made of paper, he abruptly crumpled to the ground. He twitched just once and Arno knew, without checking, that this man was toast. 'Empty the trunk, Rachel.'

Rachel looked up from where she'd being trying to make room. 'What?'

Arno started emptying the trunk. 'We don't have a driver and I'm not getting into the cabin.'

Rachel looked around, stunned and annoyed, then saw the driver collapsed in a heap on the ground. 'But...'

'It's not a heart attack. I've seen it happen too many times. The virus got him. Shit, he didn't get near you did he?'

Rachel was dazed. He just dropped dead? They were going to leave him there? Perhaps she didn't know Arno as well as she thought.

'We can use a shopping cart, there's enough abandoned around here. It's not too far to the marina is it?'

'People have been shot carrying a lot less,' Rachel told him. 'It's not a great idea, Arno. Have you any idea how much this cost?'

Arno held up his hands in self-defence. Clearly he had no idea about prices. 'I'll go tell them inside and call a cab, ok. Just empty the trunk and spray everything with disinfectant. Shit. I just want to get out of here. Every hour it's going to get worse.'

Rachel watched him go inside. Clearly he was used to getting his own way. Typical man then. All sweet when he wanted something. She hauled out the rice and then thought of her father. How he'd always leave every decision up to her Ma and then bitch about everything. Arno was never going to be like that. She had wanted a decisive man. It was going to get tougher out there. She glanced across at the cabbie lying on the tarmac and felt remorse, but only for a second. If they'd gotten in the cab he would have infected them. Bastard. Must have known he wasn't well. No one could die so suddenly without any symptoms.

Arno was back with two guys from the hotel in space suits. He immediately started helping her with the unloading. 'They're going to take the body. They got a refrigerated truck out back waiting to go to the city incineration pit.'

'I thought the pit was just a rumour.'

'Every town's got one now, Rachel. All part of the Emergency Powers Act. Only way to deal with it. Burn the bodies and lock up anyone with symptoms.'

'It's like the middle ages.'

'This is the middle ages. Every man for himself and burn the rest. I called the cab driver who brought me in last night. He said he was off duty but he's coming for two hundred.'

'Two hundred to drive us to the marina? It's not even a mile.'

'It's safer. You said yourself...' Arno got the last of the food out and then started on his suitcase. 'Got the disinfectant?'

Rachel nodded and held her mask tight against her face as she sprayed all the cartons and the case and everything that had been in the trunk. Arno took the can from her and sprayed his shoes and her own. 'Go inside, wash your hands twice. I'll go when you return. Watch out for a red cab. Driver's called Deka. We don't go with anyone else. OK?'

Rachel felt dizzy with all of this pressure but she ran back into the hotel. She badly wanted to shower all over again, never mind wash her hands. A thought brushed her mind. It was just a flash, but it was there, an unspoken fear: was she ever going to reach thirty? Would she live that long? How fucking virulent was this virus anyway?

By the time she was back Arno had loaded the food and his case into the back of a red cab and he signalled her to wait whilst he went in to wash. He was thorough. She might not like this version of Arno, but he was thorough.

The cabbie sat patiently – mask on, hat on, sweating slightly. But he was alive at least. Rachel didn't get into the cab until Arno returned, and even here Arno sprayed the interior of the cab before they got in, just to be sure.

'I don't think that stuff actually works, but it makes us all feel better I guess.' Deka remarked. His throat was very sore now, but he was sucking on a powerful cough drop and it made things easier.

Arno was looking at his face in the mirror. Or at least his forehead. 'You OK. Your voice...'

'Got a sore throat. I admit that, but it ain't the virus. I hope. You seen the guy who owns that yellow Chevrolet?'

Rachel looked at their former cab, now pushed to one side. 'He died.'

'It was very sudden.' Arno informed him. 'I mean, very sudden. He looked pretty surprised. You knew him?'

'Ya. Reece swore blind by Margi's chicken soup from the Korean café we go to on Main. Nothing was going to get him. Ate the chicken soup every day.'

Arno sat back in the rear seat. It was just like his mother. She swore on chicken soup to cure almost anything. Not this time. 'Well I guess we all need to believe in something.'

'That we do. That we sure do.' Deka agreed. He started up and they pulled out onto Burrard. Rachel was looking at the cabbie more closely. She was nervous now. 'Sorry to be rude, but I don't think you look well yourself.'

'Got out of bed to come here, Miss. It's getting tough out there. Going to need the money.'

Arno put a hand on Rachel's and shushed her softly. 'It's OK. We're just spooked that's all. Your pal died right in front of us.'

'He wasn't a pal. But I'm sorry he's dead.' He really was. 'Reece was a bastard, but no one deserves to die from this.' He wondered what they'd do with his cab. 'The marina right? Five minutes.'

'You seen any dead dogs today?' Arno asked him, remembering his ride in.

'No, but I saw a woman being burned to bring her back to life.'

Rachel pulled a face and looked at Arno to check she'd heard right. Arno wasn't phased.

'It work?' He asked.

'Yeah. Like a miracle. Doc Borov works miracles all the time.'

Arno smiled, disbelieving. 'Well I'm glad there is at least one who can.'

Deka nodded. 'Just one.'

Rachel shuddered. She just didn't like anything that was happening this day. Nothing.

Arno was musing on the cabbie's accent? 'South African, right?'

Deka smiled. Few ever recognised it. 'Ja.'

Arno smiled. 'Spent a year in the Cape – in Stellenbosch. Thought I wanted to learn the wine business. Turned out I didn't have the nose for it.'

Deka had a sudden warm feeling for home, for a place he left and forgot to go back to. 'Ya, it's all in the nose they say.' He laughed a moment but it hurt and he had to stop.

They rode across the bridge, making the turn after the Molson brewery. He noticed that it looked empty. When a brewery closes you know you are in deep trouble. Deep trouble.

'Be there in a couple of minutes. You know where the boat is?'

'Granville Island Marina. Right outside the boatyard I'm told. Can you get close?'

'Close enough,' Deka told them. 'Surprised there's any boats left. People been leaving all week. I heard they were trying to stop people leaving. My advice is to wait until dark and make for Point Grey as fast as you can. They're pretty lax after 10 o'clock, I hear.'

'Thanks. Useful advice.'

Deka looked back at Arno in the mirror briefly. 'Wish I'd gone myself. You save her. She's beautiful.'

Rachel was surprised. How anyone could tell anyone was anything behind a mask beat her, but she didn't protest.

Deka swung the car towards Granville Island, sweeping past the empty galleries and an abandoned Starbucks. He couldn't remember a time when it was deserted, ever, not during the day. Now there were no tourists, no business, no nothing.

'Be good to go somewhere where they don't burn the houses at night.' Deka remarked as he slowed down to ease them towards the tiny marina harbour.

'You saw that?'

'Saw the smoke. Drove by earlier. It's a tragedy. Never get it back. That's where the first big money settled, where they built some grand houses, places with character. It was a real community, y'know. People talk about community, but that was one for real. First place I settled when I came.'

Rachel remembered Tasha and took out her phone to make a call. She frowned as she looked at her cell. 'No signal.'

Arno looked at her cell and shrugged. 'Signal might be blocked around here, might be the bridge? More drop outs everyday now. Hard to get the engineers out there to keep it all maintained I guess.'

Deka pulled the cab to a stop outside the Specialty Yachts office beside the boat yard. There were just four yachts in the harbour behind a rudimentary security fence, only recently erected. There used to be a hundred or more yachts for sale or to rent. Where the hell had they all gone? Now he thought about it Coal Harbour Marina was pretty empty as well. The rich leaving a sinking ship, or something like.'This is it.' Deka told them. He felt like shit now, he wondered if it would be OK to take some of the Doc's magic potion. At least enough to get him home and back to bed.

Arno thrust two-hundred dollars into the box and muttered thanks. Deka popped the trunk.

They unloaded quickly, keen to get all this food out of sight, not that there appeared to be anyone around. Deka stayed in his cab, pondering all the time as to whether to risk just a little taste of the potent medicine.

'We're done,' Arno was calling out. 'Get home safe.'

Deka started the engine again and turned the cab around, fighting a sudden wave of nausea. He managed to drive up to the market buildings and then panicking as it rose up his gorge, hit the brakes, opened the door and vomited. Big time. He stayed there, unmoving, transfixed, looking at the vomit; the engine running, sweat pouring off him. Was this it? Die here, just fade out. Like Reece did?

No, he was still here. And Reece died instantly without warning, they said, he was – well he was different. Maybe it was the inoculation fighting it. Maybe it wasn't. He wished to hell he was on a boat leaving town, but then again, perhaps it was already too late for anyone to leave.

Arno had a key for the gate and a key for the yacht and with accustomed efficiency he was ferrying as much as he could to the yacht, urging Rachel to do the same. Rachel was puzzled though, looking back to where Deka had stopped about fifty yards away.

'The cabbie hasn't left.'

'Sure he has.'

'No, I mean, I can still hear his engine. He's still here. You think he needs help? He looked pretty sick.'

Arno was about to say something glib, but the look on her face changed his mind. She had seen one man die in the last hour already. 'He's taking a leak or something.'

Rachel shook her head. All her instincts told her that that man was in trouble. 'I've got to take a look.'

Arno really didn't want her to go. Equally he didn't want to go either but...

'Get the stuff stowed, OK. Don't switch any lights on. I don't want anyone to know we're here. Not yet anyway.'

'You don't have to go.'

'No, you're right. He's a human being. If he needs help, he needs help. But if it's the virus I am not touching him. Understand? It's us or it now. We have to be vigilant.'

'Vigilant' Rachel repeated, thinking that it was the first time she'd ever heard anyone actually say that word.

Arno left the yacht and made his way towards the sound of the car engine.

Dekka watched him approach. Still sitting in his seat, the bloody vomit spread out below.

'Don't come near,' Deka warned him.

'You want me to call 911?'

'Don't come near. Don't help. I'm not dying. It's the stuff Doc gave me. Body is fighting it. He said...' Deka spewed up again. Not as much as before but it hurt. Hurt real bad. There was a lot of blood there. Bright, bright red.

Arno didn't like the look of this one bit. Was everyone infected in this city? Had he been infected already? Was their flight useless?

Deka suddenly felt incredibly light. He could fly. He was sure of it. He gripped the car seat, in case he started to float. He had no regrets. He'd made his choices. This was it then. At least there would be a witness.

'Hang on,' Arno told him.

'Go.' Deka whispered. 'If they see you, you will be quarantined.'

Arno backed off. Yes, the driver was right. Whoever they were, they might be watching.

'Use your radio,' Arno told him. 'Call someone. Get help.'

Deka wondered. Would they even come? Or wait till he was dead. He watched a seabird circle above him. He'd never see any more birds. Never see Doc... He flipped the radio switch. Turned back into his seat. Turned off the engine, no need to waste fuel. He called it in. He didn't know if they acknowledged it. Didn't care. This was his time. Whatever sins he had committed, this was it, time to pay. No time to regret – always promised himself he'd die back home in the Cape, but this was a good place to die, good as any.

Forty-five minutes later Arno and Rachel saw the ambulance approach across the causeway road and they hid on the boat, making sure they weren't visible.

He'd relocked the gates, connected the cable to charge the yacht's batteries, got the water tank topped off. Now it was a question of waiting until it was time to leave. No need to draw any attention to themselves.

'He could tell them where he dropped us off.'

'He won't.'

'They will wonder where his fare is. If they are rounding people up to quarantine, they will be looking for his fare.'

'He did it off book. He's probably already dead, or near it.'

'We breathed his air.'

'We didn't touch him and we wore masks, disinfected his seats, we're fine. OK? We couldn't do any more. Strip and wash. That's all we can do. Bin these clothes. We have more.'

Rachel looked at him, realised he was talking sense and began to strip off, hitting her hand on the ceiling. 'Shit, got to get used to this.'

The yacht was smaller and much older than they said it would be. An old thirty-three-footer Chris Craft, but well built with a reconditioned Cummins diesel. He squeezed Rachel's shoulder to reassure her. 'We're fuelled up, so we're good for around three – four hundred miles if we take it easy. It's our new home, Rach. Got a decent galley kitchen and a shower, not too bad. It's good.'

Rachel wondered about the cabbie for a moment, then shivered. She had to wash. She had to learn to survive. Must get better at needing to survive.

Arno was looking for the instructions supposedly left him by the owner. 'We'll leave at ten like the cabbie suggested. Run real slow out of harbour and then head across the bay without running lights. We don't want them hauling us back now.'

They both heard the ambulance siren start up. Exchanged glances. Heard the second unmistakable sound of a cop vehicle then. Perhaps it came with the ambulance.

Arno put his fingers to his lips and signalled for her to sit down. He whispered. 'Just stay quiet. You were right, they are looking for his fare. Put this on.'

Arno handed her a huge man's dressing gown and she slipped it on, hugging it to herself. They just sat there. Quiet, unmoving, listening for anything, scared a little, strongly aware of their own hearts beating loudly.

Rachel realised that she needed to pee. She had no idea where the toilet was. Right at that moment she heard the dock gate rattle, a male voice, clear and distinct calling back 'It's locked. No sign of anything. Did he say how many?'

Through the porthole they saw the ambulance leaving across the causeway under Granville Bridge. Poor bastard would be taken to the pit most likely. Arno signalled for her to wait some more. He knew the cops would be checking everything for signs of recent activity. She heard boots on the floating dock outside, some banging as something else was moved. Her phone suddenly began to ring. Stupid ringtone. Why hadn't she put it on silent? Why had she ever thought Alanis on her phone was cute? She frantically sought it out to silence it. Couldn't find it. They'd hear it for sure. Arno dug it out of her jeans and shut it off. They both stood there in silence, hearts pounding. Had the cop heard it? Rachel mouthed 'sorry' but Arno just put his fingers to his lips.

Rachel tried to squeeze. Her urge to pee was growing in intensity. Why didn't she go when she washed her hands back at the hotel. Double stupidity. Both of them could picture the cop outside pausing to listen. He must of heard it.

Moments later they heard the cop car back away, saw the sweep of its headlights across the water. It had grown dark so quickly, they hadn't noticed, even though, now they thought about it, they couldn't see each other so well.

'Got to pee. Now!'

'Behind you, door.' Arno pointed, whispering. 'No lights.'

Rachel moved as fast as she could. Got the door open and only just made it to the can. It stank of chemicals, but it didn't matter. Nothing mattered other than having that pee.

'We can wash now,' Arno told her. 'Then let's get this old tub ready. We have to leave. They might come back. Someone might have seen us from the apartments across the water. Always someone watching.'

Rachel tried the tap. The water didn't smell so good, but stale water was better than nothing she guessed. She hoped. Arno didn't mention the phone though she knew it must have pissed him off. Telus would be cutting her off soon anyways. Just one more bill she hadn't paid.

'Hey, excellent, they left instructions on how to start the engine,' Arno was calling. 'Looks complicated.'

'You ever sailed something like this before, Arno?' Rachel asked.

He didn't reply immediately. That worried her a little. She flushed and was surprised to hear a pump kick in and dispose of the waste. She noticed a little red light was on and wondered if it was supposed to do that. 'Arno?'

She felt a hand on her shoulder and jumped, air escaping her chest. Arno was stood there, grinning. 'Sorry.'

'Hell, Arno.'

'Sorry. But look, a whole lot of instructions. Is there a red light on in here?'

'Yeah I was going to...'

'When it goes orange it means the hot water tank is ready for a shower. It will only last only ten minutes and uses a lot of water. Showers for emergencies only I think.'

'Can we shower before we leave?' Rachel pleaded. 'That way we can replenish the water before we go.'

'It's not orange yet.'

'We haven't left yet. I can hear water boiling, I think.'

'I guess.' She was right. They had to take every precaution. 'We should. We've been exposed, you're right...did you bag your clothes?'

'Did you?'

'Er. Oh, sorry, I started but...' He shrugged, there was no excuse. 'Anyway, got more, I buy two of everything. Sometimes three. Anal, I guess.'

Rachel looked at him then sighed and laughed at the same time. 'Shit we're going to have to learn a lot about each other pretty fast.'

Arno took a deep breath and grinned again. Rachel liked the way he grinned, it looked genuine, unlike some people who sort of faked it all the time. Something clicked behind her and she turned.

'Hey light's gone orange.' Arno remarked. 'I say we shower together.'

'Have you seen how small the space is?' Rachel protested.

'Tomorrow we can swim in the ocean. Big enough for two I hear.'

'Now you are being sarcastic. Strip off, Arno Lakis, get in the shower and hope to hell there's soap.'

Arno began to undress. 'You don't think we should do this once we are out at sea?'

Rachel shook her head. 'Shower now and then we can refill the tank before we leave. We dump the clothes and scrub ourselves stupid here and now, Arno. I don't want anything on us and that means your shoes as well.' She had a determined look on her face.

'My five-hundred dollar shoes?'

'Your damn five-hundred dollar shoes too. You buy two or three at a time remember, so there has to be spares.'

Arno looked at her and narrowed his eyes. 'Ouch. You think I spend too much on shoes?'

'Just take them off and put them in the trash. This is the future, Arno. Nothing is worth shit anymore.'

Arno removed his shoes, his pants, stuffed everything into the trash bag. 'You're tougher than I thought.'

Rachel ignored him, opened the door, turned on the mixer tap, and climbed in to the tiny shower space. 'Was the guy who owned this a dwarf? If we shower back to back, I think we can both get in here, but it's going to be tight.'

Arno watched her slide under the water, watch her gasp as she adjusted the temperature to make it cooler. 'Ow... Get in here, sailor... now.'

Arno squeezed in beside her and somehow, crouching down managed to soap her down as the water dribbled on his head. Rachel turned and began to soap him down as she rinsed, hoping to God that whatever might be clinging to them would be gone. 'You think that cabbie is dead?' She asked.

Arno had his eyes closed to avoid the soap. He saw the cabbie, the vomit smeared with blood and the utter disappointment in the cabbie's eyes.

'He's a fighter. If anyone was determined to beat it, he was.'

A face stood at a window looking across the marina. She'd seen the cab arrive. The ambulance come and go, the couple load their stuff onto the boat. She'd thought about calling the *'Influenza Hotline'*. It was a talk show sponsored number for you to call anonymously if you thought someone had the virus and weren't observing quarantine. A snitchers charter. But there she was – watching, as she had watched a hundred boats slip away over the past few days as people in the know left town. She sat there with her five hundred bottles of water and a stack of canned food and the front door triple bolted. She was going to survive this thing – see them on the other side. She'd cleaned out her bank account and the cash was right there in the safe under her bed. She had one of the best views in the city and she wasn't going to give it up. She'd taken unpaid leave from work and knew that if she got through this, however long it took, they'd need her back one day – city accountants were a dime a dozen right now, but she had a reputation. It you wanted value for money from competitive tendering, you put Alice Gutermann on the job. She was proud of her hardnosed aggressive accounting methods, and as long as wasn't the Mayor's cousin you were putting out of business, she was secure in her job.

Another Place to Die

She'd planned this self-imposed siege the moment the first wave of the influenza had gripped Canada. When it subsided and momentarily faded from the news, she was sure it would be back. Experts on CNN and Fox News had been saying there could be a second wave – any day soon, and this might be the big one. She began to stockpile. Day after day she'd bring stuff home, mark it off. She'd need sixty to seventy days of stuff. Kitty needed stuff too. Her cat Felice had his stash in the guest room. Kitty litter, a ton of tuna and chicken cans and another ton of IAMs for cats. She wasn't going to go short, no matter what. And she made sure she had new shrubs on the balcony so they'd have something to care for outside the apartment.

Alice didn't understand why everyone was still walking around. She listened to the news – same as everyone else, and even if they had all been inoculated, people were still dying – so clearly it wasn't working. Didn't anyone else have a desire to live? Were they all so stupid they didn't know the shit was hitting the fan or just didn't think it was going to happen to them?

That's why she didn't call when she saw the boats leave. Good luck to them. If they could get out whilst the going was good, then that was two more lives saved. All those people back in Montreal and Toronto who didn't leave – well back East they had gotten the message at least. Stay home or stay dead.

She continued watching. How many others were there she wondered, just like her, sitting at home wondering if they had gotten enough to last them through. How many could last without going crazy. That would be the real test. Living with yourself day after day – that was going to be the hardest thing of all.

6

The typical incubation period (interval between infection and onset of symptoms) for influenza is approximately 2 days. Persons who become ill may shed the virus and can transmit infection for up to one day before the onset of symptoms. Viral shedding and the risk of transmission will be greatest during the first 2 days of illness. Children usually shed the greatest amount of virus and therefore are likely to post the greatest risk for transmission. On average, infected persons will transmit infection to approximately two other people. In an affected community, a pandemic outbreak will last about 6 to 8 weeks. Multiple waves (periods during which community outbreaks occur across the country) of illness could occur with each wave lasting 2-3 months. Historically, the largest waves have occurred in the fall and winter, but the seasonality of a pandemic cannot be predicted with certainty.
Source:http://www.pandemicflu.gov

Death Row

Deka opened his eyes.

He was in his worst nightmare. Hospital quarantine. He'd die for sure now. A nurse in a full HAZMAT space suit was checking his pulse. She could see he was awake, staring at her through his bloodshot eyes. She attempted a smile. 'Well you're not dead, Mr Fortun. That's got to be good, right?'

Deka found that he couldn't speak. He had a golf ball in his throat and he was sweating profusely. The nurse prepped his arm with alcohol and then injected him with something. She put a pill onto a plastic ice cream spoon and forced it into his mouth.

'Swallow.' She gave him a bottle of water with a straw attached to suck. 'Swallow now. Might bring down your temperature, Mr Fortun. You're one hundred and two and that's bad. Doctor says your strong and good news; you're in the orange ward. Sixty percent chance of surviving here. Listen, nod if you understand. I need you to move your legs as often as you can. Just twirl them. Understand? It's for your circulation.'

Deka nodded. The pill went down. He sucked on the water and it felt good to get something down. It really felt good. He was feeling drowsy again.

'Circulate your legs, keep the blood moving, Mr Fortun.'

The nurse left, moving on to another man who looked in terrible shape. Surely not a sixty percent chance there. Deka heard... 'Still here, Mr Thomas. Didn't expect that did we? Good for you. Here, open your mouth.'

Deka looked beyond him to the rest of the ward. It was filled with men and women, coughing wrecks, groaning, gasping, wheezing, open sores, weeping noses and eyes. He suddenly realised that he couldn't hear them anymore. His ears just clicked off. He couldn't hear a thing. Not even the nurse beside him talking to the man just there. He could see her lips moving, but nothing. He'd never been deaf before. For some reason this terrified him more than anything else.

He suddenly thought of the Doc. He wondered if he was OK or feeling like Deka. He wondered about all the people the Doc had inoculated, how they'd thought they'd be OK and survive this thing. How bloody disappointed they'd be. Who'd look after the Doc's dog? Who was looking after any of the dogs and cats in the city? He turned, felt warm liquid slosh out of his left ear and it clicked back on. He could hear again. He turn his head the other way and more liquid flowed out of his ears. What the fuck was happening to his ears? 'Nurse...' he rasped, something like a sound escaped his mouth.

He didn't think she heard him but she saw him and he could see she was startled. Saw her press a button on her space suit arm and start talking to someone. She came towards him, a look of disgust and pity on her face.

'You're full of surprises, Mr Fortun. Can you hear me? Bleeding from the ears is a new one. You want me to clean that up? Looks worse than it is – I hope.'

Another nurse appeared at the other side of his bed. A male nurse in another space suit. 'Jesus.' He didn't say anything else. He roughly raised Deka's head and yanked out the blood soaked pillow. The other nurse mopped his head and neck. Stuck cotton wool in his ears so now he couldn't hear again and another pillow appeared. A yellow sticker was put above him on the wall. He didn't know what it meant but he guessed it wasn't good.

'Oh...' the nurse suddenly remembered, taking the cotton wool out of his left ear for a moment. 'I was to tell you that your cab is in quarantine too. You can claim it when you're discharged.'

Deka heard something else in her voice now. It wasn't hope. She knew he wasn't in the sixty percent anymore. He felt himself slipping under, into a dreamlike state, tripping on the edge of a chasm. Below him, a thousand feet below was a tiny river. He knew, somehow, that when he jumped he had to land precisely in the centre of that river or be crushed to death on the rocks below. He focused on the river, heard the shriek of seagulls to his left and almost as graceful as the birds around him, began to fall and fall...towards that river.

Rachel was looking under the bed she had just made up for them both. 'Arno. Is there supposed to be water under here?'

Arno came down and shone a flashlight at her feet. 'Shit. I'll check the pumps. Get anything down there up as high as you can. We're half way across the bay.'

He went back up and swore. Things weren't working as well as they should be. He'd got the engines going OK, but he didn't like the sound of one of them. He'd found more diesel fuel and taken two spare ten gallon cans with them, but there wasn't much storage space. Certainly he'd been led to believe the yacht was bigger than the thirty-three footer he'd got. He thumped the control panel and a little green light came on. He heard the pumps start up immediately.

'Hey, great.' He heard Rachel call out.

He was embarrassed. He'd thought he'd be more competent than he was at this. 'Loose wiring.'

'Water's going.' Rachel added. 'Does this mean we've got a hole'

'No. Water gets in naturally via the prop. I think. Anyway it's been standing a while and y'know... '

Rachel didn't know, but she figured it was like a car that hadn't been started in a while. Cars hated that, so she guessed boats hated it more. She'd pretty much avoided sailing despite being surrounded by water all her life. She wasn't scared, just avoided it, that's all.

Arno was reading the manual by flashlight. 'I think we have a fuel line blockage. It's not getting through to the engine properly. When we get into open water I'm going to shut off and try and get the pipe unblocked.'

Rachel appeared at the hatchway. 'How?'

'Got to suck whatever is blocking it out.'

'Suck diesel?'

'Suck diesel.'

'Fuck.'

'Yeah.'

Rachel nodded. It sounded like he knew what he was doing. She started on the kitchen. Food had to be put away, make something to eat, be organised. She had to work out how long the food would last and that meant planning some meals. Just like camp. If she told herself this was like camp it would be an adventure. She looked at the kettle. Decided it had to be boiled with seawater. Had to take every precaution, just in case. She took it up to Arno, thrust it at him.

'Fill it with seawater. I want to sterilise stuff. Don't want to use drinking water.'

Arno looked at her a moment, realised she was speaking sense. 'Good idea. Any chance of tea afterwards?'

'If you're lucky sailor.'

Arno smiled and took the kettle to the stern, kneeling down to fill it. They were taking it easy across the bay, just five-six knots, running quiet as possible without lights so not to draw attention to themselves. He could see Point Grey and the flickering lights from the streetlights and homes. He wondered how long they'd keep up the pretence of everything being normal. How many people were sitting in those homes too scared to leave already?

He filled the kettle and brought it back to Rachel who was admiring the city, still illuminated at night, just like normal.

'Loved this sight all my life. Used to beg my first boyfriend to drive me to the beach at night to watch the sunset and then we'd sit real close to keep warm and just watch the city come to life.'

'What happened to him?'

Rachel looked at Arno a moment and took the kettle. 'Went to Winnipeg to play hockey. Never heard from him again. Not once.'

Arno nodded. 'Winnipeg's like that. You get depressed then you sort of drop off the edge of the earth. Had to spend three months there once working for a finance company. Never been so cold in my life.'

Rachel took the kettle and went back down to the galley.

Arno corrected the steering and noted a tanker at anchor, lights on, but silent, about two hundred yards off. 'Lot of ships in the bay.'

'No business for them.' Rachel called out. 'I guess ships are tied up all across the world right now.'

But Arno knew that already, he'd seen the trade figures from South Korea and China. They caught the economic chill first as orders from the West got cancelled. Whole fleets of container ships were inactive right now. Nothing like this had happened since the world slump of 1929, or maybe during wartime. There would be no business for quite a while. He wondered where he and Rachel would end up, how long they could stay ahead of this thing. 'Moon's rising,' he told her. 'I think it might rain.'

Arno's cell rang. He looked at it. Decided to take the call. Rachel looked at him quizzically. 'Vancouver call. Another unhappy client. Got to take it. Sorry.'

Rachel nodded and went below to clean. Whoever had rented this yacht to him clearly hadn't bothered much with maintenance. She sighed. This was it. The great adventure. She was in love, or at least she thought she was. Not much room for that sweet stuff since they'd got up. It was all a downer so far, but would she prefer the alternative?

Before she was just like everyone else, not thinking about much, wondering how she was going to pay bills, resigned to losing her apartment and generally just letting everything happen to her. Pretty much everyone she knew just let shit happen and you dealt with it later. But that wasn't Arno's style. He had plans. It was kind of shocking to realise that they were so different. Why did he like her? What was he seeing in her that others hadn't? Why did he love her? Why that big rock? It had belonged to a Princess for god's sake. Was she worthy? She'd done jack shit to prepare for this big pandemic that was going to change everyone's lives and he'd been in the thick of it. Why had he sought her out? Weren't there any other girls in Toronto? Why had he fallen for her?

She sighed. This was typical Rachel stupidness now. She could talk herself out of anything, especially if it was good. She listened a moment as Arno was arguing with his client telling him stuff he didn't want to hear. Yeah, pretty much no one wanted to hear that everything they had worked for was going to be worthless any day soon. She made more tea. Just like her mother then, anything you couldn't solve, make tea. She smiled. Fuck it. Now where's the Darjeeling?

7

November 2007 news leaked out of China that there had been a major outbreak of a virulent and deadly flu. China vehemently denied it, arresting and possibly executing persons who alerted the World Health Authority about the outbreak. (They had jailed Qiao Songju a goose farmer in Jiangsu province for three and a half years for reporting a bird flu outbreak the previous October.)

China had recently conducted an emergency whole virus mass vaccination program using inactivated H5N1 virus with an adjuvant [additive] containing 10 micrograms of aluminium hydroxide. In controlled tests of the antiviral, the researchers report (first cited in the *Lancet* online September 2006) had produced 78% protective antibodies to stimulate an immune response. Over 675 million dosages were distributed nationally. Estimates are that a million people have died. An International Red Cross spokesperson has indicated that these deaths could be a natural reaction to such a large vaccination program. The largest ever attempted in the world in such a short period.

Editorial in Vancouver Business & Investor News: Jan 2008

Family Ties

'I'm on the phone and I say no. Tell her no.'

Shania sulked some more and swore under her breath at her father. It just wasn't fair. She needed to see Mitch and her father was being a fuckin' tyrant – as usual. Her mother Nancy took his side – as usual.

'I just want to see him for an hour.'

'It takes just one minute to pick up the virus, Shania – less even.'

Her father was still arguing on the phone out by the pool. 'I paid good money to your group, Lakis and your fuckin' solution is to have a fire sale? Are you stupid? You guys are nothing more than crooks.'

Nancy looked pensive. This was a family which had everything and everything to lose. The ten million dollar home right on the water near Horseshoe Bay – a house so big there was room for a dock inside the house. The huge motor-yacht sat there, testimony to their wealth. Twenty sports stores on the mainland, another hundred nationally, they were the first choice for professional and leisure sports consumers.

Now everything was going sour all at once.

No one was buying sportswear – no one was buying anything but supplies and camping stoves to get through the pandemic. The banks were screaming for money and her husband Bob had the idea of getting this Toronto based outfit 'Futuretank' outfit to figure out a solution for them. It wasn't happening.

Bob came back in, still angry. 'Fuckin' Arno Lakis is a clown. Says sell everything, close or sell the stores for whatever we can get. He's predicting a huge retail property crash.'

'What if he's right, Bob?'

Bob looked at his wife as if she was crazy. 'Then we're fucked. He can't be right. We're all taking this antiviral stuff, right? We're safe. We live in Canada for God's sake. Canadians haven't gone so soft they can't survive a fuckin' bad cold.'

'Why don't we sell the stores back East? We had that call from G&R Sports.'

Bob pulled a face. 'They're bust. As of yesterday. That's the bitch of it. Fuckin' Lakis might be right, but who would be stupid enough to buy now? Everyone can read the same newspapers, Nancy.'

'Then close. At least stop the haemorrhaging. We've got staff costs, inventory. We can just close and stay closed until it blows over. They said it would only last two months.'

'If we close now we'd have to pay off everyone, give them all notice and the banks will just jump in. We are cash poor right now, Nancy. You know it. We have to head into bankruptcy. We've got to get some protection. At least we'd keep the house.'

'And the monthly payments?'

'We cash in our pensions. At least they're solid. When Frank said buy gold, he wasn't kidding. It's over $1000 an ounce now and rising.'

'That's our retirement, Bob. I'm not so sure. If commercial property is going to dive, then real estate will crash too. I'm the realtor, remember. No one is buying anything right now. This was a tough sell in a good market. We got a steal, remember?'

'This house will retain value, Nancy. Shit we paid five million for it and it's worth ten. We have a cushion. It's everything we worked for twenty years. One crappy little store in Richmond to this. We owe ourselves this, at least.' He turned around suddenly. 'Where's Shania?'

Nancy pointed to the kitchen. Bob walked towards the kitchen. Nancy followed him. She knew how quickly things developed into shouting matches between them.

'She's not going to like this, no way we can pay her university tuition now. She'll have to go to Community College.'

Bob didn't find her in the kitchen. He frowned and shouted her name. 'Shania?'

Nancy looked out through the window and saw with a sinking feeling that her car was gone. She knew he'd blow his top now.

Bob went to Shania's room and found it empty. He instinctively went to look for her Mini and the moment he opened the front door and saw the gates were open he knew.

Quietly but decisively he strolled across the yard to the security gates and closed them – talking a few moments to change the security code.

He was back in the kitchen a moment later. Nancy looked at him with resignation.

'I told her no. You heard me right?'

Nancy nodded.

'Well that's it. The stupid bitch. Doesn't she realise...?' He shook his head. 'Well that's that. I told her, she goes out of this house she's not coming back and I meant it.'

Nancy had heard this before. Bob hated Mitch and not just because he was from a poor family.

'Mitch is her boyfriend. They are close.'

'She's seventeen and I told her no. He lives on Main. That's exactly where people are dying. Don't you listen to the news?'

'Your store's still open there.'

'You see me setting foot in it? I don't go anywhere, Nancy. That's why we have video phones.'

It was true. Bob was running his business from home now, ever since some Chinese family died in the Lougheed store and he was forced to have it sterilised and all the stock destroyed.

'Call her,' he told her. 'Turn her around. She won't be there yet. Tell her it's us or him, Nancy. No one gets into this house from this day forth unless they are wearing a government space suit. You hear me?'

Nancy had seen him in this kind of mood before. He's snap out of it, but it would be nasty. Always went like this when they had a financial crunch. They weren't the only retailer in trouble but that was no comfort. Bob picked up his cell and dialled again. He'd made a decision.

'I'm going to sell the yacht. David Turner says there's a hot market in ten berths. Lot's of people think they can ride this thing out at sea.'

Nancy said nothing. She hated the yacht and the people who came to freeload on it. If he could get rid of it, then great. Might save the mortgage at least.

She picked up her own phone and dialled Nancy's cell. She answered almost immediately.

'I'm not coming back Mom. You can't keep me prisoner. I'm going to Mitch's.'

Nancy said nothing for a moment. Shania loved Mitch, but Mitch hadn't had a job since quitting college, didn't even show any signs of doing anything serious with his life. God knows what he lived on, but he always seemed to have money.'

'Shania, your father says that if you go – you can't come back. You can turn around now. But if you go to him you can't come back. He wanted you to know that.'

Shania shook her head in the car, negotiating traffic. 'I'm not coming back Mom. Ever. I'm nearly eighteen now. I can do what I want.'

'Yes honey, you can, but your father says you can't come back. Not whilst this virus is...'

'You don't get it, Mom. I'm NOT coming back. You should leave too, Mom. You know you want to.'

Nancy was momentarily shocked that she'd say that. 'I love him, Shania.'

'Yeah sure. You love the cat, Mom. That's about it. Got to go. I'm over the bridge. Leave him, Mom, while you still can.'

Bob said nothing when she told him Shania had gone for good. Didn't seem to affect him at all. He just went into his office, checked his emails and talked to the store managers about the days takings. It was all he could focus on. A business worth millions going down the fucking tubes over a touch of 'flu. Didn't make any sense.

At ten-thirty that night Nancy was already in bed watching the news. None of it was good and Bob was still working on the accounts. They heard the horn. They both knew who it was. Nancy called out without thinking, an automatic response.

'Can you get the gate, Bob? The thing must be on the blink again. Shania's home.'

She didn't get a reply. 'Bob?'

Nancy heard nothing. She got out of bed and slipped on her dressing gown and went to the front door. It was already open.

Bob was stood just outside in his shorts and t-shirt, illuminated in Shania's headlights. The engine ticked over but Bob was doing nothing.

'Bob? Let her in.'

Nancy took a step outside.

'Stay out of this, Nancy,' Bob hissed

Nancy looked beyond him to the glare of the headlights and her daughter's Mini Cooper. She could see Shania had the window down and was waiting patiently, keeping quiet, knowing just one word would set her father off on one of his rants.

'What's going on, Bob?' Nancy asked.

Bob said nothing as Shania killed her motor and the lights. She got out of the car.

'Dad?'

'Your Mother told you that you couldn't come back?'

'Yes, she said...'

'Then you know these gates aren't going to open, Shania.'

'It's Mitch's birthday, Dad. I just went to see him. He's my boyfriend for god's sake. He's not sick.'

'Then why aren't you with him? Your mother made it clear I hope. Us or him.'

Nancy didn't like the tone in Bob's voice. It was too quiet.

Shania looked beyond him to her mother in her dressing gown. 'Mom?'

'I told you, Shania. I wasn't joking. Your father wouldn't joke about a thing like this.'

'You made a choice, Shania,' Bob said. 'You're almost eighteen now. Now you got to learn to live with the choice you made.' He turned, headed back to the house, gathering Nancy on the way. He made her turn around.

Shania kicked the gate in anger. 'They wouldn't let me in his house. Ask Mitch. He's right here. They won't let him in either.'

Bob took Nancy's arm and pulled her into the house.

'Bob,' Nancy was protesting, but he'd got a good grip and forced her inside.

'Dad. Mom. You can't do this. This is my home,' Shania yelled, sensing defeat.

Bob closed the front door behind them. Nancy looked at him, a little scared.

'Bob?'

'No, Nancy. We said no. No means no. We're going to survive this thing. We have to survive this thing. We don't know where they've been, who've they've seen. We know nothing and she knew the rules. She goddamn knows the fuckin' rules.'

Nancy slept in the guest room that night.

In the morning Bob was up early, as was his custom – surprised to see his daughter's Mini still parked at the gates. He was a little ashamed of her for not having the spunk to go to a motel at least. He felt mean, but he'd had to make a stand. He went to the kitchen, made coffee for everyone. He'd have to let them in. They could sleep in the pool house, it was far enough away from himself and Nancy. Couldn't have his own daughter sleeping rough. She might have learned a valuable lesson though. No meant no.

He took two cups of coffee out to the gates – then stopped, five feet away.

'Nancy!' He yelled. The urgency in his voice was enough to cut right through the walls.

Nancy awoke. She'd heard her name. The nightmares were still with her. She'd heard Bob shout her name again. She knew that call. He wanted her attention immediately or there would be trouble.

She ran to the master bedroom but it was empty. She scurried to the lobby and saw the front door was open already, sunlight casting sharp shadows in the hallway.

'Bob?'

'Out here.'

Bob was standing at the gates, two cups of coffee spilled at his side. He was shaking. Nancy ran to his side.

Shania and Mitch were both in the car. Nancy found it hard to comprehend what had happened.

Mitch was dead, his skin was almost blue and he was covered in blood. Shania was in the driving seat, slumped to one side, blood and vomit all over one door and down the outside. It dawned on Nancy that her one and only daughter, the one she'd given birth too and raised to not quite eighteen had blown her brains out – over a boy. A boy who very much looked liked he'd died of a very bad cold. Where had she got the gun?

Bob took her hand. Nancy shook it off.

'Don't hate me,' Bob said softly. 'If we had let him in we'd be dead too.'

Nancy felt it coming and she quickly turned aside and spewed, a searing pain in her stomach and heart. She heaved again. She wished that it was her dead, instead of Shania. She wished a lot of things, but mainly she realised that although Bob was right, she hated him now and would always hate him.

Bob turned away to get his phone. Someone would have to come and clear this mess away.

8

The First Wave

Winter Update 2008: Two hundred thousand confirmed deaths in China and
lax controls in neighbouring countries meant that the so called 'Jiangsu Flu'
cut like a knife through parts of former Russian territories and East Asian
nations. The devastation in Burma and, it is rumoured, North Korea where the
populations are already weakened by a lack of nutrition, is horrific. The World
Health Authority estimates the numbers infected for this phase is between
four million to as many as eight million, with many survivors left incapacitated
with acute respiratory problems.
C.S.M. 3.3.08

Ark Island

It might have seemed to her dad like an adventure before they started out, but now
they had been a month in the cabin and now it felt more like some hell-on-earth
reality show! Frances hated it, hated them, hated every living moment. The bugs,
the shower that was only hot when the sun was hot and it had been raining for
weeks now and, most of all, she hated Mercer's cooking. Frances didn't cook, had
never learned, wasn't about to. Cooking and cleaning were demeaning in Frances
world and it made living in a tiny cabin total shit.

When they had been here in summer, May and Fen had slept outside under the
mosquito net; but now it was November and pretty much everything around them

was pure mud. It was too cold to sleep outside, even in the extension Mercer had hastily erected when Frances began her moaning. Now all the cooking and sleeping had to be done inside and, what with them relying on solar to heat and cook and run the macerator for the toilet, it wasn't a happy situation in the incessant rain and grey clouds.

Back on the mainland they had told Mercer that solar worked in daylight and it did, as long as you just wanted to boil a kettle. The batteries didn't seem to charge at all in this light. Then there was the issue of privacy. Frances sulked every moment May and Fen were in the cabin, even if they were just listening to music or reading. The cess pit stank and no one liked the walk to the outhouse. May didn't use it at all preferring to go somewhere private and hope there weren't any snakes. Fen had taken to roaming and finding broken branches for firewood. She had become and expert at chopping and sawing, building fine calluses on her hands. She, at least, was warm beside her bonfires. Everything stank, but she kind of wore her old army jacket covered by spark burns with pride. She took to lighting a fire down by the rocks overlooking the water and fishing there, spending hours alone with Red.

Sometimes they caught something. Herring mostly, catfish once, but it was a bitch to gut. Those were the good days when she and Red just cooked it over the fire and ate it right there, not sharing with the rest of the 'family'. If they couldn't be bothered to come and speak to her, she wasn't going to go out of her way for them.

Some days, if it wasn't too cold or wet she and Red just curled up beside the fire and slept there. Occasionally, May, despite herself and her antipathy to Fen, came out to stare at the fire and escape the constant bickering inside the cabin. She'd read a book about how Canadians lived when they first came out West, a hundred and fifty odd years before and it wasn't much different to this. Only, as May explained it, they had God with them and that's what kept them safe. Fen wondered when May 'got religion', but other than this one observation she'd never mentioned God again. Fen thought about what May said from time to time and realised that there was a flaw in her argument. The early settlers had all of Canada to roam over and if they didn't like someone they could move to the next hill and settle there. They didn't situate themselves on the smallest god forsaken Gulf island and just wait. It had only been like, two months and they were all crazy already.

The island was small. Only five families lived on it. There was no ferry connection. They'd left the truck at Gibsons, bringing all the supplies over on three separate trips to the cabin. Mercer loved this place. Family legend had it that his Grandpa had won it in a card game. One whole acre with a rotting cabin on it, long since gone back to nature. Brought Mercer here as a kid to fish and escape the wife. Now it was their survival plan. Isolated, it never had any visitors and only three of the houses were inhabited.

Another Place to Die

The Manley's had the biggest place with a small helipad and a yacht moored by the inlet jetty they had built. Fen had never met them. She knew they were there because she saw lights come on sometimes and smoke from the fire from time to time. She assumed they were snobs.

Then there were the Delahayes, an older couple. Old man Delahaye he was a real bible thumper and like Mercer kind of believed the world was coming to an end. Couldn't wait. Mrs Delahaye sometimes would come across her as Fen looked for firewood. Probably wanted to say something about that as clearly Fen was stealing firewood from their trees, but she never said anything and Fen knew they had a heatpump in their house, some kind of thing where they used the natural heat of the earth to warm the home. People had come and drilled holes deep into the earth the summer before and Mr Delahaye had bragged that they'd never have a heating bill ever again. That's when he told her that her zits were caused by 'bad thoughts' and only when she turned to God would they heal. Fen figured then that this would be perfect. The only people who would survive would be the religious nuts and hippies. It made her ill to think just how fucking boring this crazy world was going to be. Even worse to think that she was now one of the hippies.

The last family occupying the island were the Hertzogs, Will and Manina. They were retired too, but still young, in their late thirties. They'd seen this shit coming and sold out their business and built a fortress into the cliff. Got a great view and he was into studying the stars and searching for extra-terrestials and she was into growing vegetables. They had a basement where they grew mushrooms and stuff. Totally organised and together people. Will had even come down and given her a range of small fish hooks and told her the best fishing spot from the rock over the bay. But they didn't come out of their place much and she guessed they were busy doing their own thing.

This was the island she liked to call Noah's Ark. Fen and Red had taken to discussing the island as the Ark and although Red didn't say much, she knew he thought it was pretty strange how they just waited and watched the sky most days. She walked Red as much as she could, but it was a small island and there wasn't a path right around it, you'd had to go through other people's property and they probably didn't like it. Not that she cared either way – they couldn't exactly call the cops. Fen pretty much did as she liked and no one stopped her. What bugged her was exactly why she never met anyone outside. Didn't they know fresh air was good for them? She didn't care how rich they all were, if you couldn't get out and breathe, then you might as well be dead.

Little by little, she and Red had gotten to thinking that this was their island. They were the only two who knew where all the best places were and what grew where. She even found the Hertzog's secret apple tree and she was careful to climb right up into it and get just the best ones from the top. They couldn't miss what they couldn't see.

Mercer was listening to the radio when she got back with three small herrings, grilled ready for them to eat. Frances wouldn't touch them, of course, but Mercer and May devoured them. Red flopped down in the corner to dry off and Frances scowled at them both. 'You stink.'

'It's just smoke.'

'When did you last take a shower?'

'When did you?'

Frances went back to her book and Mercer turned up the radio, never happy unless the news was bad, and it invariably was. He was busy plotting the progress of the virus on a wall chart he'd drawn. May wouldn't even look at the wall, but Fen noticed pockets of Vancouver were red now.

'Commercial Drive burned down and there's been a major outbreak in Richmond. Got the whole area locked down.'

Fen noticed that even interior towns were shaded red on Mercer's map now. She checked the progress of the virus, despite herself. She had this idea that if she ever got off the island she'd need to know where the safe areas were, if indeed there were any virus free places at all by then.

'Riots in Seattle again,' Mercer mused, offering Fen some herbal tea. She took it, needed it to warm up.

'I saw a ship go by,' Fen offered. 'Not close, but looked like a cargo vessel to me.'

Frances looked up. 'Cargo? Can't believe there's any trade going on.'

Fen sighed. 'It was high in the water. I guess that means it's empty.'

Mercer nodded, noting it down in his diary. He kept a note of everything now; tracking normality he called it.

May offered her some liquorice. Exchange for the fish. May didn't like to be beholden to Fen for anything. She was smiling, it unnerved Fen it was such a rare sight. 'It was on the radio. Some guy sneezed in a movie theatre in Istanbul and two hundred people got crushed in the rush for the exit. Gross huh.'

'Stupid. Why are people still even going to the movies? I bet they still go to mosques too. Don't they know there's a plague out there?'

'That's not all. The King died. Well first the Queen died, then Charles, he was the new King, he died right after and so did both his sons. People in England are in shock, crying an' stuff.'

Fen looked at her sister with amazement. 'I have known you for like, your whole life and I have never seen you take the slightest bit of interest in the Royal family; or Istanbul. May, you are a crazy bitch.'

Mercer moved towards the door, calling Red. 'Fen, help me with something will you while we feed the dog?'

Fen frowned, she was just getting started on her tea.

'Bring your tea. It's just...' Mercer whined and Fen just sighed all over again and called Red and they both went outside.

Mercer scooped some biscuits into Red's bowl and then signalled Fen to follow him down to the shed. Fen sipped her tea and told Red to stay and eat as she followed Mercer down the path, laid with flat rocks now so they didn't track mud into the cabin.

'What?' Fen asked, as she stood firm and watched him fiddle with his hands. 'What?'

'You don't ask to speak to me unless at least two hundred people died so...what.'

Mercer banged his head on the shed door. A very bad sign from Fen's experience.

'Frances wants to leave.'

Fen felt a sudden surge of relief. 'She does? That's good, right?'

Mercer gave her a 'look', it wasn't the remark he was looking for. 'She hates being cooped up.'

'Well shit. I'll just go and cure the virus and bring back everyone from the dead and maybe she'll be happy right? No one likes being cooped up, Dad. She could leave the cabin once in a while. The air won't kill her.'

'She wants to go to Victoria.'

'So?'

'She wants me to take her.'

Fen didn't say anything. She knew what was coming.

'I said I would but...'

'You can't go ashore, Dad. You can't risk it.'

'I'd have to refuel.'

'Don't let anyone near you.' Fen had a sudden intuitive moment of foreboding. Clearly they had been discussing this stuff behind her back for some time. Definitely not spontaneous. 'You are coming back, right?'

Mercer picked up a stone and threw it into the woods. A bird flew up, startled and they heard its wings flapping hard in the panic to get away.

'Of course, I am coming back.'

Fen heard the hesitation in his voice. 'Right away?'

'I want to get stuff.'

'We got stuff, Dad. You said we could last six months if we wanted to.'

'Food, yes. But May is going crazy with boredom and I'm...'

Fen understood now. This was about May. Frances was just an excuse.

'You aren't bored. You're stoned 24/7 Dad. Give her some. She'll soon forget being bored... Shit, May could learn to fish, cut wood. She's nearly fourteen for Christ sakes. She doesn't do anything. I'd go crazy too not doing anything.'

'I'm going to Victoria, Fen. You have to stay with May.'

Fen didn't say anything. She wondered why she wasn't surprised by this. But she didn't like him leaving May behind.

'I'd be gone two days max.'

'Two days? How would I know you didn't get it, Dad? What's to stop you coming back with the virus?'

'It's safe in Victoria. They shut it down real early. I checked Fen. No incidences in six weeks. No ferries, no planes, no one off or on the island. We'd have to sneak on and off in darkness.'

Fen continued to say nothing. She was thinking it through.

'I'd get stuff and...'

Fen finished her tea and handed him the mug. She turned to call Red who'd finished his supper already. 'Go, Dad. Take her. Take May too. She doesn't belong here. I'll be OK. I'll be fine.' She turned to her father with a smile. 'Just bring me back some magazines and some fucking bait, right? Some DVDs maybe. Don't let May choose them, no Disney shit. Nothing with Owen Wilson in it either.'

Mercer looked relieved. 'You think May would come?'

'She's desperate to do something. Take her. I'm the only one who actually likes it here.'

Mercer looked at her more carefully now and then nodded. 'We'll leave in half-an hour. Got to do it in the dark.'

'And some long-life milk,' Fen remembered as she walked off back down the slope. She wanted to be alone a while, think this through, be warm again. She picked up some sticks as she went. Half-an-hour? Like he was actually going to ask her permission then. They would have probably snuck off and left a note. Fuck 'em. Didn't need them. Never had.

Thirty minutes later, almost to the minute, she heard the little motor on the boat start up. It was dark now and she could see them go, but she heard May shout something, it might have been goodbye, it might have been rude. She didn't care. They were gone.

'Red?'

There was a delay, but Red came bounding up. Probably been to see them off. He brushed up hard against her, most likely to make sure she was real and hadn't gone too.

'It's OK, Red. We're here to stay.'

It was at that very moment as she knelt with Red beside the stumbling fire that she had that strong feeling again and goosebumps all up her spine. Dread and excitement mingled. She knew they weren't coming back. Whatever intentions they had, they weren't coming back.

She didn't know how she knew, but she knew and she wasn't sad at all. She threw the sticks on the fire and watched them catch alight. 'We can live without 'em, Red. Might even get that shower to work now she isn't using all the power to heat the fucking cabin.'

She watched sparks fly up into the sky and noticed for the first time in days that the clouds had gone, she could see stars. Red abruptly licked her face and then, for no reason at all, she started crying. Whether she cried because was alone at last or because she knew she'd never seen them again, she didn't know, but she cried and for a long time, curled up with Red beside the fire, she was warm but cold inside.

The morning sun was unexpectedly warm. Fen busied herself cleaning out the cabin and removing all traces of Frances. She aired it and then, because she could, she took a long hot shower, luxuriating in it and spent glorious minutes washing her hair with Frances's really expensive shampoo. She even got Red in there and gave him a long needed wash too. He wasn't best pleased but Fen felt it was her right now, she could be clean and civilised. She began to think of ways to improve things, make the place more like a home. It was as if a dead weight had been removed. No Frances, no sulky May, just her and Red – and now sunshine. Perfect.

He arrived sporting a bandage. Caught her off guard as Fen was still naked. Will Hertzog, looking nervous was hovering outside the window. He had a rash on his neck that looked as though it needed urgent treatment.

'Hi,' Fen yelled through the door. 'Just dressing. Finally got a shower.'

'Oh...' Obviously Will Hertzog was impatient to talk to her, but it would have to wait. 'Oh yeah, I see. Solar. Must have been hard with the rain. Your Dad here?'

Fen opened the door and stepped out. She stared at him, wondering if it was a coincidence that he was here the moment Mercer had gone. That rash looked real bad. Looked like a poison ivy reaction to her. 'Mercer's taken them fishing. They were getting stir crazy.'

Will nodded. 'Oh right, yeah.' Made sense to him. He wasn't sure how to give his news to her, he'd expected to meet Mercer. Didn't know how she'd react. 'Look, I don't want to get you upset, but we heard there's some people attacking the islands. Want you to know that if anything happens, you must come to us. Don't even try to defend this place. Come right to us. Understand? We've got protection.'

Sam North

'Attacking? How?' Fen was puzzled. All the shit in the world going on and now they had crazies as well.

'Home invasions. There's stuff out there on the radio and the Web. Says we've all got money and gold and...'

Fen looked back at their primitive shack and laughed. 'Well we're hiding it pretty good.'

'Just be warned, Fen. Tell your Dad. He's got a gun. If they come, use it. Then run to us. We can accommodate you.'

Fen nodded. It was news to her that her Dad had a gun. She wondered where he hid it. 'Thanks. For the warning and stuff. I'll tell Dad. You OK?'

Will was rubbing his neck. 'Got bitten by a spider. I have allergies.'

'That sucks. I hope they don't find us. We're a small island though, might not notice we're here, right?'

'Things are falling apart, Fen. We can't rely on anyone coming to help.'

'Like pirates.'

Will blinked. She perhaps hadn't understood the importance of his news. This wasn't a game. 'Ruthless pirates, Fen. Killers, OK. It's not a movie.'

Fen smiled. It didn't seem to matter to her. They had nothing. Maybe she could stick a sign over the cess pit saying 'Gold Here'. She watched Will go and reflected that he looked nervous and pale, like he wasn't getting out much. What was wrong with all these people she wondered? He should be outside swimming and doing stuff, like her..

Despite Will's downer news, she had a wonderful week. The fish got bigger, the sun shone everyday and she even began to sport a bit of a tan. She had the cabin just the way she wanted it and she didn't miss them once. When the two days had passed and they hadn't showed she was sure they weren't coming back. A week kind of sealed it. She didn't mind a bit. The way it had to be. She'd wait things out and when Christmas came, she'd ask the Hertzogs if was safe to go back. They might even let her have their little sailing boat so she could go. She'd have to show Red how to sail, but that would be fun.

They came on the Sunday night. With guns and flaming torches. Red was barking outside and made sure she was awake. She called him but he was out there in the dark defending her. She saw the flames coming from the Hertzog place and heard cruel laughter on the wind. It was a cold night with a fierce wind and the flames moved fast in her direction, setting light to the trees.

Fen packed her rucksack with anything she thought she and Red needed. She didn't know if they would come to her place, but one word had stuck in her mind 'ruthless'. She grabbed a sweater, some food, a water bottle and some biscuits for

Red, as much as she could carry. She didn't look back and she didn't lock. One kick and they would be inside anyway. Two other homes were alight now and she heard screams above the crackle of the burning trees. They didn't have to come to her shack, she realised, the flames would get to it first. She called out Red's name, worried she couldn't hear him barking anymore.

Fen ran down towards the fishing rock, rushing through the woods along the path she had made in the past weeks. All kinds of thoughts were rushing through her brain. The primary one was that the source of her heat was going up in flames all around her. Even if she survived this attack, how would she keep warm nights?

Red arrived, panting, whining a little. She couldn't be sure but in the light of the flames she thought he might be limping.

'It's OK, Red. Just us now.'

Red was scared, she knew it. She was scared too, but there wasn't time to think about it.

A distress flare went up from the Manley house, but Fen knew that no one would come. Not in time anyhow. The flare illuminated the tiny jetty and there, as if by magic, was a boat. For a second she thought Mercer had returned, but when she looked again it was too big.

'Come on, Red. Move.'

She ran as fast as she could towards the jetty, Red panting beside her. She looked back and saw the flames had reached the cabin, heard the snap as the wood caught fire and things began to explode in there. Stupid waste of a good home.

It was a fancy powerboat, loosely tied up. They had come in this to burn and trash the island. Well they could have it then, have the whole island. She quickly loosed off the rope from the jetty.

'In. Now. Jump.'

Red was reluctant but she threw the rucksack in and picked him up and tossed him in there as well. The boat stank of gasoline. Cans of it were stacked in the stern. Bastards. Fucking firebugs. She figured out the controls in seconds, fired her up and backed the boat away from the jetty. Red was nervous. He didn't like the motion, or the stink of gas, but he stayed close to her as she turned the boat. 'We're going for a ride, Red.'

Fen had never driven such a big powerboat before, but sensed the power under her and was excited. Above her the island burned, all the houses were alight now and she knew they'd be coming back for the boat any moment. She shot the throttle control back and moved away from the jetty, quickly turning it. Hardly waiting to let it slow she forced the throttle control ahead and the boat lunged forwards. She heard shouts, saw a flashlight on a ridge looking for the jetty and she smiled. The boat flew through the water and she was around the bend in seconds. She throttled back a moment. There was something to do. The Manley's yacht was moored here. It was a shame, a crying shame, but it had to be done.

She slowed up by the yacht, grabbed two cans of gas and unscrewed the caps, tossed them up in the air so they landed on deck to spill their guts. She had a lighter in her rucksack. It was May's really, for her secret smokes, Fen had stolen them for her bonfires. It was at the bottom of the bag, of course. She drew out a pair of old socks, stuck a can of beans in them for the weight, soaked them in gas and lit them. They burned bright and fast. She quickly lobbed it up into the air, landing it on the yacht deck above her. At first nothing happened, then whoosh, the yacht was alight, flames hungrily licking the wooden deck and sides.

Let the bandits rot on the island they ruined, she thought. No way off the island for them now. They would freeze to death once the fires went out and that was too fucking good for them.

Fen backed the boat away, nervous a spark would set off the gas cans stacked in the stern. She took it forward again, leaving the burning yacht behind. She could see them running now, flashlights ahead of them, the flames chasing them from behind as they ran towards the yacht. They'd never get there in time; they'd not get it put out if they did. It was burning fast, already spreading into the cabin and soon the fuel tanks would catch.

Fen allowed herself some satisfaction as she pulled away from the island and entered rougher waters. Bastards got what they deserved. She wondered if anyone else survived, but didn't think they had. Six major fires and the trees were burning all over the island behind her. It would probably burn all night. She turned again when she heard the fuel tanks in the yacht go up. Everything was burning so bright now they'd be able to see it from Victoria – if anyone was looking.

'Where we going to go, Red? Where we going to go?'

The engine purred, she kept it moving at a steady speed, trying to remember what Mercer had taught her about the stars. South, north or west, which was best. Red lay down at her feet, more settled now, accepting this new change. He'd go wherever she went. Didn't much matter where.

9

Guy's Drug Research Unit is part of the worldwide effort to combat the never ending threat of influenza. We are looking for healthy men and women to help in clinical studies for new vaccines. If you are healthy 18-to-50 years old, it could be you we are looking for (ladies must be surgically sterile or postmenopausal). A simple blood test will determine if you are suitable for a study.

Studies approved by the Department of Health Ethics Committee.
Guy's Drug Research Unit is part of Quintiles ltd and is independent of the Guy's and St Thomas' NHS Foundation Trust.
Advertisement – The Evening Standard, October 2006, UK

Survival Techniques

'It's one of the small islands – looks like the whole thing is on fire. Come and see.'

Arno came up on deck, wiping diesel from his hands. He looked across the water and saw huge flames. 'Has to have been set. Whole islands don't burn so easily, especially after the rain they've been having.'

Rachel frowned. She didn't like the direction things were taking. Fires in the city, now the islands, wasn't there trouble enough for everyone? 'Who's doing this and why?'

Arno flipped the cover from the starter and depressed the button. There was a click and the sound of something turning and then, finally the reassuring sound of engines firing up. He revved them and listened carefully. 'The cough's gone. Better.' He smiled for the first time in hours, looking back at Rachel, noting how tired she looked. 'Did you find the brandy? Need something to take the taste of the diesel away.'

Rachel suddenly remembered his earlier request and went to the storage box under the stern seat. 'Sorry. You're not going to be sick are you?'

Sick was exactly how Arno felt, but he said nothing. Sucking diesel up through blocked fuel lines was not his idea of fun, but at least it had cleared it.

'It's Amaretto.' She dragged out the half-empty bottle and handed it to him.

Arno took a swig and nearly choked, spitting it out almost immediately. 'Fuck.'

'I didn't figure you for a liqueur kind of guy.'

Arno took a smaller swig and gargled with it, turning and spitting it into the sea. He pulled a face and handed back the bottle, wiping his mouth with the back of his hand. 'Phew, well it's better than diesel, that's for sure. Try it.'

Rachel shook her head. 'I'm saving it for when we need it. Last rites or something.'

'Yeah, it's got that going for it. I read somewhere about the monks who first made the stuff. They tried to keep it secret and when they wouldn't sell it to the locals the peasants tried to burn the monastery down. The brandy stock was saved, even though the barrels were singed. When they tasted it, it had this smoky taste and people liked it even more.' Arno grinned at her. 'At least that's what I read on *Wickipedia* or someplace.'

'Then it must be true.' Rachel remarked smiling at him, bending down to put the bottle away. 'Hey, there's about twenty cans of tuna down here and some vodka.' But Arno's attention was taken by a flare up on the distant island. The sound of a muffled explosion hit them a moment later.

'A lot of people will be trying to escape to these islands, Rach. If some bastard's burning them out, it's either because they want to rob them, or it's fucking end-of-worlders. Probably just thieves. They'll burn people out then go back for the buried treasure. Happening back East, everyone is burying stuff because the banks are folding.'

'How do you even know this stuff, Arno?'

'That's what we do at Futuretank! Or what we did. Run scenarios – day in and day out. Companies hire us to imagine the worst and best scenarios of any given situation. Governments want to know what the effects of a prolonged drought or flooding will be, or a company want to know if they add capabilities to a product, will people pay more for it or switch to a rival? It's the intellectual end of market research I guess. Freakanomics some people call it.'

'And they came to you about the virus?'

'Lots of people worked on this way back when the SARS epidemic hit in 2003, and we were predicting it would knock 6% off Canadian GDP, more in the Far East. When we told them this pandemic could possibly kill off capitalism for good, they stopped funding us. No one wants to pay the grinch. They looked for a group that would give them a better scenario, I guess.' Arno shrugged. 'That's the future business. Call it right and they hate you for it.'

Rachel suddenly needed to sleep. Arno could see her exhaustion. He knew he'd had her up all night watching out for ships whilst they were stranded out in the open water. 'Hit the sack, Rach. I'll look for someplace safe to anchor and join you. We have to make sure we find a safe place every evening in future. We can't pull all nighters anymore.'

Rachel stumbled down into the cabin. It stank of diesel but she no longer cared. She really needed to sleep.

Arno looked back at the island, still burning behind them now. Bastards. The one thing he hadn't thought to bring was a gun. They were probably going to need one – sooner or later.

Fen was cursing. Red slept at her feet but they weren't moving. It was dark and she was mad. The fuel tank was dry and she was stranded. Behind her was a stack of about fifty cans of gasoline and she couldn't use even one! The fuel cap was locked and she couldn't find a key, or any kind of sharp tool to prise it open with. She was stuck, probably dab smack in the middle of shipping lanes, miles from anywhere. If anything hit her, she'd be toast.

She sat back and stared at the waning stars and tried to think about nothing. Not her family and how easily they had abandoned her, not about the fire – definitely not the fire – or the screams she'd heard. She had to work on a plan for her and Red to get through this, assuming she was still going to be alive tomorrow.

She awoke with a start. Her neck was sore as hell, discovered she was freezing cold. Fuck. How long had she slept? Couldn't have been more than twenty minutes or so, it was still dark. She heard the unmistakable sound of dush-dush-dush, deep bass on someone's ultra loud speakers. But where, for fuck's sake? She twisted her head. Where the hell was the music coming from? She finally saw light as a boat turned side on to her. It was approaching from the East about hundred yards distant, closing all the while, the beat getting ever louder. It was huge and headed directly for her!

Red stirred, annoyed to be woken. The boat was a huge cruiser; brightly illuminated for a party, the music at maximum decibel, practically making the sea vibrate as it made progress towards her. Fen could make out people dancing on deck; they were mostly naked, painted in weird day-glo colours. As it drew closer she could see some were passed out, others screwing right there on deck. It was crazy, packed with college kids or something. Fen stared, fascinated, overwhelmed by the decadence of it. It was a fancy cruiser, eighty-five foot or more she guessed. People were yelling and fucking and even though it passed less than twenty feet away, no one noticed her and Red staring. She knew Red wanted to bark and she grabbed his snout to silence him. The bass overwhelmed her, she felt her whole body vibrate as the cruiser passed by, its engines whispering powerfully as it swept on. She saw a blonde girl, naked and painted red transfixed, astride a man, unmoving, her eyes open but unseeing and then she was gone. Fen badly wanted to be rescued, but not by them, whatever they were, whoever they were. She remained fixed on the receding boat, unable to tear her gaze away.

Fen noticed a shimmer of light on the horizon; it would be dawn soon. She was thirsty. Red would be too, but she resisted the urge to drink from her precious water bottle. She knew she had to make it last. Who knew how long they'd be stuck out here?

She fell asleep again. The cruiser became unreal, impossible, just another component of her nightmares.

The pressure in his bladder was overwhelming. By God he needed to piss. Deka suddenly opened his eyes. It was almost light. Five o'clock by his reckoning. He'd survived the night, survived to see another morning. No one was stirring, but someone on the ward was coughing in their sleep, others snoring. He discovered he couldn't move. Worse he was soaked right through; sweat was pouring off him. His throat was bone dry and the golf ball in his throat was still there – still damn painful. Hell, he needed to piss real bad. He turned his head a little, saw a bed pan on the side table but it might as well have been on Mars, he couldn't move a muscle. He felt as though he'd been strapped down but didn't think that was the case. Perhaps it was the fever. This had happened before he remembered, in Cape Town. He'd been thirteen, taken to Groot Schuur hospital in the middle of the night and the nurses told his mother he might be paralysed for life. In a panic she went to see the shaman in Tamberskloof again, to get rid of the evil spirit she was sure was possessing him.

She never came back. It was the shame of the family that she stayed with the shaman. After tests however the Doctor had diagnosed meningitis and they'd quickly performed a lumbar puncture. To this day he could recall the pain moment the huge needle dug into the base of his spine and how quickly the fluid drained from his brain. They didn't believe him, but he felt it drain, heard it trickle out. The fever left him almost immediately. When, a day later, no one had come to see him, he walked home in his hospital gown. He'd lost a stone in weight, hardly anyone in the neighborhood recognised him.

God he really needed to piss. Couldn't hold it a second more. He let go. For one glorious moment he felt warm again, then guilty. Shit, he'd pissed his bed, like he was two again. The relief was extraordinary, felt as though he'd pissed gallons of the stuff. Stank too. That's when the pain abruptly kicked in. Spurts of intense hot pain, pounding behind his eyes and in his groin. It was throbbing and he felt tremors ride up through his body, as if someone had attached electrodes to him. He arched his back and felt he was floating away on a tide of sharp nails. And then nothing. Nothing at all.

Red heard it first; he nudged Fen awake and licked her face till she opened her eyes. The sun was hard on her, already high above the horizon. The boat rocked wildly and Red whimpered, nervous.

'What'? Fen quickly looked around her, sloughing off deep sleep. 'What? I can't see anything Red. Nothing out there.'

The wave came out of nowhere, nearly flipped the whole boat over and Red lost his grip and flipped out of the boat into the sea.

'Red!' Fen screamed, sliding to the gunwales, wondering how the hell she'd ever get him back in.

Red panicked swimming in circles, shocked but in survival mode already.

It was then that Fen saw them. Orca whales, a whole school of them, casually swimming by. One must have surfaced right under the boat; unaware it was there without the engine running. She watched them go by in awe, almost forgetting Red for a moment.

Fen ran to the stern, blocked by the cans of gasoline. Instinctively she knew that the only chance she had was to get him aboard from the rear of the boat. She had to move those cans. She got stuck in, calling out to Red to keep calm; knowing that he wouldn't understand why she wasn't helping him.

Red was anything but calm, but at least he was afloat. He liked to chase sticks into the sea from the beach. It was a whole other thing to be thrown into the water miles from anywhere.

The whales had gone. Fen scrambled over the remaining cans to the stern and called Red to her. 'This way. No this way, Red. Come on, boy, come on.'

The dog changed direction, distinct panic in its eyes. It was desperately concentrating on staying afloat.

Fen couldn't see any easy solution here. She stripped off her shirt and shoes and jumped in. She came up gasping. It was unbelievably cold. Red was upon her, placing his complete faith in her.

'Here.' Fen got his paws on the short ladder at the rear of the boat. 'Got to help me, Red.' She went under again and tried to get underneath him to boost him up, but he was slippery and his legs kicked her away. Fen came up for air again. 'Got to try something else, Red. Hang on.'

Red didn't understand and slipped back under the water again, thrashing about, scared.

Fen got a grip on the ladder and when Red surfaced, coughing up seawater, she grabbed his collar and hauled him up against her. She knew she was choking him but she arched her back and fell back against the rear deck, Red coming up with her like a wet carpet, twisting to get free of her grip and right himself. Both of them collapsed back against the cans of gasoline, freezing, soaked, but alive. Fen let go. Red scrabbled up, coughing up more seawater, but he stayed close, absolutely sure he wasn't going to go back in there ever again.

'Well done, well done, Red. Get back there, move, OK? Move.' She pushed him towards the front seats and then lay back to get her breath a moment. She lay there, frozen but relieved, realising, perhaps for the first time just how precarious her situation really was.

A thought occurred to her. 'You didn't drink that stuff did you?' She knew he had. Red would be thirsty as hell soon. Damn. Fen suddenly stripped off her jeans and jumped back into the water. The world's biggest bathroom beckoned, it was hers. She might as well use it.

Wylie stood half in and half out of the sink and licked the tap. It was as trick he knew from old when he'd been left too long in the gallery. Something was coming out, but not enough to actually assuage his thirst. It had been two days now; Doc had lain there on the sofa barely moving, except to cough and spit, not saying a word, totally stricken.

Wylie understood things were different, he knew that Doc was ill, any dog could tell when a human was well or sick, but it was different this time. Doc was nothing but a shadow; not giving orders, wasn't paying any attention to him at all. It unnerved him.

He understood this at night because there was a routine. Doc went to bed and snored and Wylie slept a while and then patrolled a couple of times to make sure no one tried to get in, or even thought about it. He still glanced regularly at the window where he'd once bitten someone's finger's off. They'd not try that again. But something had changed. No one came to the front door anymore. Doc not moving was odd, he smelt different too. Wylie had an unexplained bad feeling about everything.

He turned his attention to the tap again. Didn't understand why nothing came out of it. In annoyance he head butted it. Sometimes this worked and indeed the drips turned to a trickle and he licked the tap faster. This was better. Unbalanced, he slipped in the porcelain sink and his back caught the tap hard. Suddenly it opened, gushing cold water into the sink. Wylie drank guiltily, a whole lot happier to get some water down his throat. He nearly lost his footing again and noticed that the water was rising up against him, no matter how much he drank. He began to panic. Definitely felt guilty now. Instinctively he knew the Doc would bite his head off if he knew he was up here. He was expressly forbidden to be up here. Water continued to flow out of the tap and it was rising up to his chest now and he knew he had to get off the sink. He snatched a look back at Doc on the sofa as he scrabbled to get some footing to jump down. He was going to get walloped for this, for sure. Fretting, he whimpered.

Doc opened his eyes.

Wylie shut up. Heart pounding, he leapt off the sink, afraid he'd been seen. He ran to the back door, for escape. Still closed. That was the other thing. His shit was still there. Worse he needed to go again and he'd catch it for sure when the Doc woke up. The trouble was storing up in every place and he just wanted to run away, he was so sure he'd be hit so hard.

He felt distressed, everything was wrong and he was hungry all the time. Doc had never slept this long before, never.

There was a sudden sound from the kitchen again. He glanced back and water was pouring over the sink and falling loudly onto the granite floor, spreading everywhere. Wylie whimpered some more. He was so going to get beaten to death. For absolute sure.

She discovered she was dancing. It was a good feeling. Back at the Roxy. She was sixteen, feeling cocky she'd got in with her false ID and there was Candi with Graeme, her tongue down deep, and the music just got louder and louder and she was shaking all over from the beat. She could hardly breathe it was so loud and Candi was shouting something at her and she couldn't hear because the bass was so fucking heavy and...

The kettle crashed to the floor. Rachel woke with a start and saw it rolling below the bunk. The beat was still there. The cabin windows were rattling and her chest was vibrating and then Arno was awake, startled, jumping out of bed so fast a scorpion must have been in there.

'What? What the hell?'

They both looked at the hi-fi system but it couldn't be coming from there. The dance beat was so loud now Rachel thought her head would explode. Arno rushed up on deck and Rachel stood up to grab her sweater and banged her head hard against the bulkhead. 'Ow, fuck'. Why the hell couldn't she remember it was there. Dazed, she staggered after Arno rubbing her head. She'd have a nasty bump from that.

Arno was staring out to sea with astonishment, his hands over his ears. A huge motor cruiser was approaching the lighthouse rock where they were moored. It was going to be real close and there was nothing they could do about it.

Rachel appeared at his side, hands over her ears as well. 'What the fuck, Arno? A party boat out here, now?' She figured it was about seven in the morning. Light, but the sun wasn't up yet.

The cruiser bore down on them – the music deafening, literally making them vibrate to the dush-dush-dush of the bass. How anyone on board could stand it was the bigger puzzle; this wasn't music it was a loaded weapon.

Arno grabbed her and shouted. 'It's going to be close. Brace yourself.'

Rachel was ready to jump overboard, never mind brace herself. As the cruiser loomed ever closer they heard a harsh scraping noise from under the surface as it's hull made contact with rocks. For a second they both thought that this was it, their last moments on the planet. But the rock seemed to affect the cruiser's momentum and the stern moved around by thirty degrees and it began to move left, away from the lighthouse rock by mere fractions and sail right past them.

Rachel and Arno watched dumbstruck, hands over their ears, the cruiser so close they could almost touch it. And as it receded, they could see on deck, the bodies, distorted, vile, naked, some painted dead bodies, most in their late teens, many sprawled where they had fallen, some in pools of vomit and blood, others with faces contorted with pain. Rachel tried counting but had to stop she felt so nauseous.

'Jesus,' Arno mumbled.

'Whose steering it? Someone must be still alive.' Rachel asked, looking away from the bodies.

'Automatic pilot, probably. Just going to sail until it really does hit a rock or island. Or sinks. Must have holed a moment ago. See? It's listing.'

Rachel looked back and that's when they both saw her. A blond girl, thin as a rake, sat at the stern, awake, alive, motionless, staring at them with not a flicker of recognition.

Arno looked at Rachel and she just stared as the cruiser receded, the music with it, the whole event utterly surreal.

'I'm beginning to think we might be safer on land.' Arno remarked.

Rachel suddenly sat on the deck, her legs weak with fear from the reaction. They had nearly been rammed by a plague ship in the fucking middle of nowhere. It came with a realisation that there was probably nowhere safe to go at all.

Arno squatted down beside her and gave her a hug.

'She can't be helped. She knows it. Probably they all knew it. Just went out with a bang. Don't fret, OK. We're out here to make sure we survive, that's all.'

Rachel closed her eyes. All she could see was that motionless girl sitting on the stern. 'What if she's immune, Arno? What if wasn't her turn to die? It happens. It doesn't kill everyone.'

Arno said nothing. The girl had made a choice the moment she went on the cruiser. The likelihood was the boat would sink and she'd drown. One of life's nice little ironies. He briefly wondered how many kids there had been on the boat. He couldn't believe that he'd chosen the safest place he could on the navigation chart and that cruiser had found them. It was like the finger of God mocking them for trying to outrun the virus. 'Let's party like it's 1999.' Arno mumbled. The song was the only thing that came to mind. Probably the closest to the truth.

Rachel looked at him confused, then remembered the song. 'That dates you.'

'That's what you get for going around with an older man.' He smiled and stood up, suddenly aware that he was standing in his underwear. 'Coffee? Breakfast?'

Rachel still had the images of the corpses fresh in her mind and her first thought was that Arno was being completely insensitive. What kind of man was she hooked up with? Didn't he feel desperately sorry for that girl left alive on the boat? Shouldn't they have tried to help her? She could have easily jumped. Then the reality of their situation hit her. If she *had* jumped they couldn't have touched her. She was a plague carrier, immune or not. No one was ever going to help anyone ever again. This was just the beginning. They were going to see stuff like this almost everyday.

'Yeah, coffee would be good.' She answered at last.

10

At current production capacity, the CDC assumes that we can vaccinate approximately 1% of the population per week, following a 3-to-4 months process for the first influenza vaccine to be produced. This means it would take a month just to vaccinate health care workers, assuming health care workers are first in line. So who among health care workers get their shots in week one? Who in week two? What about public officials? Workers in key infrastructure positions? How about family members of all of the above? What about the military?
Pandemic Preparedness Situation paper – Maricopa County Dept of Public Health, Arizona State.

Check In – Check Out

Mercer blinked. He took another look at Frances sprawled out on the bed, her face purple and contorted, as if in a rage, the useless drugs spilled across the pillow beside her. He'd gone to get milk. She'd wanted milk, nagged him till he'd given in and gone out to get it. He quickly discovered that the fleapit hotel they were in had been boarded up. He'd had a fight with another hotel guest who'd been drunk and had tried to rob him. He hadn't been able to get out of the building at all. The damn elevator was out, so he'd climbed back up to the tenth floor and found Frances had gone. He'd only been downstairs thirty minutes, tops. She'd been coughing all night and of course May dying earlier – silently – in death as in life, had made Frances all the more panicky.

Now here he was, in the room with Frances who had died alone, the one thing she begged him not to let happen. He glanced at May, still sitting in the chair by the door, stiff, lips blue, her expression almost angelic. He knew it was his fault. If he hadn't let Frances nag him, every day, they'd still be safe on the island with Fen. He thought then of Fen and how she would despise him even more now. How all her life she'd hated him and her mother, Catherine, almost if she wasn't their own child, as if she could have done better.

It had been his decision to check into the almost empty hotel. Rooms so cheap it was hard to resist and it had its own kitchen, so they didn't have to go out except to buy food. Frances loved it. There was a proper bathroom and they'd made plans to just stay there, wait out the virus until it burned itself out. Frances was sure it would peak and then they'd be able to live anywhere they liked on the island. They'd have the pick of empty homes right by the ocean. She had it all planned.

Then May got sick after she went to the market. She'd worn a mask and everything, but she'd come back and said she had a headache. Frances had wanted her to leave them immediately, fend for herself. She screamed the place down and May did indeed move into an empty room down the corridor. Frances wouldn't let him call a doctor because they'd close the hotel for sure and then they'd be in quarantine. Nice irony, that. He didn't even know they were already in quarantine until he'd gone down for the milk.

Mercer had to visit May in secret and take her soup. But May didn't go quickly. She just stared at him with accusatory looks. Her last words were for him to make sure he didn't forget Fen. Which, of course, they all had, and there was no getting away from that. They had abandoned her on the island and each one of them had secretly decided not to go back there. Fen was back on the island, sure, but seemed very much in the hotel rooms sending them bad vibes.

The virus didn't seem to affect Mercer at all. Took May three days to die in all. The only thing that seemed to manifest itself was the bleeding from her nose and ears, but she didn't complain much. She refused to go the hospital, because she imagined they would just put her in a plague pit. They had all heard the rumours about people being thrown into the pits whilst still alive. On the last day, when he knew Frances was dying too, he brought May back in and put her in the chair so she could be with them both. Frances couldn't scream anymore. Her voice went quickly, then her vision, and she was coughing up bits of her lungs most of the time. She wrote that she wanted milk and finally Mercer had agreed to try to find some.

So here he stood. The fool who had brought them here, just so he didn't have to listen to them gripe and moan a day longer on the island. Two dead in the room. Here he was boarded up with them, alive, and healthy, completely untouched by the virus.

He knew he wouldn't be able to get out. There were CCTV cameras on the building. On all the boarded up buildings in Victoria. It was like medieval times, abandoning the living with the dead and dying. They were shooting looters and anything that moved at night. No one cared about 'saving' the sick. Next thing they'd probably set fire to the hotel. Couldn't blame them. That's what the preacher had kept shouting on the street corner when they had arrived. Everything had to burn, be cleansed, ready for the second coming. He seemed to draw a crowd. Everyone wanted to save their soul, any way they could.

He could try to escape, get onto the roof, jump to the next building; they most likely weren't looking up there and figured everyone was dead or dying and not able to move. But even though he lived, he might be a carrier and he was responsible for enough dying. He could never be sure that he wasn't the one who carried it into the hotel, picked up maybe when he went to get food. You met a lot of strange people selling black-market stuff out there.

He looked at May again. She'd been such a strange girl. Almost resented being alive and here she was looking completely composed. Happier than he remembered her in life. A big contrast to Frances who looked so ugly in death, as if every negative thought had consumed her whole. She was just a dead stranger lying on the bed. And he was the idiot who allowed this to happen.

He raised the gun, didn't look at it, placed the barrel under his chin and angled it up towards his brain. (He'd seen this in a film once on how to make sure you really died instantly). Gun barrel felt cold. He looked in the mirror, adjusted the angle. Had to be just so. Had to do one thing right in his life. Fen would appreciate that, him killing himself right.

Fen.

Last thought for the girl who never believed a word he said. Fen. Here I am letting you down again, girl. One last time.

He fell. No one heard. No one cared. He'd died the moment he'd checked them in anyway.

Oblivion didn't come instantly. For some reason he thought of Red, thought the dog was there in the room with him licking his face.

11

For the H5N1 virus to mutate so that it can spread from human to human, it will, most likely, have to learn how to infect the upper-respiratory tract (nearer the throat). Then coughs and sneezes will expel much more of the virus. More immediately worrying for US Government Health organisations is the increasing spread of Vibrio vulnificus – the flesh-eating marine virus growing more widespread north of the Gulf of Mexico in response to rising sea-temperatures due to climate change.
Medical News Today

No Requiems Required

Deka's eyes snapped open. Something had just gone 'click' in his head – as distinct as a light switch flicking on – one moment he was dead, another wide-awake. Not just wide-awake; alive. He could feel it. Somehow the electricity was back on and he knew it was over.

Of course he wasn't well – he could barely make his arms move at this point, but he knew the worst was over. He had beaten it, just like Doc said he would. He felt like he'd been beaten to a pulp, he was so weak, but mostly all he felt now was…hunger. Damn, he was hungry. How long had he been in here? It was still dark, but instinct and years of rising early in the taxi business told him it was around 4.30 am. He'd been rising at 4.30 am for the best part of twelve years now; getting on the road by 5.15 to collect the first customers of the day. The airport run. Under threat now from the Skytrain link from downtown. Some people still liked to use a cab no matter that the Skytrain was cheap, quick and hard to beat in traffic. The stuff they were putting in for the Winter Olympics was changing everything. Then he remembered, there would likely be no Olympics. All this building was for nothing. No one was coming now. No one was going anywhere.

He turned his head. Yes, it was dark but the blue ultra-violet lights were still burning at the far end of the ward. He didn't know why there was UV light everywhere in hospitals but he assumed it inhibited the virus somehow. But then again, surely UV light killed things. He'd seen a programme on TV. Prolonged UV light could kill healthy tissue cells. How long had he been exposed to it? He could make out shapes but no one was moving or coughing. Only him awake then.

His nostrils kicked in as he stretched and yawned. God... he stank. Totally rank. The bed was soaked, foetid and kind of squishy. He was glad he couldn't see just how bad it was. The bastards had just left him, changed nothing. He was lying in a pool of liquid. Fuck, if the flu didn't get him something else would. He did a body system check. Wiggled toes, fingers, raised one leg at a time. His joints felt sore. Now he considered it, he could literally feel every bone in his body. It was a terrible sensation. Each joint, each bone seemed to be protesting. He was alive, but filthy, nevertheless he was functioning, though damned uncomfortable.

The ward was ominously quiet. No wheezing, no coughing, just the sound of some engines outside – ambulances perhaps. He could hear random shouts coming up from the interior courtyard. For a second he could see a row of ambulances all waiting in a courtyard, but it was just a fleeting mental image, not real.

He was abruptly aware that his left arm was still plugged into a drip. He gripped the needle and pulled it out, feeling intense pain as he did so, holding his thumb down on the hole stop the blood. Fuck that hurt! The drip had dried out long ago. Why hadn't they changed it? It was a fucking miracle that he was alive at all.

He struggled to sit up, acutely aware of how wet and slimy it was in the bed. How long? How many hours had he been lying here? He gazed up the ward into the blue light and frowned. No nurses moving, no sound at all, not even snoring. He finally managed to sit up. And despite the sickening stench from his bed, yes, he was achingly hungry. Porridge. He discovered he had a desperate need for oatmeal. Hadn't eaten it for years.

He tried speaking, but no sound emerged from his parched throat. The golf ball was still there, but diminished – it was damn hard to swallow.

Well if there was no one around, he was going to go to the bathroom and get cleaned up. Didn't care if he had to crawl, he desperately wanted to be clean again.

If sitting up was hard, pulling off the blankets and swinging his legs over to the side of the bed was torture. For a real moment he considered they had tied lead to his feet to stop him moving. The pins and needles started then. He'd always been prone to them and being a cabbie was never a good choice for someone who needed to move about often, but this pain was worse than he ever remembered having before. He sat on the edge of the bed and waited – trying to flex his wrists and move his head on an awkwardly stiff neck. He'd become the iron man. Or was it the tin-man? ... he needed a can of oil.

The ward was too quiet. Much too quiet. He tried taking breaths but couldn't inhale much without experiencing a sharp pain. His breathing was chronically shallow he realised, and his lungs weren't even working at forty percent by his reckoning. It was just too painful to take in air, or what passed for air in this foul fug of germs. As he let his bodyweight onto his limbs he became aware of how his knee joints were on fire, his elbows too. Just how much damage had this virus done to him?

He remembered Doc telling him that after the SARS epidemic, patients who had survived almost regretted it as they tried to live with crippling pains in their joints and respiratory system. Years later they were still suffering. Well, he wasn't going to give in to it. Whether he believed in God or not, he had been given a chance to live and he had to seize it.

He lowered himself to the floor, stood with the aid of the bed and waited for the blood to circulate. He was light-headed, hungry, and dizzy but he had to go through with this. No one was coming, and if they did they'd force him back into that slime bucket of a bed. He was going to crawl to the bathroom if he had to.

'First steps, baby steps,' he muttered to himself. He reached the far wall and whether it was his movement or he'd accidentally triggered them, the lights began to come on, slowly flickering to life then dimming to about fifty percent. Now Deka knew what the sound of the motors was, generators. The hospital was on emergency power. He looked down the ward to the nurses' station. A nurse in a space suite was slumped against a desk. Asleep? He looked back again along the ward. Not a soul stirred. He stared more intently, bodies were half in half out of beds, some sprawled on the floor in a pool of bile and blood, others in bed, faces contorted, skin slightly purple. Deka didn't have to look further. Everyone was dead, nurse included. The stench of piss and decay was nauseating. He didn't have to go from section to section, he knew there wouldn't be any survivors. How long had it been like this? Did the hospital know?

He shuffled towards the double doors that led to the rest of the hospital. They were locked, he could see through the glass that this ward had been taped off. They knew. Bastards had just left them for dead. Expected him to die, just like everyone else. 'Only Suited and Sealed Personnel Permitted beyond this point' declared a sign taped to the doors.

Joy. He was locked into a death ward. Panic began to rise, he turned away breathing hard, his heart racing. He had to get out of here. But not like this, not covered in piss and shit and whatever else. He shuffled to a door with a shower symbol on it. Please, God, let the shower be working.

He pushed the door open, sweating now, forcing himself onwards.

There was a young man sprawled on the floor, half in half out of his HAZMAT space suit. Blood had spilled from his nose and ears but he didn't look as though he'd been there long. There was an ID: Ricard, Michel. Deka said nothing, didn't approach him. He dragged himself to the shower and turned it on. Mercifully hot water began to flow. Not fast, but enough. Deka peeled off his sodden tunic and stepped under the water.

There was enough of everything he needed, shampoo, liquid antiseptic soap in a bottle. He couldn't remember a time he had enjoyed a shower more. He frowned as he hosed down his backside. The water stung and he discovered that he had bedsores from lying in his own piss. Again he felt a flash of anger. They had abandoned him.

His eyes adjusted to the room and he saw a rack of clean towels neatly folded on a shelf and next to it, a new spacesuit shrink-wrapped in plastic. A plan formulated in his head. Newly revived by the hot steam, he knew he had to get out of there. Couldn't allow them to coop him up or quarantine him. He'd had it, passed through it, he was living proof you could survive and he had to get back to Doc, tell him. Help him, spread the word. His blood, their blood was something they could make a vaccine out of. No? That other stuff they were using wasn't working. Those killer T-Cells they had developed might stop chickens from dying, but it sure as hell hadn't helped people. Not this time around anyway.

He turned and half glimpsed himself in a steamy mirror. He frowned and looked down at his stomach. He had lost weight. A lot of weight. Was that possible in such a short time? At least twenty pounds, more maybe. Just how long had he been here?

He finally shut off the shower. Drank some cold water from the tap, drank a lot. Didn't matter if it was contaminated anymore. The way he saw it he was immune. He grabbed a towel. It had dawned on him that he had no clothes. He tried to avoid looking at the dead nurse but felt his eyes constantly drawn towards him and his greying flesh. He felt guilty for doing nothing and eventually lay his wet towel over the man's face.

He ripped the plastic seal off the spare suit and with great effort stepped into it, pulling it up, sliding his arms into the tight sleeves. He discovered they were made of a special kind of paper. Light and layered. He'd been worried about being naked under there but it was warm. He read the tear-off slip on the headgear. *'This air filter must be changed and discarded in an incinerator every three hours without fail. If filter turns red, change immediately.'*

Deka secured the headgear and twisted it into place. This version of the HAZMAT suit was tight, particularly around his thighs and crotch, but he was ready. He just hoped his strength would hold out. He suddenly remembered the door was locked. His eyes turned back to the dead nurse. Did he have a key? He moved over toward him and looked more carefully, better equipped to do this now the man's face was covered. There was a patch pocket on his left side of the suit, just like his own. Deka bent down and although it was difficult to do anything with gloved hands, his fingers made contact with a plastic key card, just like at the Holiday Inn. He slipped it out and put it into his own pocket. He had to appear confident, look as though he belonged.

Back in the ward – he was acutely aware of his perilous situation. He could see that someone had made a conscious decision to let everyone die here. Had something got out of control? How bad was it out there? He was strongly aware that it was his own personal miracle that he was alive, but could he get out? And if he did, what was out there waiting for him?

He reached the double doors, fumbled with the card, nearly dropping it. Steady. Stay steady. He concentrated, pushed it into the slot. Immediately a voice came from the speaker. *'Exiting Orange Ward. Only suited and sealed personnel can leave. Give your name now.'*

Deka panicked. Of course he couldn't give his name. The lock would freeze for sure. He had a vision of the dead male nurse on the shower room floor. Saw again the ID. 'Ricard, Michel,' he croaked.

There was a moment's hesitation. Deka began to feel sick with tension. Should he have said Michel Ricard? Or just Ricard? What if they asked his date of birth or some other question? He felt queasy.

The lock opened. He opened the door and stepped out, quickly closing the door behind him. A smaller HAZMAT suited figure was coming down some stairs holding a chart.

'You coming off shift?'

Deka looked up, aware that sweat was pouring down his forehead behind the mask.

'Off.' Deka looked into the obscured face of the new arrival and was surprised. Looked like a kid. Not more than eighteen, if a day. Couldn't be a doctor but he had an offical ID. Jowett. S. He noted the kid kept a safe distance away from him, seemed wary.

'I thought Orange Ward was off limits.'

'You left nursing staff in there. I had to check...'

The kid frowned cutting him off. 'There's staff in there?'

'Two. Both dead. I touched nothing. Someone should get them out.'

The kid shook his head, making a note on his pad. 'Too late. Clean up detail will be here at six. You shouldn't have gone in. You'll have to go to Decom. It's moved to the first floor, East Wing. 062.'

Deka nodded and headed to the stairs.

'You can use the elevator. Generators are back on till eleven. Only six hours of power today until we get some fuel. You'll need to register with the MP's for a permit to get home. We went to martial law at midnight. Admin will let you know your next shift.' He left then, walking down a long corridor, checking doors on the way.

Deka paused by the elevator. He was dizzy with hunger and all this information. Martial law? Jesus. How long had he been in there? Seemed just hours since he was down at the marina. He thought of his last passengers. Did they get out? Had they escaped or had he killed them?

Deka pushed the elevator button, resting his head against the wall. He had no ID. What would happen down there? Decom. Did he really have to go to Decom? How old was that kid in the space suit? Had they run out of doctors already? Or had they run for it, knowing what was coming. He was aware that his ass was sore, he needed some cream for the bedsores. The elevator arrived. He got in. Pushed a button. Doors closed.

There was a sign on the elevator wall:

Attention Citizens of Greater Vancouver.

Martial Law is now in effect.

Movement about the city between the hours of 10pm and 6am without a valid pass will result in immediate quarantine. All citizens are hereby informed that, as of this date, food and gasoline rationing are in effect. Individuals are directed to pick up ration books from specially-designated distribution vehicles which will visit each neighbourhood and announce their presence via loudspeaker. Any attempt to gain entry into a distribution vehicle will be met with lethal force.

By authority of Roger Samson, Chief Medical Health Officer.

Dept.
[ref:214]
CMHO

Room 062. One section of the sterilisation section was UV lit and the space suits lit up brilliant white. Like some weird Martian clubland. He entered. Was given a number and told to strip off. He could see men and women stripping off, they were naked in those suits, like him. Not surprising since the damn things were so hot. He was scared to de-suit. They'd see his wreck of a body. He just wanted to go home.

A vision of the white-washed home in Observatory spun into his head. Even after nine years in Vancouver, home was still Cape Town. So distant, but he could still see the mountain and the famous tablecloth cloud floating on top of it every time he thought of home. Bright sun, birds, friendly smiles, hot mealies, samosas. Had the Cape escaped all this? Was his stepbrother David still alive, or his neighbours, Mamood, or little Fatima?

'Suit off,' someone was shouting in his ear. 'Shower and grab some new clothes from the pile. What size are you?'

'44 chest. 31 leg.' Deka answered quickly.

'Gap sent over a supply. Pick from the pile in the corner when you're done, ok.'

Deka nodded, unfastening his headgear. He noted there were six others ahead of him going through decontamination. Twelve cubicles – disinfectants, some kind of fine orange mist that people went through. Most had shaved heads. His hair was conspicuous in being thick, short, but very visible. Would they see how emaciated he was? They seemed to accept him as one of them pretty quickly.

'Here, drink this.' A suited man ordered him. He handed Deka a plastic bottle of liquid and Deka quickly put it to his lips. Tasted like apple. The same man turned back to him and jabbed him with a needle, pushed it in and was out real fast. 'Vitamin B12 cocktail. We're all on it now. Helps. Maybe.'

Deka was grateful for the drink and what the hell, he needed all the vitamins he could get right now. The man was going down the line giving the same treatment to them all.

Deka was naked now, moving to a cubicle, sloshing through some potent burnt orange disinfectant liquid that filled your nostrils and singed the hairs.

'It passed twenty percent today,' A woman informed him as she entered the cubicle next to him. She was naked, like him, but seemingly unconscious of it.

'Statistically it's only supposed to be two point eight percent of the population y'know. Montreal seems to have got away with it best. Less than five percent. Fucking smokers. Bet Quebec's really happy eh? Probably issuing free cigarettes with the ration packs. There's no fucking justice. Took me five years to quit and now they tell me I should start up again. The virus just walks on by smokers and hits people with healthy lungs. I hate irony. It's hit nearly twenty percent infection rate now. Although they say it's levelling off fast.'

Deka was confused. 'Twenty percent of what?'

'The population. They can't bury them in pits fast enough. They started burning the bodies in the parks.'

Sam North

His new friend in the cubicle seemed to agree. 'If they had told us that smoking is a defence, we could have all started. Hell you probably don't need the antivirals at all if you smoke thirty a day.'

Deka was trying to make sense all this. 'Are you kidding? We're dying out west because we don't smoke?'

'That's what they say. Hell they stopped counting out of town. Not as bad as Winnipeg I hear. Things broke down real fast there.'

'And Chicago.' The guy on the chair interjected. 'We don't know if troopers killed more than the actual virus trying to stop the food riots. No news coming out of there now. Feds put in like wartime censorship I heard.'

Deka's shower stopped. He stepped out and moved towards the clean towels lying neatly folded on a table. The guy on the chair still had something to say.

'The fuckin' experts said it was statistically probable that two point eight percent would die because they based their figures on the 1918 flu pandemic. But we got six billion people in the world now; they had just two billion back then. We got airports, just-in-time delivery and all that shit. They couldn't even begin to shut it down. Everything was done too late. They said this T-Cell vaccine would stop it in its tracks. Twenty percent is lucky. But it hasn't even peaked yet.'

Deka was figuring it out. Vancouver was a city of 600,000 people with around two million in greater Vancouver. At a minimum 120,000 infected in Vancouver alone, so far. Jesus. Had they kept it quiet? Was this why they weren't reporting the deaths on the radio anymore?

'Richmond is like the dead zone,' the woman remarked as she emerged from the shower. 'Went like wildfire there. I guess they had the Feng Shui wrong or something.'

Deka heard someone laugh. Yeah, laugh. All the Chinese die in Richmond and it's good for a smart sly remark.

'Anyone want pit shift. Triple pay. Cash.'

Deka was reeling. These people were so casual, like they had been doing this shit all their lives. So many dead. Pit shifts. How could they get so indifferent so fast?

He found himself at the Gap stack. The woman was already sifting through it. 'I hate picking through clothes in UV light. I step outside and I discover I'm wearing orange and green or something. Just grab anything honey, it doesn't matter, they're only going to burn it when you come back for the next shift.

'Isn't the Army burying the dead?' Deka asked.

'What Army? They got wiped out in the second wave. I heard one guy went AWOL to see his girl and came back with it. Took the entire barracks out.'

'You hear about Orange Ward?' A newcomer to the room announced.

'Everyone dead. Two nurses as well. Red wards gone critical too. They say it's in the air-conditioning. Can't switch it back on until we get new filters.'

'Could be what's spreading it right through the city,' the short, acne scarred guy next to Deka pointed out. 'Especially since they don't build anything with windows you can actually open anymore. Dr Kulka reckons the virus has mutated about ten times this month. H-5 doesn't even slow it down anymore.'

'H-6 is here now. We're all getting it before we start the next shift.' The boss on the chair remarked. 'It's been proven effective in Washington State and Calgary.'

But you could see from all the eyebrows raised around the room that no one actually believed that. Probably didn't believe anything anymore.

The woman was dressed and trying to find shoes to fit. Deka has pulled on a sweater to go over some pants that he swore had flares. Fuck when was the last time he'd worn flares?

'I was reading about the pandemic of 1889.' The woman remarked to Deka. 'It's got direct links to the Asian Flu virus in 1957. It's the same fucking thing, comes around every thirty years or so. Center for Disease Control and Prevention in Atlanta has all this data on these things and no one ever took it seriously. Screw finding a cure for cancer – this thing is the biggest killer since the great plague in Europe. They weren't ready for it and now they're covering their backs. Got millions of us all vaccinated. 100 percent protection they said and then whoopsie, the virus goes right around it and bites us in the ass. Not only that, but thousands of people have developed this epilepsy thing now. It's almost as bad as the virus and gives you chronic arthritis.'

Deka was thinking that there was a vaccine that worked. He'd just proved it.

'Let's face it.' The short guy declared. 'There's no vaccine for this. You get it, or you don't get it. If you get it, it's just not worth surviving it.'

'Where are the survivors?' Deka asked.

The woman shrugged. 'I hear they ship them out to the Okanagan. When they can find drivers. Bus drivers get out there and won't come back. Can't blame 'em. It's safer and warmer there. The survivors will need a lot of therapy. Gets them in the joints. I've seen them. They can't believe they're alive and then wish they were dead.'

Deka held his tongue. He was a real survivor. They should be studying his immune system right now. Could help them understand it. 'There any cream? I got sores.'

'Yeah, me too.' Someone griped from a cubicle. 'These fucking HAZMAT suits totally suck.'

'Japanese, that's why,' someone remarked. 'Of course they're too small, they weren't made for our sizes. Makes your crotch sweat, grabs you in the crack, not surprised you got sores. On the shelf, left, middle.'

Deka followed the instructions and opened up the first box he found. He dropped his pants and applied the cream. Fuck his ass was sore, but at least he had something to soothe it with now. He was still reeling from the twenty-percent figure. What does a city with that many people cut out of it look like?

'You look like shit, Mister. Come on. Let's go to the canteen.' It was his new female friend.

'I'm hungry. Real hungry. Feel as though I haven't eaten for a week.'

'Canteen sucks but it's virtually the only place to eat now. You hear they are issuing ration tickets?'

'I saw the notice.'

'Got to get me a ration book. They're restructuring. No more Superstore. You just use your tickets at the designated store to get what you need and go. No argument. They've got armed guards at every outlet. There's no gas either. We're all going to have to walk until they get new deliveries. Only three gallons per vehicle this week. Maybe none next week. Got people car-jacking in broad daylight – shootings you wouldn't believe. Ambulances crew won't even go out there anymore without armed guards.'

'Three gallons?' Deka was thinking that his cab used that much in a hour.

They left Decom for the canteen. Deka smiled at his reflection in a glass window. He was wearing green khakis and a multi-striped sweater. His companion was wearing yellow and purple. She sighed. 'I never get it right.'

They walked across the yard to the canteen where several people were lining up. Deka noticed the dump trucks, motors running, waiting for the bodies for the pits. Noticed too the vacant expression on the driver's faces as they sat there smoking – a good six feet apart from each other. How close had he been to being one of the many dumped in the pits? Reece would be already in one, probably half the people he knew as well.

'Dogs.' His companion was saying. 'Watch out for dogs on the way home. I was nearly attacked yesterday. Lots of abandoned pets out there and they are learning to go around in packs. They're starving. Coyotes are having a field day.'

Deka didn't doubt it for a second. 'You ever hear anything about Africa? I mean the Cape.'

'That where you from?'

'Ja. I want to call home. I'm a bit scared to.'

She shook her head. 'No, seen nothing on the news, but then again, they don't show much now. Of course since the Pope was assassinated they haven't talked about anything else. Seems they were a little bit disappointed with him.'

Deka started. 'Shot the Pope!'

She looked at him, puzzled. 'Just how long a shift have you been on?'

'Forever. Don't ask.'

'Well it's Sunday tomorrow. If you're a believer you'll have to pray at home. The churches are closed.'

Sunday. Deka was thinking. He'd gone into hospital on the Monday. Five days. No wonder he was so hungry.

12

Influenza: 1918

The usual symptoms of influenza, including rapid onset with high fever, chills, headache, muscle ache in back and legs, and dry cough, were reported and the vast majority of those infected recovered within a week following bed rest, though many experienced a "depression" which took months to overcome. Some individuals showed signs of infection and were dead within twenty-four hours, and there were reports of people who literally dropped dead in an instant. Others died within two to three days, essentially by drowning as their lungs filled with blood and fluid due to haemorrhage; the majority of those who died did so as a result of pneumonia often caused by secondary infection with bacteria. Many of those who were to die showed outward signs of blueing of the lips, ears and face generally, as well as finger tips and toes, a condition called cyanosis which results from oxygen deprivation. At autopsy, it showed lung and heart damage was common with frequent occurrence of internal bleeding. Other organs, such as liver, spleen and kidney often showed abnormalities and a few cases showed swelling of the brain.
National Institute for Medical Research archive

The Scavenger

David Framer had always been a gofer. Go for this, go for that. He'd reached twenty-five years and never quite found a niche in life. Had quit school early, never committed to his apprenticeship in the Main Street Honda service department, been pretty much fired from every job for a lack of enthusiasm or moral turpitude. He just didn't pay much attention to anything, couldn't get interested in the details and very little got his interest anyway. He never quite descended to the gutter though, had no appetite for being a wino, dope made him nauseous, sex gave him pains in the head and he couldn't keep a girlfriend interested beyond a couple of weeks anyhow. Any chick could see that this guy had no ambition at all. His mother had long ago resigned herself to his failure and she'd provided a place for him to stay these past years, having all but given up hope he'd change.

The pandemic did interest him however. Somehow he found it exciting. Perhaps because you no longer needed ambition or a mortgage to be important or successful. Success was measured in how well you survived. David Framer, it turned out was pretty good at surviving, and even helping other people do the same.

David was good at getting stuff. He could focus on specific requests and, perhaps because he was so anonymous, he could steal anything to order. 'Get me a pair of jeans size 8, get me an 18-speed bike or a new hi-fi system'... he would always come back with whatever you asked for. It was just a question of locating it and strolling away with it. He never got stopped, people said that he had such an innocent face. He was always careful never to look like a bum. He did his best to look like the good Christian he was, at least on Sundays.

The virus had provided David with opportunities that had really begun to pay off for him. Whilst others were afraid to go outside and risk contact with other people, he couldn't see the problem. You met less people outside now than in. David had discovered that his talents were finally being appreciated. He had a bike with a trailer and he took orders, daily. From rice, noodles, flour, antibiotics, even baby formula, to cans of gas, he took orders, decided on a price (like Robin Hood, who was his idol, he decided the price depending on what he thought you could pay) and did the rounds of everyone he trusted.

So he was on a gasoline run. Had orders for twelve gallons. Francine and her partner Holly had decided to get out of town and go to Hedley, which was about as remote and safe as they could figure, deep in the heart of BC. They needed as much gas as they could get to move their old Toyota that far. Twelve gallons at fifty miles an hour would get them about 330 miles by their reckoning. They had made calculations and promised David that he could come too. David didn't really want to go, but he said he would so they wouldn't be offended. He was enjoying his new role as entrepreneur. He even had savings now. Never had savings before and respect. People knew he was good at this and he enjoyed their respect. Of course few would actually touch him or let him get close seeing as he was 'out there' and they were safe behind doors. But it was a good feeling to be needed.

He was in the underground carpark of the medical centre on South Granville. He'd long ago discovered that people had left their cars in 'safe' places, off the street to collect later. And since there was no power, there were no cameras to spy on him. No light either, but he didn't care, he had flashlights and worked fast, in secret, siphoning from quality cars only. David has this theory that if you could afford a Lexus or a Jag you'd put good gas into it, rather than the low octane stuff.

He'd pretty much excelled this particular morning. Got twenty gallons of gas. More than enough for the girls at twenty bucks a gallon – the going rate. Of course balancing twenty gallons on the little trailer behind his bike was tricky, as well as the other stuff he'd been commissioned to find. As many Pampers as he could carry – never could supply enough Pampers! Babies never stopped pooping.

He was on the way to Main Street when he saw the kids throwing stones at windows. He wasn't the only one out there these days, but he'd noticed a lot of bored kids would go out and cause mayhem. They didn't care about the virus. They just liked throwing stones, burning cars and shit. No one was stopping them and it kinda provided amusement he guessed. He didn't think much of them. They looted stuff just to destroy it, didn't think strategically, like who might want the stuff they were ruining. He just didn't get it. Why destroy something when you could make a buck off it?

He knew enough to keep his distance, but he was slow today and although he ducked down to Tenth Avenue, they had seen him and they could keep pace.

A girl dressed in Goth attire was running beside him now. Black dress over black jeans and black Caterpillar boots on her feet, large pins through her face and a red gash from a sore that hadn't healed over one eye. She looked mean even though she was smiling at him.

'What you got there? Something precious?' She smiled again, but David wasn't buying. He knew girls like her. All smiles and then the knife goes in. He sensed real danger. He tried to ignore her, but he couldn't get any speed up, he was going slightly uphill and the gasoline weighed him down.

'I'm busy.' David told her.

'Busy. Fuck, man. No one is busy anymore. You stole something and I want to see what you got.'

'I got to make a delivery.'

She ran ahead of him then suddenly stopped and turned. He couldn't brake, he had to swerve and swerving with twenty gallons in the back could only mean one thing. His load spilled and he crashed into the side of an abandoned truck. It knocked all the breath out of him and he cut his knees too.

The girl was staring at the Pampers strewn across the road and the cans of gas, one of them spilling it guts over everything.

'Shit, Pampers. You're delivering fucking Pampers?'

Other kids arrived, breathless and began mocking David, kicking the Pampers all over. Another tipped gasoline over them and him.

'You're a thief – know what happens to thieves?' The girl was saying with a sly smile. 'Cops shoot 'em. Call 'em vermin. You are vermin.'

The other kids grinned and watched her. She was obviously their leader.

David tried to stand, but he was entangled in the bike and the gasoline fumes were confusing him. He looked at the girl, tried reason. 'You don't understand. People need this, babies need this.'

The girl looked at her friends and laughed, kicking gasoline-soaked Pampers at him. 'Babies. The fucking world doesn't need babies anymore. Everyone is gonna die. We're all gonna die. Fuck the babies.' She turned to look at her friends. 'Anyone got a match? Vermin needs teaching a lesson in law and order.'

A kid struck a match. Someone at the back laughed as they moved away.

'You see, we're here to make sure the street stays clean. You made a mess. You gotta pay. Cops would just shoot you anyway.'

The match dropped on the gasoline spreading on the road. It ignited immediately.

David with one last surge of effort tried to separate himself from the bike, attempted to get up, but someone threw a stone and he went down again. He looked up and saw them running away laughing. The flames were all around him now. He had one chance. He stood up quickly, but his head collided with the wing mirror of the truck above him and he saw only stars. He staggered, clutching his head, feeling the blood flowing, saw the flames reach the unopened cans and then with horror saw flames running up his jeans. He was on fire.

The girl watched the entertainment from across the road. Saw the cans explode, watched the man on the bike scream and burn, the abandoned truck with him and she turned away. It wasn't as much fun as setting dogs alight.

'Come on. Let's go. He's so boring.'

Sam North

13

Post-Traumatic Stress Disorder
Approximately 10-to-20% of rescue workers and 5-10% of the general
population may experience Post-Traumatic Stress Disorder symptoms,
including: flashbacks, recurrent dreams of the event, survival guilt and hyper-
vigilance. A review of studies conducted in the aftermath of disasters during
the past 40 years shows that there extensive repercussions from PTSD among
people who experience a disaster.
Epidemiologic Reviews

Drifting

'I can't get a fix on our position,' Arno muttered, itching his face again. He now
regretted his decision to let his beard grow. He was annoyed with himself for being
unable to get a position fix from the stars. Of course it helped if you knew their
names! Although he had a compass, he felt a tad out of his depth on this. 'We're
either due south of Salt Spring or ...who the fuck knows.'

Rachel grabbed his arm. 'You hear that?'

Arno looked at her and frowned. He could hear nothing but the water slapping
against the hull of the yacht.

'Again. I can hear barking. Here...' She handed him a bottle to open.

Arno was looking at the bottle of extra virgin olive oil. 'We can afford this? I know this stuff, it costs about fifty bucks a bottle.'

'Maybe it did last year, but try a hundred. You said get pure everything. It's pure.'

'So is gold but we can't eat it.' He was gripping the metal cap when he finally heard it himself.

'Barking. You're right I can hear barking.'

'Seals maybe?'

Arno was listening. It wasn't consistent, but it was definitely coming from the west. He snapped the cap off the bottle and handed it to her.

'It is a dog. It has to be,' Rachel declared.

Arno grinned and pulled her close to him, kissing the nape of her neck. 'At least we're going crazy together.'

The barking came again and it was clearer, much nearer. Arno stepped back to the wheel and turned it towards the sound. He strained to see but the sun had set thirty minutes ago and everything was hard to see in twilight.

Rachel went back down to the cabin but was back up again with the binoculars in an instant. 'If it's a dog...'

'There must be a master with it. Dog's don't usually go sailing.'

Rachel looked back at him a moment. 'Do dogs get the virus?'

Arno shrugged, but his guess was that they would, living so close to man. They'd get something. He heard the dog bark again and adjusted their direction by five degrees.

'I think I see something. It's... so hard to see with binoculars. Can you see it? A long flat boat.'

Arno was thinking about what they would find. A live dog with a dead master? What could they do?

Rachel was thinking about it too. She put the binoculars down and looked back at Arno. 'What are you going to do Arno?'

Arno throttled back. 'The dog sounds healthy, but it will be thirsty and hungry Rachel. Get some food and some water. Got to find a way of giving it to him without going on board. We can tow the boat to shore maybe. Oh yeah, get the flashlight as well.'

Arno steered towards the sound of the dog growing ever nearer. He was worried. He was all for helping a dog in distress, but what if it was a carrier? He hated to have to keep making judgements like this.

Rachel was in the cabin getting food and water. She was relieved that Arno was at least considering saving the dog. She felt very emotional all of a sudden. It was so weird. Thousands of humans die and here was one helpless dog out at sea and she was ready to burst into tears.

'We're close. Got the flashlight?' Arno was calling.

Rachel handed it back out and Arno started sweeping the water, wondering how exactly a dog could be out there at all.

'I've got some stew in a can,' Rachel called out.

'Perfect. Open it. We can lob it over. It'll find a way of getting it out.'

A gust of wind swept by and Arno was taken aback by the smell of land. He definitely could scent pine.

The flashlight found the speedboat and the dog which now barked more excitedly, bouncing up and down with joy that someone had found him.

Arno brought them closer, putting them into neutral about five feet apart. He didn't want the dog getting too close... in case. 'Hey, boy. Good boy, we're here now.'

'You don't know it's a boy,' Rachel argued as she appeared with water and food. She saw the chestnut coloured dog and just how seriously exhausted it looked, but she could tell from the way it was bouncing on all fours that it was pretty much healthy. Nothing with the virus could do that.

'I saw a shrimp net, someplace' Arno was saying. 'Cut in half one of those empty plastic two-litre Coke bottles.'

'Already thought of that,' Rachel answered, reaching back for the rod strapped to the side of the cabin.

Arno swept the boat with the light and could see no one with the dog at all. It was impossible it had got out there on it's own. Rachel had the shrimp net ready and he quickly placed the can in so it wouldn't spill and the base of the Coke bottle filled with water.

Arno looked up at Rachel with a grin.

'Someone's been camping before.'

'Just once, but...'

Arno took the shrimp net and gently swung it over between the boats and then over to where the dog stood whining expectantly for its reward. 'Damn.'

Arno couldn't get the net to flip over and before he could do much about it the dog was on it, totally undecided as to whether to go for the water or the food. It went for the water and lapped it as fast as it could, clearly desperate.

'Well it doesn't have any troubling swallowing.' Arno remarked. He flipped on the flashlight again and swept the boat again. He stopped by the stern, surprised to see just how many cans of gasoline were there. Dozens. 'Shit, what were they trying to do, cross the Pacific?'

'They empty?'

'Doubt it. See the boat's heavy in the water. They're full. Perhaps they had engine trouble.'

'What they? All I see is a thirsty dog.'

'He is thirsty. Fuck.'

Suddenly a wave passed under them, lifting the speedboat higher than the yacht for a second. Arno fell back and Rachel only just hung on. 'Shit.'

The dog carried on drinking, guarding the shrimp net with one foot so it wouldn't disappear with the can of stew. Rachel picked up the flashlight and was looking at the speedboat again. Suddenly she was aware of a body between the seat and the footwell.

'Arno?'

Arno had seen it too. 'Small. It's a girl.'

'Is she...?'

The dog was struggling with the can, frustrated by it. He barked at it as he tried to get his snout into the food. Both Arno and Rachel saw the girl's body twitch. She was definitely alive then.

Rachel was looking at him, scared now. If she was a carrier they would have to leave. Arno was thinking. Nothing here made much sense. A girl and dog on a high powered speedboat loaded down with gas. If she was sick, then why wasn't the dog ill, or dead? If the engine had malfunctioned, she might have been out here for days and was just out of water.

'I think the kid stole the boat.'

Rachel was puzzled. 'You won't help because she's a thief?'

'I didn't say she's a thief or that I wouldn't help. I'm just trying to figure out why she is out here, clearly prepared for a long ride, but there's no food or water. She wasn't planning on a long trip, that's all.'

'What are we going to do?'

Arno made a decision. 'She's got guts. I might regret it but instinct tells me she was running from it. I know I said we had to take every precaution, but she doesn't look like the others when they got sick. I'm going on board.' He began to strip off.

'Arno?'

'If she is a carrier, which we don't know she is, I'll be wearing a mask and gloves. As soon as I have given her water, I'll jump into the sea. Salt-water will fix just about anything Rachel. You just be ready with the towel. OK?'

'Jesus, Arno. It's a risk. To both of us.'

'And she might not be infected. Thirst can kill you just as easily. Rachel I need a bottle of water, a straw and get some soup heated up. If she's been out here for days she won't be able to take solids. Mix that vitamin C powder we've got into the bottle. OK?.'

Rachel went back down into the cabin as Arno took off his jeans and shoes. She wanted him to save the girl but, then again, she didn't. She was genuinely scared now.

'She's going to be seriously dehydrated judging by the dog. Rachel?'

Rachel re-emerged from the cabin with a plastic drinking bottle and drinking straw, shaking it as she stood there. She threw Arno a small tin. 'Vaseline. Her lips will be cracked. You sure about this Arno?'

Arno stood in his boxers and nodded. 'I keep these on, I didn't want to freak her out.'

'She'll be freaked out anyway. Put your mask on now. OK. Gloves too.'

Arno complied, taking the bottle from her. 'It's OK. Bring the boat closer but keep a couple of feet away. I don't want the dog jumping.'

Rachel nodded, her teeth clamped on her lips, a childhood habit when she was tense. 'Arno?'

Arno looked up at her. 'What?'

'I love you. Thought you should know.'

'I know. I'm sorry Rachel. I can't walk by this one.'

Rachel nodded, then remembered something, dashing back into the cabin for it. She reappeared with an orange. 'Squeeze this under her nose. It'll wake her. My grandmother's trick, works everytime.' She frowned. 'Unless she's dead of course.'

Arno looked at her with surprise. 'You made a joke.'

Rachel just shook her head, smiling, hiding her fear. 'Be careful, babe. Please.'

Arno waited until their boats were closer and then jumped. 'Hope the dog is friendly.'

The dog eyed him, but didn't move, growling a little, protective of his can of food.

Rachel shone the flashlight on the girl and Arno approached gingerly. He didn't like it that she was lying on her stomach, but he guessed she had been seeking shade under there, there was precious little of it on the boat. He set the water down and looked back at the dog. 'It's OK, dog. Eat your dinner. Good boy.'

The dog did just that, holding the can between two paws licking the food out as fast as it could.

Arno flipped the girl over – careful to avoid touching her flesh. She was young, but badly sunburned, her lips swollen and cracked. He took Rachel's tin and eased the lid off. He smeared some vaseline on a gloved finger and then rubbed it on her lips. She was breathing normally, that was a good sign and there was no blood or vomit anywhere.

'The orange,' Rachel was telling him from the yacht.

He brought the orange to her nose and dug his fingers in, the citric acid spurting over her face and up her nose.

Fen started, felt as though someone had stabbed her with an orange on her nose.

'Red?' She rasped, but no intelligible sound emerged from her parched throat. She almost gagged on her tongue that seemed to be twice its normal size.

'Hey,' Arno was saying in a soothing voice. 'Swallow this kid, swallow.'

Fen started. She could barely see. Her eyes were out of focus. Someone was close, real close. Red wasn't barking.

Arno pushed a straw in between her lips and squeezed the bottle some so she'd get some water into her mouth. 'You're dehydrated, kid. Drink. You have to drink this.'

Fen began to suck and she was amazed she could move anything, but she pulled the cool water in and she could feel it slide down her throat and into her empty stomach, actually feel the entire journey of the water, it was a totally weird sensation. She sucked harder and the water was flowing. She questioned nothing, still barely conscious.

Rachel kept the flashlight on them, still fretting. 'Arno?'

'She's just dehydrated, Rachel. I'm sure of it. Kid? Can you hear me? Your dog's fine. You got a name?'

Fen swallowed some more, desperate to get the water down her. The voice beside her sounded calm, unthreatening. Sounded like Uncle Casper. Couldn't be, but she imagined it was Uncle Casper. He lived above a coffee shop on Mayne Island. She loved the herring fishing there. Good old Uncle Casper. He'd come to get her.

Arno looked at the girl's hands, she had broken nails – her clothes were dirty, plain, sensible. Nothing about this girl and dog belonged to this speedboat.

'Make some soup, Rachel. I'm going to come back on board.'

'Don't leave, Uncle Cas,' Fen tried to say, but nothing came out. She could hear him fine but she didn't seem to be able to control her own body at all.

'Keep drinking, kid. We're going to make you some soup. You're safe now. Take your time, keep sucking. We'll get you some more.'

Fen heard a splash, heard a man shout 'Fu-u-u-uck it's cold.' She remembered how cold it was. So cold. Cold nights, she and Red snuggled together to keep from freezing and they were so hungry and thirsty. How long had it been?

Arno reappeared at the stern and tied a rope from the speedboat to their own yacht. It could drift to one side of them about ten foot distant. It would be enough until they were sure. He hauled himself up onto the yacht and Rachel was there with a big towel. 'Jesus, honey, it's like the fucking Artic in there. You got my clothes?

'Get dry, come on, rub.' Rachel was telling him, standing a good three feet away from him, unsure of her own situation now.

Arno rubbed himself down with vigour. 'She's been out here for about five or six days without water my guess.' Arno pulled on his sweater and rubbed his legs as dry as he could.

Rachel shone the flashlight onto the kid. 'She's still drinking.'

'Good.' It had been a real risk going on board. He couldn't explain it, he just felt he had to. Couldn't just let everything go to hell.

'You look frozen. Better fix you some soup too.'

Arno tugged on the jeans and stood to zip up. 'We got a spare rug? I think there's one under the other bunk.'

Rachel smiled, showing that she'd already thought of it. 'Just get warm. Go see to the soup. I'll get this to her.'

Rachel went to the stern and pulled on the rope. The speedboat was heavy but eventually the two came close. She threw the rug to the girl, which landed across her long spindly legs.

'Something to keep you warm,' Rachel announced.

The dog barked once, but immediately went back to the can, which was probably empty by now, but a dog lived in hope. Fen felt the rug against her legs, reached out for it and was astonished at how weak she was, could barely pull the rug towards her. But a rug. A real thick rug. She felt a rush of pleasure. She was no longer alone.

Arno was in the kitchen, stirring the soup. Minestrone. Good enough against all colds and 'flu according to his much missed mama. She had grown up in Nice and probably never cooked as much as an egg all her life, but she knew how to supervise a cook. What would she have made of this virus? Probably expected it. She always knew the world was going to end – told him so enough times.

He looked up and did a double take. 'Hey, Rachel. Did you buy these?'

'What?' She came back to the cabin. 'I think the dog is still hungry.'

Arno was looking into a box on top of the galley shelves. 'Throw him these. Might be a bit old, but chicken-flavoured dog bones look like dog food to me.'

Rachel looked in the box. 'They're still hard. You sure you want to give them up? We might get desperate?'

'That, I think, might be the very definition of desperate. Give them to the dog. Let me feed the girl.'

'You going back onto the boat?'

'I'm sure she doesn't have the virus, Rach. She's suffering from exposure.'

'You know that for sure?'

'I...' Arno shrugged. 'My guess is still firm. She ran from someplace. I think she grabbed what she could and got out of there. Didn't think it through. But at least she was smart enough to run.'

'Like we did.'

Arno nodded. 'We got anything to put the soup in? I was thinking a beaker. Need something she can suck on. Too hot to hold it.'

Rachel rifled through a cupboard and came up with a long plastic cup. 'Best option, if she holds it, it will keep her warm. You sure you want to go back on the speedboat?'

'Yes, but I'm not going to touch her and we will keep her and the dog ten feet back until we know for sure.'

'How will we know for sure?'

'If she can tell us how long ago she saw another human. We can calculate backwards from there. Five days back and we're safe. OK?'

Rachel looked at him and took a deep breath. It made sense. But if that girl had been nearly a week at sea without water, how the hell had she survived? 'You take the soup, I'll deal with the dog.'

Fen finished the water. Felt almost human. She pulled the rug up around her and managed to push herself up to a sitting position. She could hear Red whimpering behind her, but it wasn't a bad sound. He was playing with something. She couldn't believe the both of them were actually alive. She looked up. A man was standing some distance from her, but not on the boat. It wasn't Uncle Casper.

'Kid? Can you see me. Got some soup for you. You're safe now. Name's Arno. We figure we're gonna get you to Salt Spring Island. You'll be safe there. Just hang on. Dog's got food, water. Just hang in there. OK. Soup's incoming. Use the straw. Nod if you understand me.'

Fen nodded. But something was worrying her. Something wasn't right. Salt Spring. She was going to Salt Spring?

He was there, got the straw in her mouth again, a warm plastic cup of soup in her hands. 'Hold it steady. Don't drop it.'

It tasted harsh in her mouth, she discovered she had sore gums. 'Drink it slow.' He was saying. 'You'll be fine. Everything is going to be fine now.'

She heard something fall beside her and Red jump for it. Heard him chewing on biscuits. Red curled up beside her, still chewing. She felt his coat, how thin he was, bones sticking through already, but he was there and they were together.

'See that?' A woman's voice shouted excitedly. 'Shooting star. Make a wish.'

The man laughed and she laughed too. Sounded like happy people. Fen sucked on her soup. She had been rescued by happy people. She felt quite light all of a sudden. She felt strangely safe, like another time, another Fen, a child in San Francisco living in a place where people laughed all the time.

'God, I love it when you can see the stars like this,' Arno was saying to Rachel. 'Reminds me of why we want to stay alive.'

Deka woke with a start: again.

He was sitting on a leather sofa. He blinked, something about his surroundings was wrong somehow. He took a deep breath, found he could breathe better than before – although he badly needed to spit right afterwards, damn phlegm was still gathering and he had to dump it in a nearby ashtray. Ashtray? He didn't own any ashtrays. Didn't smoke. Where the hell was he? Why was he here?

Last thing he recalled was feeling tired. So damn tired.

He looked about him and knew right away that this sofa, the metal tubed chair and just about everything in this living room including the window were way beyond anything he could afford. It wasn't his living room, so whose was it? He glanced to the sides and realised with surprise that he wasn't in a living room at all.

A military truck drove by, its tyres noisy on the cobbled surface. He watched it go past with a passive gaze, a soldier sat on the passenger side with an automatic pistol at the ready, he didn't seem to register him sitting there on the sofa. Deka realised two things at once. One, there was no glass in the window and as he glanced behind him, two, he realised that he was sitting on the sofa of a designer furniture store on Water Street in Gastown. A goddamn showroom.

He couldn't believe how long it had taken for him to register this information. He'd eaten at the Water Street Café a few times on dates and drunk at Lamplighters Pub across the way. Somewhere in the next block would be Rossini's. The manager was generous to cabbies that brought business there. He remembered staring in at this very store window a month back looking wistfully at the sofas and textiles on display.

Deka suddenly felt guilty. Had he smashed the window? He had gotten so tired he'd seen the sofa and... he checked his hands. Not a scratch. He had no recollection of how he'd got there. Slowly his situation came back to him. He'd eaten at the hospital, but pretty much thrown up directly after. Weirdly they had paid him for his week's shift. (Still believing him to be Male Nurse Ricard) No cash; food and clothing vouchers were the real currency now. They had told him to take two days off and report back at 6pm the next. They would be disappointed. He looked for his watch, then realised he'd left it at the hospital, along with anything else he might have had. ID, credit cards, shit. He couldn't go back and collect it now. It would be in a pit somewhere with all the others who died in that ward. Did they keep records? Would he listed as dead already? That was going to be awkward – not having his fucking ID an' all.

He wondered how long he'd been asleep. Judging from the light it was late afternoon. His eye caught sight of the tag on the sofa. $4,500. Even in good times that would have been considered extortionate. Now the world would be awash with unsold sofas – and everything else. Almost all his life he'd lived with inflation, particularly back home in Cape Town, where everything went up in price, sometimes 25% a year, a decade before, and now what would a world be like where prices went down all the time? He guessed some kind of slump, unless they opened the floodgates up to new immigrants. It was too hard to think about such things in his condition. And if this many were dying in Vancouver, how bad was it really in China or Africa? Didn't really bear thinking about.

The street was quiet now. He could hear the distinct crackle of automatic fire in the distance however. A food riot? Who knew? It wasn't his problem. But then again, what exactly was his problem? Where had he been going?

He stood up, with some effort, his legs still weak. He needed to piss again. He was aware that something had happened to his bladder with this virus. Constant pressure there now and it was painful to pass water. What was that? Cystitis. He remembered a girlfriend who was prone to it and he'd never properly appreciated what she was going through.

He suddenly remembered where he was going. Doc Borov. Fuck, the bastard was probably dead if he'd been through half of what he'd been through. He had to go and see for himself. He owed that man big, couldn't have survived without his magic soup, wouldn't have stood a chance.

He stepped out through the open window into Gastown, noting this time the broken glass on the sidewalk from the store window that he hadn't seen before. He looked towards downtown and there was smoke coming from a tall building, but it looked more like a fire burning out than starting.

He hadn't gone more than three steps when there was a huge explosion from the dockside area. Deka threw himself to the ground as glass shattered in the buildings around him. He dove into a doorwell, just in time, as shards of glass fell from the higher floors and showered the street around him. He rolled up into a ball shaking with surprise and fear, his heart racing and stayed like that for several minutes, knowing that some things took longer to fall or work loose. He had no idea of what had exploded, but there were all kinds of fuel bunkers down on the quays. Whether it was deliberate or just neglect, this kind of thing could be happening everywhere. A shower of oil droplets began to fall. His question was answered. A fuel bunker had ignited. There was a whole row of buildings between him and the docks; he couldn't imagine how much damage there was on the other side. He knew he'd been lucky not to be walking on the exposed side.

A siren was already sounding, but few alarms, which told Deka that the city hydro power was still out. He opened his eyes. The street was knee deep in glass. Must have blown every window out. Cost millions to replace it. He saw movement in the corner of one eye. An animal moving slowly. A cat? Bloodied. Poor bastard. Nowhere safe for a cat in a sea of glass. Deka stood up, had to lean against a wall for a moment to wait for the bloodrush to subside. He looked for the cat again, but couldn't see it. He stepped out onto the glass and realised he was wearing canvas shoes. They'd last about five minutes in this.

He remembered the tourist store was on this block beside the Steamclock. God, how many tourists had had to lie to about this stupid clock that actually did not run on steam, but they gathered around it anyway to pay respect to an invented past. Luckily for him, the booty in sweaters, souvenirs of Canada and hiking boots for all was still there. He wouldn't be a looter, just borrow them until someone cleaned the place up.

The store was a mess. The back wall has been blown in and the oil rain was falling heavily now. He walked to the gap in the wall and stared at the fuel bunkers dockside. Three were on fire, no way in hell would they get those out. Could burn for days. Bunker fuel for the ocean liners and they used a lot of fuel.

It's one thing to want a pair of boots, but in the best of times finding a size 44 Timberland that he found comfortable was hard, now when all the boxes were scattered everywhere, damn impossible. He took his time. He didn't want to go out in this oil rain anyway. Not without some slickers for protection.

Someone was shouting something from the street, but Deka didn't go and look. He had to find boots and get out of there before he was shot for looting. He found one, size 44. But not another in the same colour. Shit, what the hell. A suede one and after a search, a blue one. At least they were comfortable. He found a plastic raincoat and a hat with a bear emblazoned upon it. He'd be the last tourist in Gastown for a long while by his reckoning.

Walking on glass in an oil rain isn't to be recommended. Slip and you could be sliced. He looked for the cat again but saw nothing. Anything out in this was going to die he figured. He'd saved himself, couldn't save anyone else apparently. He looked up; the whole street was a ruin. Some bewildered people were looking down from their loft apartments. They had probably thought they were safe until now. You pay half a million or more for 'lifestyle loft living' and you probably didn't look too close at the possible hazards you get with living by a working harbour. Some of those people up there were bleeding, some covered in oil. They'd be in shock. Deka felt sorry for them but they'd have to deal with it. Everyone for themselves in this twilight zone.

Who would put all this back together? If this was happening in Vancouver, exactly how bad was it further down the west coast? San Francisco? LA? How were they dealing with it or had everyone gone crazy. He sighed and made his way towards Alexander Street to pay his last respects to Doc.

At the junction of Carrall Street and Alexander he saw some kids running from the Irish Heather pub carrying loot. Pretty well all the windows of the coffee shops and restaurants were smashed there. A dog howled somewhere from within the old *Glory Hotel* – it unnerved him.

The key was exactly where Doc said it would be. Hidden under a rock under the bridge. It had taken some searching but he'd found it; that was the main thing. Certainly no one was answering his knocking and Wylie wasn't even looking out from the door – ears pricked ready for trouble. Doc could have left but then again where would he go? Deka opened up the Alexander Street door expecting the worst.

The water was at least three-foot deep spread right across the whole gallery floor. A lethargic Wylie barely acknowledged him as Deka waded in. It stank too, a mixture of paint, shit and various unidentified floating objects. The tap that had caused all this was only emitting a trickle of water now, but Deka shut it off to make sure. He then opened up the deck door at the back, allowing the water to surge out to the yard below. From here he could see the damage in the docks from the burning fuel tanks. A cruise ship had taken full force of the blast and the hull was blackened, the superstructure was on fire. A chopper was circling and he guessed a fire crew was on its way but no one was going to save that ship, not from that heat.

'See that, Wylie. Millions of dollars of junk.'

The dog slowly climbed down from its dry perch on an old armchair and Deka could see just how emaciated the boxer dog really was.

'Got to get you something to eat boy. Seen Doc? Is he here?'

Deka took satisfaction as most of the water was leaving the gallery, reflecting that it was good that this was an old building and on the tilt. He went looking for Doc.

Wylie tried to follow but was slow, unwilling to walk on the wet floor.

There was no sign of Doc anywhere. The sofa was saturated and he could see blood stains on it. He wondered if someone had taken Doc away? If so why had they locked the dog in. The least they could have done was let him out to fend for himself.

'Doc?'

Deka paused at the kitchen. He opened all the cupboards until he found something he could give Wylie and opened up a tin of luncheon meat. He winced as he wound the key around the top and peeled away the metal. He'd always hated the smell of luncheon meat, but the dog would appreciate it, he was sure. He set it down and poured a bowl of fresh water for him as well. He didn't have to call. Wylie was there. Practically finished it in one bite and then lapped all the water.

'That's it for now, dog,' Deka told him. 'Here, try these, but I don't think you'll like 'em.' He tossed some water biscuits down as well and these too Wylie devoured. It wanted more but Deka had moved on.

He had to check the rooms upstairs. There was a gallery space and a huge loft space up there. Doc must have gone to dry ground there.

He pulled back the curtain, tugged on the heavy door and mounted the stairs instinctively looking for a light switch. Nothing. He looked up towards the light and there he was. Doc sat upright, half way up the stairs, leaning up against the wall. Deka was uncertain at first. Was he dead? He climbed the stairs slowly wishing there was more light. He came face to face with his saviour and with sudden surprise realised that Doc was breathing. Shallow breaths with a rasping wheeze, but still a breath was a breath.

'Shit. Doc. You're alive!'

He scooped him up. He wasn't the heavy man he'd been a week ago. He stank, but Deka knew nothing could affect him now. He carried him up the remainder of the stairs and straight to the bathroom. This man needed a wash and he needed fluids, really badly.

There was still water in the hot tank and it was even warm from the last time the power had been on. Deka turned on the shower and put Doc down under it.

The water registered. His eyes opened, but he could neither see properly nor move his arms.

'Don't worry, Doc. I'm going to fix you up. You'll see. My turn to save you.'

He met no resistance. But Doc was trying to say something. Wasn't sure what at first. Deka stared at Doc for a good ten minutes to make sure. The man was almost in a coma, as good as dead, but he'd said it quite faintly but distinctly – twice, a good five minutes apart. 'Red Caps – Blue Door'. No doubt about it.

It didn't mean much or it meant a great deal. He'd gone down to the kitchen area twice but seen no blue door anywhere and no red caps or capsules. Not at the front or the back of the building and definitely not on the top floor. He retraced his steps to make sure. In all his visits to the Ironworks, he'd never been to the basement and he was pretty sure it was flooded anyway thanks to the dog, but it was worth a shot.

He took himself to the back deck and stared out at the stone garden – the weird faces carved into giant stone blocks. The harbour beyond was totally still. He looked up. Thought he saw a face in a broken window of the apartment block that loomed alongside. There were going to be hundreds of faces at windows in all the high rises across the city, most people too scared to leave and each day there'd be less water, less food and then desperate or crazy they'd have to come out and ...

There was a door at the bottom of the stairs. It was locked, of course, but he had Doc's keys, kept in the tea caddy, as ever. He tried them one by one. Nothing. He tried again. One of them had to work. Fifteen keys on one ring. Personally he hated keys and the type of person who wandered around with a bunch attached to their belt. God knows why Doc needed so many keys but at least he didn't wear them.

 Eventually one key seemed to be right and Deka tried lifting the warped door a little, he hoped it would do the trick, abruptly the lock clicked over.

Deka opened up and entered a virtually empty room, save for a computer perched on a tall desk and a stool lying on the ground. As Deka's eyes adjusted to the light he could see a yellow HAZMAT suit hanging by the second door and a flashlight. There was a sign on the door – *Hazardous Chemicals – Do Not Enter* and a skull and crossbones for emphasis. Nice: Doc clearly didn't want people in there. Deka tried the keys and quickly realised that it could only be one given the Medeco deadbolt. Doc really didn't want people in here. Deka looked at the space suit on the wall and decided he'd best be protected. Who knew what was behind the door.

Suited up, he cautiously opened the door and put the flashlight on.

Deka was astonished. He didn't know what he expected, but a fully fitted laboratory wasn't on his list. Sophisticated equipment in neat rows, two microscopes, all kinds of equipment for testing and making up chemicals, he didn't know exactly what he was looking at but it looked expensive. In the back there were cages. All empty now. He didn't care to speculate what had been in there. There was a row of refrigerators, all silent now – Doc had been busy. (*Property of St Paul's Hospital – Do Not Remove*) was written on some of the boxes of vials and other glass tubes). He'd known Doc had volunteers and other people keen to get something developed that might work as an antiviral and gave protection, but he'd never really thought about how Doc had done it. The man was a scientist. There had to be thousands of dollars worth of stuff here. And now, he saw, a blue cupboard door above the freezer.

Deka moved clumsily in the HAZMAT suit and carefully opened the cupboard door. Red Capsules in a glass bottle clearly visible. Batch E056A -5.3.09. They were the only capsules he could see and he grabbed them. He felt a little creeped out down here now. Didn't want to touch anything in case...the power had been off and then on and anything he'd been keeping in the fridges were probably quite dangerous now.

He closed up the lab with care – removed the suit and then locked the basement door again. Still amazed none of the water had penetrated the membrane above. Someone had done a good job of sealing the upper floor – almost as if they had anticipated problems.

He went back upstairs aware that it was one thing getting capsules, quite another getting them down an unconscious man's throat. So easy to choke him to death and who knew what the pills would do anyways? Too little too late? What was the dosage? Were they the right pills even?

'You're not going to like this, my friend,' Deka told him.

Straws are useful things, he'd last done this for his own dog Solly that had been so ill back in the Cape many years before. Then, like now, he literally ended up blowing them down the back of Doc's throat and flushing some water down there to make him swallow. Doc nearly retched them back up, but Deka got two capsules down the man's throat, pinched his nose for a moment and they stayed there. He almost felt proud of himself.

Half an hour later Doc was in a comfortable bed, clean, wrapped up warm and being fed tepid chicken soup with a spoon. 'Sorry, Doc, it's not like your mother made it, you try cooking soup over a candle.'

He had to pinch the man's nose again to make him swallow, but over a period he got it down him. Wylie was up here now, happier, still hungry, but at least moving again and showing he was alert.

Doc said nothing, but Deka knew he was in there, listening. At least he hoped he was. All Deka could think of was to get him warm and fed. He'd found all kind of 'cures' in Doc's bedroom medical chest. Most of them marked up in Russian which he couldn't read, but he did manage to identify the mixture the Doc had given him earlier and made sure that he gave his patient a dose along with the capsules. He smeared some on his chest to help his breathing. It seemed like the right thing to do. Smeared some on his own chest too, to help with his own breathing. The reduced lung capacity was the most crippling aspect of this virus he was discovering. Every movement you paid for in pain.

'I survived, Doc. Left for dead, like you, but I'm here and I got to get you right because we've got something that can save the world. We can save a whole lot of people, Doc. You made that stuff in your lab and we just got to get you well enough to tell them.'

Before curfew, Deka had snuck out to the top of the road and broke into the old café on the corner. The freezers had failed and the place stank of rotting food, but he did find industrial sized cans of soup and spam, as well as cans of coffee, packets of tea, flour, sugar, and necessary things. When he was sure no one was looking, he made two trips back and forth back with them to the gallery, making sure all the doors were secure again.

That night, Deka found some sheet metal in the back yard and fashioned a barbecue which he placed on some bricks there. He made a decent fire to keep himself and Wylie warm, burning some of the chairs that had been ruined by the water. Didn't matter about the smoke, as long as they kept warm. That was what the virus left you with, a fucking big chill. Doc continued to say nothing, but he did begin to drink the water Deka brought him.

Deka realised that he'd be here a while and couldn't rely on the hydro coming back on any time soon. Water might get shut off too; he'd have to make sure he collected the run off when it rained again. He wondered how other people were coping. The streets were empty, so maybe they were all sat at home guarding their last cans of food.

He prepared a goulash. Gone were his pretensions at being a vegetarian. Now he had to eat whatever he could. Wylie and him feasted on it, slipping only a little down the Doc's throat, but enough so he could at least gain some nourishment. Deka resolved to stay there until Doc revived. Might take a few days, but he had nothing else to do.

The next day he cleaned up the gallery, aired it out a little and occasionally watched the oil tanks burn in the docks behind them. The wind had shifted again. A fine oil haze was falling, making everything sticky. This would continue until the fires burned themselves out. The air stank. He contemplated his future. It wouldn't be any future he had planned for, but at least he was in it. Hundreds of thousands weren't going to get that option at all.

14

Local authorities throughout Great Britain are estimated to be able to bury and/or cremate approximately 48,000 flu deaths over a period of three months. A death toll of 320,000, which can be expected in a worst-case scenario, would push back burial and cremation schedules by around seventeen weeks. A pandemic death rate of 2.5% would, therefore, overwhelm burial and cremation services. Five mass burial sites have been selected to serve England. Scotland and Wales and Northern Ireland are to find suitable sites for themselves.
United Kingdom Home Office report.

Salt Spring

'What she doing'?

'She's hugging her dog.'

'I don't understand.'

'What don't you understand? That she's hugging her dog? The dog saved her life.'

'No, what she said about Salt Spring.'

'She just said that she heard something on the radio that suggested Salt Spring isn't a good idea, that's all. She can't remember why.'

'She got a name?'

'Fen.'

'Fen?'

'That's what she says. Dog's called Red. She's from Coquitlam. Went to Centenial, same as my cousin Sara. She's feeling rough but she's a tough cookie. She'll pull through.'

'You like her, huh. Any explanation as to why she's out here?'

Rachel passed him a chocolate cookie. 'You were right. She stole the boat from firestarters. Apparently there are crazy people going from island to island burning people out. She stole the boat they came in.

'Hence all the gasoline.'

'It ran out of gas and she couldn't open the cap. Needs a key.'

'Shit. Poor kid. Can't believe there are people out there destroying everything. Why? We should all be pulling together, thinking about afterwards. There will be an afterwards you know. If we go crazy and destroy everything, it'll be that much harder to recover.'

'Some people don't give a shit about the future, Arno. You're unusual.'

'I care about everything. That's why I care about the future.'

'Yet you want to dump this girl on the island.'

Arno frowned. 'I'm not dumping her. We just saved her life. I'm giving her and the dog a chance to live, Rachel. Salt Spring Island is huge. She'll find refuge there. She must have been heading somewhere.'

Rachel said nothing. She looked back at Fen and Red sat on the speedboat some ten feet back of their stern. She felt bad for the girl. What exactly was her future? She hadn't mentioned her family yet, but you just knew she was alone.

'It's out there,' Arno was saying. 'Can't see much, but the island is there. I guess they have no power. Something everyone is going to have to get used to for a while I guess.'

Rachel hovered, uncertain what to do next. Arno glanced at her and sighed.

'Take the wheel OK. I think we're about five miles from land, my guess. Let's approach quietly; keep her at eight knots. My guess is we are going to sneak up on them. Be good if we could take on some fresh water but I guess...'

'Thanks, Arno.'

'For what?'

'For going to talk to her.'

'I...' Arno shrugged. 'Keep your eyes peeled. No running lights, OK. Let's be as invisible as we can be.' He looked back at Fen and frowned. Clearly she wasn't sick with the virus, but how could they know she wasn't a carrier? How would anyone ever know who was safe? Worse, he could be shipping her off to protect themselves, merely to infect a whole island. Or was he being selfish, using the virus as an excuse?

Damned either way. 'Throttle back a second so I can reel her in.'

Rachel did as commanded and Arno pulled on the rope to the speedboat, quickly closing the distance between them. He looked at Fen and smiled. 'Hey, Fen. Permission to come aboard?'

Fen looked at him bewildered and he jumped onto the speedboat anyway. Her voice was slowly coming back. A voice, not Fen's voice, but something harsher; at least she could communicate now.

Red barked. Arno dug out a biscuit and tossed it to him. He pounced upon it. Arno sat some feet away from Fen, still exercising proper caution.

'Hi, Fen. Feeling a bit better?'

Fen nodded, wondering what he wanted. She already knew they wanted to dump her and Red onto Salt Spring. No need for any 'chats'.

'Any folks?' Arno asked.

'Went to Victoria. Got a bit stir crazy on the island.'

'You not heard from them since?'

Fen shook her head. If he was going to offer to take her there she was going to reject it. Didn't want to go anywhere where this virus was.

'You any idea who these people were who attacked your island?'

'No. We knew they were coming though. There was a warning out.'

'You outsmarted them at least.'

'Yeah and I hope they starve to death out there. They torched everything, the island, the trees, houses, and probably killed everyone there.'

Arno nodded. Good to see her angry. She was coming alive again. She'd need that anger to survive. 'Anarchy is evil. Things are falling apart. Nothing is going to be certain or safe for a long time now.'

Fen registered the word 'anarchy' and realised it fitted perfectly. She sipped her water. Yes, anarchy was what she had been through. 'You're running too.' She remarked.

Arno smiled. 'Yeah, we're running, but not so sure where yet.'

'Nowhere's safe. I was making a map. Before, y'know. Every place it broke out. Just about the whole of BC. All of Washington State and beyond.'

Arno nodded. Rachel was right, this kid was smart. 'But there will be places of safety. Always pockets of places that disease skips over. Happened in the plague and before, in the great 'flu epidemic of 1919.'

Fen nodded. 'I know. Mercer, my Dad, made us read about it. He was obsessed.'

'Good. Now you know he wasn't exaggerating.'

Fen thought about it for a while. 'He was full of shit most of the time but about this I guess he was right. He got us out. My sister and me. My Ma, she died back in Toronto in the first wave last year. Took her in a day they told us.'

'I'm sorry. I guess we're all going to be missing someone we love now. It's what a pandemic does. So, Rachel tells me you don't like Salt Spring? Is the virus there? I didn't think...'

Fen shook her head. 'Something else. A warning, but I can't remember.'

Arno looked at her more carefully. She was a tough cookie, Rachel was right but she wasn't evasive. She had heard something.

'When did you leave the mainland?'

'September. For the last time. We'd been getting the cabin ready before that.'

'Just before the major outbreak hit the West Coast.'

'Yeah. But we were ready for it since the outbreak in China. When they started talking about cancelling the Olympics Mercer became fanatical. He said it would go worldwide. Just like the bird flu did. He said it would come just when everyone thought it was over.'

Arno nodded. 'Yeah. As soon as everyone got vaccinated, that's when it turned nasty. Your Dad saved your life, kid.'

Fen shrugged. 'But he went to Victoria.'

'He might still be there. He...'

Fen cut him off. 'He's dead. They all are. Frances and May. I know it.'

Arno realised that this girl had been abandoned by her family. He didn't know why, but certainly she had been left behind. He didn't argue with her. Bad luck for her if they were dead, but equally how could they have left a teenager alone on an island to fend for herself.

Fen looked directly into his eyes. 'I don't want to go onto the Islands yet. It isn't over. I know it isn't over. Mr Hertzog said wouldn't peak until way after Christmas.'

'Who is Mr Hetzog?'

'They built a mansion on the island with underground caverns and everything. They must have died in the attack. He told me I mustn't go back until the spring. February would be the worst month. Statistical fact.'

Arno smiled. Whoever he was, he was right. All the models he'd seen pinpointed February as the peak moment in the virus trajectory in the West and September in the Southern Hemisphere. The peak must have already happened in Australia.

Rachel was calling them. They both turned. She was pointing and they followed her gaze. 'Arno?'

Fen and Arno could see the bonfires along the shoreline. These were not random but carefully spaced 500 metres apart, more burning off into the distance. Arno knew instinctively that this was not a welcoming sign. This part of Salt Spring was patrolled. They were organised. It was going to be like this on all the islands.

'Throttle down,' Arno called out.

'I guess they don't want visitors,' Fen mumbled. 'Red?'

The dog quickly came to her and leaned up against her. Two survivors ready for anything.

A shot rang out. They heard it ripple in the sea and die in the waves.

Arno, heart beating wildly suddenly was acutely aware that they were sat on a boat stacked with gasoline. One lucky shot would send the whole thing up.

Another shot rang out. They were trying to find range. It was dark, but in starlight they must be visible somehow to those on shore. Arno stood up.

'Kid, grab your dog and get on the yacht. Now!' He turned towards Rachel. 'Rach, turn left, full throttle. We have to ditch this speedboat.'

Arno jumped back to the yacht and began to work on the rope. Fen was trying to make her legs work and to calm Red who sensed danger. Arno was telling Rachel to ease off the throttle a moment so he could get the rope loose and Fen took a step towards him. She figured she could jump the gap, but getting Red over was going to be hard. She knew she lacked the strength to carry him. Red was whining. Another shot rang out, hitting the boat to no effect. That did it. Red ran, jumped clear over Arno tugging at the rope and was on the yacht, skidding to crash stop by Rachel.

Fen would have laughed another time, but she still had to make the jump herself and her legs were like Jell-O.

'Jump, Fen,' Arno was yelling. 'Now, kid.'

She jumped, but hardly enough and she saw herself plunging under the yacht, but Arno grabbed her, pulled her over, got her on the yacht. No time to think about who and who wasn't carrying now. He threw off the rope and the speedboat immediately began to fall away.

'Get us out of here, Rachel.'

Fen was shaking. Red had found her, practically sat on her, licking her face. Rachel was moving them out of range as fast as they could. They rounded a bend and they could see another bonfire. Salt Spring meant business.

Arno stood up to get a better view. Another shot was fired from the beach and it found the speedboat. He turned just as the gasoline cans exploded. The boat lay forty feet away. The explosive blast was so great Arno was flung violently off the boat and into the sea.

'Stop.' Fen was yelling. 'Stop.'

Rachel turned back, her face bright red in the flames. Arno was gone. Fen, weak, exhausted Fen, had just jumped off the yacht. Red was astonished, too scared to bark.

'Arno!' Rachel screamed.

Another Place to Die

The flames illuminated all around them and she heard cheers floating towards her from the beach. Bastards. She swore, she didn't know what to do. She frantically looked for the liferaft. There had to be one.

Someone was shouting. Red barked and ran to the stern. More cans of gasoline exploded on the speedboat and although it was burning bright it was sinking fast.

'Over here,' Fen was yelling as best she could.

Rachel had to elbow Red out of the way but she could see Fen and she was clutching Arno. Rachel tossed off her canvas shoes and jumped in. It was freezing. All the air was knocked out of her but she twisted around to find Arno, dazed, barely conscious, Fen keeping his head above water.

'I can't...' Fen was saying.

Rachel grabbed Arno and dragged him towards the stern ladder. 'Get on board, Fen. Get out of the water.'

Fen was struggling to do just that. She could hardly move, but she pulled hard, gritted her teeth and somehow she was up, spitting out seawater. Red, anxious, whining, dancing around her.

Rachel got a foothold on the ladder and pulled up Arno behind her halfway. She knew with sinking despair that she didn't have the strength to haul him out totally.

'Arno? You're going to have to wake up. I can't lift you.'

Arno was in Florida. He was lying on a beach. Too hot. Should have turned over ages ago and he was going to be burned. Should have put another layer of suncream on by now, but...

'Arno?' Rachel screamed in his ear.

Fen reached down and grabbed an arm. 'I'll hold him. Get up here. We can haul him in together.'

Rachel took Fen at her word. Another shot rang out but they were too far away now and the speedboat had sunk, the flames spread on the water, struggling to survive.

Rachel was out of the water. Frozen to the core, but thinking of only one thing, she had to get Arno back on board. Fen kept her word and held him above the water.

Fen looked at her. 'We can do this. He's not so heavy.'

Rachel got a grip with one hand and held onto something on the yacht with the other. 'One, two, three...' They hauled. Arno came up. Fen was struggling, but Rachel got him turned around and at least half of him out of the water. She quickly stood up and pulled him clear out. She turned back to the wheel and was aghast to see that they were headed directly towards the island. She throttled up, spun the wheel and got them out of there. Let Arno rest a moment until they were safe.

When she got back to him Fen was there. 'He's stunned. The blast. I don't think he's hurt. I think his face is a bit burned though.'

Rachel nodded. She looked at Fen and although she wanted to hug her to say thanks, she just smiled. 'Thanks, Fen. I couldn't have done it without you.'

Fen said nothing. She was still wondering what they were going to do with her and Red.

'Arno?'

Arno was still out. She had to strip him, get him wrapped warm, into the bunk.

'Help me get him undressed. We're have to get him warm.'

'You shouldn't leave the throttle open and...'

Rachel knew Fen was right. 'You steer. Get us away from the island. Go South. I'll deal with him.'

Fen was happy with that. She would steer. Red followed her. She looked back at the island, the fires mere pinpricks now. Now she remembered why you couldn't go to Salt Spring.

'Arno?' Rachel was calling. 'Come back. Wherever you are. Come back. We need you.'

The Captain seemed to know what to do. A few suspected that his skills at seafaring were hazy at best but his organisational skills were beyond question. Salt Spring Island had to be defended and the Captain knew how to do that. The island was like a long string in the gulf and impossible to shield from all comers, but you could isolate them and unite the settlements between. A census was taken every village, every remote cabin, so they knew exactly who had a right to be there and who didn't. Phone communications could continue as many had satellite links and generators. It was possible to knit this island tight. Indeed it had to be done.

He'd gone from settlement to settlement from the town of Ganges and beyond, organising bonfire duties, communications and a complete 24 hour rota system to defend the many miles of shoreline.

'We can't defend all of the islands, but we can damn well make sure no one reaches the settlements that aren't already here. I don't care if they own a house here or not. If they aren't here now, they ain't coming on shore.'

The Cordon Sanitaire was set up and pretty much everyone and his dog signed up to it. Day or night, no one on or off the island. Artists and poets, hippies and pot growers united by a common cause – life itself.

The night of the 15th was like any other. The moment Ben Hinkel had had spotted the yacht he lit his fire and ten minutes later another fifteen bonfires were burning, up and down their piece of the coast. Men and women with guns hurried from their homes to the rocks overlooking the ocean.

Another Place to Die

They didn't have to wait for the Captain. They had his orders. If strangers get within a two hundred feet of the island, you open fire. If anyone swims for the shore, you make sure you get 'em clean. The ocean and the fishes would soon take them, diseased or not.

You had no choice in the matter. It was them or us. No one was going to come around later and ask questions. You just did what you could to make sure no one infected the island. It was the same on Mayne and Galiano and Hornby, you name it. No one was going to spread this thing. On the Islands at least it could be stopped – cold.

When the boat had exploded, they all cheered. They knew they had got the bastards who'd been firebombing the smaller islands. Sure they needed the gasoline, but fuck 'em, death was too good for them. Everyone wanted to take a shot then and it was a free for all. The Captain had been right. God's justice was cruel and harsh but entirely necessary and later there was a renewed enthusiasm to rebuild the bonfires. The defence of Salt and it's many, many inlets was paramount.

To be sure there would be more invaders to come. They would be ready.

Three hours later Arno was still unconscious. Fen was shivering, holding tight to her dog that looked pretty exhausted and God only knew where they were headed. Suddenly Rachel began to cry. Couldn't stop. It was stupid but fat tears rolled down her cheeks and she felt big and hollow inside. The enormity of this new life was just now hitting her hard. People were dying in the thousands behind her, others living in terror of coming into contact with someone who might have the virus. People with guns every which way you looked. She'd never even said goodbye to her mother, not one call from her friends and she'd taken off with this guy who had promised to take care of her. But there he was with burns, out cold and she'd felt she made the exact same mistakes as before. She'd trusted her father when a kid and he'd betrayed her, time and time again. Now here she was putting all her faith in another man again – based on what? A one night stand where neither one of them bothered to ask each other names or phone numbers? What was that about? Nothing comes from lust – how many times had her mother said that. Did lust actually matter when the whole fucking world was going to shit. She felt stupid, useless and guilty for investing so much in Arno. Why hadn't she gone to find *him*? Why hadn't she organized a cabin on Mayne Island. Cousin Jake lived there; he could have taken them in. Nice big cabin – they would have been safe. She should have made them take a float plane to Mayne and none of this would have happened.

She shook – her thoughts zinged from one place to another in a dark place. She began to think she was coming down with a fever.

'You ok?' Fen whispered.

Rachel glanced at her. Fen was a wreck, she and the dog looked as though someone had squeezed all the life out them.

'I'm a bit down – sorry.'

Fen stared at her a while, digesting this information. 'You got any chocolate?'

Rachel blinked. She had to think. This kid had been through so much yet... 'Sure. Want some?'

'No, but you do.'

Rachel let loose a little nervous laugh. Fuck, it was like Fen could read her mind or something. She looked like freaky enough to do that.

'Eat some chocolate. Helps me when I'm down...most of the time anyway.'

Rachel rolled over to the food cupboard and opened it up. She rooted around until she found a multi-pack of Kit-Kats.

'Kit-Kat?'

'It's chocolate.' Fen answered.

Rachel pulled the pack down and broke it open. She tossed a bar to Fen and began to unwrap one for herself. 'Wonder how long it will be before they make these again.'

'People left will still be hungry.'

'You have a very pragmatic personality, Fen.'

'Whatever. Eat. We'll be fine.' Fen peeled off the wrapping and broke off a piece for her dog, looking up at Rachel. 'Dog's get depressed too y'know.'

Rachel smiled putting two chocolate fingers into her mouth. It tasked good. Real good.

Fen tried smiling but it hurt her chapped lips. 'It's good stuff. You think you could help me pee? I can't seem to move my legs.'

'Shit yeah – your legs?'

'Pins and needles.'

'Oh shit, yeah. You've been like not moving and then suddenly...'

'I have to go.' Fen said urgently.

Rachel opened up the door to the head and flipped up the table to make it easier for her to get through. 'Take my arm. You, I can cope with. What happens when your dog wants to go?'

'He's trained. He'll let us know.'

Fen winced as she hopped towards Rachel. 'I think you'd better stay close. I'm still dizzy.'

Rachel nodded. 'It might hurt. I mean if you haven't been for a while. If you have to yell, let it out, girl.'

Fen made it to the can and dropped her shorts, a sudden wave of nausea sweeping over her. She desperately needed to pee. 'Ow – fuck it. Sorry.'

Rachel could smell it. 'Like acid when you haven't been for days. Hold tight girl. Going to hurt.'

'Bastard!' Fen yelled and then just let it all go. Rachel was right. It was fucking sore. She slumped forward, momentarily losing herself. Rachel clung on, suddenly thinking of her mother. How many times had she had to help her to and from the can at night when she had particularly low blood pressure and couldn't manage on her own.

Fen stirred and it felt like she was done.

'Better?'

Fen didn't say anything, but some colour was coming back into her face.

'You miss them?' Rachel asked her.

'Who?'

'Your family.'

Fen shrugged, indicating that she wanted out of this cramped space now. Rachel backed away.

'They made a choice.'

Rachel heard the anger in her voice and didn't press it.

'You're brave, Fen.'

'Hey, Red – bad boy. Bad boy.'

They both looked. Red was eating the rest of Fen's chocolate. He dropped it like a stone, instantly looking guilty.

Fen looked at Rachel, her eyebrows raised. 'I guess he was a bit more depressed than I thought.'

Rachel laughed. She suddenly realized that she didn't feel so down anymore. She gave Fen her last finger of chocolate. Fen ate it, thanking her with her eyes. Arno stirred momentarily then fell silent again. Rachel went over to his bunk and felt his brow. He was still totally out, but that was probably what he needed most – sleep, sleep without nightmares. Something they all needed.

'Vitamin E cream. That's what he needs or aloe vera. Best for burns.' Fen told her.

Rachel looked at her and smiled. 'Next London-Drugs we see, I'll loot some,' she replied. Fen looked back at her puzzled for a moment then smiled. Yeah, she thought to herself, all the jokes were going to be like that now.

Sam North

15

A 2006 study from Boston Children's Hospital of air travel patterns discovered that, after 9/11, the unique and significant drop off in air travel in the US delayed the peak of flu season by two weeks.

Countries and experts are split, however, on whether restricting air travel would delay the impact of a flu pandemic. Dr. John Oxford of the University of London said stopping almost all flights into a country would have the effect of killing the economy, rather than stopping the virus. Many country's pandemic plans include restrictions on international air travel. But the US data shows that domestic travel also plays a significant role in the spread of flu.

Canada's pandemic flu plan does not call for restrictions on air travel, but Dr. Ron St. John of the Public Health Agency of Canada says people will stop travelling by air anyway in the face of a pandemic, as was evidenced during the SARS crisis.
Report on CBC Television, September 2006.

The Island

Rachel found the island. Just a postage stamp at the fringe of the gulf. She didn't know if it was in Canadian or US waters and didn't care. It was a refuge, way off the ferry routes and no one was firing at her when she docked. One big home hidden behind trees, a long wooden dock in need of repair and a boathouse that housed a small two berth motor boat. A very private island. A sign posted on the dock declared that strangers were unwelcome and it was signed by A.S. Becora. Rachel thought that she knew the name, but couldn't place it and besides she had other things to think about. They needed fresh water and all of them needed time to recoup.

Fen went gathering firewood. She too was happy to be on land again, even if it was temporary. Red was especially happy running crazily up and down the stony path that led up to the house. Arno was sore and blistered on his face and hands but able to walk now. Nevertheless Rachel worried about him. Anyone who had been unconscious for more than three hours was at risk. He had a bad headache and a stiff neck, but that was most likely associated with the burns. He'd been lucky. They all had.

Arno sat on the dock watching the bright moon – already at the apogee of the evening. He felt foolish wearing two layers of suntan lotion and he knew he looked weird with his eyebrows singed, as was his hair, but he knew how fortunate he'd been to have been blown into the water and how much he owed Fen for keeping him afloat.

Fen was back by the dock on a small shingle beach building a fire. She saw him watching her. 'You still seeing spots?'

Arno shrugged. 'A little, but the ringing in my ears has gone at least.'

Fen nodded, concentrating on her fire. The wood was dry and caught easy. She was happy to be in a familiar role. 'We can cook here. Save gas on the boat.'

'Yeah. Good idea.'

Rachel returned with a bucket in her hand. 'Hi, you're up then.'

Arno smiled but realised quickly that his face was sore. 'What have you found?'

'No water yet. I thought there might be some by the boathouse but...'

Arno indicated the house behind the trees, the roof shining silver in the reflected glory of the moon. 'Try there?'

'Not yet. To tell the truth I came to get Red. It's stupid I know but, it's a bit scary.'

Arno wanted to laugh but Fen turned and agreed. 'It's the Addams family house. I can't even look at it. Truly spooky.'

Arno shook his head. 'Guys, we need water. I don't care if Count Dracula lives there, we have to ask. If no one is there, great. We can stay a while. We need to work out some kind of plan anyways.'

'Take Red.' Fen told her. 'Red. Go for a walk with Rachel. OK. Go.'

Red looked at Rachel and she looked at Red. She still couldn't get used to how much control this girl had over her dog and how willing he was to do whatever she asked.

'Well, here goes. If I scream you will come running, right?'

Fen laughed, but Rachel wasn't kidding.

Arno tried to move but found he was still too sore to follow her.

'Take the flashlight, Rach. It'll be fine. Red is a good guard dog.'

'Well he's good at barking,' Fen remarked. 'And running away. If he runs, you be sure to be right behind him. OK?'

Rachel knew she was being mocked now. She left with Red for the house.

Fen looked up at Arno and grinned. 'Best you come down here – the fire's getting warm now. Bring a rug.'

Arno could manage that and realised that he was cold. He lifted a rug out of the yacht and a family sized tin of something; he wasn't sure what in the dim light.

Fen took the can from him when he got there. Noting how much effort he had to make to get his body moving. 'That blast from the boat hurt your legs?'

Arno spread the rug out on the pebbles and sat himself down, realising he'd broken out into a sweat. 'Bruised my legs when I was falling I guess. I don't think anything is broken, but for some reason my hips and my left leg feel like lead.'

Fen frowned. 'Yeah, sounds like bruising. You hit the side of the yacht and bounced into the water. Like you'd been knocked over with a huge stick. See it in movies, never seen it real before, real fast.'

'And I thank you again for jumping in after me. You took a risk considering what you'd just been through.'

Fen shrugged. She wasn't used to being thanked for anything and felt awkward.

Arno looked up at the house in the distance. He called out. 'You alright, Rachel?'

They didn't get a reply. Fen could see the worry in Arno's eyes.

'Keep it burning, OK. I'll go look. She'll need help carrying the water anyways.'

Arno was happy she volunteered and let her go. Rachel had the dog with her but sometimes you couldn't count on it doing the right thing.

'Red?' Fen called.

Red came bounding out of the trees and sat quiet right beside her.

'Where's Rachel? Where's Rachel, Red? Show me.'

Fen didn't like this. 'Rachel?'

Red suddenly darted away and Fen realised that he was headed towards the bluff overlooking the water. This house had a pretty garden developed on the westerly side and she could smell roses and sweetpea. 'Rachel'?

A door slammed in the house and Fen turned around. 'Rachel?'

'Go away,' a woman's voice yelled. 'Get off my island.'

'Where's Rachel? What have you done with Rachel?'

'Go away. I haven't got anything. Go away. I'll shoot.'

Sounded like an older woman to Fen. A terrified woman. She ran after Red.

Rachel stood by a well. She waved. Red bounded around her. Fen began to breathe a little easier. She slowed to a walk. 'I thought you were in trouble.'

'There's a woman in the house. She's scared. Told me where the water was. I'd be scared too.'

Fen gave Red a hug. 'She has to get water from a well?'

'They don't pipe it in from the mainland y'know. It's alright, sweet, I tasted it.'

Fen took one canister, surprised at the weight of it. 'Shit, you couldn't have carried two.'

'Four gallons each. Water's heavy huh. We'll get some more tomorrow. Got to fill the tank up. There's three of us now.'

'Four. Don't forget Red.'

Rachel looked at the dog. 'Sorry, Red.' She looked back at the house.

'Anyway we can't get back to the dock without going by the house. She says she has a gun.'

Fen smiled. 'Yeah, think I'd want one out here too. You think she lives alone?'

Rachel hauled up the other canister and twisted the cap back on. 'My guess is yes, but we don't know that for sure. I'd go crazy out here.'

Fen looked back at the house. 'I wouldn't. Red and me would be happy I think. You think she owns the island? How do you even begin to own an island?'

They made their way back to the dock, skirting through bushes to avoid the house. They both had mixed feelings about the woman in the house.

'A.S. Becora?' Arno was asking when they returned. 'Really?'

'You know who she is?' Rachel wasn't entirely surprised; Arno seemed to know a whole lot of disconnected things.

'What about... 'Home in a bodybag? Sweet Dead Mama? House of Record? Alyce Stevens Becora – anyone?

Fen knew. 'Murder mysteries. She wrote them? House of Record was gross. I saw it on TV. I thought it had been written by some sick kid. This is her island? That little old lady wrote that?

Rachel hadn't read any of them but she had seen some of the movies. It made sense. The spooky house was a perfect setting. Maybe she felt safe here, away from all the terrible people and horrible crimes she wrote about.

'You want to hope the well isn't poisoned,' Arno declared. 'I seem to recall a lot of her victims die horrible deaths from poison.'

'Great,' Rachel declared. 'Now I'm too scared to drink it. Thanks, Arno.'

Arno grinned, instantly regretting it as his skin cracked. 'It'll be fine. We'll talk to her in the morning.'

'No, you'll talk to her now.' A voice declared from the darkness.

Red barked; they all turned around and there on a rock above then stood an old woman dressed in a large man's coat with a rifle pointed at them.

'The sign says visitors unwelcome. If you can't read, I'm here to make a point. You are trespassing and you've got to put that fire out and leave. Now.'

Arno stood up.

'Sit, you move when I say so.'

'We know who you are.' Arno told her. 'We just needed water and a rest. We had an accident.'

'You think you can come here, take my house, take my life. I know who you are. Disease carriers. There's a plague out there and you're taking it from island to island. You think I don't listen to the radio? You think I don't know what's going on.'

'We just wanted to rest and get some water,' Rachel repeated. 'We haven't...'

'You're going to put that fire out.'

'You going to shoot us, Ms Becora? 'Cause if you are, that's dumb. We pose no threat to you. We'll move on in the morning. You want trouble, killing us will bring plenty of it and how can you be sure they won't bring the virus with them? You go back to your house and leave us alone and we will leave you alone.'

The shot went wide and ricocheted off the dock.

'More slugs where they came from,' she told them. 'You're leaving now. You understand?'

Fen wasn't afraid. She turned around and stared at the women. 'The thing about this virus is that we all had it. Even Red here, my dog. We had it and survived it, but we still got it and you can shoot us lady, but can you shoot my dog in the dark? One bite and you'll be dead in two hours, less probably. Red? Git her, go on git her.'

Red bolted for the woman on the rock and instantly her bravado disappeared. She turned and ran, slipping on a rock, losing a grip on the rifle which fell into the darkness. She picked herself up and ran, but almost immediately Red was there, barking, harrying her, panicking her and she scrambled and ran for her house shrieking with terror.

Arno and Rachel watched with fascination and Fen just turned to them with a sly grin on her face.

Red did what he normally did, harried and nipped at her ankles. It was the game he'd played with Fen all his life and the faster they ran the more he enjoyed it and this old lady could move pretty good. He chased her right into her house. Even by the dock they heard her screams as she ran down into the cellar and bolted the door behind her, keeping Red out.

'He really bite?' Arno enquired.

'Just nip a little,' Fen told them nonchalantly. 'You're supposed to chase him back. He loves that.'

Rachel just shook her head. 'But she doesn't know that.'

Fen shrugged. 'Right now she thinks she's been bitten by a dog with the virus. You might want to go speak to her. She'll be frantic I guess.'

'Find the rifle first.' Arno told her. 'Then speak with a soft voice.'

'I get it,' Rachel said. She suddenly turned to Fen and gave her a hug. 'You are a wonder girl, you know that. I was just going to shit my panties and you just calmly set your dog on her.'

'Red and me are survivors. Not going to let some little old lady frighten us. Even if she does write creepy stuff.'

Arno put some sticks on the fire. 'Let's eat first. Better call Red back. I think it's best.'

Fen shook her head. 'Uh-huh. I'll go up. Straighten it out. Red will get confused if I don't. I reckon we got beds to sleep in tonight.'

Arno looked at Rachel and acknowledged that Fen knew what she was doing. 'What did you cook anyways?'

'Seems we have a family sized can of hot asparagus.'

Fen laughed. 'Well save me some. Asparagus. You guys really brought some weird survival food.'

'It was on sale,' Rachel declared and Fen laughed some more as she went up into the rocks to retrieve the rifle.

Arno sat down and Rachel stood watching him, confused. 'She's pretty independent.'

'She is and she's right. She knows more about surviving than we do. We should stay on this island for a few days until we have some kind of plan, OK. Until my hands and face stop being so raw anyway.'

'What about the old lady.'

'She'll either co-operate or hide. To be honest, I think she's overrated as a writer. But at least we know we are still in Canadian waters. She is a fierce independent Canadian. Won't even go across the border to do book signings. She's from Tofino, I think. I read an interview with her in *Macleans*. She was complaining that Western Vancouver Island was too crowded, Japanese fans kept finding her and pestering her, so she bought herself an island.'

'Probably a good idea,' Rachel remarked. 'I've been to Tofino often. Had a surfer boyfriend when I was seventeen. Best place to be when it's hot everywhere else. You can count on it being cool. Most of the year it's like you'd pay for someone to come and talk to you it's so quiet. But in summer, with celebrities an 'all, buying up Long Beach ocean front and the tourists. I could understand wanting your privacy. You do get a hell of lot of Japanese there – whale watching. Salivating probably.'

She looked back at the house and then remembered the food. 'Be good to have the asparagus now.'

'Sorry, thought I was grabbing beans.'

Rachel smiled. Then sighed. 'You think things will ever return to normal, Arno? You think we might wake up one day and be able to talk to strangers without wanting to shoot them?'

Arno shrugged. 'Long term, of course. Short term, no chance. We have to be aware that strangers are going to be as frightened of us as we are of them.'

A shout went up from the house and they heard some barking, but Rachel didn't stir. Fen could handle it. She realised that she was slightly jealous of the strange girl. Fen had courage and a real will to survive. She realised that half the time she just wanted to curl up and sleep, pretend none of this was really happening. She didn't of course, but she was aware that even running away wasn't a solution and it kind of scared her. There were no safe places. None at all. She wasn't even sure they had a future.

Fen returned with some fresh bread. They ate it with the asparagus.

'She's crazy as a loon but she can bake good bread. She's still in the cellar. Won't let me in. I told her to put zinc on her scratches. I told her I'd get some for her, but she still thinks she's going to die tonight. I told her I made it all up but she isn't listening.'

Arno took that on board. 'When she wakes up in the morning she'll realise she's OK and then she'll feel stupid, but at least she'll be alive.'

In the morning however there was no answer. Arno beat on the door a while.

'Ms Becora. It's Arno Lakis. Open the door please. None of us have the virus. Not one, nor the dog. Fen just said that to scare you. We just wanted a safe place to spend the night. We'll be gone soon. You are quite safe. There is absolutely no need to be afraid.'

There was still no answer. That's when Rachel came downstairs holding a medicine bottle. 'Arno? You need to get inside. She's taking isosorbid mononitrate – big doses. Means she has a weak heart. My Mother took these. If she hasn't taken them and she's got herself worked up she could die. I've seen what happens to heart patients when they panic. The pills speed up the heart, Arno. She's got nothing to drink, she's scared, might even have passed out by now. Break the door down, Arno. You have to.'

Arno looked at her a moment as if he didn't quite understand then started on the door. It was tough, like the whole house, built to last. He took a run at it.

When he finally broke down the door they found her dead, lying in a pool of urine at the bottom of the stairs. Rachel had been right. Being in the cellar all night and fearing that she was about to die must have been a big strain on her heart. It was a stupid death. Entirely preventable and all of them felt a tad guilty, even though she'd shot at them. It was made all the more grisly by all the objects in the cellar. Hanging saws, rusty blades, hundreds of things in various states of repair. It was a terrible damp place to spend your last hours and it compounded their sense of guilt.

Arno helped Rachel and Fen dig the grave beside the sweetpeas in her garden, despite his hands being sore. They all felt bad about this; it seemed to contaminate them all.

Fen found the kitchen garden when she went to look for a grave marker.

Lettuce, cabbage, potatoes, onions and a whole hedgerow of unpicked blackberries. They had more than enough to last them and seeds too for the next season.

Arno said a simple prayer for the old lady's soul and they left it at that. They all felt a guilty, but this was the situation and they had to live with it.

'We stay for now.' Arno declared. 'This island is defensible and we have food, shelter and water. That going to be OK with everyone?'

Rachel was entirely happy with it and Fen too. It was small, easy place to get bored, but there was a garden to maintain, fish to be caught and the days would look after themselves.

Arno looked back at the freshly dug grave and regretted the island couldn't have been shared in a civilised manner. But needs must, as the English would say. They had set out to outrun the virus and this was as good a place as any to do just that.

'Fen. Pick out a room. Rachel see if she had any short wave radio or satellite dish, she probably had some means of communication with the mainland. Someone was keeping her supplied with stuff. If they come, they'll be expecting her to be here, so we need a good story.'

'She caught the virus.' Rachel suggested.

'Not here she didn't. We didn't bring it either, so...'

Fen shrugged. 'Heart attack. It's the truth. She died of a heart attack. Besides, who will come now? Might as well be in the middle of the Pacific. People aren't going to be delivering anything anymore. Not for a long while anyway. I found some hooks and a stick. I'm going to try fishing.' She looked around for her dog. 'Red.'

The dog was there beside her instantly. Then she was gone. Arno found himself admiring her. She just had all the right instincts. He wondered what the hell had happened to her to be so well prepared for this harsh life.

'I'm going to do a wash,' Rachel declared. 'I don't think she ever cleaned a damn thing.'

16

Novartis announced today that it would invest $600 million to build the first U.S. based plant to develop flu vaccines. The Swiss drug maker's investment comes as companies rush to develop faster techniques for making flu vaccines as the spectre of pandemic avian flu looms. The plant's new advanced cell-culture techniques are intended to replace fifty-year-old vaccine technology that requires fertilized chicken eggs and six months production time. Novartis' investment is partly funded by a recent $220 million contract from the Health and Human Services Department. HHS distributed a total of $1 billion in grants in May to vaccine makers who are developing cell culture based techniques.

Once the North Carolina site is completed and approved, Novartis said it would produce as many as 50 million doses of seasonal trivalent flu vaccines for use in the U.S.

Health and Human Services Department

City for Sale

'Do you want shallots with that?' Deka shouted out from the backyard, listening for a reply.

Wylie was curled up in the corner watching him prepare the food, hoping for scraps. Deka had taken to cooking outside permanently now since the hydro had failed to come back on. Been six or seven days with no electricity at all. He'd found a stack of offcuts from the furniture maker next door. Enough to keep his barbecue going months if they wanted.

He was nursing a sore ankle from his latest raid on a couple of stores in Chinatown. There were guys with guns protecting most of what was there, but several stores had been left to their own devices and he'd had to force the shutters to get inside. He didn't even recognise half the stuff in there and much of it was rapidly going off, but this was his private stash now and he was careful to close the metal shutters after him when he left to deter others. Water chestnuts, bamboo shoots, assorted weird and wonderful mushrooms, basmati rice, sugar, handfuls of fresh ginger and whatever he could find in a tin and could vaguely identify. He grabbed whatever he could carry and they had enough now to last a month maybe.

A door slammed. Deka heard footsteps and suddenly Doc appeared at the basement doorway, blinking in the glow of the evening light. He'd been in his lab for an hour. Deka couldn't believe he could stand for that long.

Doc was gaunt, a pale shadow of the man who had once lived here. His eyes bulged slightly, a side effect of the virus; he'd lost a minimum of forty pounds, if not more, his body mass visibly diminished. Deka had lost hope for him many times in the first three days he'd been nursing him, but little by little signs of life flickered. Doc had sworn at him, protested every time he'd made him move his legs and arms and turned him to stop him getting bedsores, but the more he swore, the more confident Deka had been that the man was getting better. On the fourth day when he'd woken and asked for liquorice and if he was feeding Wylie, Deka knew for sure Doc was back from the dead. He'd practically had to force him to swallow his red capsules and some soup every day, but despite the protests, he'd got it down him somehow.

Now he was dressed in a shirt that looked two sizes too big for him, but he'd shaved for the first time and was at least recognisable as his old self – aside from the blood on his chin. He was feeling his teeth.

'How are your teeth, Deka?'

Deka frowned. It wasn't a question he'd been expecting. But now he thought about it, they had been bugging him for almost a week now. 'Sensitive, my gums bleed when I brush my teeth in the morning, why?'

'My gums are bleeding too. My piss still stinks. My shit is white. Like a dog. I saw this in Mozambique. Did I tell you I went there? 'Bout fourteen years ago. Hospital was worse than anything I've seen in Chechnya. People got some kind if bug, made your belly swell and your shit white. We didn't have antibiotics. Lot of people died.'

Deka wondered where else this man had been, what he'd seen? 'I've been to Maputo. Must have been nice once, thirty years ago before...'

'Before the Marxists fucked it over you were going to say. Everywhere they went they sucked out the life of the country. Just like they did in the Soviet. I know.' He smiled, a small wheezing chuckle escaped. 'Now everywhere will look like Soviet Russia. How's that for a cosmic joke.'

He handed Deka a small cup of liquid. 'Sluice this around your mouth, OK. Keep it there for five minutes, then spit it out.'

Deka took it and sniffed. 'What's in it?'

'Like everything else I use. It's from the Nime tree in Thailand. It will help your gums recover. I use it all year around. Tastes bitter.'

'Everything you use tastes bitter.' Deka emptied the cup and sloshed it around his mouth. It was exactly as he described. Bitter and antagonised his sore gums. But if it fixed them, it was well worth a try.

Minutes later, he spat it out. 'Disgusting. Tastes vile. I hope it works Doc.'

'It will. Believe me. They were using this stuff in India two thousand years ago. Tree won't grow here. Hates the frost.'

Deka shrugged. 'I just know everything will be different now; as for your shit, shallots and chestnuts will take care of that. We've got noodles, some mystery sauce and mushrooms that look like shrivelled lettuce. I hope you're hungry.'

Doc nodded. 'Sounds good.' A momentary dizziness took him and he had to lean up against the wall. 'I think my appetite is back. Thought I'd never want to eat again.'

Deka tossed the shallots and mixed in the chestnuts, adding some soy sauce and herbs. 'You begged me to kill you for two straight days. Even offered me money.'

'Why didn't you do it? I would have killed you if you had asked.'

Deka chuckled. 'I know you don't have any money. And as long as you kept asking, I knew you were still alive. Besides Wylie kept giving me the evil eye.'

Doc wagged a finger at the dog. 'You better be feeling guilty, Wylie. I have to keep living now because of you.' He slid down the wall and Wylie got up to greet his master, burying his head in his lap and snorting. Doc rubbed his ears and gave him a hug. 'Best dog I ever had. Knows everything.'

Doc was remembering stuff now. 'You were inside my lab?"

'Red capsules, remember? You were quite insistent.'

Doc nodded. Somehow he'd thought that part had been a dream. He'd tried to send Deka a mental picture of the blue cabinet door. Hadn't realised he'd actually said something. 'What dose?'

'Two everyday. Was that right?'

Doc smiled briefly. 'I guess. I'm still alive. Experimental batch. They worked.'

'What were they for?' Deka asked after a moment hesitation.

'Oxygen saturation. They help the lungs absorb oxygen which passes it onto the tissue. That's what the virus does, reduces your ability to absorb oxygen. The virus uses a key cell surface molecule to gain entrance into the cell where it reproduces. I was experimenting with an entry blocker which will stop the virus from attaching to the cell surface molecule.'

'I guess I should have taken some. I can barely walk up three stairs now without wheezing.'

'I'll make up another batch, but I think the damage will have been done. You might find this stays with you a long time, my friend. I'll think about it. We will both need something to repair the tissue damage to our lungs.'

Deka didn't doubt it. A lot of things were going to be harder to do now. Even twisting open a jar hurt his wrists. He looked inside the gallery a moment.

'Your patient here yet?'

Doc shook his head. 'She'll come. Always comes on the fifteenth. If she's alive she'll come.' He stood up again, taking a grip on the doorframe. 'You think there are many doctors who survived, Deka? Must have been tough out there. Them all thinking they were protected by TCH-5 and the booster doses. Fuck. This is some tough virus. Look at us, just skeletons now. I thought I was going to drown. Fucking virus gets so deep into the lungs. Did I turn blue?'

'Yeah. Everyone does. But, we're here, Doc. We made it.'

'Da. We're still here.' Doc nodded towards the barbeque. 'Smells good.'

'Ja. It does.' He grinned, then felt a familiar pain. He needed the bathroom again. 'Going upstairs. Need anything?'

Doc shook his head.

Deka went inside, struggling up the outside stairs like an old man, the tight pain in his chest quite distinct. He decided to get a bottle of wine whilst he was up there. Doc wasn't much of a drinker, but he did keep a good stock of wine in the place and if had learned one thing from this virus, it was that this was no time to be a saint. If wine was there, it had to be drunk. That or traded for food.

Moments later the gate rattled at the back behind them and Doc struggled to rise as Wylie raced to the gate barking.

'Hello?' A timid female voice was calling out. 'Hello?'

Wylie paid close attention as Doc ambled to the gate and unlocked it. 'Stay, Wylie. Friend. OK. Friend.'

A petite, well-dressed middle-aged blonde carrying a large Mulberry bag came in, looking a little spooked. She looked a bit overdressed for a pandemic and had made quite an effort with her make-up. Doc let her in and locked the gate behind her. They didn't say a word. What she thought of him and how he looked she kept to herself. She meekly followed Doc up the stairs into the building. She was wearing an obligatory facemask but it was of an unusual design and bright yellow.

Doc had taken his patient upstairs, away from the stink of the damp that still hung around on the ground floor. Deka emerging from the bathroom glimpsed both of them sitting on chairs in a pool of evening sunlight at the back. She, shaking and crying, Doc listening. Deka moved silently, not wanting to disturb them. She didn't look like one of Doc's normal patients at all. Too rich, too neat. But then again, where else was she going to find a doctor? There were probably a thousand doctors out there that weren't practicing anymore. He wondered about those medical workers he'd met at the hospital. How they all said the virus would peak in like sixty days. How would they even know? Was anyone counting? How would anyone know anything if there was no electricity? No news. No radio. Was everyone in hiding from one another, all waiting week after week for an all clear?

Deka was back tending the food when Doc came out on the deck briefly with a brown paper parcel, throwing it down to him in the yard with a smile. 'Guard this with your life, Teacher, might be the last fresh loaf of bread we see in a long time. You see what doctors get paid with now? Bread. It was like this in Soviet times – I feel almost nostalgic.'

'Can you help her?' Deka asked as he unwrapped the parcel. What lay before him was a heavyweight stoneground brown loaf that smelled delicious. Something precious indeed. It was odd, but he couldn't remember the last time he'd seen fresh bread, let alone want to eat some. 'This is a good loaf, Doc. She's paid you well.'

'Then I am sorry I cannot help her much. She has shingles. Painful, right across her back and down one side. Stress probably.'

'Well having half the city die might count as stress.'

Doc agreed. 'She's Leyla Aronovich.'

Deka frowned. 'The lawyer's wife? He owned most of Whistler...'

'She owns it all now. He's dead. Her whole family died. That's the little problem I can't fix. She said almost everyone in Whistler died even though they closed the whole city off months ago. She lives in West Van now in a big mansion, all by herself and her guns.'

'Guns?'

'She's a champion shot. Olympic standard. Never guess, huh? Russian girls are full of surprises.' Doc smiled briefly then noticed Deka had opened a bottle of Linderman's Shiraz.

'Pour me two glasses.'

'For her? You're treating shingles with red wine? Now I know you're a quack.'

Doc grinned. 'The wine is for her depression, the pills are for shingles. We live in strange times, Teacher. Besides, we should drink all the red wine we can, it's a cure for gum disease and strengthens the heart. Ask any Italian.'

Deka poured three glasses. He was short of a handy Italian to verify these 'facts' but if the wine helped, it helped.

Wylie came looking for something to eat and Deka let him sample their supper. He ate it. Wylie ate anything now. He'd learned one thing of late. Eat anything if offered, it might not get offered again.

The woman left half an hour later. She looked a little happier than when she had arrived. Deka put it down to the wine, but then again, she must have been happy to have found someone who at least knew what her problem was. He heard a car start up and drive away. It was immediately astonishing because Deka realised he'd gotten entirely used to the city being silent.

'You let her drive?' He admonished Doc when he returned.

Doc laughed, sitting heavily on the weather beaten bench by the barbecue. 'In Russia it is unusual to drive sober. Of course, not everyone makes it home.'

Deka laughed. 'Of course.' Deka stirred his concoction and realised that it really did smell good. Perhaps in the next life he could be a chef. 'Noodles are ready, we need plates. Want to eat out here?'

'I'm still cold. All of me is cold. You?'

'I'm getting better. Besides this wine is doing something.' He laughed briefly, taking a sip. 'I haven't drunk wine in nearly twenty years, Doc. Never drank at all.'

Doc did a double take. 'That's the saddest thing I ever heard.'

'My father drank. It wasn't pretty. He got violent. When I was a kid I used to stare at a sign by the railway in Saltriver. 'Wine gets you up, but always lets you down'. Or something like that anyway. I didn't know which I hated most. My dad out of his gourd on Lieberstein or in a funk beating the shit out of us all if we made a noise.'

Doc didn't comment. He was feeling dizzy again. He realised that he needed food. 'Cut me some bread. I think my sugar levels are crashing.'

Deka quickly cut him a slice, appreciating the fresh aroma of new bread. He dipped it into the pan and handed it to Doc. 'Eat slow, remember this is your first day up and your belly is nearly empty. Go easy on the wine too. It's got nothing to work on.'

Doc ate the bread, tossing Wylie a corner of it. He leant back against the brick wall. The bread was good, he could feel it working and Deka was right. This was his first day; he had no strength at all. Nothing. The smell of the food was doing it. He realised that he craved food. An empty Doc was no Doc at all.

Deka served up the meal, realising he'd cooked way too much, even for the three of them – regretting there was no fridge to put leftovers in now the power was off. He had a sudden vision of a million fridges filled with rotting food and wondered how everyone else was coping. Everyone was going to be hungry real soon if they couldn't store food.

The colour in Doc's face slowly returned. All three of them ate in silence, hungry and appreciative of what they had here. Wylie was still nervous, eating quickly in case they took it away from him, but Doc and Deka just concentrated on every mouthful, savouring the odd combinations and chewy texture.

Doc asked for more bread and mopped the remains with it, eating everything slowly, as if in a trance. He looked at Deka, shaking his head with a rueful smile. 'I don't know what I ate, Teacher, but I can tell you, that was the best meal I ever had. The best.'

Deka laughed. He almost felt the same. It was hot, it was tasty and he should probably write the recipe down. Deka Fortun's Pandemic Cookbook. Sure to be a best-seller.

Someone began pounding on the front door about then and Wylie was up and barking, back on duty. Deka looked at Doc and they both shrugged. Neither man was expecting anyone.

'Someone desperate to buy art?' Deka joked half-heartedly.

Doc signalled that he would go. 'Get a stick, you never know.'

'Maybe we should ignore it.' Deka suggested. 'It's gone nine. Curfew at ten.'

Doc began to shuffle towards the gallery lobby.

'Ask who it is, Doc, before you open up. There's a lot of crazies out there.'

Deka began to look for a good solid weapon. He found a block of wood with nails protruding and felt a little happier.

Wylie was excited, sniffing and snorting at the door. They knocked again and he barked, to make sure they knew that this place was protected.

Doc arrived there but didn't unlock. He was listening to voices. Russian voices. 'Dimitri?' He queried, not quite believing his ears.

There was a sudden shout of recognition from the other side. 'Alexi Borov? It is you? Dr Borov? It is really you?'

Deka heard a heavy Russian accent and saw Doc's spirit visibly lift. He unlocked the door quickly, keeping an excited Wylie back. He swung the door open and stood face to face with a pale slight balding man with smiling eyes and an elaborate red facemask. He was wearing a powersuit and wore gold rings on both hands.

'Is it OK we say hello?' He asked, uncertain of Doc's changed countenance.

Doc gave Dimitri a hug. The man hugged him back. Deka approved, this is how men should greet each other, no distance between them.

Dimitri stepped back a moment and took a longer look at his friend. He shook his head. 'Alexi, you look like shit.'

Doc laughed and stepped back to let the man in. Dimitri turned briefly to signal to his driver to wait and entered the gallery, closing the door behind him. Wylie chose not to say hello and parked himself on the stairs for a moment, wary of this new visitor.

Doc turned to Deka and smiled. 'Deka Fortun, meet Dimitri Kolata, entrepreneur and my brother-in-law.' He turned back to Dimitri. 'Deka saved my life, got me through it. Couldn't have done it without him.'

Dimitri surveyed Deka and perhaps decided he wasn't a threat. He signalled a hello and Deka did likewise. No hug for him then.

Dimitri was looking at Doc again, shaking his head. 'You had this virus?'

'Survived it, Dimitri Kolata. Both of us survived it. Lost a little weight, but...'

Dimitri still didn't like it. 'You still look like shit.' He looked at Doc with a sharp gaze. 'You say I am safe?'

Doc nodded. 'Completely. You have no risk of contagion here my friend.'

Dimitri stood still a moment, looked back at Wylie and made a decision. He began to remove his mask. 'The word of Dr Alexi Borov is my guard.' He removed the last of his mask and revealed a small moustache and a scar from his chin to his nose, not quite disguised by the facial hair.

Doc saw Deka react to the scar and smiled. 'He served in Chechnya with me. When they bombed the hospital he carried on helping me treat the wounded even though the shrapnel sliced his face open.'

Deka was impressed. 'Must have hurt.'

Dimitri laughed and produced a bottle of vodka from his coat. 'Didn't feel a thing, the angel in a bottle took care of that.' He laughed again, handing Doc the bottle. 'From Valentina. She knows this is your favourite.'

Doc took the bottle and grinned. 'My sister remembers everything. She is well?'

'She is. She is a good mother, Alexi. You were right. I might be a terrible husband, but she is an excellent wife. I have a letter for you from her.'

Doc was puzzled. 'I still don't understand how it is that you are here in Vancouver. Surely no planes are flying. Not even diplomatic... And how will Moscow survive without you?'

Deka remembered the food. 'We have food. Just cooked it. If you're hungry.'

Doc and Deka could see he was pondering if it was safe to eat here, amongst men who had had the virus, but then he smiled – nothing could be worse than Chechnya.

'Offer accepted. You have enough for my driver? We expected to eat in Vancouver restaurants, but there is nothing. In Moscow, the restaurants are still open.'

'They are? Things are not so bad there?'

Dimitri shook his head. 'No inoculation, no pass. Sometimes the old way of doing things makes things work better. We developed THN-9. Every citizen in every city and town and we have stopped it cold my friends. Stopped it cold. In China I hear it is a disaster, India too, but we cut it down. Russia survives.'

Dimitri removed his coat and took out the inevitable businessman's Blackberry (even if there was no signal, few businessmen could be parted from them in Deka's observations). He extracted letters from his inside pocket and handed them to Doc. 'From Valentina and Nona. Read. Not all good news. I am sorry.'

Deka saw Doc's face change. 'Nona. Nona Guerrin?'

Dimitri smiled looking at Deka. 'He thinks he is forgotten, but Russian girls, they never forget a lover. She is single again by the way. Still looks good.'

Doc went over to the stairs and sat with Wylie to read his letter and Dimitri joined Deka in the gallery. 'Something smells good. You cook outside?'

'No power. We're running short of candles. Come out back, Dimitri, I'll warm the food for you and your driver.'

'Open the vodka. This is a time to celebrate.'

Deka took some glasses with him out back and tossed some wood onto the fire. It took in seconds. 'I don't understand how you got here.'

Dimitri found a chair and sat, careful not to crease his suit. 'Do the cell phones still work here? I had a signal in the city...?'

Deka shrugged. 'It's like everything else. When there is power... but I guess they are having problems with getting men to keep it running, or something. Several days now without any hydro now. I'm getting used to it, and the clear skies. No planes, no industry, keep this up and we'll cure global warming.'

Dimitri smiled. 'Ha, the silver lining. I hear about this all the time now.'

'But you got here.' Deka persisted. 'Somehow. No ships docked. We would have noticed.' He put the three glasses on the table and went back into the gallery to get the vodka. Doc was trying to read by candlelight and shaking a little. Wylie came over to Deka, still unsure of the situation and the stranger. Deka stroked his head and he accepted that. Wylie had decided that Deka was a friend, but this new guy smelled entirely different.

Deka returned with bottle and poured Dimitri a shot.

'Not drinking?'

'I had wine. I don't think I can handle...'

"You have to drink. We are all friends here and this is a big occasion. Pour Alexi a shot and yourself. We must drink to friendship.' It was an order, Deka discovered. Despite himself, Deka poured the shots.

'So,' Deka asked right out. 'How did you get here?'

'I think you'll find submarines are still operating and the Russian Navy needs investment, should I say.' Dimitri smiled, like he actually owned the sub.

'Ah.' Deka smiled at Doc as he joined the party. 'He came by submarine.'

'So I have discovered,' he waved his letters. 'And my mother is dead. Old age, Valentina says.'

Dimitri shrugged; indicating there was another possibility. 'She wouldn't get inoculated. There were scare stories. She chose to believe them. She left for Kiev to stay with Gunter. She died in her sleep, Alexi. Nothing dramatic. I am sorry for your loss.'

Doc nodded. He preferred the truth. He discovered the vodka and raised his glass, indicating to Deka to raise his. Deka complied.

'To Nina Maria Borov, a good mother and friend.'

They drank. Dimitri refilled their glasses. Deka hastily busied himself preparing more food. He didn't want to get caught up in any drinking games. He knew about Russians and vodka. He knew everyone could drink him under the table, he didn't need to prove his manhood to anyone.

'Valentina is worried about you, brother-in-law. She thinks you are wasting your life in this country.'

Doc shrugged, pulling Wylie towards him and giving him a rub. Wasting away perhaps, but...' He changed the subject. 'So you sneak in by submarine to deliver a letter to me, huh? Such a grand gesture my friend, such a grand gesture.'

Dimitri laughed, rubbing his neck, which seemed to be causing him irritation. He lifted his glass again and Doc followed suit. 'To opportunity, my friend. To opportunity.'

'Opportunity, my mother used to say, is another man's misfortune,' Doc informed him.

Dimitri smiled, knocking his glass back. 'Your mother was a perceptive woman Alexi Borov. This is a special time. Like the seven plagues of Egypt. Each one brings misery, misfortune and death. But each time someone made a fortune. In famine it is the man who has the grain, in drought, the man who has the water, in pestilence... who knows?'

'The man who has the cure?' Doc ventured, but Dimitri laughed again and shook his head.

'No, too easy. They tell me that when San Francisco had the big earthquake, what just over a hundred years ago? A man ran up and down the city streets buying up deeds of those fleeing the fires. By the time the army had put out the fire he owned most of the city.

'This virus is my earthquake, Alexi Borov, brother-in-law. It is your earthquake too.' He poured more vodka into their glasses. Deka pointedly declined and began to serve up the reheated food. 'Raise your glass to opportunity, my friend.'

They drank. Doc felt a heat building in his stomach. He knew he'd not be able to drink more without spewing.

'Eat, Dimitri, eat. Deka has made something special.'

Indeed Deka had two plates prepared and he gave one to Dimitri and took the other out for the driver. Doc steered their guest over to the table inside and lit a new candle.

Dimitri was looking at the abstract modernist paintings on the wall. 'I never cared for this kind of art. It's ugly, Alexi.'

Alexi could only agree. 'They don't matter anymore. The artist is dead – most likely and we will need them for the fire soon enough. People won't be coming to any galleries anytime soon. Not to buy art anyway.'

Dimitri tasted the food and was pleasantly surprised. 'Good. Very good. Of course I have been eating Navy food for a couple of weeks.'

Alexi smiled. 'So, you come by this submarine. A long way from Moscow. You must have come to buy something. Something very important to risk so much.'

Dimitri ate some more, realising he was hungry. Deka returned with the food still on the plate. He pulled a face. 'He says he's not hungry.'

Dimitri laughed. 'He eats only tinned food. He told me. Trusts nothing.'

'Where did you meet him?' Doc asked.

Dimitri watched as Deka gave the food to Wylie, who ate quickly, not quite believing his luck.

'He's with the embassy staff. Only three survived out of fifty. They didn't use the vaccine we sent them. Or didn't get it. Who knows.'

'I'm worried about you, Dimitri. You say you are protected but...'

'I have taken everything, Alexi Borov. I am immune. Believe me. Moscow thrives. It is the world that has died, not us.'

Deka filled the old metal kettle to boil water on the fire. 'But you took this risk and came to buy something here. Is it a secret?'

Dimitri smiled waving his fork in the air. 'No secret. No secret at all. I did not come to buy something; I came to buy *everything*. I've come to buy your city. Maybe two cities – depends upon the price. Didn't you know? Everything is for sale. Everything.' He beamed at Deka. 'Your food is good, very good. You're hired.'

He turned to Doc and laughed, short and slightly annoying. 'You're hired too. That's why I'm here.'

Doc shook his head. 'This is a ghost town, Dimitri. Nothing to do, things falling apart. No one trusts doctors anymore.'

'Did I say I needed a doctor?'

'Even billionaires need doctor's, Dimitri. No one is immune.'

'You're the only man I trust in this whole continent, Alexi Borov. You're an honourable man – a man who has never cared enough about money, but always treats everyone with respect.'

Doc sat down, sending Wylie off to the corner. 'I'm no businessman, Dimitri.'

'Yes. True. I am the businessman. You will run my office. You will be my partner. You will keep everyone honest and for that...' He ate his last mouthful of food, pushing his plate to one side. 'For that I will pay a million dollars a year.'

Deka looked at Doc. He wanted to laugh it seemed so absurd. But Doc wasn't laughing. Dimitri was about to charge their glasses again but Doc stopped him. 'Tea, Dimitri. You want to kill us. We have very intolerant stomachs. We will celebrate with tea – like the Arabs.'

Indeed the kettle boiled at that moment and Deka busied himself with making them tea. Dimitri put up his hands in surrender. 'Of course. Of course. You are right. You are still recovering. I was just excited to be here at last. I have so much to do and I need good friends with me. Tomorrow I will buy Robson Street. I am told it is the street to own.'

'Robson Street is full of shops and hotels, Dimitri. No shoppers, no tourists, no profit. You may not be getting the best advice.' Doc told him, concerned.

Dimitri shook his head. 'Precisely why it will cost nothing. They are desperate to sell. I have already been approached, my friends. I have lawyers and landowners desperate for my money. I will buy the leases for almost half a mile of buildings for next to nothing. Imagine that.'

'But there will be no tourists, Dimitri.' Deka protested. 'Not for years now.' He offered Rooibos tea to him in a blue porcelain cup, pouring some for himself and Doc.

Dimitri smiled knowingly. 'Remember the man in the earthquake? Everyone thought he was mad. Now everyone thinks I am mad. The world has changed but do you really think they will stop shopping and fucking? Will Vancouver be less attractive? Will they take away the mountains, the ocean? Everything is empty now, but in a year? Eighteen months?'

Doc shook his head. 'Might take more than a year, Dimitri. Deka thinks up to 100,000 people died in this city alone. Almost all of Whistler died. We are talking a lot of empty real estate from here all the way back to Calgary. For that matter I hear Halifax is a catastrophe. You probably know more than us about what happened elsewhere.'

'Elsewhere is elsewhere. I have seen the pictures from Paris and Rome. It is too much. Too much. To hell with the old world, Alexi. I want this world.'

'I never got to Paris.' Doc sighed.

Dimitri drank some more of his tea. 'It was overrated. Here, on the other hand. I can do something. And there's millions back home, with money and ambition who'd rather be here my friend. I already spoke with the Government. Anyone with money they will let in when this outbreak is over. They need us. The tax base is gone. They want us. We will replenish Canada and America with good middle-class Russians. Doctors, dentists, businessmen and their families. We have survived for a reason, Alexi Borov. Now we will buy their cities and treble our fortunes. You will see.'

Doc and Deka exchanged glances. It sounded crazy and yet so damn plausible.

'You do know the virus hasn't peaked yet, Dimitri. It is still killing people and we haven't had the full effect of winter yet. Might not peak until February.'

'And I am here, in hell, buying lots. This is my risk. I have come at the moment people least expect me and I will own this city by the end of the month.'

Deka sipped his tea. He had often wondered what it would be like to come face to face with a megalomaniac and this, he realised was the moment. He sipped his tea, relishing the aromatic flavour. 'You ever hear of Cecil Rhodes?' He asked.

Dimitri looked at Deka more closely, a little surprised by the question. 'He is my personal hero. A man with vision, a man who knew he had to unite Africa to make it rich. Small minds tried to defeat him but he triumphed. If only his great railway to Europe could have been built. Cecil Rhodes was a very great man.' He turned to Doc, looking into his face most directly. 'You trust this man, Alexi Dimitri?'

Doc smiled. 'He's a fucking saint. Worse than a saint. I trusted him with my life and he made me keep the bargain. Tough son of bitch, Dimitri. Thought I had died but he saved me, and Wylie here. Yes I trust him.'

Dimitri adopted a very serious gaze and turned to Deka, raising his cup of tea.

'So – half a million and your job is to keep him safe. Understood?'

Deka nearly choked. They clashed cups and drank back the hot tea. Doc gave him a look but Deka wasn't sure he knew how to interpret it.

'Deal?' Dimitri declared, relaxed now. This business was over.

'So we are bought too, along with the city.' Doc remarked.

Dimitri didn't flinch. 'Everyone is bought or sold, Alexi Borov. Some for more than others.' He held out his cup for more and Deka quickly complied. 'This tea?'

'Rooibos. Tick-Tock tea from South Africa. Kept many a Boer alive though hard times.'

'He started me drinking it a year ago. Said I was too tense,' Doc added. 'But it works.'

Dimitri though about that a moment, he could see these two men really trusted each other. He was almost jealous of their friendship. Then seemed to brighten up and smiled again. 'Tomorrow I will show you your offices. Before then you will need suits.'

'No shops open,' Deka informed him.

Dimitri waved his hand, this was no problem. 'My shops will open for you my friends. Money is the key to anything in hard times. But,' he smiled at Deka a moment. 'Tea also has its uses.'

Deka reflected upon how surreal this was. How one man can see an opportunity in the middle of a pandemic, whilst everyone else, including himself, could only see death and misery.

Doc was probing Dimitri's red facemask and its multi-layers with a knife, curious to its construction and texture. He noted that it had a small active tab on it that was ticking down to zero.

'It tells you when it is expired?'

Dimitri relaxed. 'My company makes them. Micro filters, three layers, kills bacteria you inhale and kills bacteria you exhale. Guaranteed. 48-hour limit from the moment you put it on. Our own government made it mandatory to wear one outside your own home and at all times in offices and factories, inside or out. We make millions over them every day. The profit margin on those numbers is amazing. In three months I made my first billion, in a year I am one of the richest men in Russia.'

'And it stops the virus?'

'It stops the virus spreading. It has stopped it Alexi.'

'But no one is claiming to have found a cure?'

He dismissed this idea with a wave of his hands. 'That's not my business. My business is to stop it spreading.'

Doc understood the distinction. 'What would a cure be worth do you think?'

Dimitri laughed, revealing gold back fillings. 'Who has that? No one. You think you have a cure, Alexi Borov?'

Doc shrugged. 'We survived.'

'Yes, you survived. Your friend here survived. Some people survive. You know of course that it kills the most in people aged twenty-four to thirty-six. The healthiest die first. One of the ironies. One of God's little jokes, I think. But, then some people survive cancer, Alexi. You think there is a cure for cancer?'

'No.'

'But if there was?'

'People would start smoking again,' Deka interjected.

Dimitri laughed, sat back and roared some more. 'I like you, Deka Fortun.' He chuckled again. 'Start smoking again. Funny. Very funny.'

But they never discussed a cure again. Doc knew then that Dimitri would never allow such a thing. Not when there were billions to be made from a mask. It was ever thus. No cure for the common cold if they could sell you pills and potions they absolutely knew could not and would not ever cure it.

'I must go.' Dimitri declared. 'Tonight I will sleep in a soft bed and dream of submarines.' He paused. 'Tomorrow. Meet me at the Derbyshire Hotel at eight thirty. I have the top floor.'

'It's still open?'

'I bought it this morning. Bring the dog. I'd like to have a dog living there. Dog's have good sense.'

Doc showed Dimitri to the front door whilst Deka cleared up. He noted Wylie hadn't gone to the door with his master. 'What's up, Wylie? Cheer up, you got a job too you know. We all did.'

Deka glanced over towards the Harbour a moment – a shooting star caught his eye as it streaked across the sky. He couldn't remember if it was a bad omen or a sign of good luck. A sign either way.

'Come on, dog. Help me with the washing up. Life goes on you know.'

17

Researchers at the University of Warwick are developing the 'protecting virus' that completely prevents flu symptoms developing by slowing influenza infection rates to such an extent that the harmful infection becomes a vaccine against that very form of influenza.

Experiments so far show that a single dose of protecting virus can be given 6 weeks before an infection with flu virus and be effective using a drop of saline containing the protecting virus, squirted up the nose. This could also have a substantial advantage over anti-viral drugs that only give less than 24-hour protection. The Warwick research team has now filed a patent on the protecting virus and has established a company – ViraBiotech – to help advance those aims.

http://www.innovationsreport.de/html/berichte/agrar_forstwissenschaften/ bericht-71409.html

An Easy Way to Die

Arno was working on the yacht, trying to fix a slow leak and do general maintenance. He knew they weren't likely to be going anywhere soon, but he was acutely aware that he was bored. He could understand why a writer might want to shut herself away on an island for months at a time, indeed it might be essential. Certainly their deceased mystery writer had lived in comfort, tending her garden which was important, but probably also a good distraction on days when she was blocked. It was certainly ambitious and must have been developed over years. He felt guilty they had robbed her of her life and her island, but these were the times they lived in now. Few people trusted strangers, with good reason. But Arno was also conscious that he missed his regular morning latté and newspapers – the *FT* in particular. Then there were the guys in the office, Rita, his associate, who had a weird sense of humour but a sharp analytical mind; he even missed the regular updates from *Bloomberg*. He was aware that not only was it likely that way of life was gone for his entire generation but there could be a complete political change. The world couldn't experience a plague like this and not undergo some kind of revolution in thought.

At one time he had considered that he could just walk away from the job, the data, the heated debates, the massive pile of reading and the endless redrafting of the runes of a future Canada. But now he realised, with deep regret, that he would have never been able to leave that world. Not for long, not voluntarily. It was what defined him. Loving Rachel was great, but there would have come a day when he would have had to drag her back with him to share his crazy life there.

Now there was nothing to go back to; and nothing going forward either.

He tried the radio. No FM out here. He flipped to AM and there they were – the preachers, the men with poison on their lips.

'God has visited this plague upon the earth and we, the survivors, await the glory. This *is* the Second Coming my friends, salvation is nigh, paradise awaits us. This is God's world now with him at the centre beckoning you. Heed his call and you never need be afraid again. We shall live in a Christian world with Christian values and...'

He twisted the dial again.

'It is true, my friends. The Rapture index is now standing at 190 – the highest number on record. It is time, my friends. Pretribulation rapture is here and now is the time of the Second Coming of Christ. It is written: You have forgotten God your Savior; you have not remembered the Rock, your fortress. Therefore, though you set out the finest plants and plant imported vines, though on the day you set them out, you make them grow, and on the morning when you plant them, you bring them to bud, yet the harvest will be as nothing in the day of disease and incurable pain.

(Isaiah 17:10-11)

Arno twisted the dial once more but could only find a broadcast in what sounded like Chinese. There was no music, no news, nothing he wanted to hear at all.

Fen suddenly appeared at the hatch. She looked apprehensive. He looked up and smiled at her, inviting her in. She stayed where she was, a question clearly poised on her lips.

'Something's troubling you. Want to share?' Arno asked.

Fen shrugged and stared up at the blue sky a moment before answering. 'What will the world be like, Arno? I mean after.'

Another Place to Die

Arno looked at Fen with surprise and then frowned, thinking about this question with the seriousness it deserved. He didn't answer her immediately. It wasn't easy.

They had studied this, argued a great deal over it back at the Futuretank Institute. They had been asked to work up a worse case scenario for Montreal six months previously and they had been astonished at how the model revealed how quickly things would stop functioning. The argument was about how fast everything could return to 'normal' after a major virus attack, the scenario ranging from weeks to months. The client didn't like the response; certainly not months. But the reality was that although you could get the power on, so to speak, you had to assume that a high percentage of key personnel would be dead or incapacitated. Restoration would take time. A lot of time in the case of training doctors, even nurses and teachers, at least a solid year in either case. So many professions would have gaps and filling them would require people to be trained and in many cases it would be hard to find the trainers and teachers. Layman could fill gaps but could you ask a layman to do operations? Run a nuclear reactor? Even managing ground transportation needed skills built up over time. Wither pilots? Cops? Even lawyers, damn it. Where would the plumbers, electricians, chefs, bus drivers and many more semi-skilled professionals come from? Someone would have to retrieve and restore the many thousands of databases (and eliminate the millions who would no longer be on them). The cost of data recovery would be prohibitive and so much could go wrong. Everything was so dependent on software and systems being up and running and maintained. From traffic lights to tax data, from hospital records to credit card statements, getting it all straightened out just couldn't happen overnight.

'The short answer is six months, Fen. But whereas some things might come back quickly, there will be so many gaps and potholes in our delivery systems, it might take two to three years before everything is functioning normally.'

'Normal? You think anything will be normal ever again?'

Arno shrugged. 'People are resilient. Correction, survivors are resilient. During World War Two, the Germans killed six millions Jews – right? Not killed in action, but deliberately rounded up and murdered. You know this from history. But it also took a huge logistical effort to organise this, and a lot of people were involved from death camp architects to railway workers, a great many people. But right after the war life returned to normal in Europe pretty quickly. Of course it was chaos at first, but once reconstruction started, very rapid. The Jews had been all but wiped out in Germany. The doctors, lawyers, artists and artisans they had been had already been prevented from working for years before the war began – so their roles in life had already been supplanted by others. Those that could left to rebuild their lives elsewhere.

'It's a harsh lesson but what it tells us is that everyone is replaceable. In Germany it was a different kind of virus, fascism is a vicious, virulent virus, but even so, our virus is much more efficient at killing than even the Nazi's. And unlike post-war Germany, there is no one to take the place of our doctors and lawyers and engineers. No teachers or builders or plumbers. Millions with real skills will have died and we will have to train new people to take their places.

'The good news is, it means as soon as you graduate school there will be a job for you. You'll have the pick of professions to train for and governments desperate to pay you to learn. In this new world, companies and Governments will pay you to go to University. It might not seem it now, Fen, but surviving the virus is going to be a lot like winning the lottery.

'It will be a smaller, better world and you'll be one of the people in charge of it.'

Fen was surprised. She had not thought about the positive side of this catastrophe. But he was right; the competition had been decimated. Suddenly Darwin's concept of 'survival of the fittest' made terrible sense.

'Feel better?'

Fen shrugged. 'It's like being told it's OK to cheat.'

Arno laughed. 'It won't be all smooth sailing. Crime might get a lot worse, I am sure of it. Politicians will still suck as people look for people who will promise solutions. We might get stuck with right-wing demagogues or socialist dictators, there will be endless disputes about property, intellectual copyright, banks will go under. Many people will survive but find they are now destitute. 'I'd say things might get pretty violent and we will live under curfew and restrictions longer than necessary.'

'That makes me feel a lot better,' Fen declared, smiling. 'What about you and Rachel?'

Arno thought about that for a moment and smiled. 'We'll have kids and hope they grow up to be as smart as you.'

Fen blushed. It was a new sensation for her to get any praise.

'Or, Red,' Arno added seriously. 'He's pretty smart too.'

Fen stood up, smiling now, appreciating his addition. 'Red's the smartest person in our group I think.'

Arno nodded. It was probably true. 'OK, conference over. We need to get stuff out of the yacht. Need all perishables off and anything useful we can carry. Alright?'

'I'll get a box.'

'Two boxes,' Arno called after her.

It was about three hours after supper when things started to go wrong. Arno was in the study tidying up, making sure that A.S. Becora's personal effects were all bundled together, in case one day someone cared enough to find out what happened to the writer..

He heard running footsteps outside and finally Rachel appeared at the door breathless, looking frazzled and pale. She had to take deep breaths, she could hardly speak.

'What?' Arno asked. He'd never seen her look so panicked. 'I thought you were going to bed?'

'It's Fen. She's sick.'

Arno frowned. 'How sick?' Though he knew the answer from her face. He couldn't believe it. Why now? How had this happened?

'It looks like the virus, Arno. I'm scared...'

'You sure, Rachel? We haven't had contact with the virus for...shit we've been here six days now. Fen wasn't sick three hours ago at dinner, she had no symptoms and besides the incubation period is less than three days, at it's weakest. It can't be the virus, Rachel. It just can't.'

Rachel frowned. She wasn't used to him not believing her. 'She's feverish and vomiting, there's blood in her spittle and Red's sick too.'

Arno blinked at that. He moved quickly towards the kitchen next door. He'd need the first-aid box, some antibiotics, and his briefcase with the all-important phials of TCH-6 in it. At the last moment he remembered some re-hydration packs. How the hell had this happened? It made no sense at all. 'You touch her?'

'I was washing her hair when it started.'

'Disinfect yourself?'

'Real fast. But...'

Arno looked at her and smiled. 'Don't panic OK. It might not be the virus. Could be anything. What do we really know what might be on the island? Did you check for a spider bite or snake bite?'

Rachel shook her head. She had been so spooked she hadn't checked Fen at all.

Arno was frowning though. 'But Red has it too?'

'Bad. Just lying there puking and he's shat all over the carpet. Stinks too. More than normal that is.'

He followed after Rachel. Was this it? This was fast. If it was the virus they were all as good as dead right now. No matter what they did. He didn't want to let her go. Not now he'd found her.

'Rach, boil up some water. If it is the virus, we can't do anything much. If it's something else, we will have to deal with it. What did we have for supper?

159

We all had the same right? I don't feel sick. You?' She shook her head, but didn't mention the discomfort in her stomach because she sensed it was just panic, a reaction to Fen getting sick.

'Where is she?' Arno asked.

'Top room.'

They parted at the bottom of the stairs, pausing only to stare at each other a moment. Uncertain of their future now, scared of what might come.

'Boil that water, Rach. No matter what. I love you. OK. I will always love you.'

Rachel briefly smiled, took comfort from that and went to the kitchen, aware that she had desperately wanted to hug him, but was suddenly afraid that she might infect him. She may have already unwittingly done so. She hated this life. Hated the virus.

Arno mounted the stairs feeling angry. They'd saved that girl and her dog. She was brave, she, of all the people he'd met, deserved to live. He couldn't believe she had the virus. Refused to believe it. It just wasn't possible. Now he and Rachel were at risk. More than risk. If Fen had it, then they'd be showing the symptoms within hours now, if not sooner.

Red was groaning, he completely ignored Arno's arrival and was still shitting from a prone position. Rachel hadn't been kidding about the stench. Fen lay on the bed in a sodden T-shirt, her face bright red and there was a rash across her neck that disappeared under her shirt. A pool of bloody vomit lay beside her and her sheets were soiled. He could see that she was gripped in a vice of pain, her face and body arched as if under attack. There was no point in trying to protect himself anymore. They'd had breakfast together, meals, sweated together in the garden, her breath was his breath when they'd been digging over the soil yesterday and they'd laughed together at just how tough gardening was. Whatever she had was also building in him. Impossible that it was not. Her eyes were strangely bloodshot and the fever was burning bright. She had looked and sounded so normal at dinner.

'Fen? Can you hear me'.

Fen groaned in reply as she clutched her stomach.

Arno made a decision. 'Fen, I'm going to get you cleaned up, OK. I'm going to remove your T-shirt; you're soaked OK. I'm going to wash you and try and cool you down a little. You've got a high temperature. You think you could swallow some soluble aspirin?'

Fen didn't reply. She didn't care what he did. She for one didn't think she was going to live another hour. Whatever this was, it was killing her, boiling her alive. She shivered and shook almost uncontrollably as the high temperature held sway.

Arno kept his word. He stripped her, put her under the shower, warm water; he didn't want to shock her to death. He went back to the bed, stripped it, found new sheets, cleaned up the room and the dog mess. Red was past caring what happened to him, but Arno decided to administer the same treatment and somehow, he wasn't sure how he got both Red and Fen to swallow and hold down soluble aspirin. He realised that they'd probably puke it up, but if he could get their temperatures down for a while.

He dried Fen off. She was barely conscious. He noted the scars on her back, briefly wondered where they had come from. Just as he had finished he could tell it was all about to begin again. He only just got her to the can in time as her bowels let loose. He nearly passed out from the stench but at least she wouldn't be lying in it this time. He hosed her down again and dried her off, and rubbed E-45 cream everywhere that was exposed to give her skin some protection. As he did so began to realise something. 'Rachel?'

He put one of his own T-shirts on Fen and wrapped a big towel around her before putting her back to bed. She lay curled up like a little child, no longer shivering – warm and momentarily safe. It seemed to him that her skin and eyes had taken on a jaundiced look. Did she have hepatitis? If so heaven help her. Arno placed a bowl within easy reach for her. He made her drink some of the re-hydration mix to replace lost fluids. He made sure there was a jug of water beside her bed for when she woke again.

Arno called out to Rachel once more. 'Rachel? I don't think this is the virus. It's something else. I really don't think...'

Fen was trying to say something to him. 'Red...'

'It's OK. I've cleaned him up too. Fen, just hang on, OK. You're our family now. You're part of us. You just hang tight – don't give in. You hear me?'

Fen nodded, her eyes closed.

Arno checked on Red who was sleeping now. He made sure an old ashtray was cleaned and filled with fresh water for him when he woke up. He'd need it.

Arno went down to his own bedroom, stripped off, took a quick shower as a security measure. He expected the worst any moment, but for the time being at any rate he remained unaffected. Dressed in T-shirt and shorts he went looking for Rachel. He didn't blame her for not coming up to help. She was probably afraid and she had every right to be.

'Rachel? I hope you've got that kettle boiled. I desperately need a cup of tea.'

Arno walked into the kitchen, saw the kettle boiling and turned it off. Rachel wasn't there. He frowned. 'Rachel?'

He looked out through the window, saw the trees swaying. A breeze was getting up. He briefly thought about making sure the yacht was secure. He thought he heard something in the back. He turned and walked towards the downstairs bathroom. 'Rachel? Babe? Are you OK? Rach?'

The stench was immediate and horribly familiar. Rachel was unconscious – still sat on the toilet, sweating, bloody vomit down her chest.

'Jesus.'

As Arno grabbed her to clean her off, he knew for certain that he'd be next.

18

Spanish Flu 1918-19
The first case can be traced to Camp Funston, Kansas, USA on 8 March 1918. This heralded the start of the pandemic which spread around the world in three waves. The first wave, in March to July of 1918, was relatively mild, causing only a small increase in the death rate. This was followed by the most devastating wave between September and December 1918, the virus having changed its character, perhaps in the rotting trenches of embattled France where thousands of unfortunate soldiers wallowed in filth for months at a time. The final wave came February to April 1919 – a virulent stage producing a sharp rise in death rates.

Dealmaker

Wylie sat in a small patch of sunshine watching the sky. He was still getting used to his new way of life on the Derbyshire Hotel roof garden. But you could tell from the sheen on his coat that he was beginning to recover and he wasn't so anxious anymore. Some weight gain was evident too.

Doc stood looking at a spreadsheet behind a plate glass window. He too felt strange in this environment, slightly awkward in his Armani suit although he stuck to his Converse sneakers – he rated comfort over appearance, despite his elevated position. Clean, well groomed, he was virtually unrecognisable from the shamonic man he had been before. He wasn't too happy keeping bankers' hours.

Or at least Dimitri hours, which ran on London time – New York time or whenever time, he wasn't entirely consistent. He'd noticed he was recovering, but far less quickly than his dog or Deka. Like his friend Deka, he'd discovered that he had been left with a persistent shortness of breath, entirely consistent with lung damage but annoying, particularly when it came to climbing stairs.

Two weeks had passed by in a blur. Power had been partially restored and was available for at least six hours a day, but rarely at night. The city was slowly getting organised, rationing was firmly enforced and although deliveries of foodstuffs and other items was still sporadic, the emergency services were still intact and functioning, again, mostly in daylight hours. The mayor had made it work, bashed a few heads together and if one lynchpin went down, was completely dispassionate about replacing people. It was what worked.

Vancouver was learning to live with some kind of tolerance and although people were still dying, to be sure, the numbers were falling and Doc knew, from experience that within a month it would be over completely. No one was going to come back from the dead, but at least then people could stop being afraid.

Deka appeared, wearing his cooks apron. He too was out of breath. 'Damn elevator is out again.' He collapsed into a chair to get his breath. 'Where's Dimitri?'

'Still with the Hong brothers. They're trying to get a better price out of him.'

Deka chuckled. 'Good luck to them, they've got no chance. Never met anyone so keen to get a deal. I still can't believe your sister married him. Not that I know what she is like.'

Doc shrugged. 'She wanted everything. She got it.'

Doc put the spreadsheet down and opened up a bottle of sparkling water, pouring both of them a glass. Deka nodded towards the spreadsheet curious as to its contents.

Doc took the bait. 'It's from the Mayor's office – City Disease Control'. Doc passed a glass of water to Deka and sat down opposite him. 'They're talking about a secondary problem developing all over the city. Salmonella. So much food has either gone off or contaminated good food. People have mostly discarded their frozen food but some of the dried food gets mixed with untreated water and...'

'The shit finally hits the fan.'

Doc smiled. 'Exactly. But if you got it bad before you could take someone to hospital. The stomach cramps can be pretty bad and jaundice can develop and liver failure. Combine that with people getting dehydrated and the almost total lack of hospital beds...'

Deka understood. 'We talking hundreds?'

'Thousands probably. There just aren't the hospital staff anymore and the virus took away most of the doctors and nurses. We don't have enough antibiotics, dressings or blood. You've seen the hospitals – they are choked with the virus survivors.'

Deka was surprised about that. 'How many survived the virus? I mean how did they?'

'Not many. Less than eight percent and they are in bad shape. They need 24 hour care. But they aren't getting it and with the power going out all the time. We're talking 25,000 in this city alone. My guess is…most will die.'

Deka agreed. 'They'll have to put them in schools, hotels. God, it's a second nightmare. I had heard they were shipping them out to the Okanagan.'

'No fuel, no drivers, no buildings to put them in. It was never going to happen.' Doc answered, then remembered his news. 'I heard from Leyla Aronovich.'

'The woman with the big house and guns?'

He smiled, happy Deka remembered. 'She's agreed to sell. Dimitri owns pretty much all of it. The bank called and they confirmed Dimitri's line of credit. He has access to billions, all backed by gold. He wasn't bullshitting, but…'

Deka smiled, gulping down some water and letting loose a giant burp as it hit the spot. 'You think it really is his money?'

Doc shrugged. 'Do I think he is honest?'

Deka pulled a face. 'I guess, I mean, do you trust him?'

Doc didn't answer at first, sipped his water and thought about it. 'A little, but I'm not sure he understands this city. He has ambitious plans, but I came here to get away from Russian life and people.'

'And now he's going to swamp us with them.'

'It's the way they do things. Never subtle.'

'You heard what he was saying last night.' Deka remarked. 'About the virus starting in Rügen in the Baltic Sea. That's where the swans all died of bird 'flu a few years ago. Dimitri says they were doing biological warfare experiments there back in 1951. Never cleaned up.'

Doc shook his head. 'Everyone knows they did experiments, but that was over fifty years ago. The swans have been breeding there for decades and never got sick before. This virus is the same as all the others in history. It comes, it goes. Sometimes it kills millions, sometimes it doesn't. This one started in China but it could have started anywhere. Don't look for conspiracies.'

Deka didn't respond. Sometimes Doc didn't like to see bad in anyone and anything, but Dimitiri had seemed pretty convinced all the same.

'I need to take a shower in a minute. Lock up behind you.' Doc told him.

Deka sighed. He still had to pinch himself that he was here, staying in the Derbyshire in a suite all to himself. Of course it was a ghostel, as Doc liked to call it.

No staff, no service, but it was comfortable. Deka had discovered that his role was to try to keep people well fed and watered. He was happy doing that. As long as he could get the raw materials. Luckily the Russian driver Dimitri had hired mostly stuck to himself, ate little and drank vodka in silence whenever he wasn't needed.

Doc's cell rang. He answered quickly, something Dimitri was quite insistent upon. The man lived for phone and email communications and was basically unbearable when the power was out.

Doc was listening and trying to squeeze in some answers. 'Of course. The money went to Kidbroke and Allen in London at 1pm our time, as instructed. Did you hear about the riots in Paris? The Government's fallen. They got the army out on the streets.

'The Agneau consortium made contact. I think they are very keen to sell. Beekman defaulted on the towers on Burrard and they got stuck with a $500 million hole. They will throw in their West Van and False Creek investments as a sweetener. They have about a billion dollar exposure in Vancouver all told and my guess is that they are desperate to do a deal.'

Dimitri laughed down the phone. 'Let them default, Alexi. We will pick it up for a fraction from Citibank. The point of this game is to find out who is left holding the cards and deal with them. They will be shitting themselves. No one gets it, my friend. Prices are falling like a stone and they are going to stay that way – for now. We closed the deal on Metrotown, Alexi. You were right, it's a good location. You should have seen how happy they were to get out from under. Pathetic. These people think it's the end of the world.'

Doc was reading the Mayor's bulletin. 'By the way, you're right, the Mayor's Office thinks this wave of the virus peaked on the 12th. You'll need to work fast before everyone works it out. But of course we haven't had the full effect of winter yet.'

Dimitri swore at something in the car he was travelling in and then came back to the phone. 'I'll be back at 5.15pm. Make sure Pittman is there and keep him happy.'

'He's already phoned. He's ready.'

'Excellent. Good work.' Dimitri disconnected. Doc glanced back up at Deka. 'I think we should have asked for more money, Deka Fortun.'

Deka laughed. 'Ja, people like him don't stop. I've seen them in my cab. Can never resist a deal. It's a sickness.'

Doc didn't disagree. Deka was right, but nevertheless here they were, in suits, helping a man buy their whole city from under them. It was like some crazy joke, any moment they expected a TV crew to burst in and say 'ha fooled you.' But then, right now there was no TV and it was all too real.

'I'm going to get rations. How many for dinner do you think?' Deka asked.

'Eight, maybe eleven, but they might not eat. Just make sure there's wine and some bits to nibble'.'

'Bits to nibble? Never thought I'd ever hear you say that, Doc. I'm not sure they offer 'bits' at the ration store, but I'll see what I can do. OK.'

Deka left shaking his head. Life had taken a strange turn here.

Doc went outside for some fresh air. Wylie turned, looked pleased to see him. Doc went over to the dog and sat beside him in the diminishing sunlight and stroked his fur. This was what he really wanted. A simple life – the sun with Wylie. Not this gangster world where desperate people sold out their futures to a man like Dimitri. Valentina had told him the day before she married the man that he was ambitious – Doc's complete opposite. That's what she wanted. A man who knew the price of everything.

It was gone past six pm already and the lawyers seemed nervous. They were all gathered in the restaurant. Deka hosting, keeping the 'bits' going and the wine flowing.

They all drank now. Somehow a rumour had gotten started that red wine was a good prophylatic against the virus and it steadied nerves in tough situations. And this was tough. Together the assembled group represented a large group of real estate owners and bankers representatives from the city and greater Vancouver. They were desperate to get a price, almost any price for their pieces of it. This was the only pawnshop in town and not a man or woman in the room didn't think that when times were back to normal they'd be able to redeem their possessions for a price less than what this crazy Russian was prepared to pay for it now. They were simultaneously nervous and smug in this situation. Sure of one thing, whatever they sold, land or buildings, the Russian couldn't exactly take them away with him.

The biggest sellers were the banks, looking to balance their books with Russian gold. Doc figured they were looking at several billion dollars of real estate here in good times. But good times had gone forever. Now they would be lucky to get ten cents on the dollar.

What chance did an ordinary guy with a mortgage to pay and no job have in this bear market? Dimitri was buying up mortgages wholesale too. He really aimed to get it all. A lot of people would get a shock some day soon. He wouldn't hesitate to foreclose on anyone.

'He is coming?' A banker queried with impatience.

'Delayed by a roadblock.' Doc reassured them. 'Seems some people are taking the law into their own hands. But he's through now.'

Others were sympathetic. 'No one obeys the law now. Houses are being looted, there aren't enough cops to go around and half the time it's them helping themselves.'

Everyone agreed on that. 'I thought they were supposed to shoot looters.' Was a common complaint.

Pittman, the big gun lawyer with a finger in everything was holding forth. Drinking too much, Doc thought, but then again, let him. Dimitri would eat him for lunch later.

'This cop comes to our offices. This was back in November right, when things were just falling apart. He's on duty, driving his vehicle alone, doing his regular patrol route through the city, when he got a call about a possible robbery in progress at Leverman's.'

'The gold dealers?' Someone asked.

'Yeah. Anyway, he arrives, and he knows his route pretty well – so he goes to the underground car park where he knows they take deliveries. There is a robbery in progress all right. But get this, it's cops. He recognises one of them and there they are loading up bullion, gold coins whatever there was. The alarms were ringing, but they knew no one was coming. Now my cop, names not important, he is in a quandary. But the other cops just nod. They politely give him a choice. Join them or die. The cameras are out, no one else is coming, they could shoot him and suffer no consequences or he could share. His choice.

'He agrees to a share, naturally. And by my auditors reckoning they walked out with something like 200 million in gold at today's prices.

'Next thing we know is that the cop comes to us, with the gold. He wants to protest his innocence 'protect his pension'. I try to tell him that his pension went south with the virus and he should probably just take the money because that's the last he's going to see for a while, but he is insistent.

'I asked him why he didn't go to Internal Affairs or whatever they're called and he tells me that two of the cops in the robbery run it. He'd actually gone there first and recognised them both. Luckily for him they didn't see him.

'So now we've got the gold, his statement of innocence and we make contact with Leverman and he's gone. Not dead. But gone. He knew this thing was going to blow up in our faces and he went to his place in Hornby Island to wait it out, thinking his gold was pretty secure in the time vault. No way to contact him of course.

'Then the cop's wife calls. He's dead. She says he left some money for her with us. We point out that it's stolen goods and she threatens to sue us.

'We meanwhile have alerted the Chief of Police about the theft and the names of those involved. He says, add it to the list. Turns out that some renegade cops have been systematically looting the city, block by block. Got calls from every company. You name it – jewels, gold, share certificates. Just helping themselves.

They arrest them. Find nothing. Nothing. Only evidence is my dead cop's testimony and the gold we are holding from Leverman's.

Cops are suspended. Can't put them away – the jails are closed and the law courts aren't in action either, so they can't even be prosecuted. So what happens? They disappear. All but one leaving their ugly wives and kids behind to face ignominy. End of story.

'My guess is, when things get back to normal, there's going to be a whole lot of collateral that people thought they had that isn't going to be there. Then they are going to turn to the insurance companies and they won't be there either. And then there will be foreclosures you wouldn't believe and major bankruptcies. It'll be like dominoes, one falling right after the other. And that's why, Dr Borov, I'm sitting here with you tonight, awaiting Dimitri, because I want to meet the man who thinks real estate is going to be worth something when this shit is over. Because frankly, I don't.'

Doc suddenly saw Dimitri and his driver go by in the outer lobby. He got a signal to come outside. Doc turned to Deka and gave him a sign. 'Those samosas ready? You have to try his samosas. Best I've tasted.'

Deka went to the pizza oven and their guests were momentarily distracted as Doc left the room.

Dimitri was lying on a sofa in the back room – his office when the electricity cut out. He looked washed out, pale, thoroughly exhausted.

'Meeting was tougher than I thought, Alexi. Those Chinese bastards really like to take it to the wire. Got it though. All signed. In my briefcase.' He winced as he swallowed. 'Never had to talk so much in my life. My throat is sore. Fix me up. That stuff you make. I have to stay on top of this. Big deal tonight.'

Doc frowned. 'How sore? Show me.'

'It's nothing. Just sore. Get me that stuff? Your magic soup. I need it.'

Doc sighed turned and left the room. He had his bag of tricks in the lobby. He'd already learned the hard way when the elevator stopped earlier in the week that he had to keep it with him on whatever floor he was on.

He returned. Dimitri was washing his face and hands.

'You're doing too much Dimitri. A body needs sleep, needs food. Your eyes are bloodshot. Did you eat anything today at all?'

'Fucking Chinese food. You know I hate dim sum. They get so offended when you won't eat their shit, but I drank the tea. Drank so much fucking tea.' He smiled briefly. 'I screwed 'em good. Not too tired for that.'

Dimitri wiped his face then and shrugged. 'Tonight, after this, I will sleep OK. After we sign. I will take a whole morning off. Have a sauna when the power is on. Do it right.'

'I'll hold you to it.'

'Now fix me up, Doctor Borov. I have deals to make and I've got a fucking headache and my wrists are sore. You're right. I'm tired. I never know when to stop. Valentina always makes me lie down, makes me rest.'

'Valentina was right. We often make bad decisions when we are tired. Now swallow this. Don't drink any alcohol tonight, OK? Let them drink, you nothing.'

Dimitri swallowed the liquid, made a proper grimace as he reacted to the foul taste, then calmly put his jacket on and adjusted his collar. He didn't like to wear a tie. It annoyed the bankers and distracted them. He liked anything that distracted them.

'You make proper Russian medicine, Alexi. That is disgusting stuff. Disgusting. Did I tell you we signed a deal for the Government offices? Tax, health, hospitals. They sold the lot; they are so desperate for money. Leaseback, guaranteed six percent for fifty years with inflation reviews. Like robbing the blind. I love doing business here.'

'You checked they hadn't already mortgaged them I hope? You can't trust them just because they are the government.'

'That's what took so long. But we got this city by the balls, Alexi.'

Doc said nothing. He often wondered if any of this stuff would hold up in court when the dust settled. Who was conning who in this game? He never got to see the actual financial transactions. He shrugged. Wasn't his business. Let his brother-in-law play king until the real prince appeared.

Dimitri felt his throat. 'Works. Damn stuff really works.'

Two tense hours with Dimitri on top form, Deka and Doc watched him with astonishment as he worked the room, picking one off, then another, pitting one against the other. Hard-faced lawyers pulped to mush with piss poor deals, all sweetened with backhanders (diamonds, gold bullion, whatever it took), pulling every trick and some no one had seen before. They watched as a city changed hands, lot by lot, street by street. Dimitri had done his research. Whatever they thought they could get per square foot six months before was just fantasy island now. Dimitri liked to knock noughts off in this new situation and it hurt everyone in the room.

'In 1886', Dimitri told them, 'Vancouver burned to the ground. It all vanished and just a few days later people were building, laying out new streets and lots and it was open for business. That's the kind of city I love. You'll see; the city will live again, it will build again. You will all come back to me and beg me to sell you back your office blocks and your hotels and shopping malls.'

Pittman smiled at that fantasy. 'And we'll offer you ten cents on the dollar Dimitri and see if you like it.'

Dimitri laughed, but no one else did. The room was full of men and women who had the distinct impression of having been thoroughly fleeced.

Doc gathered signed documents, witnessed all, date stamped them and the warrants that guaranteed their validity.

Dimitri had arranged for a security officer to come and escort them out – get them through curfew. He was particular about all the little details. Their guests left bewildered but impressed. Confident in their judgement that the Russian was a fool with his money.

It was only afterwards, when Doc and Deka had tidied up and secured the building that they noticed Dimitri was gone. Doc went to the back room and found him lying on the day bed clutching his head. He was sweating, his hands shaking. Doc didn't like the look of him at all.

'Sleep here, Dimitri. Can I get you something?'

'I'm just exhausted.' But it didn't sound like that to Doc.

Deka appeared at the door. He had some hot chocolate in a mug. 'You look beat. I thought this might help you sleep.'

Dimitri took it and sipped, but his throat was closing up and it hurt too much. Doc frowned. 'You wore your mask today, Dimitri?

Dimitri pointed at it lying on the table. 'Still got some hours to go. It's good.'

'Did you shake hands with anyone?' Doc asked.

'No. Never. You know I took precautions.'

'But you ate something?' Doc queried, seemingly keeping it casual.

'I told you I only had tea. Fucking endless cups of green tea.'

'Was anyone sick there? That you know of?'

'No. Look this is exhaustion. That's all. I'm forty-five now. I get tired. I just need a little sleep. You'll see, I'll bounce back tomorrow.'

Doc looked at Deka, he could see he'd reached the same conclusion he had. 'Deka, go check on his driver. Room 214.'

Deka nodded and quit the room. Doc waited a moment then felt Dimitri's pulse. It wasn't good and he was clammy.

'Listen to me. I can make you up something. The same stuff I gave Deka and myself. It protected us. Didn't cure it, but we lived through it. I know it works, Dimitri.

Dimitri opened his eyes. 'I am protected. This is exhaustion. I have taken everything I need. I know you want to help but THN-9 works, Alexi. I have a booster upstairs. Get me the booster. They warned me in Moscow. Told me to expect this.'

'Our virus may be a different mutation to what you are used to. You've been exposed for two weeks, a bit more now. You haven't rested, you don't eat properly and you run risks meeting people.'

Dimitri struggled to sit up to face Doc. He was shivering and distinctly feverish now, sweat pouring around his eyes and neck.

'You feel nauseous?' Doc queried. He could see Dimitri was struggling with something. Doc grabbed an ice bucket standing in the corner and rushed it over. Dimitri suddenly lurched forward violently vomiting into it. Doc noted the bright blood from his lungs.

Dimitri stared at the contents of the bucket with horror. 'No.'

'Yes. You must let me inoculate you. I know it works, Dimitri. It is proven.'

'Get my booster.'

'It's probably too late for that. It might make you worse.'

Deka returned, breathless from the run up and down the stairs. He entered the room, could smell the vomit, it was all too damn familiar.

'Shav is dead. Been dead for at least an hour, my guess. It's the virus, for sure.'

Doc knew something else now. He knew that everyone in that room who'd made a deal with Dimitri this very evening had been lethally exposed to him. They had all breathed his air, had argued with him, pressed their points home and even if they didn't shake on it, they had used the same pen, done countless small things, any of which could have been lethal to them.

'Dimitri, let me help you.'

Dimitri responded by vomiting again, but still shook his head. 'Get me my booster. Alexi. My Blackberry. Get my Blackberry. Guard it well.'

Deka went to Dimitri's jacket on the wall and dug in his pockets. Pulled out the beloved Balckberry. 'Got it. It's safe.' He gave it to Doc.

Doc shrugged, looking again at Deka. 'I'll get your booster dose. But I have to walk up to the top floor. I'll will take thirty minutes. You understand? My chest is weak Dimitri. It's a long way. Try and get some sleep OK. Just lie back, try to sleep. Deka will stay nearby. Right? It will take time. It's a long climb.'

Deka nodded, taking the bucket to empty it in the bathroom next door.

Doc left. He knew it was a wasted journey. A booster wouldn't do anything but give him more of the virus. Who knew what was in it?

The generator packed up when he was less than half way up the stairs and the lights failed. He swore, but he wasn't going to go back down to the basement to fill up the tank. He continued upwards, knowing with every step that Dimitri was closer to death. The virus acted quickly and he'd had a long run of luck. Whatever they had in the Russian vaccine was potent stuff, but clearly not resistant to the Canadian strain of the virus. It was worth observing that there was a difference.

A vaccine could be made easily enough now, but not quickly enough for their dealmaker.

He reached the top exhausted. His chest hurt, as if a spike had been driven through it. His eyes were watering. He knew he wouldn't be able to go down again for a few minutes, his legs would simply give way. It would take months to get his strength back, he knew that now. His chest pounded, he could barely fill his lungs with air and he felt nauseous. He realised that he had to get some candles lit, he couldn't see a damn thing. Dimitri would just have to hang on, there was no choice in the matter.

Deka had cleaned up when he finally returned. Doc was sweating profusely from the climb down – his head and chest tight with pain. He stood at the door lighted candle in hand, reacting to the stench of bleach. Doc staggered to a chair to sit and collapsed, legs shaking quite visibly now.

'Where is he?' Doc whispered, looking around the room.

Deka nudged his head towards the back of the room. 'Over there.'

Doc strained to see in the gloom and was astonished to discover that Deka had already wrapped Dimitri in a tablecloth and tied both ends.

Deka poured Doc some tea, poured himself a cup as well. 'He died about five minutes after you left the room. I called after you but you didn't hear I suppose.'

Doc took up his tea and held it tight between his hands, glad of the heat and steam on his face. He said nothing for a moment. Deka sat opposite him, seemingly composed. Doc felt a lump in his pocket and took out Dimitri's Blackberry. He realised now that Dimitri had realised he was dying, wanted him to know that his Blackberry would be needed now.

A shot rang out outside. They could hear shouting. They knew the hotel doors were secure. Neither one of them could be bothered to check it out. Happened all the time now. Deka sipped his tea and looked contemplative.

'You remember when you told me that one day we'd have a choice on who gets to keep which side of the city?'

Doc frowned looking at Deka, then slowly he began to smile, remembering.

Deka poured more tea and smiled. 'I think that time has come, Doc. Which side do you want?'

Doc lay back in his chair and thought about it, then suddenly, he laughed. Deka joined in. The absurdity of their situation, all the more funny because it was so stupidly real.

'The sunny side,' Doc said at last thinking of his bones. 'I want the sunny side.'

Deka grinned. They toasted with the tea and sat back, silent, pondering their future.

Sam North

19

Spanish Flu 1918: The Spreading
Disease spread could be traced to routes of individual ships, along railway lines and even to the postman delivering mail to isolated communities. Reports of whole families dying, up to ninety percent of individual communities, and sixty percent of the total Eskimo population, can be found.

Many cities and towns ground to a halt as there were insufficient healthy people to run services; medical facilities were overwhelmed with sick people and the number of deaths led to a shortage of coffins and introduction of mass burial in some areas, to remove the chance of further public health problems.
National Institute of Medical Research (NIMR)

Nightwatch

Red woke her, barking in the garden below. She stirred in her bed, her nostril assailed by the stench of her soiled sheets and the dried vomit beside her. Her mouth was desperately dry, her eyes practically glued together and she felt like a truck had dragged her a couple of miles, but whatever it had been – it was definitely gone.

She crawled out of her bed, unable to remember where the T-shirt she was wearing had come from. Her legs felt like rubber and when she sat up and looked at her stomach and arms she knew she had lost a lot of weight; she was vaguely pleased about that.

Red was still barking but it was his frustrated bark, not a scared one and a good sign that he was better too. Fen staggered to the window, gave it a shove and looked out. The air smelled fresh. Red was chasing a butterfly, looking well, didn't seem to have a care in the world. Fen wondered where Rachel and Arno were. There was a vague feeling of panic then. What if she was alone now? What if they had got whatever she had and died? She instantly dismissed this thought – if they had died or thought they were dying they would have left her a note.

She wondered too how long she had been out of it. Then she saw herself in the mirror and got a shock. She'd lost way too much weight, her hips jutted out, her face was pale, her hair looked lifeless. She could have been a ghost. Just how ill had she been? She let out an involuntary moan.

There wasn't much water pressure, but she took a lukewarm shower and it felt astonishingly good to be clean. She saw that she had scratch marks on her chest where there had been a rash, just the remains of it still visible but her skin felt rough and she didn't like the feel of her flesh under her fingers at all.

She towel dried her hair and then stripped her bed, did her best to make the room smell sweeter, opening every window, discovering there was quite a stiff breeze outside. She knew she was being a coward now. At any time she could have called out Arno or Rachel's name, but there was one part of her that was afraid to discover the truth. The silence downstairs didn't help any.

She found the note from Arno in her sneakers. It took her ten whole minutes to pluck up courage to read it.

Fen,
We all have salmonella poisoning. I figure it was the chicken fritters we defrosted. Do not touch or eat any frozen food.

If you are reading this you are well again. Great.

Eat little at first, have plenty of fluids. Rachel took ill soon after you did and I expect the worst to happen to me any moment now.

There is a distinct, but slim possibility we could die. I pray not.

If we are alive when you awake, get fluids into us at all costs. This isn't the virus; you can touch us without fear. Make sure the turbine switch is on – it has a tendency to switch itself off. If on your own, make sure the yacht is secure.

Survive here as long as you can. Do not go back to the mainland until you get an all clear on the radio and even then make sure it is legit.
Be strong, be well. I am very proud of you, Fen.
All my love
Arno x

Fen read it one more time, realising she was crying and shaking. She sat down on the floor – suddenly intensely scared that she was alone. Almost too scared to go downstairs to check. She heard Red barking again and that reassured her a little. Not alone as long there was Red to care for and he had her.

Salmonella. She knew about that. Knew instantly why she had been in so much pain. She remembered May had been in so much pain she had wanted to die. She'd eaten eggs and in the middle of the night they had rushed her to the hospital. For a second she could see May, twisted with pain in the hospital bed and their mother crying, Mercer pacing, only for the image to dissolve to Mercer taking May away in the boat to Victoria. She wondered if they were still alive. She didn't think so, down deep, didn't think about them at all now.

But what if she really was alone? Just her and Red. That was scary, like being the last person left alone in the world – a century of loneliness opened up before her.

She ran downstairs; she had to know. Didn't want to be alone, not now, not now she had been found. 'Rachel? Arno?'

Rachel lay in a foetal position on a mat by the bathroom door. She was awake but chronically dehydrated, barely able to move. Fen could see in her eyes that she was desperately glad to see her.

'Arno, you must help Arno' Rachel croaked. Fen ignored her. She hauled her up to a sitting position, made her drink water. She opened a window, emptied the bowls of vomit and flushed the toilet a few times to get it working again, prodding at it to force stuff down. Rachel was surprisingly clean. She'd chosen her spot well, managing to get to the toilet each time. She was painfully thin now, she seemed to have shrivelled. They both had. When Fen removed her nightshirt she had the same rash that she had, but brighter more livid, right across her chest and half way down her back.

Fen found a clean shirt to put on her and once she'd made Rachel pee, she walked her gently to her bed, where she crept in and fell asleep almost at once, just like a child.

'I'll go and find Arno,' Fen whispered. 'I'll be back OK. Sleep now.'

Fen washed her hands, wishing she had taken the first-aid course they had offered at school. She wondered what state Arno would be in, prayed he would be alive.

She found him lying naked on the floor in the generator room. He was out cold. He'd probably had been trying to get the generator back on. Fen flipped the switch and it immediately kicked in. It made her feel more in control; there would be hot water again and electric light.

Arno was freezing cold. She had no idea how long he'd been lying there but strangely there was no sign of vomit or excrement, but he did have the same rash on his chest. She found herself staring at him and his nakedness, so vulnerable and so cold. She noted the tiny tattoo, a little Tin-Tin rocket on his shoulder blade. Made her smile.

Fen knew he'd be too heavy for her to move him, or lift, but she remembered a game she and May used to play when they were younger and she went to get a rug.

Back in the generator room, she lay the rug down beside Arno, rolled him over onto it, which took more effort than she had thought possible and then, she dragged him out of there, took him to the dining room, just off from the downstairs toilet. She got rugs, pillows, made him as comfortable as she could and then did what her mother would have done for her, made him a hot water bottle. She had seen it in the bathroom earlier. Boiled the water and wrapped it in a pillow-case and then placed it on his stomach. It was a gentle way to wake up and take some of the pain away from his stomach. Worked for her when she had a tummy ache – didn't see why it wouldn't help him.

Indeed, ten minutes of heat and Arno began to stir. Fen was ready with some fresh water. Had a straw in his mouth and made him drink. He didn't open his eyes, but he took in a full glass of water before falling asleep again and Fen left him a while. Better to sleep, stay warm and wake when his body was ready again.

She went to the kitchen. Red was there, sat by his upended bowl. He looked at her with such surprise he didn't move for a second, then, as if launched from space, he pounced upon her, trying to lick her and bury his head in her, and whimpering like a lost puppy. He was so happy to have her back; so desperate to let her know how much he had missed her. Fen hugged him and discovered she was crying. 'It's OK, Red, it's OK, we're still together, we're still here.'

Red wrapped his paws around her and stared at her a moment.

'Yes, I know, you love me and you are hungry. You hungry, baby boy?'

Red just licked her one more time and she laughed. Fen stood up and began to hunt for something for the two of them. Naturally she found cookies but now she was pretty thorough in checking the dates of stuff. She never wanted to be sick again as long as she lived. She tossed Red some oatmeal rusks. She was going to have to be inventive.

'We got rice, we got noodles, we got hmm... God, we don't have much.'

Red didn't care at this moment. He had Fen back and that made him feel better all over. 'We have mint tea. Yay. I'll make some tea. Let's go check the garden, Red. Must be something to eat there.'

It was breezy outside, quite chilly actually, winter was coming. Fen and Red ventured to the kitchen garden and she noted some of the lettuces were going to seed. She cut one down and uprooted an onion. That would have to do. Sliced, lightly boiled and served with some water biscuits it would make something acceptable for her at least. Rachel and Arno wouldn't be eating yet.

Inside again she found Arno had already emptied the refrigerator and anything that could kill them and the freezer section was empty too. Clearly if the power wasn't regular, things could go off.

'You eat tuna?' She asked Red.

Red kinda looked as though he'd eat anything – so she opened the can and mixed it in with some more rusks. He ate without any trouble at all and then drank a ton of water. Red at least was well again.

An hour later she tried to get Rachel drinking some mint tea. 'My mother used to say it helps with cramps, calms the stomach.'

Rachel took the cup, grateful for anything. She heard music coming from downstairs. 'You got the power back on?'

'Just flipped the switch. Quite a breeze. Hope the turbine doesn't blow away.'

'I sent Arno down to switch it back on.' Rachel remembered suddenly.

'He must have fallen,' Fen informed her. 'When did you send him down?'

Rachel couldn't remember. They both seemed to have lost track of time. Suddenly she was crying, sipping her tea and crying, big fat rollers pouring down her cheeks.

'He's going to be fine,' Fen reassured her, although she didn't know that for sure. She held Rachel's hand and let her cry on her shoulder. Rachel felt so overwhelmingly sad all of a sudden, as if the whole world was on her chest. She felt stupid. They were alive; they'd survived another test. There was nothing to cry about.

'I'm going to look for a good fishing spot tomorrow. We need fresh fish.'

Rachel nodded, staying where she was, comforted by Fen's presence and her calm acceptance of everything that happened to her.

Fen let her remain until she fell asleep again. She lay Rachel back down and made sure she was warm, then headed on back downstairs. There was stuff to do.

'Red?'

Red looked up from the dining room floor where he lay next to Arno. Fen smiled. He'd remained exactly where she'd told him. 'Good boy. Come on, let's get some fresh air.'

Two more days went by. Fen nursed her charges, washed them, fed them vegetable soup she had made herself from fresh vegetables and beef stock cubes.

Another Place to Die

Arno's fever had broken but he was incredibly lethargic. He seemed to have suffered in a different way to both Rachel and herself. A high temperature and much groaning, but he'd also suffered pain in his eyes and arms, his joints in particular, his fingers felt swollen to him, although Fen couldn't see anything different. He loved the hot bottle and she kept it warm for him as it really did take the pain away from his stomach. He switched in and out of pain and slept or groaned depending on how it took him.

Rachel nursed him now, still uncomfortable and bugged by a determined headache, but she at least had him in bed beside her and they were on the road to recovery. As slow as it was. It made Rachel very conscious of how precarious island life could be if one got ill. How easily one might easily perish without someone there to care for you.

Fen realised she had lost her sense of time. It was a day or two later. Rachel and Arno were taking their time to recover, Arno most of all. The bug seemed to have affected them all in different ways. She had recovered quickly, but then she was the youngest and arguably the fittest of the three.

On rainy days she filled in time exploring the massive cellar that seemed to cough up an endless cornucopia of stuff, some of it dating back a hundred years at least. Books, objects, weird junk that seemed to have no purpose, and several typewriters that belonged in a museum. On better days she was outside tending the garden, weeding and making decisions about what she would let go to seed so they could grow more in the spring. Fen had acknowledged that she would be there in the spring and it didn't faze her one bit. She dreaded having to go back to the city or school or any part of her old life. She liked this new life just fine for now. Red loved it too and he had discovered a spot where he liked to swim out for the sticks she tossed into the ocean. Sometimes Fen joined him, although it was bitterly cold now.

She was happy, almost for the first time in her life and at peace. This little island was a secret place, unlikely to attract attention. She felt safe at last.

She and Red had explored almost every inch and that was when they found the ideal fishing rock, overhanging a sheer drop of twenty feet or so suspended over a deep inlet pool. She'd made a line and fashioned some kind of hook and although she hadn't quite perfected a bait they might like or a grip to reel them in, if they took it, she knew a good spot when she saw one and anticipated big catches to come.

It was when taking a wrong turn from the rock that Red had found an old path higher up the cliff. It was overgrown now but it once had been clearly defined. Fen made her way through brambles and tall weeds and until she found a natural space in the lee of the island where wild roses climbed everywhere. In the middle was a weather-beaten bench with a white rock set up before it as a footstool. It must have been 'her' spot. Her place to write. Even though the wind was brisk, in this oasis, it was warm, completely free of any wind. It was quiet and when Fen and Red sat on the bench they found they were staring through an overgrown fig tree at the ocean and the islands beyond, far, far in the distance. Fen loved this spot. The afternoon sun found it easily and she luxuriated in its warmth as she ate late evergreen huckleberries as sweet as any she had ever tasted. Little tight clusters of berries. They were pasty pink, curiously salty to taste on the outside from exposure to the misty ocean air.

On the second day, she had collected berries for everyone and cleared branches of the fig tree to get a better view of the ocean. It was during this reclamation project that she found the sundial and surrounding it, in a big circle the word *Giselle* spelt out in seashells set in slate. She puzzled over who Giselle might be. A daughter? Lover? A long lost pet?

She felt inspired by this place and resolved to focus her mind on all the things that had happened to her. She began a diary. It seemed time to do so.

She began a plan of how she might write her diary. So much had happened to her, it was so hard to recall dates and events precisely, but she was afraid she'd forget unless she wrote it all down. So she made a planned index of dates with cryptic sentences so that she had it right from the start. Where was the beginning of her story? Mercer deciding to build the cabin on the island or, the tragedy of her mother dying so suddenly. Or the day May decided never to speak to her again or the first day she met Red, three years earlier. She pondered on all of that – what was the beginning of Fen and what bits did you leave out and who would read it? If anyone.

She awoke with a start. Red was sat close to her on the bench, nervous about something. Fen realised she was sweaty from where Red had been sleeping leaning against her and aware that the sun was setting. She dropped the diary, guiltily realising that she had hardly written a word.

'What's wrong, Red?' Red jumped off the bench and peed, whining a little, and anxious to get her to move for some reason.

'What?'

Fen stood up stretched and then realised that the ocean had changed. It was pretty choppy out there, white crests as far as the eye could see. She took only a few steps from the bench and was hit with the full force of the wind sweeping across the island. 'Jesus. Oh my god, Red, it's a like a full on storm. Let's go. Arno and Rachel will be freaked.'

Fen picked up her diary and the plastic container filled with berries. She ran after her dog, totally amazed at how quickly the weather had changed.

Red was ahead of her, pelting down the path, jumping over anything that got in his way. Fen crested the hill and was surprised to see huge waves crashing against the jetty and the rocks by the headland. Sea spray was carried all the way to the house. The yacht, though secured to the jetty, was nevertheless heaving and straining against the timbers, as it received a heavy battering from the sea.

She reached the house, breathless and damp from the ocean spray. It took all her strength to close the door behind her. She slid the bolt over to make sure it stayed that way. The house was creaking, windows rattling as it protested against the wind.

'Rachel?' Fen shouted. 'Rach?'

She heard a noise in the living room and Red went to investigate. Fen followed, aware she could smell pine burning.

Rachel was sat on a kid's stool in front of the fireplace building a log fire. She looked like a wraith, so painfully thin wrapped in the old woman's silver dressing gown. But at least Fen could tell she had showered and done her hair. Rachel was on the mend at last, wanting to do things. She was looking at a silver framed picture of a child.

'Thought you might have been blown away out there, Fen. It's a huge storm. Did you see the waves crashing over the rocks? The whole house shudders y'know.'

'I know. What you got there?'

'Giselle. Pretty, huh. Could be her niece. Taken about five years ago.'

Fen joined her, she briefly looked at the image of a blonde girl with a funny hat staring out at the camera. How weird she'd just found her name written in sea-shells. She wondered where she was now, if she was already dead.

Red flopped down beside the sofa with a stick he'd brought in with him. 'Arno better?' Fen asked.

Rachel smiled at her. 'Thanks to you. He ate your soup. Even wanted more. I think I am going to have to get you to write your recipes down.'

Fen laughed. 'Not my recipes. Hers, the old lady. I think she really lived on the stuff she grew. There's a recipe for every kind of soup. I found her recipe books in the cellar. Did I tell you I found the pumpkin patch? We have about eight pumpkins and they'll make great soup.'

Rachel took Fen's hand and squeezed it. 'Thank you, Fen. I really don't think I would have got better without you. Really. You are an angel.'

Embarrassed, Fen stood up looking at the rattling windows. 'I have to get the shutters closed and the windows fastened. Don't sit too close to the fire, Rachel. That dressing gown might not be fireproof. It's too shiny to be safe.'

Rachel looked at the gown and realised that Fen was right. She quickly discarded it, revealing just how much weight she had lost in her illness. She was quite conscious of it. Fen took the gown from her and threw it onto the sofa where Red grabbed it and dragged it down to the floor.

Fen looked at the logs and frowned. 'You think we have enough to last the winter?'

Rachel considered it a moment. 'There's a huge pile down by the jetty. I think she had a couple of cords delivered. I know you don't want us to cut down your precious trees.'

Fen smiled. She realised that they both already knew how proprietary she had become over the island. 'There's some that have to be thinned out but...'

Rachel reassured her. 'But there's a shed that's rotting too and if the wind doesn't take it, we can burn that first. Besides, the turbine heats us and let's face it, it's pretty much windy every day.'

'Got to go.' Fen declared. 'Oh yeah. I brought these.'

She opened the container filled with the huckleberries. 'Try one.'

Rachel was nervous to try. 'My stomach's still delicate.'

'They are fresh and salty and full of vitamin C. You need to get fresh stuff inside you, Rachel. Both of you do.'

Rachel tried one. A real look of surprise came over her face. 'Wow, sweet, weird salty skin. Nice.'

Fen smiled, leaving the container for her. 'Maybe try Arno with some. Might just wake him up a little.'

'I think he's just enjoying being a lazy bum,' Rachel remarked. But when she looked up she realised she was alone.

Red stayed with her gown, gazing at the flames licking the logs. Rachel dragged the fireguard over and placed it in front of the fire. She wondered how Fen was always so practical and sensible. She had never been like that at her age. Not even now.

She looked at Red, who yawned and rolled over for her to scratch his tummy. Rachel complied. 'And you're a happy soul too. You're a lucky dog, Red. You know that? A very lucky dog.'

Fen had gone out by the back door and gone right around the house closing the shutters, making sure everything was secure. The storm doors to the cellar were a bit flappy, but she piled stones and bricks on them, which would do, she hoped. The temperature was dropping and the wind was growing more fierce. She was afraid for the yacht, but in the dark she couldn't see anything anymore and there was little she could do about it anyway.

Fen was about to go back in when lightning struck, hit a tree above the house. She waited for fire to break out, but it didn't, and in that instant, as the inevitable thunder rolled overhead, the rain broke, drenching her and the little island. Fen ran for the back door, happy the vegetables would get a soaking and that the well would be replenished. The rain fell with such force it was almost painful and she was glad to get back into the dry kitchen. Rachel was making tea and looked at her in astonishment.

'God, you're drenched.' She threw a towel at Fen who took it gratefully.

'Lightning struck a tree. Storm's right over us.'

'I heard. Arno was calling. Can you go up to him? Take the tea. There's one for you as well.'

Fen pulled off her sweater and shorts – had no qualms about being naked in front of Rachel. They were both darn skeletons anyway – pass for supermodels if they were taller. She put a coat on from behind the door. It looked ridiculous but at least it was dry.

'I'll get those dried. Take the tea up and then come back down and get warm by the fire. Deal?'

Fen smiled. 'Bet Red's there already. Can't tear him away from a warm fire.'

Sure enough, she saw him splayed out in the living room as she made for the stairs. She smiled all the way up the stairs, carefully balancing the mugs of tea

Arno was dressed in two sweaters and a pair of shorts – standing in darkness by the window. Fen took the tea over to him – stood beside him as he stared out across the ocean. She could hear his breathing, still wheezy for some reason.

'There's a boat out there. Saw a distress flare.'

Fen stared with him. Immediately she was worried. She didn't want anyone to come. No one. Ever.

'Storm's fierce. I really don't think the yacht is tied securely enough but then, neither is the jetty.' Arno continued.

'You want me to check it out?'

'No. Well, later maybe. When the rain stops. I told Rachel to keep the lights off. I don't want them to find us.' He paused a moment. 'Sorry, that sounds harsh.'

Fen was relieved. He was thinking like her. She said nothing.

Lightning flashed, forking left and right, a violent explosion in the atmosphere. For a complete second they could see the jetty, the yacht rising high as a wave swept ashore and the driving rain. Then blackness and ten seconds later another rolling crack of thunder.

'We're going to lose the yacht aren't we?' Fen whispered.

'There. Did you see it? A boat. Must be big.'

Fen saw it. Didn't like it. It was way too close, even though it was still a distance away. She began to pray in her head for them to miss the island. 'God you don't have to sink them, but let them pass by, let them pass by.'

Arno sipped his tea and stayed staring out of the window.

'Did I thank you for saving me yet?'

Fen allowed herself a tight smile. 'You saved me first.'

Arno nodded. 'We have to look after each other. This thing is a long way from over, Fen.'

'What if they come? The people on the boat?'

The lightning flashed again, further away now. Arno looked at Fen, took her hand and squeezed it. 'We have the shotgun but this isn't Salt Spring. We just have to hope they miss us.'

'But if they don't'

'We will have to hope no one aboard has the virus. We are weaker than we were. It would get us fast. You'd have to hope to die quickly.'

'Not much of a choice.'

'No.'

'I started a diary today.'

Arno drank more of his tea. 'Then I really hope that you get to continue it.'

Fen finished her tea. 'Did you want a hand to get downstairs. Rachel's got a fire going.'

Arno was about to decline when he changed his mind. 'Yeah. I'd like that.'

Fen took his arm and guided him to the door.

'I found a great spot for fishing. Not quite worked out how to make them bite though.'

'There's a fishing rod in the cellar you know and all kinds of tackle. Might be a bit big for you, but perhaps we could set something up. Rachel tells me you are quite a fisher er person, whatever.'

Fen laughed. 'Fisherman. No one is ever a fisherperson. I hope.'

Downstairs the fire was roaring, Rachel had potatoes wrapped in tinfoil beside it and it was homely. Getting Red to make space was harder, but eventually he gave way.

'This is what life must have been like before TV,' Fen remarked quite seriously.

Rachel thought about it. 'I like it. We'll have to talk to each other and sing or something.'

'Charades', Arno suggested.

Fen giggled. But she noted none of them ever referred to the boat in distress outside on the ocean. All eyes studiously avoided the front door and what might be out there.

Two hours later, the rain stopped as quickly as it started. The clouds were moving swiftly and a bright moon could be glimpsed now and then, brightly illuminating their island. Rachel and Arno were asleep by the fire and Fen wanted to keep them that way.

She put another log on the fire, replaced the guard and tiptoed to the kitchen. Even Red didn't notice her go. She ignored her shoes and just put on Arno's old Arran sweater, slipping out the back quietly.

The wind was still pretty fierce and most likely wouldn't blow out until the morning, but she wanted to make sure the yacht was still there. If they had to escape, she wanted to know they could.

It was jet black out there. Typically the moon had vanished the moment she went outside. She made her way down to the jetty and could feel and see that the waves had made a real mess of everything. Now she knew why nothing grew in this part of the island.

She reached the jetty just as the moon appeared for a brief thirty seconds. She froze. There *was* someone there. Fen's heart stopped. There was a man on the jetty. She didn't move a muscle. Just stayed there buffeted by the wind waiting for the next glimpse of moonlight.

It came at last. The man was still there. He hadn't moved. He wasn't going to move. She realised that he was most likely drowned. She looked down at the beach area and the rocks there and thought she saw another. But no one was moving or making a sound.

She didn't want to go near them, in case. But didn't want to go back either. She'd come to check the yacht, so made her way towards it. She jumped aboard and she could see immediately that the hatch was open. Accident or forced? Was someone inside? She found some loose metal on the deck and tossed it down there. She heard it clunk against something, but there was no reaction. She heard a sudden roar behind her and turned in time to see a huge wave bearing down on her and the yacht. She had no time to leap off, she jumped to the mast and gripped it hard as the wave engulfed her.

Water poured down the hatch into the yacht and if there had been anyone in there, they would drown, for sure. Suddenly, as the wave withdrew, so did the jetty. The yacht, with a wrenching groan suddenly was set free and with a rapid motion, moved away from the island, swept by the force of the ocean. Fen realised that she was adrift, every second the yacht was moving further away from the shore. Her thoughts raced. She had to save the yacht, but she didn't even know how to get it started. Didn't even know if it would start, it was so full of water.

The moon came out again and then she saw it. A face staring at her from the hatchway. A man's face. Then it was gone again. There *had* been a man in there!

This yacht could not be saved by her. She looked back at the island and realised that they had already gone fifty yards. She had to jump. She had to get back or be lost.

Sam North

She looked in vain for the lifebuoy, but could see nothing and then, the choice was abruptly no longer hers. Another huge wave hit the yacht broadside and as the boat rolled, she was flung into the ocean, plunging deep into freezing water.

She surfaced, only to discover the current was taking her away. She struck out for the island, aware that the heavy sweater was dragging her down. Taking a sodden Arran wool sweater off in water is no easy task and twice she went under trying to pull it off. She felt panic rising. She had to swim; she had to keep moving. Something hit her back. She twisted around and it was some object off the yacht. She swore, but somehow the sweater came off at last and she kicked free, crawling with every last ounce of her strength towards land.

There was a light ahead. Flashlight. She made for that. But then, as the yards closed, she remembered Arno had said no lights. Who was using the flashlight?

Now the rolling waves were carrying her forward and she picked up speed. She was aware that there were rocks ahead. The man on the jetty had made it, but perhaps the rocks had got him first. But then again, perhaps he wasn't dead? Perhaps he had been just lying there exhausted and now he was up with a flashlight waiting for her.

She heard barking. Red!

But it was to her left and she was moving right, at speed to the edge of the island. She was suddenly aware that the current was taking her past the island and out to sea. She turned, put her last energy into a spurt towards a jutting rock. A wave crashed over her, but she kept on, her strength ebbing, she closed her eyes, thought of Red, thought of the island and that warm log fire inside the house.

She hit a rock, practically knocked herself out cold. She cried out. Clung on, but was dazed for a moment. Then there was splashing, someone was coming towards her. One the zombies was coming for her. She let out a strangled cry of terror and nearly went under as she forgot to kick. The beast was suddenly upon her and Red was there, whining, concentrating hard on staying afloat, but right there, with her.

'Red. Red. I can't believe it. Red.'

Arno finally made his way onto the rocks and got a hand to her and pulled the two of them out. He fell back exhausted as a naked Fen and a slimy wet dog collapsed beside him. They said nothing. Couldn't speak. Could barely move, but they had to and they scrambled back to safer land.

Arno paused where the jetty had been. 'I don't suppose you brought my sweater back?'

Fen said nothing. She was looking for the bodies.

'The sea took probably them back. I saw one.' Arno told her, sweeping the beach area with the flashlight. There were no bodies to be seen. Not a one.

They made their way back to the house and the warmth of the fire.

'I couldn't save the yacht,' Fen finally muttered, shivering.

'Nothing could. You were crazy to try. Just get warm, Fen. We're alive. Whoever they were, they are no longer. Let's stay alive for as long we fucking can. OK? That's our job now. Staying alive.

Fen nodded. Yes as long as they fucking could.

'We need towels and blankets here,' Arno was yelling as they entered the kitchen.

20

Beneath is all the fiend's: there's hell, there's darkness,
There is the sulphurous pit – burning, scalding,
Stench, consumption, fie, fie, fie, pah, pah!
King Lear Act 1V W. Shakespeare

Tread Softly and carry a Big Stick

It was one thing being lord of your domain. Another thing making it legal. For that Doc had discovered he and Deka needed passports, birth certificates, and proof of citizenship and most likely blood types. The world dies but bureaucracy continues. Doc had already been to the gallery (and indeed secured it for posterity) and found the building secure. Doc found he was busy all the time, trying up all the loose ends left by Dimitri. He'd tried to reach his sister in Moscow but found no answer from any emails or many attempts to phone her. He preferred to think the networks were down rather than the worst.

Another Place to Die

What he had found was that Dimitri had opened a door and a lot of people were keen on cashing out of the city, not taking the long view. With Dimitri gone, the line of credit dried up. Doc was able to consolidate what they had and by trading some parts of the parcels with those who were ambitious to build their own little property empires, the books were squared. They had no actual ready cash (although Dimitri had a suitcase of Treasury Bills acquired from some dubious source that might have cash value) but then again they had no debt either. With the information stored on Dimitri's Blackberry, Doc had details of every transaction and all his contacts back in Moscow and in London that had already proved useful. If they believed they were still in contact with Dimitri, he wasn't going to disabuse them. It bought them time at least. Doc was now concerned mostly with securing legal titles, protecting 'their' investments and making sense of this New World order. To this end he found that in spite of everything the Real Estate Board of Greater Vancouver was still in business. Someone was desperate to offload the False Creek Olympic Athlete's village – at any price – back in '06 they had paid around $193 million for the 2.6 hectare site; now despite extensive development, it could be worth just ten percent of that. Doc was beginning to sense desperation out there as the banks continued to squeeze out anything they could, classically driving prices down still further.

But it was Deka who had to set out on a sunny, but chilly, autumn morning for his old apartment to retrieve personal documents. He had thought about taking one of the cars. They had acquired some new BMWs in a small transaction, but what he really needed was a Prius, or other electric vehicle, because there was no gasoline to be had anywhere in the city as far as he could determine. There were rumours of a protected depot out near the airport, but he didn't quite like the idea of going out there only to discover he couldn't get back. If there were any electric vehicles around people were hanging onto them. Of course without fuel or steady power supplies it was hard to charge the batteries and there the flaw in 'electric' cars was exposed. You wouldn't want to drive anywhere if you didn't think you could get it back safe.

So he walked, leaving Hornby and appreciating the sudden beauty of the fall colours surrounding Robson Square. The Law Courts had been closed for the duration and the foliage unchecked – now the true beauty of Arthur Erikson's concept was plain to see, concrete almost overwhelmed by roof gardens and bushes. The fountain had long ago ceased functioning but one could not take away the simple truth that at least in this Square nature would state its claim.

He was amused to see government workers in their PPE spacesuits and inevitable N95 masks lining up for coffees at the lone *Starbucks* open next door to the hotel. He'd been himself, but of course with no milk deliveries from anywhere it took a lot of guts to swallow a soy latté and he'd never been a black coffee drinker. Nevertheless if Starbucks was open, things would soon stabilise. A rare bus went by, the few passengers daring to be on it sat on separate seats and some wore spacesuits just to be sure. It would take some time to remove the fear entirely.

Most of Vancouver's drivers had perished, or were afraid to continue but there was a basic service up and running with volunteers to get emergency workers to and from destinations. The virus was diminishing rapidly according to the Mayor's office, still around a hundred per week but this was the end of the second wave. Deka was sure of it. Doc had told him it would taper off almost as quickly as it came, depending on how bad the winter would be. Of course, if winter was bad and prolonged there could be a third wave and history told them it could be the most vicious mutation of the virus of all. But most people, save Jehovahs, weren't thinking that far ahead. They were just happy hell on earth was ending.

It was eleven o'clock by his watch. He was amused to see just how many variations in time there were across the city. Just how hard would it be to get everything back to the way it was?

There were workmen fixing a broken water main on the corner of Richards which was a good sign. On Homer he was astonished to see a cop on a horse carrying out inspections of property, but then again, without gas, cops couldn't use their cars. Somehow the sight of the cop on his horse filled him with hope. The cop waved as Deka walked by. 'Think it might rain?' he asked.

'Got that feeling to it. Good to see you, officer.'

'Good to be here. Where's your stick?"

'Stick'? Deka queried but the cop was distracted by a call on his cell and Deka moved on. A little bit puzzled. Why would he need a stick? Was someone going to attack him? He'd walked a little in the city but as far as he could see most people were still too afraid to go outside, unless they had to go to the government rationing centres and scurry back.

He neared the Sportsdome at BC Place and discovered his route down Cambie was blocked by burned out vehicles and rubble. He shrugged, he'd either have to go back a couple of blocks or go the long way around through Chinatown to Main Street and double back. From habit, he chose the long way. Walking along Beatty, he noted the abandoned cars were more frequent here and beyond on East Georgia where an abandoned yellow school bus was still burning. It looked deliberate. Kids maybe, enacting some anarchistic fantasy. There was so much to clear away before traffic could flow again. Again he didn't choose the most direct route, curious now to see what had happened to the city elsewhere. He found himself on his way to Chinatown along West Pender.

Another Place to Die

He had passed Tinseltown (long since closed to moviegoers) when Deka thought he saw movement in along Carrall street to the side. Hastings was just one block away with the bums and addicts and he was thinking that he was going to get hit on for something, when he simultaneously remembered that the bums had been the first to go and now Hastings was free of human traffic of any kind. He saw movement again and quickened his pace, something was there and he could hear a weird kind of rumbling and high pitched screaming. It was disturbing and he looked ahead to the rather forlorn Chinese stores abandoned ahead. If anyone was coming for him there was nowhere to go. He turned as the sound turned into a rush and his flesh crawled.

Rats, thousands of rats were literally flowing out of a building and heading screaming and angry towards him! For a moment his heart seemed to stop, his legs froze in place and he could barely take it in. More and more rats were pouring into the street and the noise was scary, uncanny, freaky, like the wind.

He turned and began to run, instantly breathless, frantic to find some refuge. Some rats ahead of the pack leapt onto his legs and he had to tear them off, trying not to break his momentum. He realised all too quickly that he was going to be their next meal.

Behind him a sea of rats sensed a feast and their squeals were all the more intense, panicked, hungry, savage – determined.

Deka jumped through a shattered glass store window and ran to the back looking for the stairs; the rats closing in behind, easily scaling the broken glass behind him. He found the stairs and even though he sensed his heart would burst, he rushed up them, crashed through the door and slammed it behind him.

He took a moment to see if he had been bitten, rolling up his trousers and although he was scratched, he could see no major teeth marks. He moved to the window and looked out down into the street. Rats flowed like lava along what was now East Pender, diving in and out of the shops, scavenging whatever they could. The noise was too weird and eerie and he knew it would enter his dreams. There seemed to be no end to them. How on earth had they gotten so bad, so many?

He watched with morbid fascination as they moved up towards old Chinatown and the markets there. They must have long ago been stripped of anything edible. He recalled that he himself had scavenged there not so very long ago when Doc was sick. Did that make him no better than a rat?

At last they were gone. Deka's brain tried to provide some logic for this. All the natural predators were dead. Rats had had months to breed unchecked by poisons or man putting up any resistance. He remembered from classes in school so many years ago that the average rat can breed every three weeks and they can fall pregnant again just two days after giving birth. An unchecked rat population would experience fantastic growth then, until all the food had been exhausted. He had a brief image of Granville Island with the huge market there. Even in good times he'd sat having lunch there at the water's edge watching the rats in the rocks and there had been plenty living off scraps even then. Now he imagined the island stripped bare, wall to wall with the creatures. He felt momentarily sick.

'You look scared.' A female voice declared from behind him.

Deka swung around, astonished, almost suffering heart failure all over again.

His eyes alighted on a young Chinese woman sat on a chair calmly breast feeding her child. Deka staggered back a little finding a perch on a bale of cloth. He looked about him and he could see he was in an old apartment, now used as a stock room, with much merchandise wrapped in plastic on shelving along one wall.

'I'm s-s-s-sorry,' he began to stutter.

She smiled, gently wiping sweat from the head of her baby. 'There's anti-septic in the bathroom. It might be old but if you are scratched you must wash and clean it. Rats are dirty.'

Deka looked at her – still in shock that he was in someone's place. He felt embarrassed but she was right, he had to clean up, staunch the blood. Stupid to survive so much and die from something a rat might carry. He moved towards the bathroom and closed the door. He nervously pulled down his trousers and checked his legs. He was scratched in four places, no actual bites. No water came out of the tap but he looked around and found some witch hazel – good enough and there was cotton wool too. He cleaned up – accepted the sting with grace. He had a mental image of him burning out the rat scratches and the scent of the witch hazel suddenly floated a memory of his grandmother patching him up after a football game thirty years before.

He smeared some old anti-septic cream on his legs when they had dried and finally re-entered the room. He was still embarrassed and began to apologise. 'I'm sorry. I didn't mean to burst in. I was...'

She looked up at him and put her finger to her lips. 'Shush, I am trying to get him to sleep.'

Deka nodded.

'Where is your stick?' She asked. 'Can't go out without a stick.'

Deka had begun to appreciate that. Sticks were essential. He was thinking an Uzi might be more effective, but...

'You live here?'

She shook her head. She seemed to be sad and she pointed to a picture of an older Chinese woman on the wall. 'My mother's place. She wouldn't leave. So stubborn. I think maybe she died some weeks ago. No sign of her here.'

Deka sat down on the cloth bale again. 'I'm sorry.'

She shrugged. 'She must have known. I grew up here. She was good. She made me go to college. Wanted me to leave. Then when I left she grew angry I wasn't there for her.'

Deka smiled. 'Mother's are like that. I'm told.'

She indicated the window. 'Rats are starving. They will attack each other soon. It's natural.'

'They nearly ate me. I've never been so scared in my life.'

She nodded and gently placed her child down on a cushion, fastening her top to cover up. She wore no bra Deka noticed and wasn't in the least embarrassed he had seen her breast-feeding. She showed no fear either.

'How did you get here?' He asked.

'Bus. There is one back to Richmond at 2pm.'

'Things getting better I think.' Deka remarked. She didn't reply.

Deka felt awkward again. 'I'm on my way to my old apartment. If it's still there.'

'Might not be,' she said softly. 'So much is gone.'

'Baby is healthy at least.'

'Always hungry, like his father.'

'He survived I hope.'

She frowned. Deka didn't pry.

'Your wife?' She asked in return.

'No wife. No family. But I survived. I was lucky.'

'Perhaps,' she returned. 'Where are you from?'

'Cape Town.'

She smiled. 'Beautiful city.'

Deka was surprised. 'You know it?

She shrugged. 'I was aircrew for *British Airways*. Went pretty much everywhere I could. Always looking for the best place to live I think.'

'But you came back.'

'Born here. Born there actually.' She indicated the little room behind the bales of cloth. Deka looked back and could make out a picture of her as a teenager getting a prize for something. She had been cute then, as now. He looked at the happy smiling face there. She still smiled like that. Something about her was good. Perhaps it was because she seemed so calm and secure sat there with her child. He felt protective over her. He knew he had to leave but was reluctant to do so.

'Funny,' she was saying, noting that Deka had been staring at her photo. 'I spent ten years running away from this place and here I am, exactly where I was born.'

'But alive,' Deka reminded her. 'Alive is good.'

'You think there is a future?' From the sound of her voice he could sense that she didn't think so.

'The world just caught a cold. That's all. It's not the end. We all have futures.'

She tried to rise. Deka could see she was struggling and in the light now he could see how painfully thin she was. He made to move towards her to assist but one look stilled him. He backed off. 'I'm not infected. No need to be afraid. I survived the virus. Some do.'

He could see she doubted him.

'I'm sorry. I'll leave. Don't worry. But...' he looked towards the window. 'I'm scared to leave you. If the rats come back.'

She pointed to a stick leaning up against the wall. 'The bus will be there at 2pm. I will wait.'

Deka still didn't want to leave her. 'My name is Deka Fortun. I live at the Derbyshire on Hornby. You can find me there. If you need anything. Anything at all.'

He could tell she was confused by that.

'Derbyshire?'

'The hotel.'

'Oh.'

'It's closed, but I live there now. Might open soon. There's a need for safe lodging in the city. The Mayor is keen to get things back to normal.'

'Nothing's going to be normal again,' she snapped. Then realising she sounded harsh she took a deep breath and smiled again. 'Eva Ng.'

Deka nodded, pleased to know her name. 'Eva. We're all alone now. If you...'

He wasn't quite sure how to end that sentence.

'Derbyshire? On Hornby.' She replied

'Yes.'

Deka began to walk towards the door.

'Fortun is a good name.' She remarked.

'I hope so.'

'Get a stick, Fortun. A very big stick.'

Deka gave her a small wave. He was totally opposed to leaving her there, but he guessed she felt safe in her old childhood home.

He opened the door. Hesitant in case any rat should still be lurking.

'Do you believe in God, Fortun?' Eva asked softly behind him.

Deka paused a moment to consider the question. 'Not right now, Eva.'

'No,' she echoed. 'Not right now.'

Deka closed the door behind him and went warily down the stairs. Now he looked more closely he could see it specialised in sleepwear. Nightgowns were strewn on the floor and pretty Chinese models in nighties were depicted in posters on the walls.

He exited through the broken window. Ultra cautious now in case of rats.

As he walked up the street he turned to look up at the window, where the sign read Sleepshop. She was staring at him from the window, baby in her arms.

Deka had a curious feeling that he'd see her again. He felt light of foot. Full of strange hope again. Eva. Eva Ng.

Deka reached his old Victorian red-brick apartment building fifteen wary minutes later. It had begun to rain and threatened more judging from the black clouds. He'd kept an eye out for the rats and although he hadn't even seen even one, everywhere you could see where they had been. Each shop had been systematically cleaned out; they had eaten anything and everything, chewing through doors if they had to.

His old five-story building stood like an indestructible beacon on 2nd Avenue. One of the last survivors in the face of the Winter Olympic bulldozers. It wasn't looking well however. The rain exposed a broken gutter and water was cascading down the brickwork into an open top floor apartment window. Left unattended during the winter the floors and plasterwork below would rot. The quarantine stickers were still in place but this did not faze him. He wondered how many had survived.

He entered

The green glazed tiling was fully intact. The mailboxes stood firm, unforced. Even though three of the ground floor apartment doors had been kicked open and the furniture inside tossed around, other doors remained locked. In general the old girl had weathered the crisis, if not the elements. A sign on the Bennett's door read: We have evacuated to Maple Ridge. There is nothing of value in this apartment.

There were similar signs on other doors. So many had gone. But Deka knew that Maple Ridge had been hit hard – not exactly the right place to hide in this scenario.

The stairs had been blocked with some refrigerators. A lot of fridges. He looked at them with irritation. No way he could squeeze past. He'd have to try and remove or at least get under one and worm his way up. For once in his life he was happy to have lost so much weight. Clearly someone up there wanted to deter looters.

He worked at the first fridge, getting it upright and then tilted it left so he could get at another. It took the best part of half an hour and he worked up quite a sweat but slowly he found a way through. No looter would have been so determined he felt. Unless they wanted a fridge.

Exhausted, keenly aware of how fragile his lung capacity was now, his heart thumping, he finally reached the first floor landing. He had to sit for a few minutes to get his energy back and steady his nerves. He took time to examine his scratches and was happy to see that the witch hazel had done its job, there was little swelling and he didn't think he had a problem. He'd set Doc on them when he got back. They had a stock of antibiotics now for these kinds of emergencies.

Sam North

He looked back along the corridor, similar notices on some of the doors. He wondered all the time as he was thumping the fridges around if anyone had heard him and were now cowering behind their doors. But no one appeared. He realised his own stupidity. If there had been anyone up here, they would most likely have starved to death given that they couldn't actually get out of the building past the blockade on the stairs.

He climbed to the second floor and opened his door. The smell was pretty bad. Like someone died. One look in the kitchen and he knew why everyone threw out their fridges. Food rotted inside the fridge and outside, on the table, the maggots had long ago eaten the fruit. He turned away to his living room. Suddenly amazed that he had once lived here. Must have been the home of a monk. No pictures, no plants. The Deka Fortun who had inhabited this place was poor; everything looked old, serviceable, but tired. He realised that he didn't miss the place one bit. Or the life he lived in it. Now he was almost a wealthy man, if you skipped over the bit where he actually possessed no cash and everything else he had was on the whim of Doc and a dead Russian guy. No, the man who had lived in this place had surely died along with everyone else.

'It that you, Mr Fortun?'

Deka went to his open front door with surprise on his face. He was confronted by Mrs Hoffsteader, in curlers and barefoot (with blackened malnourished skin) standing there in her pink shorty nightie, almost half the size she used to be and carrying a shotgun with surprising confidence.

'Mrs Hoffsteader, you're alive!'

'That's your opinion, Mr Fortun.'

'Well, I think it's a miracle.'

'You're the miracle, Mr Fortun. Where have you been?'

'Hospital.'

'I can see you shrunk. Can't believe you got out of there alive.'

'Didn't eat the food. That's the secret.'

'I heard. And worse. Talking of food...' She looked past him towards the kitchen. Deka followed her gaze and for a second there thought she going to mention the stink but then realised that she was probably after something else.

'How you getting in and out, Mrs Hoffsteader?'

'Fire escape,' she answered, as if it was a stupid question.

Deka realised that he should have thought of that himself. You could easily hook the ladder and bring it down if you stood on something.

'Are you alone in the building?'

Mrs Hoffsteader shook her head, one curler coming loose as she did so.

'No. Mr Alex and his sister Shelia are still in 24.'

'There's a broken gutter out front. Water pouring into 56 or 58. There's a window open.'

Mrs Hoffsteader made a mental note of that. 'I've got keys. I'll take care of the window. There's a few things going wrong, but at least we got water back and hydro for some hours of the day. Nights are cold though.'

Deka looked at her and could see she was pale and just plain looked ill for someone who hadn't been sick, that is. 'I guess most other's died huh?'

'Some left. Some died. You look like shit. You had the virus?'

Deka nodded.

'You lost sixty pounds I'd say. At least. What do you weigh now?'

'No idea, but if it's ten stone I'd be surprised. You do know there are ration coupons now. Just have to show your ID.'

She looked at him as if he were stupid. 'I get my share.'

Deka looked back into his apartment. 'Just come to get some things, but I'm not coming back, Mrs Hoffsteader. Take anything you want that isn't rotten – except the tea. I need my Rooibos tea.'

Mrs Hoffsteader put her shotgun down, leaning it against the wall.

'You're not infected?'

'Cured. Virus can't get me now. It damn well tried though. Get some garbage bags from the cupboard and load up. There is bound to be pasta, some sauces, tuna, quite a load of tuna.'

She didn't need a second invitation.

Deka went into his bedroom and lifted the carpet, then the loose floorboard under that. He pulled out his passport, his birth certificate and his letter of confirmation of citizenship with all the important numbers. He pulled out five hundred dollars in cash as well; completely surprised, he'd forgotten he'd put it there.

Mrs Hoffsteader was clattering about in the kitchen. 'I can take the coffee?' she called.

'Everything except the tea and...' Deka got up off his knees and went into the kitchen, pocketing his documents on the way. He reached up to the top shelf of the cupboard and retrieved a huge bar of *Cadbury's Fruit and Nut*. A gift some months before from one of his regulars who been to London. No need for the rats to have that.

He took one more look around and sighed. He gave Mrs Hoffsteader the key.

'Have what you like or sell stuff.'

'Nothing's worth shit now, Mr Fortun, but thanks.' She tried lifting the bags full of food but couldn't. Deka smiled.

'I'll take them up for you.'

Mrs Hoffsteader looked at him with puzzlement. 'I don't remember you being so nice but I thank you, Mr Fortun. You are an honourable man.'

'You could move to a newer place, y'know. City's practically empty. You could get squatter's rights. Find a newer place, safer part of town.' He could tell from her face that she'd never leave the building. 'How are you living anyway? They paying pensions?'

'No they are not. They issue rations and there's a soup kitchen if you can stand the fights. No one cares if we live or die, Mr Fortun, the old are forgotten. Them that can't go for rations just plain starve to death and that's a fact. I see women selling themselves for food and cigarettes and fools going for it. People are still dying y'know. It ain't over.'

'And then there are the rats.'

'And then there are rats. Heard they attacked people over by Granville Island. Ate them alive. Shot ten on the fire escape last week.' She laughed. 'Tasted like shit but a stew's a stew.'

Deka shook his head. That's why Mrs Hoffsteader was alive. It was her versus the rats and she'd win, by his reckoning.

He carried the food upstairs to her apartment as she locked up behind him.

'Get that window closed upstairs, OK?' He reminded her on the stairs.

'It'll be done. Whole city's rotting.'

'It's coming back. Coming back to life, I promise.'

'When *Jeopardy* comes back on TV, I'll know things are right again, but not until.'

Deka smiled. 'Ja, that's one way of looking at it. You stay safe, Mrs Hoffsteader. If you ever need anything. Leave a message for me at the Derbyshire.'

'The hotel?'

'Someone has to guard the hotels.'

Mrs Hoffsteader nodded her head. 'Yes, someone's got to keep stuff safe. We saved this place. We did our bit.'

Deka deposited the bags inside her kitchen. Mrs Hoffsteader had a two bedroom place with a dining kitchen. It was old fashioned but spotless, the sofa still wrapped in plastic. He could see she had been reading. There was a pile of brand new mysteries stacked in the corner.

'Found some books I see.'

Mrs Hoffsteader looked guilty. 'Rescued some, Mr Fortun. Didn't steal 'em. Saved them from the rats. I rescued what I could carry.'

'And someone will be grateful you did one day.'

She stood in her kitchen, still proud, waiting for him to leave so she could unload her stash. 'Derbyshire,' she repeated. 'But if the hotel ain't open?'

'Nowhere's actually open, but some buses are running and the water's getting fixed. Power might come back on twelve hours a day soon, maybe more. You'll see, Mrs Hoffsteader. A year from now everything will be back to normal.'

She looked out of the window across to Grouse Mountain in the distance. 'And where will my friends be, Mr Fortun. All gone. Just me now.'

Deka could say nothing but, 'stay well, stay safe.'

He left her standing, staring down at the bloated garbage bags.

He made sure the fridges were impassable once again and left by way of the fire escape. As he walked away from the building he didn't look back. It was too sad.

He avoided Chinatown on the way back, had no idea why he had gone via Main Street anyway – save that he was following the route that he always travelled in his cab. On foot you had to consider the shortest routes everywhere. Shortest and safest with the least rats. He made a mental note to find a bicycle.

It was still raining as he ambled across Cambie Bridge. He surveyed his adopted city and felt rising optimism again. It was entirely possible for it to recover. Dimitri was right. It might be empty now, but still people would want to come here and it was their duty to make them welcome, make sure it was ready for them and of course ensure there was somewhere to live. Take the long view.

There was a bus broken down at the Pacific Boulevard junction with Cambie. The masked passengers were standing around, each maintaining a careful distance between each other. He thought of Eva back in Chinatown. He wished he could see her again. She'd been so pretty, despite her emaciated state. There was something about her that calmed him. As he approached the bus he saw a rat scuttle by, disappear down a drain. He realised that he still had no stick.

The bus driver was arguing with a passenger and everyone was looking glum, as if they knew this bus wasn't going anywhere today.

'Still no stick, Mr Fortun.' A voice remarked out of the crowd.

Deka turned his head and there she was. Eva. She was standing in a flimsy red coat, her baby strapped to her back.

Deka couldn't prevent himself from smiling broadly. 'No stick yet, no.'

Eva blushed. Deka moved closer towards her.

'I can offer tea and...' he pulled out the chocolate bar and saw her eyes light up. (Saw a few others stare enviously as well).

'Fruit and Nut! How did you know? My favourite.'

'Well, it seems that an invitation is in order, Eva Ng. Tea and chocolate at the Derbyshire.'

Eva looked back at the bus, the crowd staring at them and made a decision. A big decision. 'I will come with you.'

Deka smiled and offered his arm. She hesitated only for a moment, so long since she had held an arm, been close to anyone other than her child. She hooked her arm in his.

The bus crowd murmured. No one ever touched now, ever, and they formed their own conclusions about this woman.

Deka, Eva and child walked towards the city. The rain stopped for a while.

'What is the boy's name?'

Eva didn't answer immediately. Deka was uncertain of what to say after that. 'I didn't mean to pry.' Somehow he felt he had offended her.

She looked at him with guilty eyes. 'I didn't name him, yet. I couldn't. I didn't think we would live, Mr Fortun.'

Deka stopped a moment and looked squarely into her face. He saw such sorrow there, but he wondered if she too felt the lightness he was feeling as he stared at her. He had never had such a beautiful woman on his arm, ever.

'If I had a boy I would call him Nicolas.' He told her. 'He was a friend. Not at first. He was strong and funny and everyone liked him at school and I don't think he even noticed me. But some boys picked on me after a football game and he sided with me against them. We were friends from that moment on. Even when he won a scholarship to Bishops. The best school. He was my best friend until...'

'Until?'

Deka sighed. It was a stupid story now he thought about it. 'Until he stepped on a landmine in Angola. He went to work for the oil company and...'

Eva frowned. 'Your friend not so lucky.'

Deka shrugged. 'He died instantly they say. The unlucky ones bleed to death.'

They walked on. Deka wondering why he had been so stupid to mention Nicolas. He thought too of Doc's reaction when he turned up with Eva and child. They hadn't really discussed about what everything would be like when everything returned to normal. If everything returned to normal.

Eva was clearly thinking about what she was getting into here. It was getting darker as the rain clouds gathered for another go.

'You like me?' She asked him finally.

Deka wondered why she asked that. Was she going to tell him there was someone else? He realised that that would upset him more than anything else that had happened recently.

'I hope I will and I hope you will like me too,' he answered, trying to sound much more calm than he felt inside.

Eva was clearly thinking. She stopped a moment to adjust the straps on her dress. Deka drew out a tissue and wiped dribble from the baby's mouth. Eva looked surprised but smiled briefly in appreciation. 'What do you miss most, Mr Fortun, in this great civilisation of ours?'

Deka looked at her and shrugged. 'Everything I suppose.'

'In particular.'

Deka took a deep breath; the pressure in his chest was building again as they walked up an incline. 'Truthfully?'

'Absolutely.'

'I miss the impossible, my health, of course. I wheeze now. Never wheezed before.'

'No, about life. What do you miss? And please don't say a Big Mac and McFlurry to go.'

Deka laughed, even though that too hurt his chest. 'I will never miss a hamburger if I had two lives.'

'Then what do you miss?' She was quite insistent.

'The *Vancouver Sun* I suppose – although I'd get the *Globe and Mail* most days because it lasts longer – y'know, waiting between fares.'

Eva nodded. 'That's it? Civilisation crashes and all you miss is a newspaper?'

Deka looked taken aback. 'A newspaper is everything, Eva. You got the news, sport, the classifieds, a crossword, the funnies... It's how you judge a city, by the quality of its newspaper.'

'Which is why in Vancouver you read the *Globe* – a Toronto paper.'

Deka shook his head smiling ruefully. She was sharp this one. 'Some days I read the *New York Times* or even the *LA Times*. Hell, I read all the papers. I spent a lot of time in my cab.'

'OK I get it. Newspapers you miss most. Nothing else?'

'Margi's soup. It's a Korean café at 28th and Main. Best vegan soup there is. Although, ' he smiled at the recollection, 'she was always trying to get me to try her chicken soup.'

'See now you're getting to the real stuff, Mr Fortun. Margi's soup.'

Deka looked at her askance. 'You don't like that answer either.'

Eva shook her head and smiled. 'I do. Better than I miss 'Modern Art' or being able to pop over to Paris to pick up a little black dress from Chanel.'

Deka smiled. 'I'd never miss modern art.'

'That's the point. No one would. Might miss the old stuff in the galleries, but guess what they are still there, if they haven't been looted. They looted the Uffizi in Italy y'know. I was there in Florence. Couldn't believe it. Thieves went in, they had trucks parked outside and they say the police couldn't do anything because they didn't want to shoot anything valuable. Besides they were all scared to death of going outside and catching anything. No one knows where Leonardo da Vinci's 'Adoration of the Magi' has gone or the Titians; almost half the collection has disappeared. Broad daylight; they just walked out with it and drove off.'

Deka noticed that she had picked up a British accent working for BA, he liked her direct way of speaking. 'Where do you think the art went?'

'Locked away in some bastard collector's vault forever.'

'He might be dead already.' Deka ventured.

'With luck.'

'Might turn up on Ebay.' He suggested.

Eva laughed. 'Yeah – that I can see. See now you're remembering stuff. Ebay collapsed the moment everyone realised nothing was ever going to get delivered again.

'I was in Italy just as the first wave began. People dying in Turkey and Romania by the thousands and I told my crew boss that was it. Choose the city you want to die in and go there. He thought I was crazy.'

'So you came home.'

'I was pregnant. Hadn't told them. You can't work pregnant. I wanted my baby to be Canadian, like me. Nothing else.'

Deka noticed a homemade crayon sign in a tall apartment tower window and pointed.

'HELP – Broken Leg – Need Water & Food – Apt 3434'

Eva looked at him as Deka took out his cell phone. 'Wonder how long it's been there?'

'I'll call it in. The Mayor's office has a special number for this kind of thing.'

'He or she might be dead already,' she cautioned him.

'Doesn't matter. You have to help. So many people are surviving all over the city anyway they can, but are trapped. We have to save the healthy – broken leg or not.'

Eva watched and listened as Deka made the call. He seemed so confident and they seemed to know who he was. She was impressed; pleased he had a conscience.

Deka snapped his phone shut. 'They'll be there in an hour. It's really stupid, but the thing people forget most when they quarantine themselves is water, then paper and crayons. It's like you have to relearn basic communication skills all over again. With the power out most of the time, people's cells aren't charged and of course most of the system is down. God knows what condition people are living in most places.'

He turned to Eva. 'You were living in a house or an apartment?'

'House. My cousin's. He died in the first wave.'

'I'm sorry.'

'He worked at the hospital. It was pretty terrible there. But he wouldn't leave.'

Deka knew exactly how bad it was and felt for her.

'I was hoping the child's father would come here. He has a house in Deep Cove.'

'He...? Deka didn't really want to pry.

'He went to Mauritius instead. Left me a note. Said it would be safe there.'

'Mauritius? Africa?'

'Unless there's one in Disneyworld. That one. Never fall in love with a pilot, Mr Fortun. They can't stay on the ground.'

'I'll bear that in mind.'

The baby suddenly sneezed. Eva wiped his nose, looking nervously back at Deka as she did so. 'It's not...'

Deka smiled. 'I know about babies. They turn blue you worry, otherwise they sneeze and snort and ick up pretty much all the time. Particularly in my cab!'

Eva laughed, relaxing again. Still amazed that she had stumbled across this man who seemed so immediately comfortable around her and her child.

Deka was looking ahead. 'I'll be happier when there is traffic again. Cities aren't supposed to be so quiet.'

Eva didn't agree. 'I like it. I saw a farmer with his horses on the road in Richmond yesterday. I'd like to see the whole city with horse and carriages, could happen y'know.'

Deka shook his head. 'Price of oil collapsed. When normal life comes back everyone will climb back into their cars and trucks as if nothing ever happened.'

Evan looked disappointed. 'Oh, I hope not. I really do hope not.'

Deka was concerned as they approached Granville. He didn't like Granville Street in the normal times. Never felt safe. Too many dealers and bums. But aside from a stray dog that looked nervously at them before going its own way, they crossed safely. Deka realised that Granville too would be different, until a new breed of people discovered it.

Eva's child woke up again and began to whinge a little. She paused to reassure him and they went the rest of the way with the babe in her arms.

At the hotel Deka let them in and quickly locked the door behind them. The building was silent. No Wylie to greet them. Doc had taken to going out and about with his dog. He felt safer. There was no music either. Doc liked to fill the hotel with classical music 'to fill up the space'.

'Tea, chocolate and I think I have some scones left over I made yesterday.'

'Scones?' Eva laughed. 'Real scones?'

Deka pulled a face. 'I got bored of making bread. Thought I'd try a recipe I found.'

'You're the cook?' Eva asked.

Deka smiled. 'Cook, anything you want me to be. That's me.'

Eva didn't understand, but she was happy to be somewhere safe and clean and where there was food. The old fashioned English styled restaurant with it's oak and mahogany tables looked so welcoming and civilised, like Sherlock Holmes would pop in any moment. She wondered why she had never been there before.

'Women's room over there,' Deka pointed out, handing her a flashlight. 'Might even be hot water. Toilet flushes.'

Eva rolled her eyes and laughed. 'You know how to impress a woman, Mr Fortun.'

She took herself and the child to the women's room, extraordinarily happy to find it clean. She left the flashlight on the side as she went to the loo. Here she was with a cook. She was philosophical about it. At least she'd eat. Plus he had manners and clearly liked her. She could tell immediately. She didn't know exactly why she was there, but there was something so calming about him. She was sure he was a good man. She smiled as she recalled his scared faced when he'd rushed into the old apartment. The rats had frightened him, just as she too had been sickened by them when they first began to appear.

She didn't understand why he'd never seen them before, but then again, perhaps this hotel didn't have any.

The baby cried out and she wiped herself and went to him. He'd need changing. She had a spare nappy in the pouch. She ran a tap and true to his word, warm water came out. Immediately she filled the sink and gave her boy a bath. He loved it, his little face smiling as the warm water swooshed around him and she gently soaped him.

'You like Nicolas – honey bun? You think you'd like to be a good friend to someone one day?'

The baby laughed and she felt lighter suddenly. She sensed a huge burden had just dropped away from her life.

'Nicolas Fortun,' Eva declared to the mirror. Yes it seemed to fit. It didn't matter he was only a cook or a cabbie. Didn't matter at all. Another good man was going to be hard to find.

21

Health Canada

After having studied all possible precautions for a pandemic which it figures could kill 58,000 people, Health Canada concedes that citizens can't do much to fend off infection except wash their hands. Hand washing "is the cornerstone of infection prevention and may be the only preventative measure available during a pandemic. People should have plenty of hygiene products as there may be an interruption to the supply or shortages of hand antisepsis products, soap and hand towels."

A vaccine cannot be produced until the new flu strain has been emerged and been identified. It would then take six months to produce the vaccine. Therefore a vaccine will not be available at the start of the epidemic and may be in short supply during the initial stages. Health Canada also states "a regular flu shot would be of no use against a mutated version of avian flu." *Source: Health Canada*

The Calendar and The Whale

Rachel and Fen were sat by the fire in the living room after breakfast. Neither one had quite got into the day yet. They could hear Arno chopping wood outside.

Rachel suddenly looked up at Fen and asked. 'What do you miss?'

Fen replied instantly. 'Ben and Jerry's Chocolate Chip Mint.' Then laughed, turning away her gaze to sigh a moment later. 'Actually nothing. I thought I'd miss my music, y'know. But I don't. I don't miss school, as if. I certainly don't miss 'the bitch' my father's girlfriend. I don't even miss May, my sister. I don't think I miss anything. Not even TV. Does that make me weird?'

'Nothing at all?' Rachel queried.

'Nothing – 'cept maybe dog food. Cats can survive in the wild but Red doesn't really go looking for food. He still waits for me to get it for him. When did dogs forget how to hunt?'

'Red's still a civilised dog, Fen. You can bet your life that there's a hundred thousand dogs out there right now eating anything they can, running around in packs.

'Dogs are a lot more resourceful than you think. I guess they don't say it's a 'dog eat dog' world for nothing.'

'Eew – not nice, Rachel. Red can hear you.'

Rachel smiled. 'Sorry.'

Fen picked up a small crystal ball from the table. 'I can see my future now. But you have no idea of how much I hated my past. I hated every moment. I couldn't wait to graduate high school and just get the fuck away from home.'

Fen pressed the glass object to her face a moment, closing her eyes.

'The pressures gone now. I wake up and I can't wait to do stuff. I'm happy. Even though I'm hungry a lot and could really do with some toothpaste, I'm happy. That make any sense?' She put the crystal ball down.

Rachel wrapped her arms around her legs and thought about it a moment. 'Yeah. It makes sense and ditto the toothpaste. Arno says we should rinse our mouths out with salt every day – oral hygiene.'

'Sounds gross but we got lots of salt. And you, Rach? What do you miss?'

Rachel wrinkled her nose and then smiled. 'Easy. Bean City. My local coffee shop. Best blueberry muffins in the city and of course my double shot semi-skimmed wet latte with a vanilla twist.'

Fen smiled. 'I never got into coffee. Mercer, my dad, wouldn't let us drink it.'

Rachel stared at her uncomprehending. 'No coffee? It's like – weird. Everyone drinks coffee in Canada.'

'Not Mercer. Coffee is some sort of conspiracy against the peoples of North America. Of course dope on the other hand... He liked to smoke that. Used to give it to me and May to stop us crying when we were kids.'

Rachel's eyes widened. 'And you grew up this normal?'

'I'm not normal, Rachel. I never even wore make-up yet. Another thing Mercer wouldn't let us have. Not that I actually cared, but May cared and she always put it on when she got to school. Anyways, turned out I was allergic to dope. Makes me break out. Face, arms, chest. Not pretty. Allergic to milk too.'

'Then it's pretty handy we don't have a cow.'

'Yeah.'

Fen suddenly remembered something. 'You ever see a movie called 'Right at your Door'? Starred Rory Cochrane. Some chemical bombs go off in LA and...'

'Yeah, yeah, saw it on HBO I think. Got the girl from *West Wing* in it too...Mary McCormack. Scary fucking scenario. Made me think hard about living in a city. We always think we are safer in Canada than America but it isn't true. We have our own fanatics.'

'Mercer made us watch it. I was thinking about it yesterday. About how you're supposed to listen to the instructions on the radio and obey the cops and everything and how it's all lies and I never did understand why he didn't really help her. I would have helped her. I would have gone outside – no matter what. If you love someone – you'd want to die with them.'

'You're a secret romantic, Fen. Why were you thinking about that film?'

'Like. You ever think that this virus could have been terrorists? Like it was supposed to kill everyone in one city but kinda got out of control?'

Rachel shook her head slowly. 'No. Not even Al Qaeda would be that stupid. They'd have to have an antiviral developed for this strain of the virus already developed and if they wanted to protect their own – they'd have to vaccinate millions of Shias without any western government health agency noticing. I don't think it's possible unless they just wanted to kill everyone – in which case they have done a great job.

'Plagues come and go, Fen – it's natural.'

Fen nodded. 'That film saved me. I think that's why Mercer made us watch it. You have to take care of yourself, you can't wait for help.'

Rachel shrugged. 'Just be glad we aren't back in Vancouver or LA right now.'

'Shit yeah. It would be a million times worse.'

'And they'd be shooting looters, boarding infected people up in their homes – dead or alive. The hospitals will be overwhelmed – dead zones and everyone who took the advice to stay home and stay indoors will be up to their eyeballs in shit.'

'I guess there wouldn't be any water. No power.' Fen said.

'Food rotting in your fridge and in the stores.' Rachel added.

'They've got rationing. I know that because Mercer said they had lots of emergency plans. But what about next year?'

Rachel frowned. 'Next year?'

'Well, if there's no food now, what about next year? Who's going to plant it? Who's going to pick it? Mercer said that the second year might be worse than the first.'

Rachel said nothing for a moment. She'd never really though that far ahead. But Fen was right. 'Well – I guess there would be less of us to feed.'

Fen nodded in agreement. Then looked up directly into Rachel's eyes. 'You would have left me at Salt Spring if you could have landed me there.'

Rachel was thrown for a moment. 'We were scared. Didn't know if you had the virus or not. It wasn't personal. We wouldn't have left you without food and water.

We thought Salt Spring would be safe for you. Sorry.'

Fen looked away a moment. 'I guess I would have left you too.'

Rachel bent forward to poke the fire. 'I don't like this conversation anymore. You're alive, Fen, because Red was barking his head off when he spotted our boat. Everything turns on one small thing.'

Fen knew that. Red had been saving her life ever since he had been born.

'There's something else I miss.' Fen added.

'What?'

'Leone. She went to Mexico with her family same time we escaped. Baja. You think she's OK?'

Rachel nodded. 'You'll be surprised. A whole lot of people will have survived. They're hiding out, being safe, taking precautions. Your friend will probably be swimming every day, working on her tan and won't even know or understand all the crazy things you have been through. It would seem too fantastic to her.'

Fen grinned. 'Yeah.' That much she could believe. She stood up suddenly. 'Got to go fishing.'

Rachel watched her leave – wondering exactly what was going on in that girl's head. She was never sure as to whether they had rescued her or she had rescued them, but she was glad Fen with them. She got up to join Arno. The wood would need stacking.

'Hey guess what?'

Arno was grinning as he returned with more driftwood. Rachel was stacking the firewood up against the porch wall and stood up, rubbing her sore back. All this lifting and stacking was new to her and it hurt. She pulled her coat closer to her. It was warm work but the wind was chilly.

'We got mail?'

Arno made a silly face. 'And they opened a coffee shop down by the beach.'

'About time.'

'You want to know or not?'

'Does it involve more lifting? 'Cause if it does I am seriously unkeen.'

'Where's Fen?'

'She's gone fishing. I told her it was too cold, but she's pretty dedicated and I think she wants to be thought of as useful.'

'She is useful. I think without her fish we'd be pretty damn miserable. Anyway, you know that room we never go into?'

'You mean hers.' Rachel was referring to A.S. Becora's strange bedroom with the four poster bed.

'Yeah. Hers.'

Rachel gave him a look. 'I told you that you were feeling guilty. She's haunting this place y'know. She won't be happy until we are all dead.'

'Well she's going to be disappointed isn't she. My mother would believe you but luckily I come from a long line of sceptics. No ghosts. Unless she took a shotgun with her.'

Rachel smiled. 'Funny. So what did you find? A warm duvet I hope. I can't believe she only has blankets.'

'Calendar. Electric – batteries still OK. Guess what today is?'

'Well it's winter. That I can tell you. My nipples are sore if that's a guide.'

'It's Christmas Eve, Rach.'

Rachel was momentarily silenced. She looked back at the trees swaying in the wind. Christmas already. 'Really?'

Arno nodded. 'Funny how time flies when you spend half of it in a coma.'

'You're full of them today. Shit, Christmas.' Her eyes lit up. 'Let's make it special for Fen. OK? She doesn't know right?'

'Well I'm all for making it special, but how would you like your baked potatoes? With holly on them?'

'We can make it special. God, we have to, Arno. She's been through so much y'know and we forget she's still a kid.'

'Don't let her hear you say that. But...' he thought about it. 'You're right. We need something to celebrate.'

Rachel came closer and gave him a hug. 'I just can't believe we've been gone so long already. What can we do? She'll come back with fish. We've got cabbage and some carrots and potatoes.'

Arno kissed her. 'I'll do the food.' He declared, breaking off a moment. 'Time to breakout that blackberry wine she's got stored in the larder.'

Rachel was thinking. 'We need gifts.'

Arno laughed briefly. 'You do recall that this is an island, right?'

Rachel was growing more enthusiastic with the idea now. 'What did Anne of Green Gables do? What did the Little Women do? If they couldn't buy stuff, they made stuff.'

Arno grinned, stepping back from her a moment. 'Anne of Green Gables?'

'You have read it, haven't you?" Rachel asked, one eyebrow raised. 'It's practically a Canadian citizenship test. No Green Gables, no passport.'

'Yeah, yeah, I saw it on TV. I think I was more into Pac-Man in those days and Jessica Rabbit. I spent a lot of time in Thunder Bay winter and summer. Sailing, I had a dirt bike for while, god knows what shit I got into, but it was very Canadian shit. OK. Can I have my passport now?'

"Jessica Rabbit?" Rachel queried – then shook her head.

'OK. I'm doing the food.' Arno told her. 'You're doing gifts and making the house look pretty. If you see a turkey land on the island, let me know and I'll get the gun.'

Rachel pulled a face. 'People don't eat birds anymore, Arno. Especially turkeys.'

'And I bet the turkeys are happy about that.'

Rachel was looking at the sky. 'Cold enough to frost tonight. I thought the Gulf Islands were supposed to be warmer than everywhere else. Thought that was the whole point of them.'

'You never spent a winter back East then. This is practically tropical. It will be minus 20 back in Toronto. Let's get moving. I want Fen to get a real surprise.'

Rachel moved into the house, excited now. It was time they celebrated something and Christmas was the best way of all.

Fen and Red were fishing. She was getting a lot better at using the fishing equipment now, even if was too bulky for her arms and her bodyweight. She was fly-casting using a sink tip line and hoping for spring salmon. Someone, probably not the old woman, had serious intentions about fishing off this island, though most likely from the stern of a boat. Fen had set her heart on a big salmon. Someone had told her once that the bigger fish had a thing for bright colours. She had worked out how to use the Gibbs Gypsy lure that she found in the basement and because this is what Mr Hertzog had told her months before; she had been experimenting with scenting it. Her first attempt was with pilchard and dog's blood, Had to be red, she remembered. She had some idea of what a salmon might like, and today she'd done exactly what he'd taught her using a small herring with a good shine on it. She began by cutting it behind the gills, twisting the bait knife into it to pull out the entrails and then angling the herring on the double hook, tucking one hook inside. She was fishing the traditional way. Mr Hertzog had done this with brined herring but her only choice was fresh herring. It was likely to stay on the hook longer by her reckoning and had to work, after all, that what's salmon ate. All she had was a single action mooching reel and she was in business. She longed to learn more about fishing, but Arno knew next to nothing about it and Rachel didn't even like to touch a fish, let alone filet it – although she sure liked to eat it.

Her main concern was being able to land anything she caught. Getting a grip was a real bastard on the rock. The elevated position meant she could cast well, get it out far into the island deepwater inlet, but that meant holding the rod all the time and it was designed to be slotted into something, she was sure of it. Waves rolled in beneath her driven by the persistent wind.

She was freezing to death slowly. Despite wearing three old sweaters and some dungarees she'd found. Red stayed close, trying to steal warmth off her.

'Another half hour, Red, and then we'll call it quits. OK?' She cast again and it landed in good water where she'd seen something pop up earlier to mock her fishing skills.

Red was all for calling it quits immediately, but he knew his duty was to stay. Fen could hardly concentrate she was so cold and found herself drifting off and making wishlists.

One: She wanted a fully-loaded iPod with everlasting batteries.

Two: A winter jacket that actually fitted her and kept out the cold and would keep her feet warm in the bed at night.

Three: She wanted to sit in a dark cinema, watch a great movie – get totally lost in it. Maybe get a little bit sick on Coca-Cola and chocolate at the same time.

Four: She wished she could stop dreaming about Arno.

This was her guilty secret. She had developed a crush on Arno and felt stupid about it because she knew he was obsessed with Rachel and he was old. She could rationalise everything. Her hormones was were kicking in, she was going to be sixteen in February, whenever February was and she kept having these huge erotic dreams about her and Arno. Couldn't stop them. If he as much as touched her accidentally she had a hot flush and sometimes, when they sat by the fire at nights, he let her sleep on his lap as he stroked her head. But then, just to confuse things, Rachel let her do the same thing. She told herself that this was all normal, she was a girl, this was what girls did, fantasise about having sex, but sometimes it was so real it was embarrassing having breakfast with Arno in the morning.

Arno seemed totally oblivious of course.

Her line twitched. She braced herself.

'Red. Can you see it? We got something.'

Red had already noticed the line go taut and stood excitedly watching the water. He was just as keen as she was to get the fish reeled in. He was getting used to grilled fish for dinner and anything that got them back to the warm fire was good by him.

'It's big.' Fen shrieked. 'Don't think I can hold it.'

She jumped backwards into the crevice between two rocks and leaned back, doing her best to reel whatever it was in. It was resisting and she fought hard. Her hands were raw, numbed from the cold. She pulled and reeled in a little more. The line was going crazy, but whatever it was had been hooked good and they couldn't lose it now.

She called up to Red who was still looking out across the water. 'Can you see it, Red?'

It was heavy. For a moment there she thought she had a shark on the line but, if it had been a shark, it would have ripped the line out from her hands by now.

Red was getting very excited. Fen was doing her level best to hang onto the rod but it was getting tougher and she lacked upper body strength.

'We're losing it,' Fen wailed. 'We're losing it.' Nevertheless she reeled it in a little more, astonished she could do anything at all, feeling the pressure in her face and shoulders as she pushed up against the rock to get better leverage.

Suddenly the rod was yanked out of her hands and ran away, but instantly became wedged in the crevice, she experienced a rising thrill. Whatever it was wasn't going to get away. Not this time.

Fen dashed up to the rock beside Red and saw her catch, thrashing violently on the edge of the inlet. It was fucking huge. Chinook salmon by her reckoning.

Fen made a big decision. There was no way she could reel it in now, but she could grab it. She peeled off all her clothes, jeans, old boots, everything. The biting cold wind didn't matter a fig right now. She was one very skinny, goosepimpled kid who was going fishing to catch the biggest fish of her life.

She jumped. The inlet was about fifty feet deep or more below the rock. She plunged in, surfaced seconds later, screaming from shock it was so cold, then struck out for her catch, still hoping to get away.

Fen wasn't sure exactly how you grabbed a fish that was so intent on surviving and she realised with amazement that it was at least sixty pounds. Huge. She couldn't grab its tail it was thrashing so hard, but she could at least get her arms around it and tug the whole thing closer to the rocks.

'Got you. You're mine.'

Red was barking, there was blood in the water and she was in battle with a whale.

It was at that exact moment that Arno arrived with a hot drink for her.

He was stood on the rock staring at a naked wild child covered in fish blood wrestling the biggest fish he'd ever seen outside of a fish stall. Fen was like a savage; a rare beautiful savage. He loved her for it.

'I think you won, Captain Ahab.' He called out.

Fen looked up, triumphant, grinning like a crazy girl, the fish half in and half out, still fighting. She was aware she was naked, that blood was dripping off her hair and face but she didn't care. She'd caught her fish.

Arno grabbed her clothes and clambered down the rocks to join her. He dumped the clothes and the cup of tea on dry rocks and shed his own shoes.

'Fen, if there's ever an award for 'Survivor of the Year' make sure I put your name down for it, OK? I'll pin it on your chest. Of course it might hurt a little.

Fen laughed. She was on a high. She'd won. Better yet Arno was there to witness her triumph. She noted with a tiny thrill that he was staring at her.

'Let's get this ugly sucker out of the water,' Arno told her. 'Get that hook out as well.'

He looked at her again and shook his head in wonder. 'If you don't actually die of pneumonia tonight you'll get to eat this thing.' He put a hand on her shoulder, an earnest look on his face. 'Baby. You're the toughest, craziest, greatest girl I have ever known.'

Fen could only grin.

'Now go back in, wash the blood off before Rachel thinks there's a murderer on the island.'

Fen plunged back into the water and headed for the cleanest part.

Arno grabbed the fish and took the struggling creature up to the higher rocks.

He felt sorry for it. Probably thought it was safe these days with all of Vancouver's fisherman most likely out of action. He wondered how long it would take to die, if there was something he should do to put it out of its misery. Fen had really excelled. She'd never starve out here. Never.

He looked back down. Fen was already out of the water. She looked blue with cold but happy, doing her best to pull her clothes back on over a wet body.

Fen felt Arno's eyes on her, but she didn't turn around, let him look. She wanted him to look. She finally got her sweater over her head and their eyes met. Arno just smiled and returned to wondering what to do with the fish.

Fen sat down to pull on her dungarees and pull on her boots. She was shivering now, the adrenaline was receding.

Arno dropped down out of sight to examine the trapped rod and after a struggle he got it out of there, but cut his fingers in the process. 'Jesus, it's sharp. You bent the handle, but it's still serviceable I think. Yeah. Still works.'

He reeled in the line until the lure appeared. Then stashed the rod up above the tide line where Fen liked to keep it under some bushes.

Fen was down at the water's edge washing her hands. Arno joined her, hoping the salt water would fix his cuts some.

'You sliced your fingers too, huh.'

'It was biting hard. I couldn't let go.'

'Got to get you some gloves. Make some maybe. Fuck. I'm sore.' Arno held his hands in the salt water for as long as he could stand it.

'I'm not sure whether to praise you or spank you. Jumping into the sea like that – with no one around? What if you'd succumbed to hypothermia? You'd be dead, Fen, and we wouldn't know until too late. It's winter. I know we need the fish, but, you know what? We need you more.'

Fen didn't say anything. He was right. She'd been excited, but now she thought about it, it had been damn cold in there.

Arno handed her the tea he'd brought. It wasn't so hot anymore but it was welcome.

'You think we could make something to ship the rod into, so it holds it?' Fen asked.

Arno thought about it a while. 'There's a plastic drainpipe down by the shed. We could wedge it into that crevice and put a lot of rocks around it. As long as the base doesn't come away, you could slot it in after you cast and it might hold.'

Fen smiled, leant up against him. Arno put an arm around her and squeezed. 'Damn big fish, Fen.'

'Chinook. You can tell by the black gums and it's spotted tail.'

'So happens it's my favourite.'

They hefted the silver fish up onto Arno's shoulders and began the walk home. Red already released from his duties was on his way there.

'Rachel's got a surprise for you when you get back. Get in, shower and find a party hat? OK?'

Fen was puzzled? 'Party hat?'

'You'll see. How come you don't feel the cold? Jesus, it's freezing now.'

Fen stuck close, happy, way colder than she cared to admit, but happy.

Fen disappeared to take a hot shower the moment they got inside, pausing only long enough on the stairs to hear Rachel, who was in the kitchen, squeal with amazement when she saw the fish. 'My God, Fen, you're amazing, absolutely amazing.'

Fen ran upstairs with a big smile on her face. It was pretty amazing. She looked at her hands, they were still bleeding which was annoying but these were the scars of victory.

Arno left the filleting to Rachel as he too noticed he was still bleeding. He cast about for bandages and anti-septic cream. Put some aside for Fen too, she'd need them for sure.

Rachel looked up at him with a big smile when he returned. 'I know your secret.'

'Hey I told you not to peek.'

'Where did you find it? Plum pudding? You sure it's OK?'

'They last forever and it's a Dutchy pudding, a last relic from Royal England. One year old, but it doesn't expire until 2012 apparently. I hope you aren't allergic to nuts. It's got everything in it.'

'I'll find some brandy. Can't serve it unless it's covered in blue flames. It's like a real Christmas. My daddy used to insist on Christmas pudding with brandy sauce.'

Arno went outside a moment to the rear porch. It was their fridge now. He'd never quite figured out the fridge in the larder, which worked off the wind-turbine.

Nothing ever really got cold. It was certainly cold enough outside now to keep most things fresh. Everything was going back to the old ways of doing things.

He came back in with a tray of food he'd made earlier. Vegetable rolls topped with half-chestnuts. 'We could salt vegetables next year,' he stated. 'I found blocksalt in the basement and a stack of old canning jars, you know, the ones with rubber seals.'

Rachel looked at him with surprise. 'You're kidding right?'

Arno shrugged. 'No. My grandmother used to do it. We had fresh garden beans in winter, all kinds of things. You'd be surprised how people coped before refrigeration. Of course you had to soak them a while to get the salt out but it worked. She made jams, bottled fruit, you name it. I can still remember slicing French beans fresh from the garden.'

Rachel stared at him a while, then finally smiled. 'You're enjoying this back to roots thing aren't you. Never figured you for a woodsman but you like it. Admit it.'

'Come on, I know you're enjoying it too. No office hours, no phone calls, no emails. This is real freedom. This is the new frontier, Rach.'

Rachel thought about it a moment, looking askance at the huge fish that Fen had caught. 'Maybe – but if she brings in a shark, I quit. Hear that. I quit.'

Arno laughed, put his food tray down and gave her a hug. 'Yeah, you're enjoying it.'

'Light the candles before she gets down, caveman. Now, exactly how do you expect me to cook this fish?'

'Already taken care of. Look outside, Rach.'

Rachel glanced up and out of the window and she could see smoke coming from the barbecue. She smiled. 'You've been camping before, haven't you.'

'Had to cook for fifty hungry academics at a Futuretank weekend in Thunder Bay. Learned fast. Didn't learn much about the future but an awful lot about barbecues.'

Rachel went to select some knives. Orca needed fixing.

Fen couldn't find a party hat, but she found a chest full of old clothes – some dating back thirty years or more, at least they looked old to her. She wondered who Mary Quant was. No label she had ever heard of. Retro stunning stuff that was strange but impressive. She licked out a pair of purple cords, a big spotted blouse with a droopy collar, both of which were just one size too big for her. There was a sequin vest jacket and big plastic fake jewels. A real treasure chest. She put it on and thought it looked pretty cool, even if the cords were a bit short in the leg. She wondered whose it had been; not the old woman's surely. Maybe Giselle, the name she'd found by the sundial.

She caught sight of herself in the mirror and laughed. Ridiculous but people had actually worn this stuff.

Red came bounding up the stairs to find her stopped short when he saw what she was wearing.

'Yeah, it's me. Cool, huh.' She hugged him and he licked her face.

She felt her hands were sticky and realised she was still bleeding. She broke off and rushed to the bathroom. 'Sorry, Red, bit yucky.'

She was running her hands under the cold tap when Rachel knocked on the door.

She did a double take when she saw what Fen was wearing. 'Wow, Janis Joplin. You seen Fen any place?'

Fen grinned. 'Cool, eh?. Who was Janis Joplin?'

'Singer, white soul, *'Take another piece of my heart baby'*, great voice, died of an overdose. It was the thing to do back then.'

'Song sounds familiar.'

'Probably because they use it to sell soap. You look really cute. Here, I brought you these. Arno said you cut your hands.'

Fen showed her cuts to Rachel and she pulled a face. 'Dry your hands. I'm going to dress them. You'll not be fishing for a few days after this anyways. Shit, Fen, you look great. You look just right.'

'You did something to your hair.'

'Tried. Arno didn't notice though.'

'What's the occasion anyway? Your birthday?'

Rachel took Fen's hands and rubbed anti-septic cream onto the cuts and tightly wrapped bandages around them, fastening them with tape. Fen was impressed.

'Like a real nurse.'

'Had to nurse my father for a while. Had to learn. He was a terrible patient. Made me understand in five minutes flat why my mother left him.

'There. That should hold them. Don't even think of washing your hands until tomorrow, OK and I'll dress them again.'

'So is it your birthday?'

'It's someone's birthday. You ready to go down?'

Fen nodded. 'I didn't get you a present.'

'You don't think that whale in the kitchen is enough of a gift? Come on, girl. You are the hunter-gatherer around here. I'm real proud of you.'

Fen appreciated Rachel's words. Sensed they were genuine. She didn't really know Rachel well yet. Despite seeing her everyday. She sensed there were two sides to her. One a bit dreamy, the other, like a mother, easily annoyed by silly little things. But she liked her. She guessed there were two sides to everyone.

Rachel pulled her out of the bathroom towards the landing. 'You ready? She hollered down to Arno.

'Thirty seconds,' he answered, running to the far end of the living room to flip a switch. Music began to flow. *Fossils*, a track from *Carnival of the Animals* floated across the house.

Fen began to smile as Rachel pulled her further towards the landing. She could see candlelight flickering down the stairs.

Arno appeared at the bottom of the stairs in a Santa hat and Rachel turned to her and invited her to go down the stairs. 'Happy Christmas, Fen, Happy Christmas.' Arno and Rachel chorused.

Dazzled, Fen slowly walked down the stairs, sensing tears and she had a constricted feeling in her throat. When she got to the bottom of the stairs Arno gave her a big hug and Rachel was right behind her, hugging her too. All three of them held tight and Fen could see beyond, in the living room filled with beautiful music, there were more candles, a blazing log fire and little things to eat, just like a real Christmas.

Fen couldn't say anything. Fat tears rolled down her cheeks onto Arno's shoulders. He checked her to see she was OK, and realising her dilemma, pulled her towards the living room and sat her down by the fire. Red, of course, was already there, soaking up the heat.

'It's...' Fen looked at the little decorations that Rachel had hung about the room. 'It's really Christmas?'

'Absolutely. Rach, get the wine. We're going to risk Madame Becora's blackberry special. Stay here. I just got to check the fish.'

'Check the fish?'

'Barbecue,' Rachel answered for him as Arno dashed outside.

Fen was just plain astonished. Couldn't believe they had kept all this secret from her.

Arno was suddenly back via the front door, which swung open with a clang, nearly putting out the candles. He was beckoning them. 'Come see, come see.'

Rachel put the bottle down and took Fen's arm and they went to the front door.

It was snowing. Arno was standing outside in the snow twirling around, laughing.

'See, this proves it's Christmas,' he was saying.

Fen loved seeing him look so happy and looked back at Rachel who clapped.

'Bravo. You made it snow, Santa. Did you check the fish?'

'Oops.' Arno nearly fell flat on his face as he dashed around the corner to attend to the barbecue.

'Gifts.' Rachel said firmly. 'Time for the gifts.'

Fen was amazed all over again. 'We have gifts?'

'Santa came earlier. Couldn't stop, was busy. Lot of people to cheer up this year.'

Rachel shepherded Fen back in the house and firmly shut the door; a tad annoyed all the heat had gone for the moment. Fen didn't care about that. She went back to the fire with Red and just felt slightly overawed by it all. They had gone to so much trouble, made it feel like it was all for her.

'Have to get Arno to open the bottle. Cork's riveted in I think.' Rachel pulled a couple of packages off the sideboard. She gave one to Fen.

'Just so you know, you can't send it back.'

Fen laughed. She carefully pulled the packaging apart and extracted a book.

'Womans' Guide to Shooting and Fishing,' she called out. 'Wow.'

'Look at the date.' Rachel pointed out.

Fen looked inside the flyleaf. 1928. Almost a hundred years – double wow. It was truly a guide to shooting and fishing – what to wear to the hunt and how to cook stuff you killed. She was stunned. It was going to be funny to read and yet, really, really useful.

'Thanks, Rachel, thanks.'

'There's a certain old lady who collected this stuff, so I guess we should thank her.'

Fen didn't know how to respond to that. They almost never talked about the writer whose house it was.

'I feel bad I didn't get anything for you and Arno.'

'I told you, the fish is the best gift ever girl. Eat one of Arno's rolls. Amazingly they taste good.'

Fen picked one out and ate. She was impressed. 'Hmm, good.' Red was looking at her with imploring eyes, so she snuck one for him too. After all it was Christmas.

Fen looked into the fire, suddenly feeling sad. 'You think anyone else is celebrating?'

Rachel thought about that. What was Christmas going to be like in the city? How many people didn't make it this far? How many survived and had to live with breathing difficulties and no help.

Arno came back after a few minutes, shaking snow off his hair. 'Barbecue in the snow is a new one for me, but we have the best fish in the whole world guys. Enough for dinner, breakfast and probably five more dinners. Be in the kitchen in five before Red gets it.'

Fen looked around for Red and saw that he was gone. 'Red!'

Red suddenly appeared from the direction of the kitchen, looking guilty. They laughed and he tentatively wagged his tail, hoping he wasn't in trouble

They found Arno had laid four places, which puzzled Fen, but not Rachel, whose eyebrows were raised only a moment.

'Expecting someone?'

'She's already here,' Arno answered. 'You can't celebrate Christmas in this house without paying respects to the person who made it possible.'

Fen checked with Rachel, but Rachel seemed to think this was entirely normal. She handed Arno the bottle to open, which even he struggled with.

He poured four glasses of a very dark cherry red liquid.

Rachel raised her glass and Fen followed. Arno made the toast. 'To Fen, for providing the feast, to A.S. Becora for providing the venue, to Rachel for being wonderful and to all, Happy Christmas.'

'Happy Christmas,' they chorused and then drank.

No cups rattled, no wind gushed through the kitchen, nothing happened save Arno set his wine glass down and narrowed his eyes. 'Well now I know why we let California make the wine.'

'It's not so bad.' Rachel declared.

'Sweet,' Fen added. 'Very sweet.'

'We will have it with the pudding.' Rachel decided.

'There's pudding?' Fen exclaimed.

'It's Christmas, Fen. What kind of Christmas would it be without plum pudding?'

Fen just shook her head. Didn't seem possible. She took Arno's and Rachel's hands suddenly and squeezed them (even though it hurt Arno and herself a little).

'I just want you to know I never once felt I belonged anywhere before. Never loved anyone. I love you both. I really do.'

Rachel squeezed her hand back, as did Arno.

'We both love you Fen. Owe you a great deal.' Arno answered. 'Now, this fish should be eaten hot, so let's eat.'

They ate. Arno careful to put some salmon on A.S. Becora's plate. It seemed best to take precautions.

22

The risk-of a 'bird flu' pandemic has been downgraded as a major health-risk to the nation. We have been advised the chances of H5N1 mutating to an 'active' virus that places the UK at risk is no longer a viable scenario. Therefore, we have taken the decision that scarce financial resources that have been diverted to this preparedness campaign are to be redeployed back into the NHS as we prepare for a normal winter influenza season.
Health Spokesperson for NHS Pandemic Preparedness – UK October 2006

A Big Decision

Snow didn't arrive in Vancouver until two days later and it didn't get cleared. No one came to salt, no plough made a space for traffic. Fuel was still in short supply and besides, there was little traffic save the buses and they would have to wait. It fell heavily too and the temperature dropped to five below. Without power most homes couldn't heat, most new homes had no fireplaces and the ones that had mostly had gas fires and there hadn't been gas for months. Fires broke out in North Van and in Burnaby, but no fire trucks went out there, as the roads were impassable.

For every moment you could tell yourself that the city was coming back to normal, something like snow told you it was a lie.

Doc knew what was working and what wasn't. He'd met with the Mayor a few times now and the new guys running the city and they'd come up with a strategy of concentric circles of functionality. Each week, one block, then another would be made secure, residents recorded, empty places noted and where power and services could be reconnected, they were, where they couldn't, shut off, it was done and bit by bit the city was being reclaimed.

It was this process that was revealing good news about those who had survived and taken heed of civic warnings and kept a low profile subsisting on the rations. It also revealed horror stories of whole families found dead in their apartments and homes, left to rot where they lay.

By December 31st they were getting a clearer picture of what would be needed and just how devastating the virus had been. And it wasn't over. Clearly it had peaked, but now it was so cold – everyone in the city office and the hospitals knew that normal winter colds and 'flu would set in. With a weakened population, respiratory illnesses would soar and the old would be vulnerable without any heating at night. There would be panic all over again and it would allow the virus to expand its footprint once more. Doc still held to the idea that it would be February before they would see the back of it in BC and most likely later in the East where it stayed cold until late March, early April.

Doc surveyed his new home with mixed feelings. He had found himself a pretty impressive townhouse on Richards. Home of a former movie director he heard. Four bedrooms, a screening room, small swimming pool and a roof garden leading off the master bedroom. What had attracted him to it most was the fireplace in the enormous vaulted living room, no doubt illegal in a city that forbade open fires, but he could burn logs (in this case wooden pallets he had to saw by hand in the small back yard). But could keep the place warm at least and Wylie in particular was pretty keen on it.

The best part was that he hadn't even known that he owned it until Deka had done the inventory and discovered they owned a whole raft of townhouse leases along with a slew of retail spaces that probably wouldn't produce any income for some years to come now.

He'd tried to encourage Deka to take it, but he'd decided on Kits. He wanted to live by the bay and now he had Eva and the kid with him, it made sense he would want a family home. The hotel was now billeting for priority government workers and officials and that worked out pretty well. The Mayor was all for getting the Courts up and running again and instituting the rule of law in the city. He had full respect for the guy; he was tough, but absolutely determined to get Vancouver back on its feet. Everyone had heard the stories of anarchy in some American cities and back East in Canada. It was going to be a case of tough love and anyone who could was put to work in whatever expertise they had. It was the opportunity Doc had been waiting for and now he had some influence to make things happen.

The oven dinged in the kitchen. He checked his watch. Exactly right. He was getting in tune with the idea that power would be available for just six to seven hours a day. They had been promising twenty-four hours but with staff shortages, so many places to make safe and now the snow, he recognised the magnitude of the problem of getting services back to normal. Maintenance was the key and maintenance workers were exactly what they were short of, in almost every sphere.

He moved to the elaborate kitchen with its marble floors, granite tops and central dining and workspace. He had laughed when he first saw it. A Russian Czar should have such a kitchen, that it was now his amused him. It had everything and of course, without electricity, almost nothing worked most of the time.

He opened the oven and after grabbing a cloth, took out a loaf of bread in a baking tin. Doc was impressed. His first loaf. Sure it was a bit misshapen, but it smelled pretty good to him. Deka had taught him how to do this and it was a good skill to have.

He switched off the oven and put the kettle on. His visitors would be here in a moment. The snow would delay them, but he knew they would come.

Indeed moments later Wylie's ears detected something and he ran for the front door.

Wylie sat by the door twitching expectantly. Once he had been frightened of Deka, but now he missed him. How he knew it was Deka was just a mystery, but that's dogs for you.

Two big knocks on the door followed. Doc ambled over, patted Wylie and opened up the vast steel-lined oak door. (The film director had installed bulletproof glass at ground level as well.)

Deka was stood there, covered in snow, Eva and child too, but they were smiling and entered the house in good spirits, stamping their feet and shaking off the snow. They even had a gift for Doc, handing over a bottle of vodka.

Doc embraced them both, planting a big kiss on Eva's cheeks. She busied herself wiping snow off her child, trying not to be overawed by the place.

Deka was studying the lobby and was impressed, more so when he saw the fire burning in the living room. 'Lekker, Doc. Nice. I remember now when they built this. People would make me slow my cab down so they could stare.'

Doc laughed. 'It's like the Czar's palace. There's even a screening room that can seat thirty people. Pool is a bit icy though.'

Eva stared at it all in wonder as she shed her coat at last. 'It's beautiful. So many mirrors.'

Doc shrugged. 'Well I shan't be bothering to look in them. Come on, to the kitchen, it's the warmest room at the moment.'

'Something smells good. You've been baking.'

'In your honour, Deka Fortun. My first loaf.'

Deka laughed, slapped Doc on the back. 'First loaf is special. Must be a big occasion. We are going to celebrate the New Year in style, hey?'

Doc smiled, inviting them to sit as he busied with the tea.

'Impressive kitchen.' Deka remarked with just a hint of jealousy. 'Must have cost thousands. Doc, you have to find yourself a good woman to share this with. Can't live here alone.'

Doc grinned. 'I would have to consult with Wylie. He gets jealous.'

Eva laughed, but then realised he was serious.

Wylie heard his name and came up to Deka, rested his head on his lap.

'He missed you.'

'I missed him.' Deka rubbed Wylie's ears.

Eva looked at them both with surprise. 'That is a very special dog.'

Doc shrugged. 'He is my friend. A good friend is hard to find.'

He poured tea as Eva lay a blanket on the floor for her child to lie on. It seemed happy and made little squeaks as it looked up at the many implements hanging from the ceiling rack. Eva still hadn't gotten used to the idea that she had met a cook one day who turned out to be one of the richest men in the city, although, like most other people, they had hardly a dollar in cash to spend.

'I got lucky,' Deka remarked, looking back at Eva squatting by her child.

Doc nodded. 'I'm really happy you decided to stay Eva. Deka is a good man. Now, which knife, chef? I am ready for the bread.'

Deka was frowning however. 'You should let it cool a little before we cut it, cuts cleaner that way.'

'I should?'

'We will drink the tea and if you wrap it in a tea towel and put it on the window ledge there by the cold, it will be ready to eat in fifteen minutes.'

Doc bowed to Deka's advice and did as he was told.

'It must be a big occasion if you are baking bread Doc. I know you. Always cook something before a big decision.'

Doc laughed, returning from the window. 'You know me too well, Teacher. Always looking after me.'

'It's just bread but...'

Doc held up his hands as Eva rejoined the table. They drank the tea and clinked cups together for luck. Eva smiled.

'You look different.' She ventured. 'Happier.'

Deka had noticed this too. But he was worried, behind his smiles. He had been waiting for the second shoe to drop for some days now. Doc had been talking to a number of people; different people, important city people and he hadn't involved Deka in the meetings. It didn't seem to be about property though, although most certainly about money. Power was shifting in the city and he had had to juggle what they had, negotiate with desperate and some pretty vile people as well. He was glad the hotel was being used and staffed now. He had never been comfortable living there and when he found that he could exchange one parcel of property for another in a consolidation move, he took a prime waterfront property off Cornwall for himself and Eva to live in that came with the portfolio. He'd moved their offices to a block they owned on Burrard, taking most of the first two floors. Everything was different now, the top floors were too big a risk and ground floor was the place to be. He'd got himself a bicycle too, and meant to use it when the snow melted.

Doc meanwhile had been listening to 'experts' and Deka was now worried that Doc would pull in professionals to run everything, who probably wouldn't think much of an ex-cabbie heading up the organisation.

Doc poured more tea. Eva was watching him. She'd only met Doc a few times and he had always been very polite. She didn't think he looked well. Way too thin, but then Deka too had been through hell and it would be a while before he gained weight again she sensed. She liked him but did not yet love Deka. Nevertheless he was the kindest man she had ever met and she knew she had to learn to love him, for it was obvious he loved her and her child.

'Big change, happy change,' Doc was saying. 'I'm going back to work.'

Deka was confused. He and Doc worked practically 24/7 on their little real estate empire, surely that was work enough?

'Work?' he queried.

Doc laughed, revealing a white tongue, part of him had not yet fully recovered. 'Yes work. I am going to the Resident at the City General Hospital.'

'Doctor?' Deka queried. 'You can finally be a Doctor?'

'Of course. I know they are desperate for doctors now. I am going back to work on the virus Deka. Going to run things different now. Going to make it the best hospital the city ever had. It has 500 beds choked with patients who survived but they all regret it. Lung capacity at thirty percent, oxygen absorption minimal, blood counts low, their tongues split. I think it will be a long time before they recover. We must clear them out, find places for them to recover where they will get care, but the virus will come back I think. We have your blood and mine to work with. I have already talked to the lab on 2nd Avenue to start producing a vaccine. There is no need for anyone else to die of this thing. No one.'

Deka was amazed. 'That's... that's just great. Finally you can show them what you can do.'

Doc smiled. 'Yes. I can make a big difference. They will listen now. Nothing else has worked.'

'And me? Deka asked, as calmly as he could.

Doc took his hand and squeezed it. 'You my friend have Dimitri's empire to run. We sell nothing, unless we have to, we sit on everything until we are old men, then sell to the highest bidders.

'You and Eva will run it, make it work, provide money for the hospital and that little boy down there, who will go to University, he will become a great teacher or Doctor. We shall make sure that we rent fair and that no one gets fat or lazy and we pass it on better than we found it. It's all we can do, pass it on to the next generation.'

Deka looked at Doc, gave a quick glance to Eva and wondered how it was he had ever found himself such a good and honest friend. 'Thank you, Alexi. Thank you.'

'No thank yous. We earned it. We survived. Someone has to own stuff. Well it's us and we shall respect it. That's all. Respect it.'

'Where are the people going to come from who will rent?' Eva asked quietly.

Doc and Deka both looked at her.

'And that,' Doc declared, 'is why you will marry her, Deka Fortun. She asks the hard questions. You must find the answers.'

'I guess there's still a lot of Russians who'd like to move here.'

'And people from Taipei,' Eva remarked, thinking of her own relatives in Taiwan.

Doc smiled. 'You see, answers can be found. I start at the hospital tomorrow. This snow is like Moscow snow, you will see, they will start coming in with coughs and sneezes and we need to be ready. They will panic, some will have the virus, many will not. People are nervous now. I want to get the whole city vaccinated with DAS1.'

'DAS1?' Deka asked.

'Deka Alexi Strain1.' Doc replied with a grin.

Deka appreciated his name being used. 'Dr Borov's killer soup. Maybe they'll build a statue of you, Doc. You and Wylie in Robson Square'. He glanced back at the window. 'I think we can eat the bread now.'

Doc went over to get it. Wylie sensing something was about to happen looked excited. Doc told him to sit. He did so instantly.

Eva poured more tea into their cups, sizing both the men up. 'You are both very different,' she told them quietly. 'Businessmen aren't like this. I've met a lot flying and you two are quite different.'

Doc returned with the loaf and unwrapped it before them. 'I'm hoping that that is a compliment, Eva.'

Eva blushed. 'It is. Believe me, it is.'

Doc cut the bread. It was perfect. He handed each of them a slice and revealed honey to go with it. He beamed with pleasure as they spread the gold liquid over the still warm wholemeal bread. He tossed some to Wylie who ate it quickly, glad to be included.

'We eat bread for a long, long, friendship,' Doc declared.

'And a long life,' Deka added, raising his cup.

'Long life.' They chorused as they drank the tea.

Outside it began to snow again and the city was perfectly quiet.

23

Almost half the US soldiers that died in World War I died of flu. Almost thirty-thousand of them died in October 1918 alone. Rival trenches were so close together that the wind carried the virus to both sides of the War. It wasn't the development of the airplane or tank, that ended World War I – it was HN51 – influenza.
History Today

Contact

'Apparently the garden should be turned over one spit deep.'

Rachel was reading up on 'The Compleat Amateur Gardener by H.H. Thomas' – a volume so old and mouldy it had practically reverted to vegetable matter on its own. But even though published in 1924, good advice still held, even if they were a bit short of horse manure and a heated greenhouse. 'One spit deep I take it is a technical term?' Rachel asked.

'I think it means a spadeful – but don't hold me to it. It have any useful advice on how to generate and preserve seeds?'

'No, but it's big on pests and paraffin emulsion – if that helps.'

She stared at Arno as he was mending the old frames, filling in cracks before the really bad weather took hold.

'I was thinking about Helena,' Rachel remarked.

'Helena?'

'She's with EDF in France. Atomic power. She was at Uni with me, went on an exchange to Paris and never came back.'

'What about her?'

Rachel shrugged. 'Well, y'know. France. It's a big country right, sophisticated health system, lots of organisation, more than us. I just can't believe they'd let everything get so bad as it did here, that's all. They have a huge tourist industry– I guess so does Spain next door. How the hell do they get through this?'

Arno didn't answer directly as he screwed a new piece of wood to the weak window frame. He hadn't really given too much thought to France, but Rachel was right, Germany, France and Spain, they all had a great deal to lose by this virus. The longer it went on, the harder it would be to get everything started up again. The economic effects were going to be like there had been a war and keeping civil control would be a bitch as millions would need financial and food support. The whole of Europe would be desperate by now.

'Remember 9/11? Then the big scare back in 2006 when you couldn't fly with hand luggage for a while? Each time people predicted that people would stop travelling, that tourism was dead. But you know what? People still need vacations. Maybe after this it will be like that. Everyone will be so happy it's over, we'll all go travelling. My guess is that oil will drop below $10 bucks and the airlines that survived (if any) will be so pleased to see us they'll give tickets away. Just a hunch.'

Rachel wasn't convinced. 'But this is bigger than 9/11, Arno. You're right it's like a war. A World War. Everyone is affected.'

'And after WW11 tourism really took off – well fifteen or so years after.'

'Fifteen years after. Say it slowly, Mr Future. I'll be over forty. I'll be pushing you around in a wheelchair. You're really saying it's going to take fifteen years for us to get over this virus.'

Arno put the screwdriver down and glanced out of the window, saw Red spread out in a patch of sunlight. He looked happy at least.

'Everything will look really bad for a while and the banks will probably wind up owning everything, but the sun will still rise. The six hundred miles of beaches in France will still be there, Rachel. The ocean will still pound the coast and kids will still surf. Indeed swimming in salt water will probably keep them from getting the virus. Shit, we saw a fishing boat out here yesterday. People have to eat. Things will return to normal as fast as it can. People will need to find and grow food and kids will need to swim. Summer will still come as it always does and we will all want to take a break. France will welcome whoever wants to come, as it always has.'

'You should work for the Government. That's their kind of bullshit.'

'It's not bullshit, Rachel. You asked about your friend. Well, she works in atomic energy. Assuming they have kept all those reactors going, or at least shut some down safely; assuming she took the vaccines and didn't come into contact with the virus, she'll be in an ideal situation to help France recover. She'll be happy as a lamb when you finally make contact with her and let her know that you too survived.'

'Aren't you the sudden optimist.'

'On the other hand, I'd be scared to live in France because people still live near to chickens and cows and other animals and everyone had big families. But outside the cities, which will suffer the most, there are many places for people to go and wait it out. They have a history of surviving plagues, wars, political intrigues and religious bloodlettings. I'd be heading to some lone farmhouse at the base of the Pyrenees, far from anyone else.'

'With your deadly chickens.'

'Not exactly. Grippe Avian isn't my favourite way to die. Personally I hope your Helena ran away and is hiding in that huge farmhouse – probably pointing guns at strangers that come her way.'

Rachel sighed. 'That's what everything comes down to isn't it, pointing guns at strangers.'

Arno smiled. 'History would seem to indicate that. You seen the varnish? I put the tin down...'

Rachel reached over to the chair and picked up the tin. 'This?'

'Yeah.'

'Rachel suddenly frowned looking up at him. 'You ever actually fixed a window before?'

Arno grinned. 'My stepfather was a great believer that boys should be able to change a plug, fix flat tyres, change engine oil and be independent. I never saw him lift as much as a hammer, but he was an expert supervisor.'

'I detect a sarcastic note.'

'You cannot supervise well if you don't understand the task at hand. So I assume his father tutored him accordingly. He also taught me how to plow a straight furrow, ride horses, several of his polo ponies actually, and polish silver. The latter was saved as a punishment for anything I did wrong, which was often, apparently. Either that or there was way too much silver. First thing I sold when he died.'

Rachel laughed. 'First time I've seen you look miserable. I can see you as a little boy stuck in a cellar with piles of silverware. Your bottom lip all down, just like now.'

Arno shook his head. 'No cellar. Well there was a cellar, but the polishing of silver would be done in the gun room so he could keep an eye on me as he read his *Financial Times*. He'd give me a running monologue on politics and business and I guess some of it stuck. He was an ogre but he often meant well and I never hated him. May the bastard rest in peace.'

A shout rang out. Red instantly jumped up and gave a warning bark.

'Another fishing boat I should think. Fen is vigilant, I'll say that for her.'

'She's the best thing about this whole mess. I adore her. She's so damn happy here.'

Arno nodded. 'Yeah. Makes you wonder what her life used to be like though.'

He picked up his tools. 'Right. On to the next window. Damn, I could sure use a cup of coffee right now.'

Rachel just sighed. She hated to even think about coffee she missed it so much.

'Hey, shut that door, it's cold out there,' Rachel hollered from the kitchen.

'Sorry,' Fen replied. 'Bringing in some firewood. There was another fishing boat out there. Not coming close though.'

'If we had a boat, we'd be doing the same.' Arno told her, putting the lid back on the varnish. 'Right. Next job on my list awaits.'

'I have more jobs for the list', Rachel shouted out.

'My dance card is full, madam. Perhaps next time.'

Arno winked at Fen as he followed her outside, noting immediately how cold it was getting.

'Damn it's cold. Hope that glue has set on the tubs.'

Fen came over with him to where Arno was installing a water cistern to catch the water run off. He'd located three polyethylene tubs in the old boathouse and figured that he could get the water to flow into them from the roof and then, using a primitive filtration system using charcoal and some wire mesh, they'd have water on hand for cooking or the plants. The well was around 90 meters deep by his reckoning and not being replenished fast enough. He wanted to take the pressure off it.

They had so little rain this winter; it always seemed to pass over them or to one side. They'd had snow, frost, lots of ice and bitter cold winds coming down the Georgia Strait, but not enough steady rain. Three people used a lot of water.

Of course the water runoff wasn't exactly going to pass the Canadian Drinking Level Standards test but hell, it would damn well have to do.

They had the radio now but no communications, the storm took out the satellite dish. There was no one they wanted to contact anyways. It was bad enough being forced to listen CBC, back on the air from Victoria. They were running news updates on the hour from across Canada, interspersed with cheery broadcasts from Stuart McLean – who unaccountably had managed to survive everything or they just had a mountain of repeats to hand. The music was pretty downbeat as well, with lots of folk songs and well... it beat the darn preachers and rapture folk on the other frequencies.

The news wasn't great. It had been a hard winter pretty much right across Canada and the US – with power restored in only a few cities. The Pickering nuclear plant outside Toronto had had problems – people were being evacuated in conditions of 30°C below. Little to envy about that.

Back in Vancouver the winter had been unseasonably cold and with so many still having to line up for rations– the virus had come back for a last hurrah. The December pause had been just that, a lull and now it was back with the snow and the cold nights in unheated homes. In cities across North American and Canada people were beginning to find a 'voice' again and were looking for answers and people to blame. It was going to be a long list.

Fen didn't listen to the news. It was always going to be bad and well, she had moved on. She had no intentions of going back to the city – ever. Once this was over, the most she would consider was going to a larger island; one that could guarantee it wasn't teeming with zombies. She was thinking Galiano. Give a little more space for Red to roam. She whistled but Red had gone to off for a walk. He liked to go up by the trees and shelter there, out of the persistent wind and watch everything from there.

'Looks OK to me,' Fen remarked as Arno inspected his handiwork.

'We shall see when it rains. It feels like rain, but let's hope it doesn't miss us again.'

'Tide's falling.' Fen remarked, moving away.

Fen took herself down to the rocks at the shoreline. She did this everyday when the tide retreated a little. She had crab traps set in tight crevices and two days before they had been lucky to get two fat Dungeness crabs to feast on. But it didn't mean that crabs came every day. She'd learned how to dig for Butter and Manila clams and then cover the holes so they could breed again. She was learning a new way to live and liked it. Even teaching Arno how to fish.

Rachel had found this great pamphlet in a kitchen drawer– the 1998 *British Columbia Tidal Waters Guide*. Told her what to look for, what poisons might be lurking and how to tell the difference between male and female crabs. It opened up a whole new world to Fen.

Realising that there would be no crabs today she returned to the old dock. Her other job was gathering firewood. They tried to use driftwood when they could, even though it spat and hissed in the grate. She was nervous of two crows that had set up home on the boathouse. Ever since she was about ten, Mercer had warned her about West Nile virus and crows falling dead out of the sky. Then along came bird flu. Crows made her nervous, they were the most likely to be the sentinels of disaster. It was an irrational fear, but one she couldn't quite shake off.

Arno was shouting something back at the house. Fen turned and saw he was pointing out to sea. She turned back and quickly her eyes found what he'd seen. A small rigid inflatable patrol boat. Moving fast towards the island. There only seemed to be one person on board.

Fen dropped her firewood. Her heart skipped a beat. Her instincts were to run, but she held her stance. The dock was smashed from the storm so he'd have a problem getting ashore. He could beach it, of course, a light boat like that. But who was he? Why was he coming directly to the island? She looked back to the trees. Red started to come down to join her but she gave him a signal to lie down and he dropped on all fours. Watching her intently now.

As the man throttled back he waved. Fen waved back. He was wearing a Coast Guard uniform. Not everything had gone to shit then.

He turned off the engine and drifted in close, the wake pitching the craft up and down.

'Hi. Alyce Becora at home?'

Fen shook her head. 'Died. Some months back.'

The man was clearly upset by that. Fen looked closer, he looked a bit tubby, and he for one had not had the virus. He showed no sign of wanting to come ashore. 'You know her?' Fen asked.

'A little. So many dead, it's like it never ends, eh?'

'She had a heart attack. Couldn't get her pills.' Fen told him. Sticking to the truth here.

'Now that makes me feel real guilty,' the Coast Guard remarked, a genuine look of shame on his face. 'I had these pills to bring over in November but – what with guarding the coast from marauders and ...'

'She died quick. You want to see her grave?'

The Coast Guard pulled a face. 'God's way I suppose. So many folks perished because they couldn't get their pills. The virus did its work in the city, but out here and on Salt, all those good people dependent on drugs to keep 'em alive, they just never got delivered. All gone, just like that, one after the other. It's God's justice they say. You can't put off what is due forever.'

This guy, Fen knew, listened to the other frequencies on the radio. Right then Fen knew he wasn't going to want to come onto the island.

'I make a regular patrol, y'know. Ms Becora was... well she had fans back on Mayne and they send her stuff.'

'That's a shame.' Fen told him. 'Wasted journey.'

The man pulled out a piece of paper and produced a pen all of a sudden.

'Name's Butter, by the way. Christian Butter. You must be her niece, Giselle. She was hoping you'd make it out here.'

Giselle. That name seemed to haunt Fen. The name on the mosaic by the sundial, and the little girl whose picture was on the mantelpiece in the living room. Shit, if he wanted her to be Giselle, she'd be Giselle.

'Anyway,' the Coast Guard continued. 'I came because I got to do this survey. Find out who's living and whose died on the islands. There's some Federal Money for some sort of recovery plan. I tried telling 'em back in Victoria that the Islands were OK. We're not the ones who need help, but I have to count heads. No one else is available. So. Besides you?'

"There's my cousin Rachel and her boyfriend Arno Lakis. That's L A K I S.'

He wrote stuff down. 'Rachel a Becora too?'

'Until she marries, she is.'

The man smiled. 'Hell, weddings. We'll know this trouble is well behind us when we start to have weddings again. That will be a blessed day.'

Fen smiled, trying to will him to leave.

'School too.' He said. 'The kids on Mayne are going insane without school. Some Government idiot in Victoria ordered all the schools closed, but we don't have the virus and the kids need school real bad. 'Teachers need jobs too. No one getting paid. Bartering only gets you so far.'

'Mayne didn't get the virus?'

'The Influenza committee made sure of that, eh. No one on or off the island from day one. Anyone with a cold shut in their house for thirty days and the whole coast patrolled, day and night, to make sure we stayed pure. It was exhausting, I can tell you that, but we saved the island.'

Fen wondered if they were shooting at boats like on Salt as well. Hard to blame them.

'You know a Casper Bowden?' She asked.

Christian, the Coast Guard visibly relaxed. 'Old Casper. He still runs the Big Cup Coffee Shack – although they ran out of coffee a month ago. He's still a volunteer fireman. One of the best. You know him?'

Fen could hardly say he was her Uncle given that he believed she was Giselle.

'Stayed there last summer in his loft. Friend and me. Kinda hope she's OK.'

"Well he most definitely is. Wife died couple of years back but I think Casper's got an eye on Jenny Brown, who runs the post office. She's sweet on him too, but her husband might have something to say about that.' He suddenly remembered his other mission.

'Which reminds me. I got letters for Ms Becora and a parcel and some sugar and herbal tea. Jenny insisted.'

Fen smiled. 'We could sure use the tea. We could use some cookies and what the hell, some ice cream too.'

The Coast Guard laughed. He hefted over a plastic wrapped parcel and tossed it out of the boat at Fen's feet. Fen noted he wore gloves. She wasn't going to touch anything if he hadn't worn gloves.

'I tried raising you on the sat phone. You got no power eh?'

'No satellite dish. The storm took it, the dock and our boat too.'

'Early December eh? That was something. Ripped the heart out of Ganges on Salt. I heard Hornby had homes blown away. Real bad winter storm.'

He started up his engine again. Began to pull away. 'You stay well, Giselle. Really sorry 'bout your Grandma. She was quite a character.'

With that he and the boat were away again. Fen reflected that she was lucky that he wasn't the brightest Coast Guard she had ever met, but at least he was a happy one. She stayed where she was for a moment. Red dashed over, unable to stay put any longer. She rubbed his ears. She didn't open the plastic wrapped parcel. Didn't really trust anything anymore. She watched the small craft until it was once again a speck on the ocean. She was thinking about Uncle Casper and the woman at the post office.

Arno arrived and looked at the parcel on the ground.

'We got mail?'

'Coast Guard paid us a visit and the mail is for her. There's tea and sugar in there somewhere, but I'm not touching it without gloves.'

Arno wasn't wearing gloves either. It could wait.

'That all he wanted?'

'He was taking some kind of census. He thinks I'm the old ladies niece, Giselle. I didn't tell him different. Gave him your name though.'

Arno looked at her with surprise. 'You did?'

'If I'm Giselle and Rachel's my cousin, then you're here by invitation. I told him the old lady was dead. He didn't seem too upset.'

Arno considered the situation. If there were Coast Guards, then things were getting back to normal. Taking a census of the Islands was a good idea. Know what you were dealing with. He suddenly noticed Fen was crying. Just a trickle of tears. It was just not like her at all. He went to her, took her into his arms. She sobbed silently into his jacket.

'What?'

'I don't want things to go back to normal. I don't want mail and I don't want to leave here. I don't want this to end, Arno. I don't want to lose this.' She nudged his chest and Arno kissed the top of her head and hugged her tight. He was aware, as Rachel was too that Fen was having feelings. Hell, they all were. Day didn't go by without each one of them needed to show some affection for each other. Red wanted in on the act and stuck his nose in between them. Arno patted him too.

He sighed, looking Fen in the eyes. Her tears puffing up her eyes. 'It will end – one day. But we don't have to. OK? You, me, Rachel, we are a family unit now. We might get booted off this island if the real Giselle turns up, but we'll go together. I made a promise. You hear me? I made a promise.'

Fen took his hand and squeezed it hard. He squeezed back to reassure her.

'Rachel's pregnant isn't she? I know she is.' Fen told him. She saw the look of surprise on his face. So he didn't know. She'd been right.

It was news to Arno. 'Pregnant? You sure? How...?'

'I can tell. She's scared to tell you.'

'She is? But why. It's great news'

'She's sacred Arno. I'd be scared. To bring a kid into this world? Things are changing. I don't know where I fit in and...'

Arno pulled her off him and spun her around, squeezing her neck with affection. 'Pick up your firewood, let's go find out. If she's pregnant, you're the godmother, hell, you're the sister, the aunt, you're family, Fen. Now, quit the tears. Let's go find Rachel and give her a big hug. No more fear in this family. We have a future to think about.'

Red barked.

'Yeah, yeah. You're the Uncle, Red. Red's the Uncle.'

Fen smiled again, picking up her firewood. The parcel lay on the shore behind them. Civilisation could wait.

Previous titles by Sam North

The Curse of the Nibelung – A Sherlock Holmes Mystery
Lulu Press 2005 USA ISBN – 1-4116-3748-8
Some reviews from the first UK edition:
"Chocolate will never seem quite the same again. With an irresistible, high-quality
Goon-like zaniness, this dynamically paced thriller follows its own larger-than-life
logic. Not to be missed." *The Sunday Express*

"A splendid spoof, even better than the author's earlier parody of Le Carré',
'Eeny Meeny Miny Mole.'" *The Sunday Telegraph*

Diamonds – The Rush of '72
Lulu Press 2004. USA – ISBN 1-4116-1088-1
"This is a terrific piece of storytelling... highly recommended for lovers of the Old
West and, more importantly, for all those who enjoy a good adventure story well
told."
The Historical Novel Society Review

Going Indigo
Citron Press, UK
"Treading really new ground in its off-beat child's-eye black comedy."
The Independent.

Ramapo
Sphere Books, UK
"A gripping, tension filled thriller."
The Mail, Hartlepool.

209 Thriller Road
St. Martin's Press, New York.
"A fine British mystery paced with whimsy and suspense."
Statesman Journal, Salem, Oregon.

Eeny, Meeny, Miny, Mole (Written as Marcel d'Agneau)
Arrow Books, UK
"Imitation of such quality zaniness is the sincerest form of flattery"
Christopher Wordsworth – *The Observer*

Also by Sam North

Diamonds – The Rush of '72
ISBN 1-4116-1088-1

Diamonds – The Rush of '72 is a true adventure set in the American West. A tale of greed, treachery and bravado. Two prospectors, John Slack and Philip Arnold, arrive penniless and near-starving in San Francisco to deposit raw American diamonds in the Bank of California, it causes quite a stir.

Rumours abound in the city of the biggest diamond find since Kimberley, with fabulous riches to be made. Slack and Arnold try to keep their claim secret. They attract the attention of California's biggest banker, William Ralston and New York's finest investors; including Horace Greeley – only to discover that these fine gentlemen intend to cheat them. But Slack and Arnold are wily men, hardened by years on the mountains. They won't be taken easily. What begins as a trickle in the Colorado mountains would grow into the great rush of '72.

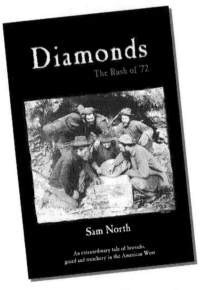

'This historical mining is an elegant and convincing novel, a novel of comic moments and dark overtones .'
George Olden
– *Falmouth Review*

'This is a terrific piece of storytelling highly recommended for lovers of the Old West and, more importantly, for all those who enjoy a good adventure story well told'.
Chris Lean
– *Historical Novel Society Review*

Diamonds – The Rush of '72
www.books.lulu.com/content/68464
Distributed by Ingrams and available from Amazon and other online booksellers.
Printed in the USA and UK

Also by Sam North

The Curse of the Nibelung – A Sherlock Holmes Mystery
ISBN 1-4116-3748-8

Revealed for the first time the great detective's role in World War II.
It is December 1939. Four British spies have perished in strange circumstances in Nuremberg trying to discover the biggest secret of the Third Reich. Winston Churchill sends Sherlock Holmes on what could be his very last case. Holmes and Watson must enter Germany and solve the mystery. Two ancient men with their beautiful young nurse Cornelia must pretend to be German sympathisers. If captured, England will disown them. Their loyalty and Holmes' skills at deduction will be severly tested. There is no one they can trust and the terrible truth of Nuremberg is far more sinister than even Holmes could imagine. Their chances of ever returning to England, very slim indeed.

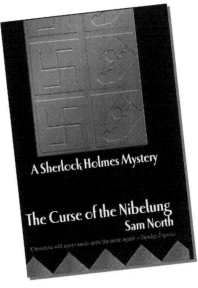

'The triumphant return of
Holmes and Watson.'
Eric Hiscok
– The Bookseller

'Chocolate will never be
the same again. With an irresistible,
high-quality Goon-like zaniness, this
dynamically paced thriller follows its
own larger-than-life logic.
Not to be missed.'
Richard Pearce
– The Sunday Express

The Curse of the Nibelung – A Sherlock Holmes Mystery
www.books.lulu.com/content/132693
Distributed by Ingrams and available from Amazon and other online booksellers.
Printed in the USA and UK

3395549

Made in the USA